Availab
from Mills

EXPECTING TROUBLE

"I don't know who I can trust. So is that why you're here, to rescue me?"

"Not exactly." But why the heck did Cal suddenly feel as if he wanted to do just that? Still, he wasn't about to let her off the hook. "Why did you lie about who your baby's father is?" he demanded.

Jenna blinked and her eyes widened. "How did you know?"

"This morning my director called me into his office to demand an explanation as to why I slept with someone in my protective custody."

"Oh, I had no idea. How did he even find out?"

"Because we've been keeping tabs on you, Jenna."

"Me? Why? Why am I suddenly so important to the government?"

"Because it seems someone wants you dead. You've been placed back in my protective custody until you and your baby are safe."

PRINCE CHARMING FOR 1 NIGHT

He handed Vera her glass-like shoes with a wry smile. "Don't lose one, Cinderella," he teased.

She snatched them back. "You know, your cousin Candace didn't like you very much."

"Now there's a shock," he said, leading her up the mansion's sweeping front steps.

"She said you're mean, stubborn and ruthless...and will do anything to get your clients off."

"Never a good thing in a lawyer," he said drily.

She met his amused gaze, so strong and confident. Not to mention devoid of shadiness or deceit. With a sinking feeling, she suddenly knew the slain heiress had been completely wrong about him. She shouldn't be surprised. The rivalry between the Rothchild family cousins was legendary in Vegas.

"Touché," Vera acknowledged, thinking just maybe *she'd* been wrong about Conner, too.

Not good. She did *not* want to like this man. Bad enough she was hopelessly attracted to him. What if he turned out to be honourable and principled, too?

He ushered her inside. "Welcome to my home."

Said the spider to the fly.

First published in Great Britain 2010
Harlequin Mills & Boon Limited,
Eton House, 18-24 Paradise Road, Richmond, Surrey TW9 1SR

Expecting Trouble © Delores Fossen 2009
Prince Charming for 1 Night © Harlequin Books S.A. 2009

Special thanks and acknowledgement are given to Nina Bruhns for her
contribution to the LOVE IN 60 SECONDS mini-series.

ISBN: 978 0 263 88206 3

46-0310

Harlequin Mills & Boon policy is to use papers that are natural, renewable
and recyclable products and made from wood grown in sustainable forests.
The logging and manufacturing processes conform to the legal environmental
regulations of the country of origin.

Printed and bound in Spain
by Litografia Rosés S.A., Barcelona

EXPECTING TROUBLE

BY
DELORES FOSSEN

PRINCE CHARMING FOR 1 NIGHT

BY
NINA BRUHNS

⟡™ MILLS & BOON®

EXPECTING TROUBLE

BY
DELORES FOSSEN

Imagine a family tree that includes Texas cowboys, Choctaw and Cherokee Indians, a Louisiana pirate and a Scottish rebel who battled side by side with William Wallace. With ancestors like that, it's easy to understand why Texas author and former air force captain **Delores Fossen** feels as if she were genetically predisposed to writing romances. Along the way to fulfilling her DNA destiny, Delores married an air force top gun who just happens to be of Viking descent. With all those romantic bases covered, she doesn't have to look too far for inspiration.

To Tom, thanks for all the support.

Prologue

A deafening blast shook the rickety hotel and stopped Jenna cold.

With her heart in her throat, Jenna raced to the window and looked down at the street below. Or rather what was left of the street, a gaping hole. Someone had set shops on fire. Black coils of smoke rose, smearing the late afternoon sky.

"Ohmygod," Jenna mumbled.

There was no chance a taxi could get to her now to take her to the airport. And worse were rebel soldiers, at least a dozen of them dressed in dark green uniforms. She'd heard about them on the news and knew they had caused havoc in Monte de Leon. That's why by now she'd hoped to be out of the hotel, and the small South American country. She hadn't succeeded because she'd been waiting on a taxi for eight hours.

One of the soldiers looked up at her and took aim with his scoped rifle. Choking back a scream, Jenna dropped to the floor just as the bullet slammed through the window.

She scurried across the threadbare rug and into the bathroom. It smelled of mold, rust and other odors she didn't want to identify, and Jenna wasn't surprised to see roaches race across the cracked tile. It was a far cry from the nearby Tolivar estate where she'd spent the past two days. Of course, there'd been insects of a different kind there.

Paul Tolivar.

Staying close to the wall, Jenna pulled off one of her red heels so she could use it as a weapon and climbed into the bathtub to wait for whatever was about to happen.

She didn't have to wait long.

There was a scraping noise just outside the window. She pulled in her breath and waited. Praying. She hadn't even made it to the please-get-me-out-of-this part when she heard a crash of glass and the thud of someone landing on the floor.

"I'm Special Agent Cal Rico," a man called out. "U.S. International Security Agency. I'm here to rescue you."

A rescue? Or maybe this was a trick by one of the rebels to draw her out. Jenna heard him take a step closer, and that single step caused her pulse to pound in her ears.

"I know you're here," he continued, his voice calm. "I pinpointed you with thermal equipment."

The first thing she saw was her visitor's handgun. It was lethal-looking. As was his face. Lean, strong. He had an equally strong jaw. Olive skin that hinted at either Hispaniç or Italian DNA. Mahogany-brown hair and sizzling steel-blue eyes that were narrowed and focused.

He was over six feet tall and wore all black, with various weapons and equipment strapped onto his chest, waist and thighs. He looked like the answer to her un-finished prayer.

Or a P.S. to her nightmare.

"We need to move now," he insisted.

Jenna didn't question that, but she still wasn't sure what she intended to do. Yes, she was afraid, but she wasn't stupid. "Can I trust you?"

Amusement leapt through his eyes. His reaction was brief, lasting barely a second before he nodded. And that was apparently all the reassurance he intended to give her. He latched on to her arm and hauled her from the tub. He allowed her just enough time to put back on her shoe before he maneuvered her out of the bathroom and toward the door to her hotel room.

"Extraction in progress, Hollywood," he whispered into a black thumb-size communicator on the collar of his shirt. "ETA for rendezvous is six minutes."

Six minutes. Not long at all. Jenna latched on to that info like a lifeline. If this lethal-looking James Bond could deliver what he promised, she'd be safe soon. Of course, with all those rebel soldiers outside, that was a big *if*.

Cal Rico paused at the door, listening, and eased it open. After a split-second glance down the hall, he got them out of the room and down a flight of stairs that took them to the back entrance on the bottom floor. Again, he looked out, but he must not have liked what he saw. He put his finger to his lips, telling her to stay quiet.

Outside, Jenna could still hear the battery of gunfire

and the footsteps of the rebels. They seemed to be moving right past the hotel. She was in the middle of a battle zone.

How much her life had changed in two days. This should have been a weekend trip to Paul's Monte de Leon estate. A prelude to taking their relationship from friendship to something more. Instead, it'd become a terrifying ordeal she might not survive.

Jenna tried not to let fear take hold of her, but adrenaline was screaming for her to run. To do something. *Anything.* It was a powerful, overwhelming sensation. Fight or flight. Even if either of those options could get her killed.

Cal Rico touched his fingers to her lips. "Your teeth are chattering," he mouthed.

No surprise there. She didn't have a lot of coping mechanisms for dealing with this level of stress. Who did? Well, other than the guy next to her.

"Try doing some math," he whispered. "Or recite the Gettysburg Address. It'll help keep you calm."

Jenna didn't quite buy that. Still, she tried.

He moved back slightly. But not before she caught his scent. Sweat mixed with deodorant soap and the faint smell of the leather from his combat boots. It was far more pleasant than it should have been.

Stunned and annoyed with her reaction, Jenna cursed herself. Here she was, close to dying, only hours out of a really bad relationship, and her body was already reminding her that Agent Cal Rico smelled pleasant. Heaven help her. She was obviously a candidate for therapy.

"I'll do everything within my power to get you out of here," he whispered. "That's a promise."

Jenna stared at him, trying to figure out if he was lying. No sign of that. Just pure undiluted confidence. And much to her surprise, she believed him. It was probably a reaction to the testosterone fantasy he was weaving around her. But she latched on to his promise.

"All clear," he said before they started to move again.

They hurried out the door and into the alley that divided the hotel from another building. Cal never even paused. He broke into a run and made sure she kept up with him. He made a beeline for a deserted cantina. They ducked inside, and he pulled her to the floor.

"We're at the rendezvous point," he said into his communicator. "How soon before you can pick up Ms. Laniere?" A few seconds passed before he relayed to her, "A half hour."

That was an eternity with the battle raging only yards away. "We'll be safe here?" Jenna tried not to make it sound like a question.

"Safe enough, considering."

"How did you even know I was in that hotel?"

Cal shifted his position so he could keep watch out the window. "Intel report."

"There was an intelligence report about me?" But she didn't wait for him to answer. "Who are you? Not your name. I got that. But why are you here?"

He shrugged as if the answer were obvious. "I'm a special agent with International Security Agency—the ISA. I've been monitoring you since you arrived in Monte de Leon."

Still not understanding, she shook her head. "Why?"

"Because of your boyfriend, Paul Tolivar. He is bad news. A criminal under investigation."

Judas Priest. This was about Paul. Who else?

"My ex-boyfriend," she corrected. "And I wish I'd known he was bad news before I flew down here."

Maybe it was because she was staring craters into him, but Agent Rico finally looked at her. Their gazes met. And held.

"I don't suppose someone could have told me he was under investigation?" she demanded.

He was about to shrug again, but she held tight to his shoulder. "We couldn't risk telling you because you might have told Paul."

Special Agent Rico might have added more, if there hadn't been an earsplitting explosion just up the street. It sent an angry spray of dirt and glass right at them. He reacted fast. He shoved her to the floor, and covered her body with his. Protecting her.

They waited. He was on top of her, with his rock-solid abs right against her stomach and one of his legs wedged between hers. Other parts of them were aligned as well.

His chest against her breasts. Squishing them.

The man was solid everywhere. Probably not an ounce of body fat. She'd never really considered that an asset, but she did now. Maybe all that strength would get them out of this alive.

Since they might be there for a while, and since Jenna wanted to get her mind off the gunfire, she forced herself to concentrate on something else.

"I believe Paul might be doing something illegal. He

uses cash, never credit cards, and he always steps away from me whenever someone calls him on his cell. I know that's not really proof of any wrongdoing."

In fact, the only proof she had was that Paul was a jerk. When she refused to marry him, he'd slapped her and stormed out. Jenna hadn't waited around to see if he'd return with an apology. She hadn't even waited when Paul's driver had refused to take her into town. She'd walked the two miles, leaving everything but her purse behind.

Agent Rico smirked. "Tolivar was under investigation for at least a dozen felonies. The Justice Department thought you could be a witness for their case against him."

"Me?" She'd said that far louder than she intended. Then she whispered, "But I don't know anything." Oh, mercy. She hadn't thought things would be that bad. "What did Paul want with me? Not a green card. He's already a U.S. citizen."

Cal nodded. "The Justice Department believes he wanted your accounting firm so he could use it to launder money."

"Wait, he can't have my accounting firm. According to the terms of my father's will, I'm not allowed to sell or donate even a portion of the firm to anyone that isn't family."

He had no quick response, and his hesitation had her head racing with all sorts of bad ideas.

"We believe Paul Tolivar planned to marry you one way or another this evening," Cal said. "He had a phony marriage license created, in case you turned down his proposal. Intel indicates that after the marriage, he planned to keep you under lock and key so he could control your business and your money."

A sickening feeling of betrayal came first. Then anger. Not just at Paul, but at herself for believing him and not questioning his motives. Still, something didn't add up. "If Paul planned to keep me captive, then why didn't he come after me when I left his estate?"

"He had someone follow you. I doubt he intended to let you leave the country. He contacted the only taxi service in town and told them to stall you."

So she'd been waiting for a taxi that would never have shown up. And it was probably just a matter of time before Paul came after her.

"I slept with him," Jenna mumbled. Groaned. She pushed her fists against the sides of her head. "You must think I'm the most gullible woman in the world."

"No. I think you're an heiress who was conned."

Yes. Paul had given her the full-court press after she'd met him at a fund-raiser. Phone calls. Roses. *Yellow* roses, her favorite. And more. "He told me he was dying of a brain tumor."

Rico shook his head. "No brain tumor."

It took Jenna a moment to get her teeth unclenched. "The SOB. I want him arrested. I want—"

"He's dead."

She had to fight through her fit of rage to understand what he'd said. "Paul's dead?"

Cal Rico nodded. "He was murdered about an hour ago. That's why I'm here—to stop the same thing from happening to you."

Her heart fell to her knees. "Wh-what?"

"We have reason to believe that Paul left instructions. In the event of his death, he wanted others dead, too. You included. Those rebel soldiers out there are after you. And they have orders to kill you on sight."

Chapter One

Special Agent Cal Rico checked his watch—again. Only three minutes had passed since the last time he'd looked. It felt longer.

A lot longer.

Of course, waiting outside his director's door had a way of making each second feel like an eternity.

"Uh-oh," he heard someone say. Cal saw a team member making his way up the hall toward him. Mark Lynch was nicknamed Hollywood because of his movie-star looks. He was a Justice Department liaison assigned to the regional headquarters. "What'd you screw up, Chief?" Lynch asked.

Chief. Cal had been given his moniker because of his aspirations to become chief director of the International Security Agency. Except they weren't just aspirations.

One day he *would* be chief. Since that was his one and only goal, it made things simple.

And in his mind, inevitable.

"Who said I screwed up anything?" Cal commented. But he was asking himself the same thing.

Lynch arched his left eyebrow and flashed a Tom Cruise smile. "You're outside Kowalski's office, aren't you?"

Cal had been assigned to the Bravo team of the ISA for well over a year, and this was the first time he'd ever been ordered to see his director. Since he'd just returned from a monthlong assignment in the Middle East and wouldn't receive new orders within seven duty days, he was bracing himself for bad news.

He'd already called his folks and both of his brothers to make sure all was well on the home front. That meant this had to do with the job. And that made it more personal than anything else could have been.

"If you have a butt left when Kowalski quits chewing it," Hollywood continued, "then show up at the racquetball court at 1730 hours. I believe you promised me a rematch."

Cal mumbled something noncommittal. He hated racquetball, but after this meeting he might need a way to work out some frustrations. Pounding Hollywood might just do it.

The door to the director's office opened, and Cal's lanky boss motioned for him to enter.

"Have a seat," Director Scott Kowalski ordered. There was no mistake about it. His tone and demeanor confirmed that it was an order. "Talk to me about Jenna Laniere."

Cal had geared up to discuss a lot of things with his

boss, but she wasn't anywhere on that list. Though he'd certainly thought, and dreamed, about the leggy blond heiress. "What about her?"

"Tell me what happened when you rescued her in Monte de Leon last year."

That was a truly ominous-sounding request. Still, Cal tried not to let it unnerve him. "As best as I can recall, I entered the hotel where she'd checked in, found her hiding in the bathroom. I moved her from that location and got her to the rendezvous point. About a half hour later or so, the transport took her away, and I rejoined the Bravo team so we could extract some American hostages that the rebels had taken."

Kowalski put his elbows on his desk and leaned closer. "It's that half hour of unaccounted-for time that I'm really interested in."

Hell.

That couldn't be good. Had Jenna Laniere filed some kind of complaint all these months later? If so, Cal had her pegged all wrong. She had seemed too happy about being rescued to be concerned that he'd used profanity around her.

"Wait a minute," Cal mumbled, considering a different scenario. One that involved Paul Tolivar, or rather what was left of Tolivar's regime. "Is Jenna Laniere safe?"

Translation: had Tolivar's cronies or former business partners killed her?

The FBI had followed Jenna for weeks after her return to the States. When no one had attempted to eliminate her, they'd backed off from their surveillance.

As for Tolivar's regime, there hadn't been enough

hard evidence for the Monte de Leon or U.S. authorities to arrest Tolivar's partners or anyone else for his murder. In fact, there hadn't been any evidence at all except for Justice Department surveillance tapes that couldn't be used in court since they would give away the identities of several deep-cover operatives. A move that would almost certainly cause the operatives to be executed. The Justice Department wasn't about to lose key men to further investigate a criminal's murder. Especially one that'd happened in a foreign country.

"Ms. Laniere's fine," Kowalski assured him.

The relief Cal felt was a little stronger than he'd expected. And it was short-lived. Because something had obviously happened. Something that involved her. If Jenna had indeed filed a complaint, there'd be an investigation. It could hurt his career.

The one thing he valued more than anything else.

He would not fail at this. He couldn't. Bottom line—being an operative wasn't his job, it was who he was. Without it, he was just the middle son of a highly decorated air force general. The middle son sandwiched between two brothers who'd already proven themselves a dozen times over. Cal had never excelled at anything. In his youth, he'd been average at best and at worst been a screwup—something his father often reminded him of.

His career in the ISA was the one way he could prove to his father, and more importantly to himself, that he was worth something.

"After you rescued Ms. Laniere, the Justice Department questioned her for hours. Days," Kowalski corrected. "She didn't tell them anything they could use to build their case against Tolivar's business partners. In fact, she claims she never heard Tolivar or his partners speak of the rebel group that they'd organized and funded in Monte de Leon. The group he ordered to kill her. She further claimed that she never heard him discuss his illegal activities."

"And the Justice Department believes she was telling the truth?"

Kowalski made a sound that could have meant anything. "Have you seen or spoken with her in the past year?"

"No." Cal immediately shook his head, correcting that. "I mean, I tried to call her about a month ago, but she wasn't at her office in Houston. I left a message on her voice mail, and then her assistant phoned back to let me know that she was on an extended leave of absence and couldn't be reached."

The director steepled his fingers and stared at Cal. "Why'd you try to call her?"

Cal leaned slightly forward as well. "This is beginning to sound a little like an interrogation."

"Because it is. Now back to the question—why did you make that call?"

Oh, man. That unnerving feeling that Cal had been trying to stave off hit him squarely between the eyes. This was not something he wanted to admit to his director. But he wouldn't lie about it, either.

No matter how uncomfortable it was.

"I was worried about her. Because I read the investigation into Tolivar's business partners had been reopened. I just wanted to see how things were with her."

Judging from the way Director Kowalski's smoke-gray eyes narrowed, that honest answer didn't please him. He muttered a four-letter word.

"Mind telling me what this is about?" Cal asked. "Because last I heard it isn't a crime for a man to call a woman and check on her."

But in this case, his director might consider it a serious error in judgment.

Since Jenna had a direct association with an international criminal like Paul Tolivar, no one working in the ISA should have considered her a candidate for a friendship. Or anything else.

Kowalski aimed an accusing index finger at Cal. "You know it violates regulations to have intimate or sexual contact with someone in your protective custody. And for those thirty minutes in Monte de Leon, Jenna Laniere was definitely in your protective custody."

That brought Cal to his feet. "Sexual contact?" Ah, hell. "Is that what she said happened?"

"Are you saying it didn't?"

"You bet I am. I didn't touch her." It took Cal a few moments to get control of his voice so he could speak. "Did she file a complaint or something against me?"

Kowalski motioned for him to take his seat again. "Trust me, Agent Rico, you'll want to sit down for this part."

Cal bit back his anger and sank onto the chair. Not easily, but he did it. And he forced himself to remain calm. Well, on the outside, anyway. Inside, there was a storm going on, and he could blame that storm on Jenna.

"As you know, I'm head of the task force assigned

to clean up the problems in Monte de Leon," Kowalski explained. "The kidnapped American civilians. The destruction of American-owned businesses and interests."

Impatient with what had obviously turned into a briefing, Cal spoke up. "Is any of this connected to Ms. Laniere?"

"Yes. Apparently, she's still involved with Paul Tolivar's business partners. That's why we started keeping an eye on her again."

That took the edge off some of Cal's anger and grabbed his interest. "Involved—how?"

Kowalski pushed his hands through the sides of his graying brown hair. "She's been staying in a small Texas town, Willow Ridge, for the past couple of months. But prior to that while she was still in Houston, one of Tolivar's partners, Holden Carr, phoned her no less than twenty times. They argued. We're hoping that during one of their future conversations, Holden might divulge some information. That's why the Justice Department has been monitoring Ms. Laniere's calls and e-mails."

In other words, phone and computer taps. Not exactly standard procedure for someone who wasn't a suspected criminal. Of course, Hollywood would almost certainly have been aware of that surveillance and monitoring, and it made Cal wonder why the man hadn't at least mentioned it. Or maybe Hollywood hadn't remembered that Cal had rescued Jenna.

"What does all of this have to do with alleged sexual misconduct?" Cal insisted.

Kowalski hesitated a moment. Then two. Just enough time to force Cal's anxiety level sky-high. "It's come to our attention that Jenna Laniere has a three-month-old daughter."

Oh, man.

It took Cal a few moments to find his breath, while he came up with a few questions that he was afraid even to ask.

"So what does that have to do with me?" Cal tried to sound nonchalant, but was sure he failed miserably.

"She claims the baby is yours."

Chapter Two

Cal finally spotted her.

Wearing brown pants and a cream-colored cable-knit sweater, Jenna came out of a small family-owned grocery store on Main Street. She had a white plastic sack clutched in each hand. But no baby.

One thing was for sure—she didn't look as if she'd given birth only three months earlier.

But she did look concerned. Her forehead was bunched up, and her gaze darted all around.

Good. She should be concerned about the lie she'd told. It probably wasn't a healthy thought to want to yell at a woman. But for the entire hour-long drive from regional headquarters to the little town of Willow Ridge, Texas, he'd played around with it.

She claims the baby is yours.

Director Kowalski's words pounded like fists in Cal's head. Powerful words, indeed.

Career-ruining words.

That's why he had to get this situation straightened out so that it couldn't do any more damage. Before the end of the week, he was due for a performance review, one that would be forwarded straight to the promotion board. If he had any hopes of making deputy director two years early, there couldn't even be a hint of negativity in that report.

And there wouldn't be.

That's what this visit was all about. One way or another, Jenna was going to tell the truth and clear his name. He'd worked too damn hard to let her take that early promotion away from him.

Cal stepped out of his car, ducked his head against the chilly February wind and strolled across the small parking lot toward her. He figured she was on her way to the apartment she'd rented over the town's lone bookstore. Judging from the direction she took, he was right.

Even though she kept close to the buildings, she was easy to track. Partly because there weren't many people out and about and partly because of her hair. Those shiny blond locks dipped several inches past her shoulders. Loose and free. The strands seemed to catch every ray of sun.

That hair would probably cause any man to give her a second look. Her body and face would cause a man to stare. Which was exactly what he was doing.

She must have sensed his eyes on her because she whirled around, her gaze snaring him right away.

"It's you," she said, squinting to see him in the harsh late afternoon sun. She sounded a little wary and surprised.

However, Cal's reactions were solely in the latter category.

First, there were her eyes. That shock of color. So green. So clear. He hadn't gotten a good look at her eyes when he rescued her in that dimly lit hotel, but he did now. And they were memorable. As was her face. She wore almost no makeup. Just a touch of peachy color on her mouth. She looked natural and sensual at the same time. But the most startling reaction of all was that he wasn't as angry at her as he had been five minutes before.

Well, until he forced himself to hang on to that particular feeling awhile longer.

"We have to talk," Cal insisted. And he wasn't about to let her say no. He took one of her grocery sacks so he could hook his arm through hers.

She looked down at the grip he had on her before she lifted her eyes to meet his. "This is about Paul Tolivar's business partner, isn't it? Is Holden Carr the one who's having me followed?"

That stopped Cal in his tracks. There was a mountain of concern in her voice and expression. Much to his shock, he wasn't immune to that concern.

He didn't like this feeling. The sudden need to protect her. This sure as heck wasn't an ISA-directed mission.

He repeated that to himself. "Someone is following you?" he asked.

She gave a surreptitious glance around, and since their arms were already linked, she maneuvered him into an alley that divided two shops.

"I spotted this man on my walk to the grocery store. He stayed in the shadows so I wasn't able to get a good look at him." Her words raced out, practically bleeding together. "Maybe he's following me, maybe he's not.

And there's a reporter. Gwen Mitchell. She introduced herself a couple of minutes ago in the produce aisle."

Cal made note of the name. Once he was done with this little chat, he'd run a background check on this Gwen Mitchell to see if she was legit. "What does she want?"

Jenna dismissed his question with a shrug, though tension was practically radiating from her. The muscles in her arm were tight and knotted. "She claims she's doing some kind of investigative report on Paul and the rebel situation in Monte de Leon."

That in itself wasn't alarming. There were probably lots of reporters doing similar stories because of the renewed investigation. "You don't believe her?"

"I don't know. Since the incident in Monte de Leon, I've been paranoid. Shadows don't look like shadows anymore. Hang-up calls seem sinister. Strangers in the grocery line look like rebel soldiers with orders to kill me." She shook her head. "And I'm sorry for dumping all of this on you. I know I'm not making any sense."

Unfortunately, she was making perfect sense. Cal had never met Paul's business partner, the infamous Holden Carr, but from what he'd learned about the man, Holden wasn't the sort to give up easily. Maybe he wanted to continue his late partner's quest to get Jenna's accounting firm and trust fund. Jenna's firm certainly wasn't the only one enticing to a potential money launderer, but Holden was familiar with it, and it had all the right foreign outlets to give him a quick turnover for the illegal cash.

Or maybe this was good news, and those shadows were Justice Department agents. Except Director Kowalski hadn't mentioned anything about her being followed. It was one thing to monitor calls and e-mails, but tailing a person required just cause and a lot of manpower. Since Jenna wasn't a suspect in a crime, there shouldn't have been sufficient cause for close surveillance.

And that brought them right back to Holden Carr.

"You've heard from Holden recently?" he asked. A lie detector of sorts since he knew from the director's briefing that she'd been in contact with the man in the past twenty-four hours.

"Oh, I've heard from him all right. Lucky me, huh? He's called a bunch of times, and right after I got back from Monte de Leon, he visited my office in Houston. And get this—he says he's always been in love with me, that he wants to be part of my life. Right. He's in love with my estate and accounting firm, and what he really wants is to be part of my death so he can inherit it." She paused. "Please tell me he'll be arrested soon."

"Soon." But Cal had no idea if that was even true.

"Good. Because as long as he's a free man, I'm not safe. That's why I left Houston. I thought maybe if I came here, Holden wouldn't be able to find me. That he'd stop harassing me. Then yesterday afternoon he called me again, on my new cell phone." She moistened her lips. And looked away. "He threatened me."

That didn't surprise Cal. Holden wouldn't hesitate to resort to intimidation to get what he wanted. Still, that was a problem for the back burner. He had something more pressing.

"Holden didn't make an overt threat," Jenna continued before Cal could speak. "He implied it. It scared me enough to decide that I need professional security. A bodyguard or something. But I don't know anyone I can trust. I don't know if the bodyguard I call might really be working for Holden."

Unfortunately, that was a real possibility. If Holden knew where she was, then he would also know how to get to her.

She paused and blew out a long breath. "Okay, that's enough about me and my problems. Why are you here?" She conjured a halfhearted smile. "Gosh, that's a déjà vu kind of question, isn't it? I remember asking you something similar when you were rescuing me in Monte de Leon. Is that why you're here now—to rescue me?"

"No." But why the heck did he suddenly feel as if he wanted to do just that?

From that still panicked look in her eyes, it wasn't a good time to bring up his anger, but Cal wasn't about to let her off the hook, either.

"Why did you lie about who your baby's father is?" he demanded.

Jenna blinked, and then her eyes widened. "How did you know?"

"Well, it wasn't a lucky guess, that's for sure. This morning my director called me into his office to demand an explanation as to why I slept with someone in my protective custody."

"Ohmygod." Jenna leaned against the wall and pulled in several hard breaths. "I had no idea. How did your director even find out I'd had a baby?"

Because she already had a lot to absorb, Cal skipped

right over the Justice Department eavesdropping on her, and gave her a summary of what Director Kowalski had relayed to him. "You told Holden Carr that the baby was mine."

Jenna nodded, and with her breath now gusting hard and fast, she studied his expression. It was as icy as the Antarctic. "This could get you into trouble, couldn't it?"

"It's *already* gotten me into trouble. Deep trouble. And it could get worse."

He would have added more, especially the part about Director Kowalski demanding DNA proof that Cal wasn't the baby's father. But he caught some movement from the corner of his eye. A thin-faced man in a dark blue two-door car. He drove slowly past them.

"That's the guy," Jenna whispered, tugging on the sleeve of Cal's leather jacket. "He's the one who followed me to the grocery store."

The words had hardly left her mouth when the man gunned the engine and sped away. But not before Cal made eye contact with him.

Oh, hell.

Cal recognized him from the intel surveillance photos.

He cursed, dropped the grocery bag and slipped his hand inside his jacket in case he had to draw his gun. "How long did you say he's been following you?"

Jenna shook her head and looked to be on the verge of panicking. "I think just today. Why? Do you know him? Is he a friend of yours?"

There was way too much hope in her voice.

"Not a friend," Cal assured her. "But I know *of* him." He left it at that. "Where's your baby?"

"In the apartment. My landlord's daughter is watching her. Why?"

Cal didn't answer that. "Come on. We'll finish this conversation there."

And once they had finished the discussion about the paternity of her child, he'd move on to some security measures he wanted her to take. Maybe the Justice Department could even provide her with protection or a safe house. He'd call Hollywood and Director Kowalski and put in a request.

Cal tried to get her moving, but Jenna held her ground. "Tell me—who's that man?"

Okay, so that wasn't panic in her eyes. It was determination. She wasn't about to drop this. Not even for a couple of minutes until they could reach her apartment.

"Anthony Salazar," Cal let her know. "That's his real name, anyway. He often uses an alias."

She stared at him. "He works for Holden Carr?"

"He usually just works for the person who'll pay him the most." Cal hadn't intended to pause, but he had to so he could clear his throat. "He's a hired assassin, Jenna."

Chapter Three

Jenna was glad the exterior wall of the café was there to support her, or her legs might have given way.

First, there was Cal's out-of-the-blue visit to deal with.

Then the news that he knew about the lie she'd told.

And now this.

"An assassin?" she repeated.

Somehow she managed to say aloud the two little words that had sent her world spinning out of control— again. She'd had a lot of that lately and was more than ready for it to stop.

Cal cursed under his breath. He picked up the grocery bag he'd dropped and then slipped his arm around her waist.

Jenna thought of her baby. Of Sophie. She couldn't let that assassin get anywhere near her daughter.

She started to break into a run, but Cal maneuvered her off the sidewalk and behind the café. They walked quickly into the alley that ran the entire length of Main Street. So they'd be out of sight.

"You didn't know that guy was here?" she asked as they hurried.

"No."

That meant Cal had come to confront her about naming him as Sophie's father. That alone was a powerful reason for a visit. She owed him an explanation.

And a Texas-size apology.

But for now, all Jenna wanted to do was get inside her apartment and make sure that hired gun, Anthony Salazar, was nowhere near her baby. And to think he might have been following her on her entire walk to the grocery store. Or even longer. He could have taken out a gun and fired at any time, and there wouldn't have been a thing she could do to stop it.

He could have hurt Sophie.

Maybe because she was shaking now, Cal tightened his grip around her, pulling her deeper into the warmth of his arm, while increasing the pace until they were jogging.

"I didn't name you as my baby's father to hurt your career," she assured him. "I didn't think anyone other than Holden would hear what I was saying."

A deep sound of disapproval rumbled in Cal's throat. He didn't offer anything else until they reached the bookstore. Her apartment was at the back and up the flight of stairs on the second floor.

"You have a security system?" he asked as they hurried up the steps.

"Yes."

She unlocked the door—both locks—tossed the groceries and her purse on the table in the entry and bolted across the room. The sixteen-year-old sitter, Manda, was on the sofa reading a magazine. Jenna raced past her to the bedroom and saw Sophie sleeping in her crib. Exactly where she'd left her just a half hour earlier at the start of her afternoon nap.

"Is something wrong?" Manda asked, standing.

Jenna didn't answer that. "Did anyone come by or call?"

Manda shook her head, obviously concerned. "Are you okay?"

"Fine," Jenna lied. "I just had a bad case of baby separation. I had to get back and make sure Sophie was all right. And she is. She's sleeping like…well, a baby."

Still looking concerned, Manda nodded, and her gaze landed on Cal.

"He's an old friend," Jenna explained. She purposely didn't say Cal's name. Best not to give too much information until she knew what was going on. Besides, she'd already caused Cal enough trouble.

Jenna took the twenty-dollar bill from her pocket and handed it to Manda. "But I was barely here thirty minutes," the teen protested. "Five bucks an hour, remember?"

"Consider the rest a tip." Jenna put her hand on Manda's back to get her moving. She needed some privacy so she could find out what was going on.

"Why didn't the alarm go off when we came in?" he wanted to know as soon as Manda walked out with her magazine tucked beneath her arm. It wasn't a question, exactly. More like the start of a cross-examination.

"It's connected to the bookstore." She shut the door and locked it. "The owner turns it on when she closes for the evening."

That didn't please him. His disapproving gaze fired around the apartment, but it didn't have to too far. It was one large twenty-by-twenty-five-foot room with an adjoining bath and a tiny nursery. The kitchenette and dining area were on one side, and the living room with its sofa bed was on the other. It wasn't exactly quaint and cozy with the vaulted, exposed beam ceiling, but it was a far cry from her massive family home near Houston.

"Why this place?" he asked after he'd finished his assessment.

"It has fewer shadows," she said, not wanting to explain about her sudden fear of bogeymen, assassins and rebel fighters.

She could still hear the bullets.

She'd always be able to hear them.

Cal nodded and eased the grocery bag onto the tile-topped table.

"You want a drink or something?" Jenna motioned to the fridge.

"No, thanks." There was an unspoken warning at the end of that. That was her cue to start explaining this whole baby-daddy issue.

She was feeling light-headed and was still shivering, so Jenna snagged the trail mix from her grocery bag and went to the sofa so she could sit down.

"First of all, I didn't know what I said about the baby would even get back to you. To anyone." She popped a cashew into her mouth and offered him some from the bag. He shook his head. "Yesterday, when Holden called, I'd just returned from Sophie's three-month checkup with the pediatrician. Right away, he started yelling, saying that he knew that I'd had a child."

"How did he know?"

"That's the million-dollar question." But then, Jenna rethought that. "Or maybe not. I stopped by my house on the outskirts of Houston to pick up some things before I went to the appointment. Holden probably had someone watching the place and then followed me. I was careful. You know, always checking the rearview mirror and the parking lot at the clinic. But he could have had that Salazar guy following me the whole time."

In hindsight, she should have anticipated Holden would do something like this. In fact, she should have known he would. He was as tenacious as he was ruthless.

"So Holden confronted you about the baby?" Cal asked.

"Oh, yes. Complete with yelling obscenities. And that was just the prelude. No more facade of being in love with me. He demanded to know if Paul was Sophie's father. If so, he said he would challenge me for custody."

"Custody?" Cal didn't hide his surprise very well.

"Apparently, Paul had some kind of provision in his will that would make Holden the legal guardian to any child that Paul might have—if I'm proven unfit, which Holden says he can do with his connections. After he threatened me with that, I stalled him, trying to think of what I should say, and your message was still in my head. It made the leap from my brain to my mouth before I could stop it, and I just blurted out your name."

Cal walked closer and slid onto the chair across from her. Close enough for her to see all the scorching blue in his eyes. And close enough to see the emotion and the anger, too. "My message?"

She swallowed hard. "The one you left on my voice mail at my office about a month ago. My assistant sent it to me, and I'd recently listened to it."

A lot. In fact, she'd memorized it.

She'd found his voice comforting, and that's why she'd replayed it. Night after night. When she couldn't sleep. When the nightmares got the best of her. But his voice wasn't comforting now, of course. Coupled with his riled glare, there wasn't much comforting about him or this visit.

Well, except that he'd put his arm around her when he thought she was cold.

A special kind of special agent.

He still looked the part, even though he wasn't in battle gear today. He wore jeans, a dark blue button-down shirt that was almost the same color as his eyes and a black leather jacket.

"Anyway, after I realized it was stupid to give Holden your name," she continued, "I thought about calling him back and making something up. But I figured that'd only make him more suspicious."

Because Cal wasn't saying anything and because she suddenly didn't know what to do with her hands, Jenna offered him the trail mix again, and this time he reached into the bag and took out a few pieces.

"I've done everything to keep my pregnancy and delivery quiet. *Everything,*" Jenna said, aware that her nerves were causing her to babble. It was either that, humming or reciting something, and she didn't want to launch into a neurotic rendition of the Preamble to the Constitution. "I don't have any family, and none of my friends know. No one here in Willow Ridge really knows who I am, either."

She didn't think it was her imagination that he was hesitant to say anything. Under the guise of eating trail mix, Cal sat there, letting her babble linger between them.

Since she had to know what was going on in his head, Jenna just went for the direct approach. "How did your director find out that I'd told Holden about my baby?"

His jaw muscles began to stir against each other. "The Justice Department has kept tabs on you."

"Tabs?" She took a moment to consider that. "That's an interesting word. What does it mean exactly?"

More jaw muscles moved. "It means they were keeping track of you in case Holden decided to divulge anything incriminating they could use in their case against him."

So it was true. Her fears weren't all in her head. The authorities thought Holden might be a danger as well.

Or maybe they didn't.

Maybe they were just hoping Holden would do something stupid so they could use that to arrest him.

"I was bait?" she asked.

"No." But then he lifted his shoulder. "At least I don't think so."

Jenna prayed that was true. The thought wasn't something she could handle right now.

"The baby is Paul Tolivar's?" Cal asked.

She nodded. And waited for his reaction. She didn't get one. He put on his operative's face again. "Just how much trouble will this cause for you?" she wanted to know.

"The ISA has a morality clause." His fingers tightened around a dried apricot, squishing it. "Plus, the regs forbid personal contact during a protective custody situation."

That was not what she wanted to hear. "You could be punished."

Again, it took him a moment to answer. "Yeah."

"Okay." Jenna took a deep breath, and because she couldn't stay still, she got up to pace. There was a solution to this. Not necessarily an appetizing solution, but it did exist. "Will my statement that I lied be enough to clear you, or will you need a paternity test?"

"My director wants a test." He stood as well, and caught her arm when she started to go past him. His fingers were warm. Surprisingly warm. She could feel his touch all the way through her thick sweater. "But I think that's the least of your worries right now."

"Because of Anthony Salazar." Jenna nodded. "Yes. He's definitely a worry. His being here means I'll need to leave Willow Ridge and go into hiding."

"You're already in hiding," Cal pointed out. "And he found you. He'll find you again. He's very good at what he does. You need more protection than a bookstore security system or a hired bodyguard can give you. I'll make some calls and see what I can do."

Pride almost caused her to decline his offer. But she knew that it wouldn't protect her baby. And that was the most important thing right now. She had to stay safe because if anything happened to her, it would happen to her precious daughter as well.

"Thank you," Jenna whispered. She repeated it to make sure he heard her. "I really am sorry about dragging you into my personal life."

"We'll get it straightened out," he assured her. But there was a lot of skepticism in his voice.

And annoyance, which she deserved.

"Okay, while you make those calls, I'll arrange to have the paternity test done," Jenna added.

Somehow, though, she'd have to keep the results a secret from anyone but Cal and his director.

Because she didn't want Holden to learn the truth. Jenna moved away from Cal and started to pace again, mumbling a poem she'd memorized in middle school. She couldn't help it. A few lines came out before she could stop them.

"What you must think of me," she said. "For what it's worth, Paul and I only had sex once, and we used protection. But I guess something went wrong…on a lot of levels. Honestly, I don't really even remember sleeping with him." Jenna mumbled that last part.

"You don't remember?" he challenged.

She shook her head. "One minute we were having dinner, and the next thing I remember was waking up in bed with him. I obviously had too much to drink. Or else he drugged me. Either way, it was my stupid mistake for being there. Then I made things so much worse by telling Holden that you're my daughter's father. And here we didn't even have sex. Heck, we never even kissed on the floor of that cantina."

A clear image formed in her mind. Of that floor. Of Cal on top of her to protect her from the explosion. It wasn't exactly pleasurable. Okay, it was. But it wasn't supposed to be.

Not then.

Not now.

She'd already done enough damage to Cal's career without her adding unwanted sexual attraction that could never go beyond the fantasy stage.

He opened his mouth to say something, but didn't get past the first syllable. There was a knock at the door, the sudden sound shattering the silence.

Cal reacted fast. He reached inside his jacket and pulled out a handgun from a shoulder holster. He motioned for her to move out of the path of the door.

Jenna raced across the room and took a knife from the cutlery drawer. It probably wouldn't give them much protection, but she didn't intend to let Cal fight alone. Especially since the battle was hers.

With his hands gripped around his weapon, he eased toward the door. Every inch of his posture and demeanor was vigilant. Ready. Lethal.

Cal didn't use the peephole to look outside, but instead peered out the corner of the window.

He cursed softly.

"It's Holden Carr."

Chapter Four

This was not how Cal had planned his visit.

It was supposed to be in and out quickly. He was only on a fact-finding mission so he could get out of hot water with the director. Instead, he'd walked right into a vipers' nest. And one viper was way too close.

Holden Carr was literally pounding on Jenna's door.

Cal glanced back at her. With a butcher knife in a white-knuckled death grip, Jenna was standing guard in front of the nursery. She was pale, trembling and nibbling on her bottom lip. *Bam!* There were his protective instincts.

There was no way he could let her face Holden Carr alone. From everything Cal had read about the man, Holden was as dangerous as Paul, his former business partner. And Paul had been ready to commit murder to get his hands on Jenna's estate.

"Go to your daughter," Cal instructed while Holden continued to pound.

She shook her head. "You might need backup."

He lifted his eyebrow. She wasn't exactly backup

material. Jenna Laniere might have been temporarily living in a starter apartment in a quaint Texas cowboy town, but her blue blood and pampered upbringing couldn't have prepared her for the likes of Holden Carr.

"I'll handle this," Cal let her know, and he left no room for argument.

She mumbled something, but stepped back into the nursery.

With his SIG Sauer drawn, Cal stood to the side of the door. It was standard procedure—bad guys often like to shoot through doors. But Holden probably didn't have that in mind. It was broad daylight and with the door-pounding, he was probably drawing all kinds of attention to himself, but Cal didn't want to take an unnecessary risk.

Once he was in place, he reached over. Unlocked the door. And eased it open.

Cal jammed his gun right in Holden's face.

Holden's dust-gray eyes sliced in the direction of the SIG Sauer. There was just a flash of shock and concern before he buried those reactions in the cool composure of his Nordic pale skin and his Viking-size body. He was decked out in a pricy camel-colored suit that probably cost more than Cal made in a month.

"I'm Holden Carr and I need to see Jenna," he announced.

Cal didn't lower his gun. In fact, he jabbed it against Holden's right cheek. "Oh, yeah? About what?"

"A private matter."

"It's not so private. From what I've heard you're threatening her. It takes a special kind of man to threaten a woman half his size. Of course, you're no stranger to violence, are you? Did you murder Paul Tolivar?"

Holden couldn't quite bury his anger fast enough. It rippled through his jaw muscles and his eyes. "Who the hell are you?"

"Cal Rico. I'm Jenna's...friend." But he let his tone indicate that he was the man who wouldn't hesitate to pull the trigger if Holden tried to barge his way in. "Anything you have to say to Jenna, you can say to me. I'll make sure she gets the message."

"The message is she can't hide from me forever." Holden enunciated each word. "I know she had a baby. A little girl named Sophie Elizabeth. Born three months ago. That means the child is Paul's."

It didn't surprise Cal that Holden knew all of this, but what else did he know? "Paul, the man you murdered," Cal challenged.

There was another flash of anger. "Not that it's any of your business, but I didn't murder him. His house-keeper did. She was secretly working for a rebel faction who had issues with some of Paul's businesses."

"Right. The housekeeper." Cal made sure he sounded skeptical. He'd already heard the theory of the runaway housekeeper known only as Mary. "I don't suppose she confessed."

Holden had to get his teeth apart before he could respond. "She fled the estate after she killed him. No one's been able to find her."

"Convenient. Now, mind telling me how you came by this information about Jenna's child?"

"Yes. I mind."

Cal hadn't expected him to volunteer that, since it almost certainly involved illegal activity. "Hmmm. I smell a wire tap. That kind of illegal activity can get you arrested. Your dual citizenship won't do a thing to protect you, either. If you hightail it back to Monte de Leon, you can be extradited."

Though that wasn't likely. Still, Cal made a note to discover the source of that possible tap.

Holden looked past him, and because they were so close, Cal saw the man's eyes light up. Cal didn't have to guess why. Holden was aiming his attention in the direction of the nursery door and had probably spotted Jenna. He tried to come inside, but Cal blocked the door with his foot.

"She'll have to talk to me sooner or later," Holden insisted. "Call off your guard dog," he yelled at Jenna.

"What do you want?" Jenna asked. Cal silently groaned when he heard her walking closer. She really didn't take orders very well.

"I want you to carry out Paul's wishes. In his will, he named me guardian of his children. He didn't have any children at the time he wrote that, but he does now."

"You only want my daughter so you can control me," Jenna tossed out.

Holden didn't deny it. "I've petitioned the court for custody," he said.

Jenna stopped right next to Cal, and she reached across his body to open the door wider. "No judge would give you custody."

"Maybe not in this country, but in Monte de Leon,

the law will be on Paul's side. Even in death he's still a powerful man with powerful friends."

"Sophie's an American," Jenna pointed out. "Born right here in Texas."

"And you think that'll stop Paul's wishes from being carried out? It won't. If the Monte de Leon court deems you unfit—and that can easily happen with the right judge—then the court will petition for the child to be brought to her father's estate."

"Sophie is not Paul's child." She looked Holden right in the eye when she told that lie.

But Holden only smiled. "I've seen pictures of her. She looks just like him. Dark brown hair. Blue eyes."

Pictures meant he had surveillance along with taps. This was not looking good.

Cal could hear Jenna's breath speed up. Fear had a smell, and she was throwing off that scent, along with motherly protection vibes. But that wouldn't do anything to convince this SOB that he didn't have a right to claim her child.

From the corner of his eye, Cal spotted a movement. There was a tall redheaded woman with a camera. She was about forty yards away across the street and was clicking pictures of this encounter. Gwen Mitchell no doubt. And she wasn't the only woman there. He also spotted a slender blonde making her way up the steps to Jenna's apartment.

"That's Helena Carr," Jenna provided.

Holden's sister and business partner. Great. Now there was an added snake to deal with, and it was all playing out in front of a photographer with questionable motives. Cal could already hear himself having to explain why he was in small-town America with his standard-issue SIG Sauer smashed against a civilian's face.

"This meeting is over," Cal insisted. He lowered his gun, but he kept it aimed at Holden's right kneecap.

"It'll be over when Jenna admits that her daughter is Paul's," Holden countered.

"We just want the truth." That from Helena, who was a feminine version of her brother without the Viking-wide shoulders. Her stare was different, too. Nonthreatening. Almost serene. "After all, we know she slept with Paul, and the timing is perfect to have produced Sophie."

Cal hoped he didn't regret this later, but there was one simple way to diffuse this. "I have dark brown hair, blue eyes. Just like Sophie's." He hoped, since he hadn't actually seen the little girl.

Helena blinked and gave him an accusing stare. Holden cursed. "Are you saying you're the father?" he asked.

"No," Jenna started to say. But Cal made sure his voice drowned her out.

"Yes," Cal snarled. "I'm Sophie's father."

"Impossible," Holden snarled back.

Cal gave him a cocky snort. "There is nothing impossible about it. I'm a man. Jenna's a woman. Sometimes men and women have sex, and that results in a pregnancy."

And just in case Jenna was going to say something to contradict him, Cal gave her a quick glance. She was staring at him as if he'd lost his mind.

"You won't mind taking a DNA test," Holden insisted.

"Tell you what. You send the request for a DNA

sample through your foreign judge and let it trickle its way through our American judicial system. Then I'll get back to you with an answer."

Of course, the answer would be no.

Still, that wouldn't stop Holden from trying. If he controlled Jenna's child, then he would ultimately have access to a vast money-laundering enterprise. Then he could fully operate his own family business and the one he'd inherited from Paul.

"This isn't over." Holden aimed the threat at Jenna as he stalked away.

Cal was about to shut the door and call his director so he could start some damage control, but Helena eased her hand onto the side to stop it from closing.

"I'm sorry about this." Helena sounded sincere. Or else she'd rehearsed it enough to fake sincerity. Maybe this was the brother-sister version of good cop/bad cop. "I just want the truth so I can make sure Paul's child inherits what she deserves."

Jenna didn't even address that. "Can you stop your brother?"

Cal carefully noted Helena's reaction. She glanced over her shoulder. First, at her brother who was getting inside their high-end car. Then at the photographer.

"Could I step inside for just a moment?" That sincerity thing was there again.

But Cal wasn't buying it.

Jenna apparently did. With the butcher knife still clutched in her hand, she stepped back so Helena could enter.

"That reporter out there might have some way to

eavesdrop on us," Helena explained. "She has equipment and cameras with her."

Maybe. But Cal hadn't seen anything to suggest long-range eavesdropping equipment. Still, it was an unnecessary risk to keep talking in plain view. Lipreading was a possibility. Plus, anything said here could ultimately put Jenna in more danger and get him in deeper trouble with the director. Not that her paternity claims were exactly newsworthy, but he didn't want to see his and Jenna's names and photos splashed in a newspaper.

"Well?" Cal prompted when Helena continued to look around and didn't say anything else.

"Where do I start?" She seemed to be waiting for an invitation to sit down, but Cal didn't offer. Helena sighed. "My brother is determined to carry out Paul's wishes. They've been friends since childhood when our parents moved to Monte de Leon to start businesses there. Holden was devastated when Paul was killed."

Cal shrugged. "Paul isn't the father of Jenna's child, so there's no wish to carry out."

The last word had hardly left his mouth when he heard a soft whimpering cry sound coming from the nursery.

"Sophie," Jenna mumbled.

"Go to her," Cal advised. "I'll finish up here."

Jenna hesitated. But not for long—the baby's cries were getting louder.

"I do need to talk to Jenna," Helena continued. She opened her purse and rummaged through it. "Do you have a pen? I want to leave my cell number so she can contact me."

That was actually a good idea. He might be able to get approval to trace Helena's calls and obtain a record of her past ones.

Cal didn't have a pen with him, and he looked around before spotting one and a notepad on the kitchen countertop. He got it and glanced into the nursery while he was on that side of the room. Jenna was leaning over the crib changing Sophie's diaper.

"Someone was following Jenna." Cal walked back to Helena and handed her the pen and notepad.

She dodged his gaze, took the pen and wrote down her number. "You mean that reporter across the street? She approached us when we drove up and said she was doing an article about Paul. She said she recognized Holden from newspaper pictures."

Cal shook his head. "Not her. Someone else. A man." He watched for a reaction.

Helena shrugged and handed him the notepad. "You think I know something about it?"

"Do you? The man's name is Anthony Salazar."

Her eyes widened. "Salazar," she repeated on a rise of breath. "You've seen him here in Willow Ridge?"

"I've seen him," Cal confirmed. "Now, mind telling me how you know him?"

Her breath became even more rapid, and she glanced around to make sure it was safe to talk. "Anthony Salazar is evil," she said in a whisper.

He caught her arm when she turned to leave. "And you know this how?"

She opened her mouth but stopped. "Are you wearing a wire?" she demanded.

"No, and I'm not going to strip down to prove it. But you *are* going to give me answers."

Her chin came up. Since he had hold of her arm, he could feel that she was trembling. "You're trying to make me say something incriminating."

Yeah. But for now, Cal would settle for the truth. "What's your connection to Salazar? Does he work for your brother? For you?"

She reached behind her and opened the door. "He worked for Paul."

He hadn't expected that answer. "Paul's dead."

"But his estate isn't."

"What does that mean?" Cal asked cautiously.

"Yesterday was the first anniversary of Paul's death. Early this morning his attorney delivered e-mails of instruction to people named in his will. I saw the list. Salazar got one."

Cal paused a moment to give that some thought. "Are you saying Paul reached out from the grave and hired this man to do something to Jenna?"

"That's exactly what I'm saying." Helena turned and delivered the rest from over her shoulder as she started down the steps. "Neither Holden nor I can call off Salazar. No one can."

Chapter Five

After Jenna changed Sophie's diaper, she gently rocked her until her daughter's whimpers and cries faded. It took just a few seconds before her baby was calm, cooing and smiling at her. It was like magic, and even though it warmed her heart to see her baby so happy, Jenna only wished she could be soothed so easily.

Not much of a chance of that with Holden, his sister and that assassin lurking around. She kept mumbling the poem *"The Raven,"* and hoped the mechanical exercise would keep her calm.

She heard Cal shut and lock the door, and Jenna wanted to be out there while he was talking to Helena. After all, this was her fight, not Cal's. But she also didn't want Holden or Helena anywhere near her baby.

With Helena gone, Jenna went into the kitchen so she could fix Sophie a bottle. Cal glanced at her, but he had his phone already pressed to his ear, so he didn't say anything to her.

"Hollywood, I need a big favor," Cal said to the person on the other end of the phone line. "The subjects

are Holden Carr, Jenna Laniere and Anthony Salazar."
He paused. "Yes, the Holden and Jenna from Monte de
Leon. I need to know how he found out where she's
living. Look for wiretaps first and then dig into her employees. I want to know about any connection with
anyone who could have given him this info or photos
of Jenna Laniere's baby."

Well, that was a start. Hopefully Cal's contacts would
give them an answer soon. It wouldn't, however, solve
her problem with Salazar.

She and Sophie needed protection.

And she needed to clear up the paternity issue with
Cal's director. And amid all that, she had to make arrangements to move. The apartment was no longer safe
now that Holden and Helena Carr knew where she was.
Packing wouldn't take long—for the past year, she'd literally been living out of a suitcase, anyway.

With Sophie nestled in the crook of her arm, Jenna
warmed the formula, tested a drop on her wrist to make
sure it wasn't too hot, and carried both baby and bottle
to the sofa so she could feed her. Sophie wasn't smiling
any longer. She was hungry and was making more of
those whimpering demands. Jenna kissed her cheek and
started to feed her.

Once it was quiet, it was impossible to shut out what
Cal was saying. He was still giving someone instructions about checking on the reporter and where to look
for Holden Carr's leak, and Cal wanted the person to
learn more about some e-mails that might have recently
been sent out by Paul's attorney.

She didn't know anything about e-mails, but a leak in

communication could mean someone might have betrayed her. There was just one problem with that. Before the trip to the pediatrician, no one including her own household staff and employees had known where she was.

Now everyone seemed to know.

Cal ended his call and scrubbed his hand over his face. He was obviously frustrated. So was Jenna. But she had to figure out a way to get Cal out of the picture. He didn't deserve this, and once she was at a safe location, she could get the DNA test for Sophie.

"So, this is Sophie," he commented, walking closer. "She's so little for someone who's caused a lot of big waves."

"I'm the one who caused the waves," Jenna corrected.

Cal shrugged it off, but she doubted he was doing that on the inside. "She seems to like that bottle."

"I couldn't breast-feed her. I got mastitis—that's an infection—right after she was born. By the time it'd run its course and I was off the antibiotics, Sophie decided the bottle was for her." Jenna cringed a little, wondering why she'd shared something so personal with a man who was doing everything he could to get her out of his life.

Cal walked even closer, and Sophie responded to the sound of his footsteps by turning her head in his direction. She tracked him with her wide blue-green eyes and fastened her gaze on him when he sat on the sofa next to them. Even with the bottle in her mouth, she smiled at him.

Much to Jenna's surprise, Cal smiled back.

It was a great smile, too, and made him look even hotter than he already was. That smile was a lethal weapon in his arsenal.

"She looks like you," Cal said. "Your face. Your eyes."

"Paul's coloring, though," she added softly. "But when I look at her, I don't see him. I never have. I loved her unconditionally from the first moment I realized I was pregnant." Sheez. More personal stuff.

Why couldn't she stop babbling?

"Helena left you her cell number," Cal said, dropping the notepad onto the coffee table, switching the subject. "She said you're to call her."

Jenna glanced at it and noticed that it had a local area code. "What does she want?"

"Honestly? I don't know. All I know is I don't trust her or Holden." Sophie kicked at him, and he brushed his fingers over her bare toes. He smiled again. But the smile quickly faded. "Helena said that early this morning Salazar received an e-mail from Paul's estate. It might have something to do with why he's here."

Paul again. "It doesn't matter why he's here. I plan to call the Willow Ridge sheriff and see if he can arrest him."

"That's one option. Probably not a good one, though. Salazar won't be easy to catch."

"But we both saw him, right there on Main Street," Jenna pointed out.

Cal nodded. "Unless the local sheriff is very good at what he does, and very lucky, he could get killed attempting to arrest a man like Salazar."

Oh, mercy. She hadn't even considered that. "Then I have to move sooner than I thought. As soon as Sophie's finished with her bottle, I'll—"

But she stopped there because it involved too many steps and a lot of phone calls.

Where should she start?

"We'll have some information about Holden soon," Cal finished for her. "Once we have that, we'll go from there. It's best if we arrange for someone else to pick up Salazar, not the local sheriff."

"We?" she challenged, wondering why he wasn't excusing himself from this situation.

He kept his attention on Sophie and reached out and touched one of her dark brown curls. "We, as in someone assigned from the International Security Agency."

But not him. A coworker, maybe.

Jenna thought about that for a moment and wondered about the man sitting next to her. She hadn't forgotten the way he'd bashed through a window to save her. "Are you a spy?"

He didn't blink, didn't react. "I'm an operative."

"Is that another word for a spy?"

"It can be." Still no reaction. "The ISA is a sister organization to the CIA. We have no jurisdiction on American soil. We operate only in foreign countries to protect American interests, mainly through rescues and extractions in hostile situations." He took his eyes off Sophie and aimed them at her. "I'm not sure how much I can get involved in your situation."

"I understand." Sophie was finished with her bottle, and Jenna put her against her shoulder so she could burp her. "Besides, I've caused you enough trouble."

He didn't disagree. But there was some kind of debate stirring inside him. "I hadn't expected to want to protect you," he admitted.

Oh. She was surprised not just by his desire to help her, but also by the admission itself. "Why?"

"Why?" he repeated.

She searched his eyes, looking for an answer. Or at least a way to rephrase the question so that it didn't imply the attraction she felt for him. An attraction he probably didn't feel.

"Why did you call my office in Houston last month?" It was something Jenna had wanted to ask since she'd received the message.

Cal shrugged. "The ISA was reopening the investigation into Paul's business dealings and murder. I wanted to make sure you were okay."

"And that's all?" She nearly waved that off. But something in his eyes had her holding her tongue. She wanted to know the reason.

He didn't dodge her gaze. "I was going to see if you'd gotten over Paul. I'd planned to ask you out."

Jenna went still. So maybe the attraction was mutual after all.

She doubted that was a good thing.

"I was over Paul the moment he slapped me for refusing his marriage proposal," Jenna let him know.

His jaw muscles went to war again. "I heard that slap. I was monitoring you with long-distance eavesdropping equipment."

She felt her cheeks flush. It embarrassed her to know that anyone, especially Cal, had witnessed that. The whole incident with Paul was a testament to her poor judgment.

"I've been a screwup most of my life," she admitted.

He made a throaty sound of surprise. "You think that slap was your fault?"

"I think being at Paul's estate was my first mistake. I should have had him investigated before I went down there. I shouldn't have trusted him."

He leaned closer. "Is this where I should remind you about hindsight and that Paul was a really good con artist?"

"It wouldn't help. I've been duped by two other losers. One in college—my supposed boyfriend stole my credit cards and some jewelry. And then there was the assistant I hired right before this mess with Paul. He sold business secrets to my competition." She paused, brought her eyes back to his. "That's why I'm not jumping for joy that you wanted to ask me out."

Cal flexed his eyebrows. "You think I'm a loser like those other guys?"

"No." Shocked that he'd even suggest it, she repeated her denial. "I know you're not. But I have this trust issue now. On top of the damage I've caused your career, I know I'd be bad for you."

He didn't say a word, and the silence closed in around them. Seconds passed.

"Remember when you were lying beneath me in that cantina?" he asked.

"Oh, yes." She winced because she said it so quickly. And so fondly.

"Well, I remember it, too. Heck, I fantasize about it. I was hoping once I saw you, once I got out my anger over the lie you told, that the fantasies would stop."

Oh, my. Fantasies? This wasn't good. She'd had her own share of fantasies about Cal. Thankfully, she didn't say or do anything stupid. Then Sophie burped loudly, and spit up. It landed on Jenna's shoulder and the front of her sweater.

The corner of Cal's mouth lifted. There was relief in his expression, and Jenna thought he was already regretting this frank conversation.

She glanced down at Sophie, who was smiling now. Jenna wiped her mouth, kissed her on the forehead, put her in the infant carrier seat on the coffee table and buckled the safety strap so that she couldn't wiggle out.

"Could you watch her a minute while I change my top?" Jenna asked.

"Sure." But he didn't look so sure. It was the first time he'd ever seemed nervous. Including when he'd faced gunfire during her rescue.

Jenna stood. So did Cal, though he did keep his hand on the top edge of the carrier. "Forget about that fantasy stuff," he said.

"I will," she lied. "I don't want to cause any more problems for you."

But she had already caused more problems. Jenna could feel it. The attraction was stirring between them. It was a full-fledged tug deep within her belly. A tug that reminded her that despite being a mom, she was still very much a woman standing too close to a too-attractive man.

She fluttered her fingers toward the nursery. "I won't be long." But even with that declaration, she gave in to that tug and hesitated a moment.

Cal cursed softly under his breath. "We'll talk about security plans after you've changed your top."

That should have knocked her back to reality. But

while his mouth was saying those practical words, his eyes seemed to be saying, *I want to kiss you.*

Maybe that was wishful thinking.

. Either way, Jenna turned before she said something they'd both regret.

She hurriedly grabbed another sweater from the suitcase in the nursery. She shut the door enough to give herself some privacy, but kept it ajar so she could hear if Sophie started to cry. Jenna peeked out to see Cal playing with her daughter's toes while he made some funny faces. The interaction didn't last long—Cal's phone rang, and he answered it.

"Hollywood," Cal greeted. "I hope you have good news for me."

So did Jenna. They desperately needed something to go their way.

She peeled off the soiled sweater, stuffed it into a plastic bag and put it in the suitcase. It would save her from having to pack it in the next hour or two. Then she put on a dark green top and grabbed some other items from around the room to pack those as well.

When she'd finished cramming as much in the suitcase as she could, she took a moment to compose herself. And hated that she didn't feel stronger. But then, it was hard to feel strong when her past relationship with Paul might endanger her daughter.

She peeked out to make sure Sophie was okay. She was. So Jenna waited, listening to Cal's conversation. It was mostly one-sided. He grunted a few responses, and started to curse, but he bit it off when he looked down at Sophie. The profanity and his expression said it all.

"Bad news?" Jenna asked the moment he hung up.

"Some." He looked at Sophie and then glanced around the room. "It's best if you stay put while arrangements are being made for you and Sophie to move."

She walked back to the sofa and sat down across from her daughter. Just seeing that tiny face was a reminder that the stakes were massive now. "Staying put will be safe?"

Cal nodded. "As safe as I can make it."

"You?" she questioned. Not we. "Your director approves of this."

"He approves."

Which meant the situation was dangerous enough for the director to break protocol by allowing her to be guarded by Cal despite the inappropriate conduct that he believed had happened between them.

"How bad is the bad news?" she asked.

He pulled in his breath and walked closer. "Our communications specialist is a guy we call Hollywood. He's very good at what he does, and he can't find an obvious leak, so we don't know how Holden located you. Not yet, anyway. But we were able to get more information about the e-mails sent out by Paul's attorney. Each one was sent from a different account, and one went to your office in Houston. Holden, Helena and Anthony Salazar each got one. The final one went to your reporter friend, Gwen Mitchell."

Gwen Mitchell? So Paul had known her. Funny, the woman hadn't mentioned that particular detail when she'd introduced herself at the grocery store.

Jenna reached for the phone. "Well, my e-mail didn't

come to my private or business addresses. I check those several times a day. I'll call my office and see if it arrived in one of the other accounts."

Cal caught her arm to stop her. "The ISA has already retrieved it and taken it off your server. It's encrypted so we'll need the communications guys to take a look at it."

That sounded a bit ominous, so she settled for nodding. "What's in these e-mails?"

"We've only gained access to yours and Salazar's. His e-mail was encrypted as well, but we decided to focus on it first. The encryption wasn't complex, and the computer broke the code within seconds. We're not sure if all the e-mails are similar, but this one appears to be instructions that Paul left with his attorney shortly before his death."

"Instructions?" The content of that e-mail was obviously the bad news that had etched Cal's face with worry. "Paul gave Salazar orders to kill me?"

"Not exactly."

His hesitation caused her heart rate to spike.

"Then what?" she asked, holding her breath.

"We're piecing this together using some files we confiscated from Paul's estate and the e-mail sent to Salazar. Apparently before you rejected Paul's proposal and he decided to kill you, he tried to get you pregnant."

Oh, mercy. She'd known Paul was a snake, but she hadn't realized just how far he'd gone with his sinister plan.

"Paul used personal information he got from your corrupt assistant, the one who sold your business secrets," Cal continued. "With some of that information,

Paul invited you to his estate when he estimated that you'd be ovulating. He drugged you. That's why you don't remember having sex with him."

She groaned. This just kept getting worse and worse. Everything about their relationship had been a cleverly planned sham. "Paul ditched the plan after I said there was no way I'd marry him."

Cal shrugged. "He intended to kill you, but he also planned for your refusal and your escape."

Jenna felt her eyes widen. "He knew I might escape?"

"Yeah." He let that hang in the air for several seconds. "He also took into account that he might have succeeded in getting you pregnant. In his e-mail to Salazar, Paul instructed the man to tie up loose ends, depending on how your situation had turned out."

"So, what exactly is Salazar supposed to do?" Jenna didn't even try to brace herself.

Cal glanced at Sophie. Then stared at her. "In the event that you've had a child, which you obviously have, Salazar has orders to kidnap the baby."

Chapter Six

Cal waited for a call while Jenna bathed Sophie. Jenna was smiling and singing to the baby, but he knew beneath that smile, she was terrified.

A professional assassin wanted to kidnap her baby and do God knows what to both her and Sophie in the process. They'd dodged a bullet—Salazar had indeed followed Jenna to the grocery store and hadn't just headed for the apartment to grab Sophie. Maybe he hadn't had the address of the apartment. Or perhaps he wanted to get Jenna first. Maybe he thought if he eliminated the mother, then it'd be a snap to kidnap the child.

That plan left Jenna in a very bad place. She couldn't go on the run, though every instinct in her body was shouting for her to do just that. Running was what Salazar hoped she would do.

She'd be an easy catch.

Cal didn't intend to let that happen. Correction. He had to arrange for someone else to make sure that didn't happen. For the sake of his career, he was going to take these initial steps to keep Sophie and Jenna safe, and then he was going to extract himself from the picture.

He checked his phone to make sure it wasn't dead. It wasn't. And there was still no call from headquarters or Hollywood, who was on the way with some much needed equipment. Cal needed some answers. They were seriously short on those.

Sophie made an "ohhh" sound and splashed her feet and hands in the shallow water that was dabbed with iridescent bubbles. Cal glanced at her to make sure all was okay, and then turned his attention back to the phone.

"Ever heard the expression a watched pot doesn't boil?" Jenna commented. "It's the same with a cell phone. It'll never ring when you're sitting there holding it."

She lifted Sophie from the little plastic yellow tub that Jenna had positioned on the sole bit of kitchen counter space, and she immediately wrapped the dripping wet baby in a thick pink terry-cloth towel.

Cal stood from the small kitchen table and slipped his phone into his pocket in case Jenna needed a hand. But she seemed to have the situation under control. She stood there by the sink, drying Sophie and imitating the soft baby sounds her daughter was making.

He went closer to see the baby's expression. Yep, she was grinning a big gummy grin. Her face was rosy and warm from the bath, and she smelled like baby shampoo. Cal had never thought a happy, freshly bathed baby could grab his complete attention, but this little girl certainly did.

Deep down, he felt something. A strange sense of what it would actually be like to be her father. It would be pretty amazing to hold her and feel her unconditional love.

When he came out of his daddy trance, he realized Jenna was looking at him. Her right eyebrow was slightly lifted. A question: what was he thinking? Cal had no intention of sharing that with her.

"Want to hold her while I get her diaper and gown?" Jenna asked.

Cal felt like someone had just offered to hand him a live grenade. "Uh, I don't want to hurt her."

Jenna smiled and eased Sophie into his arms. He looked at Jenna. Then Sophie, who was looking at him with suddenly suspicious eyes. For a moment, he thought the baby was going to burst into tears. She didn't, though he wouldn't have blamed her. Instead, she opened her tiny mouth and laughed.

Cal didn't know who was more stunned, Jenna, him or Sophie. Sophie jumped as if she'd scared herself with the unexpected noise from her own mouth. She did more staring, and then laughed again.

"This is a first," Jenna said, totally in awe. Cal knew how she felt. It was like witnessing a little miracle. "I'll have to put it in her baby book." She disappeared into the bedroom-nursery for a moment and came back with Sophie's clothes. "First time you've ever held a baby?" she asked.

He nodded. "My brother, Joe, has a little boy, Austin. He's nearly two years old, but I was away on assignment when he was born. I didn't see him until he was already walking."

"You missed the first laugh, then." She took Sophie

from him and went to the sofa so she could sit and dress the baby. "You're close to your family?"

"Yes. No," he corrected. "I mean, we keep in touch, but we're all wrapped up in our jobs. Joe's a San Antonio cop. My other brother is special ops in the military. I started out in the military but switched to ISA."

Jenna had her attention fastened on diapering Sophie and putting on her gown, but Cal knew where her attention really was when he noticed she was trembling. He caught her hand to steady it and helped her pull the gown's drawstring so that Sophie's feet wouldn't be exposed. Sophie didn't seem to mind. The bath had relaxed her, and it seemed as if she was ready to fall asleep.

"Why is Paul sending Salazar after us now?" Jenna asked. She stood and started toward the nursery. "Why wait a year?"

Cal tried not to react to the emotion and fear in her voice. "Could be several reasons," he whispered as he followed her. "Maybe it took this long for his will to get through probate. The courts don't move quickly in Monte de Leon. Or maybe he figured the e-mails would cause a big splash, something to make sure everyone remembers him on the first anniversary of his murder."

"Oh, I remember him." She eased Sophie into the crib, placing the baby on her side, and then after kissing her cheek, Jenna covered her lower body with a blanket. "I didn't need the e-mails or Salazar to do that."

She kissed Sophie again and walked just outside the door, and leaned against the door frame.

A thin breath caused her mouth to shudder.

There was no way he could not react to that. Jenna

was hurting and terrified for her daughter. Cal was worried for her, too. The ISA might not be able to stop Salazar before he tried to kidnap Sophie.

Since Jenna looked as if she needed a hug, Cal reached out, slid his arm around her waist and pulled her to him. She didn't resist. She went straight into his arms.

She was soft. *Very* soft. And it seemed as if she could melt right into him. Cal felt his hand move across her back, and he drew her even closer.

Her scent was suddenly on him. A strange mix of baby soap and her own naturally feminine smell. Something alluring. Definitely hot. As was her body. He'd never been much of a breast man, but hers were giving him ideas about how those bare breasts would respond to his touch.

"This isn't a good idea," she mumbled.

Cal knew exactly what she meant. Close contact wasn't going to cool the attraction. It would fuel it.

But it felt right soothing her on a purely physical level. When he was done here, after Jenna and Sophie were no longer in danger, he needed to spend some time getting a personal life.

He needed to get laid.

Too often he put the job ahead of his needs. Jenna had a bad way of reminding him that the particular activity shouldn't be put off.

She pulled back and met his gaze. The new position put their mouths too close. All he had to do was lean down and press his lips to hers, and Cal was certain the result would be a mind-blowing kiss that neither of them would ever forget.

Which was exactly why it couldn't happen.

Still, that didn't stop his body from reacting in the most basic male way.

With their eyes locked, Jenna put her hand on his chest to push him away. Her middle brushed against his. She froze for a split second, and then went all soft and dewy again. He saw her pupils pinpoint. Felt her warm breath ease from her slightly open mouth. Her pulse jumped on her throat.

She was reacting to his arousal. Her body was preparing itself for something that couldn't happen.

"I'm flattered," she said, her voice like a silky caress on his neck and mouth.

Uh-oh. She probably meant it to be a joke, a way of breaking the tension. But it didn't break anything. That breath of hers felt like the start of very long French kiss. A kiss he had to nix. He didn't have the time or inclination to deal with a complicated relationship.

Besides, she wasn't his type.

He didn't want a woman that was fragile, so prissy. No, he wanted a woman like him, who liked sex a little rough and with no strings attached. A relationship with Jenna would come with strings longer than the Rio Grande. And he couldn't see her having down-and-dirty sex with him whenever the urge hit.

Her breath brushed against his mouth again, and Cal nearly lost the argument he was having with himself. Knowing he had to do something, fast, he stepped away from her.

In the same instant, there was a knock at the door.

His body immediately went into combat mode, and he drew his gun from his shoulder holster.

"It's me, Hollywood," their visitor called out.

He pushed aside the jolt of adrenaline. "He works for the ISA," Cal clarified to Jenna.

However, he didn't reholster his weapon until he looked out the side window to verify that it was indeed his coworker and that Hollywood wasn't being held at gunpoint. But the man was alone.

Cal opened the door and greeted him. "Thanks for coming." He checked the area in front of the bookstore but didn't see Gwen, the reporter, or either of the Carrs.

"No problem." Hollywood stepped inside and handed Cal a black leather equipment bag. "I brought a secure laptop, a portable security system, an extra weapon and some clothes. I didn't know how long you'd be here so I added some toiletries and stuff."

"Good." Cal didn't know how long he'd be there, either. "Has anyone picked up Salazar?"

"Not yet. We're still looking." Hollywood's attention went in Jenna's direction, and with his hand extended in a friendly gesture, he walked toward her. "Mark Lynch," he introduced himself. "But feel free to call me Hollywood. Everyone does."

"Hollywood," she repeated. She sounded friendly enough, but she was keeping her nerves right beneath the surface.

Cal hoped to do something to help with those nerves, something that didn't involve kissing, so he took out the laptop and turned it on. They needed information, and he would start by reviewing the message traffic on Salazar to see if anyone had spotted him nearby. By now, Salazar knew who Cal was. He would know that the ISA was involved. However, Cal seriously doubted that would send the man running. Salazar wasn't the type.

"We're working on trying to contain Anthony Salazar," Cal heard Hollywood tell Jenna.

"And I'm to stay put until that happens?" she spelled out. She shoved her hand into the back pockets of her pants.

Cal frowned and wondered why he suddenly thought he knew her so well. Jenna and he were practically strangers.

Hollywood glanced at him first and then nodded in response to Jenna's question. "The local sheriff has been alerted to the situation, and the FBI is sending two agents to patrol through the town. Cal can keep things under control here until we can make other arrangements." He took out a folder from the bag and handed it to Cal.

Cal opened it and inside was a woman's picture. "Kinley Ford?" he read aloud from the background investigation sheet that he took from the envelope. He glanced through the info but didn't recognize anything about the research engineer.

"That file is a little multitasking," Hollywood explained. "The FBI sent her info and picture over this afternoon. She's not associated with Jenna or Salazar, but she's supposedly here in town. She disappeared from Witness Protection, and there are lot of people who want to find her."

Cal shook his head. "Please don't tell me I'm supposed to look for her."

"No. But if anyone asks, that's why you're here. It's the way the director is keeping this all legitimate. He can tell the FBI that you're here in Willow Ridge to try to locate Kinley Ford, as a favor for a sister agency. Don't worry. I'll be the one looking for the missing woman, but your name will be on the paperwork."

Cal breathed a little easier. He wanted to focus on Jenna and Sophie right now.

"I'll set up this temporary security system," Hollywood continued. "And then I'll get out of here so I can stand guard until the FBI agents arrive."

Cal approved of that. The local sheriff would need help with Salazar around. "What about the background check on Gwen Mitchell?"

"Still in progress, but Director Kowalski found some flags. According to her passport, she was in Monte de Leon during Jenna's rescue."

That grabbed Cal's attention. "Interesting."

"Maybe. But it could mean nothing. She is a reporter, after all. There's nothing to link Gwen to Paul or the Carrs. She appears to have been doing a story on one of the rebel factions."

"And she got out alive." That in itself was a small miracle. Unless Gwen had had a lot of help. The ISA hadn't rescued her, that was for sure, so she must have had other resources to get her out of the country.

"We'll keep digging," Hollywood explained. His voice was a little strained as if he was tired. He rummaged through the bag and came up with several pieces of equipment. "Are these the only windows?" he asked, tipping his head to the trio in the main living area.

"There's a small one in the bathroom," Jenna let him know.

Hollywood nodded and went in that direction to get started. Cal was familiar with the system Hollywood was using. It would arm all entrances and exits so that no one could break in undetected, but it could also be used to create perimeter security to make sure Salazar didn't get close enough to set some kind of explosive or fire to flush them out.

Once the laptop had booted up, Cal logged in with his security code and began to scan through the messages. One practically jumped out at him.

"Here's the e-mail that Paul sent you," Cal told her. "ISA retrieved it and kept it in our classified In-box so I could look at it."

She took a step toward him, but then turned and checked on the baby first. "Sophie's sleeping," Jenna let him know, as she hurried to the sofa to sit beside him.

Cal was positive this e-mail was going to upset her, but he was also positive that they needed to read it. Besides, there might be clues in it that only she would understand, and they might finally make some sense of all of this.

"Jenna, if you've received this e-mail, then I must be dead," she read aloud. *"I doubt my demise has caused you much grief, but it should. Once I have a plan, I don't give up on it. Ever. Our heir will inherit your vast wealth and mine, and will continue what I've started here in Monte de Leon. What the plan doesn't include is you, my dear."*

She stopped, took a deep breath and continued. *"So put your affairs in order, Jenna. I'll be the first person to greet you in the hereafter. See you in a day or two. Love, Paul."*

There were probably several Justice Department and ISA agents already examining the e-mail, but it appeared to be pretty straightforward. A death threat, one that Salazar had probably been paid to carry out.

She groaned softly. "Paul planned for all possibilities. Like a baby. I'm sure the e-mail would have been different if I hadn't had a child." Jenna scrubbed her hands over her face. "And when I woke up this morning, I thought my biggest threat was Holden Carr."

Maybe he still was. Cal was eager to get a look at those other e-mails. All he needed was some kind of evidence or connection that could prompt the FBI to arrest Holden or his sister.

Cal glanced at the notepad on the coffee table. Helena's number was there, and she'd wanted Jenna to call her. While it wouldn't be a pleasant conversation, it might be a necessary one.

Jenna must have followed his gaze. She reached for the notepad and retrieved her cell phone from her purse on the table next to the front door. But before she could press in the numbers, Hollywood came back into the room.

"All secure back there," he informed them. He went to the windows at the front of the apartment and connected a small sensor to each. He put the control monitor on the kitchen table and checked his watch. "I'll be parked on the street near here until I get the okay from the FBI."

Cal stood and went to him to shake his hand. "Thanks, for everything."

"Like I said, no problem. If you need anything else, just give me a call."

Cal let Hollywood out, then closed and locked the

door. While he set the security monitor to arm it, Jenna sat on the sofa, dialed the call to Helena and put her cell on speaker.

The woman answered on the first ring. "Jenna," Helena said, obviously seeing the name on her caller ID. Cal made a note to switch Jenna to a prepaid phone that couldn't be traced.

"Why did you want to talk to me?" Jenna immediately asked.

Helena's answer wasn't quite so hasty. She paused for several long moments. "Is your friend, Cal, still there with you?"

"He's here," Cal answered for himself.

It was a gamble. Helena might not say anything important with him listening. But he also didn't want Helena to think that Jenna was alone. That might prompt her to send in Salazar for Sophie—if the man was actually working for Helena, that is. But perhaps the most obvious solution was true—that Salazar was being paid by Paul's estate.

Helena paused again, longer than the first time. "Why didn't you tell us you're an American operative?"

Cal groaned softly. She shouldn't have been able to retrieve that information this quickly. "Who said I am?"

"Sources. *Reliable* ones."

"There are no reliable sources for information like that," Cal informed her. She or Holden had paid someone off. Or else there was a major leak somewhere in the ISA.

"What did you want to talk to me about?" Jenna prompted after a third round of silence.

"Holden," Helena readily answered. "The Justice Department and the ISA have contacted me. They want me to give them evidence so they can arrest my brother for illegal business practices and for Paul's murder."

Jenna glanced at him before she continued. "Is there evidence?"

"For his business dealings. Holden isn't a saint. But there couldn't be evidence for Paul's murder. The housekeeper's responsible for that."

Ah, yes. That mysterious housekeeper again. Cal had monitored Paul's estate for the entire two days of Jenna's visit, and while he'd heard the voices of many of Paul's employees, he hadn't heard of this housekeeper named Mary. Not until after Paul's body had been found with a single execution-style gunshot wound to the head. It'd been the local authorities who'd pointed the finger at the housekeeper, and they had based that on the notes they'd found on Paul's computer. He'd apparently been suspicious of the woman and had decided to fire her. But those notes had been made weeks before his death.

"Did you agree to help the Justice Department and the ISA?" Cal asked, though he was certain he knew the answer.

But he was wrong.

"Yes. I intend to help the authorities bring down my brother," Helena announced.

Jenna's eyes widened, but Cal figured his expression was more of skepticism than surprise. "Are you doing that to get Holden out of the way so you can inherit both Paul's and his estates?"

"No." She was adamant about it. That didn't mean

she was telling the truth. "I want the illegal activity to stop. I want the family business to return to the way it was when my parents were still alive."

"Admirable," Cal mumbled. He didn't believe that, either, though he had to admit that it was possible Helena was a do-gooder. But he wasn't about to stake Jenna's and Sophie's safety on that.

"What was in Paul's e-mail to you?" Jenna asked the woman. Cal moved closer to the phone and grabbed the notepad so he could write down the message verbatim.

"The e-mail was personal," Helena explained. "Though I'm sure it won't stay that way long. Cal will see to that."

Yes, he would. "If that's true, then you might as well tell me what it says."

This was the longest silence of all. "Paul said he would see me in the hereafter in a day or two."

Almost identical wording to Jenna's e-mail, but Cal jotted it down anyway. "Why would Paul want you dead?"

"I don't know." Helena sighed heavily, and it sounded as if she had started to cry. "But he obviously believes I wronged him in some way. Maybe Paul wanted Holden to inherit everything, and this is his way of cutting me out of his estate."

Or maybe Holden had gotten a death threat, too. But then with plans to have Sophie kidnapped, that left Cal with a critical question. Whom had Paul arranged to raise the child? Certainly not an assassin like Salazar.

He thought about that a moment and came full circle to the fifth recipient of one of Paul's infamous e-mails.

Gwen Mitchell.

He needed a full background report on her ASAP. It was possible that she was connected to Paul.

"Jenna, we're both in danger," Helena continued. "That's why we have to work together to stop this person that Paul has unleashed on us."

"Work together, how?" Jenna asked.

"Meet with me tomorrow morning. Alone. No Holden and no Cal Rico."

That wasn't going to happen. Still, Cal had to keep this channel of communication open. "Jenna will get back to you on that," he answered.

"Be at the Meadow's Bed-and-Breakfast tomorrow morning at ten," Helena continued as if this meeting was a done deal. "It's a little place in the country, about twenty miles from Willow Ridge. I'll see you then." And with that, she hung up.

Jenna clicked the end-call button. She wasn't trembling like before. Well, not visibly, anyway. "Do you think she wants to kill me, too?"

He considered several answers and decided to go with the truth. "Anything's possible at this point." But he did need to get a look at all the e-mails to get a clearer picture.

"I'm scared for Sophie," she whispered.

Yeah. So was he. And being scared wasn't good. It meant he'd lost his objectivity. He blamed that on holding Sophie. On that first laugh. Oh, and the cuddling session with Jenna. None of those things should have happened, and they'd sucked him right in and gotten him personally involved.

Jenna swiveled around to face him, blinking back tears, and moved closer into his arms.

And Cal let her.

"I'm not a wimp," she declared. "I run a multimillion-dollar business. And if the threats were aimed just at me, I'd be spitting mad. But my baby is in danger."

Cal couldn't refute that. Heck, he couldn't even reassure her that Salazar wouldn't make a full-scale effort to kidnap Sophie. All he could do was sit there and hold Jenna.

A single tear streaked down her cheek, and Cal caught it with his thumb, his fingers cupping her chin. And he was painfully aware that he was using his fingers to lift her chin. Just slightly.

So he could put his mouth on hers.

And that's exactly what he did.

The touch was a jolt that went straight through him like a shot. It didn't help that Jenna made a throaty feminine sound of approval. Or that she slid her arms around his neck and drew him closer.

Cal cursed himself for starting this. And worse, for continuing it and deepening the kiss. French-kissing Jenna was the worst idea he'd ever had, but that jolt of fire that her mouth was creating overruled any common sense he had left. She tasted like silk and sin, and he wanted a whole lot more.

He heard a ringing sound and thought it was another by-product of the jolt. But when the ringing continued, Cal realized passion wasn't responsible. His cell phone was. He untangled himself from Jenna and checked the caller ID screen.

It was Director Kowalski.

"Hell," he mumbled. Cal quickly tried to compose himself before he answered it. "Agent Rico."

"We might have a problem," the director started. That wasn't the greeting Cal wanted to hear. "First of all, I just read the e-mail that Paul Tolivar supposedly sent Jenna. You think it's legit?"

Cal had given that some thought. He should have given it more. "I'm not sure. Anyone close to Paul could have composed those e-mails and sent them out. Anyone with an agenda." He glanced at Jenna. There was no surprise in her eyes, which meant she'd already come up with that theory.

"You have someone in mind?"

This was easy. Cal didn't even have to think about it. "Helena or Holden Carr. Both inherited a lot of money from Paul. Also, those flags on Gwen Mitchell might turn out to be a problem."

"Yes, we're working on her. But something else has popped up." The director took in an audible breath. "We might be wrong, but there are new flags. Ones within the department."

Everything inside Cal went still. This was worse than bad news. "What's wrong?"

"We think we might have a leak in communications who could have been responsible for alerting Gwen Mitchell and the Carrs as to Jenna Laniere's whereabouts."

"A leak might not have been necessary for that. Holden or Helena Carr could have been watching Jenna's estate and then followed her when she went there." Of course, that didn't explain how they'd known about Sophie, unless the person watching the estate had seen the baby in the car. That was possible, but it sounded as if the director thought someone or something else might have been responsible. "Who do these flags point to?"

"Not to anyone specific, but if it's true, the source of the information has to be in ISA."

Oh, man. The bad news just kept getting worse. They might have a traitor within the organization. "Who in ISA would have access to the pool of information that would affect all the players in this case?"

Kowalski blew out an audible breath. "Mark Lynch is a possibility."

That was not the name he'd expected to hear the director say. "Hollywood," Cal mumbled.

"I know he's on the way there with equipment. And I know you two are friends. I didn't learn about the flags until a few minutes ago."

And that in itself could be a problem because it meant someone was trying to cover their tracks. Or else set someone up. "What exactly are these flags?"

"Hollywood monitored the message traffic pertaining to Jenna Laniere. Faxes, e-mails, telephone calls. The info in question went from Paul Tolivar to his lawyer. It was her detailed financial data, including passwords and codes for her business accounts."

Cal knew about those messages that'd been sent a year ago while Jenna was in Monte de Leon. Paul had gotten into Jenna's laptop the first day she was at his estate and had copied her entire hard drive. Though Paul had only sent those messages to his lawyer, it didn't mean that someone else couldn't have learned the contents, saved them and now sent them out again. But why do it now, especially since the information was a year old?

That led Cal to his next question. "Why do you think Hollywood's the one who compromised this information?"

"Because we intercepted an encrypted message that was meant for him. The message was verification of receipt of Ms. Laniere's info and details about the payment for services rendered. We checked, and there has been money sent to an account in the Cayman Islands."

Cal tried not to curse. He didn't want a gut reaction to make him accuse his friend of a crime he might not have committed. "That still doesn't mean Hollywood's guilty. One or both of the Carrs could be trying to set him up to make it look as if he sold Jenna's financial information. And they might be doing that to get us to focus on Hollywood and not them."

"Could be." But the director didn't sound at all convinced of that. "It's a lot of money, Cal. If the Carrs had wanted to set someone up, why wait until now?"

That timeline question kept coming up, and Cal still didn't have an answer for it. Was it tied to Sophie? And if so, how?

"There's a final piece to this mess," the director continued. "We accessed Hollywood's personal computer, and we found several encrypted messages from Anthony Salazar. In the most recent one, Salazar asks Hollywood to help him with the kidnapping."

Cal couldn't fight off the gut reactions any longer. He felt sick to his stomach. Yes, it could all be a setup, but it was a huge risk to take if it wasn't. Hell. Had he been that wrong about a man he considered a friend?

"We tried to stop Hollywood before he left to go see you. But when he gets there, tell him he's to report back to me immediately. Don't let him in," Kowalski warned.

Cal groaned. "He's already been here. He installed the equipment and left."

The director cursed. "He wasn't supposed to be there yet. He had instructions to arrive at 9:00 p.m."

Cal got to his feet and glanced around. At the equipment bag. At the laptop he'd used to read the e-mail Paul sent Jenna. At the security systems that Hollywood had activated a full hour ahead of schedule.

"What are my orders?" Cal asked. He motioned for Jenna to get Sophie.

"We might have a rogue agent on our hands. Get Ms. Laniere and her daughter out of there," the director ordered. *"Now."*

Chapter Seven

The nightmare was back.

This time, she wasn't in Monte de Leon, and there were no rebel soldiers. Jenna knew this was much worse—her precious baby was in danger.

"Bring as little as possible," Cal instructed in a whisper. He stuffed diapers and some of Sophie's clothes into her bag and added a flashlight. "Hurry," he added.

Not that she needed him to remind her of that. Everything about his movements and body language indicated they had to move fast.

"What kind of flags did you say the director found on Hollywood?" Jenna whispered. Cal had told her that Hollywood might have bugged the place. He might be listening to their every word.

"They don't have a full picture yet." Cal looped the now full diaper bag over his shoulder and motioned for her to pick up Sophie. "You'll have to carry her. I need at least one hand free."

So he could shoot his gun if it became necessary.

"Does your car have an infant seat already in it?" he mouthed.

She nodded and scooped the sleeping baby into her arms. Thankfully, Sophie didn't wake up. "I'm parked just behind the bookstore. The keys are in my purse."

Jenna wanted to ask if it was safe to take her car. But maybe it didn't matter. They had to take the risk and get out of there.

Cal drew his gun while she swaddled Sophie in a thick blanket. The moment she finished, she motioned for them to go. He paused a moment at the door. Then he opened it and glanced around outside.

"Let's go," he ordered.

Jenna grabbed her purse. She stuffed her cell phone into it, extracted her keys and stepped out into the cold night air. It was dark, and there was no moon because of the cloudy sky, but the bookstore had floodlights positioned on the four corners of the building.

Cal kept her behind him while they made their way down the stairs. He stopped again and didn't give her the signal to move until he'd glanced around the side of the store. Once he had them moving again, he kept them next to the exterior wall.

It seemed to take a lifetime to walk the twenty yards or so to her car. She unlocked the door with her keypad, but instead of letting her get in, Cal motioned for her to stand back. She did. And he used the flashlight to check the undercarriage for explosives.

God. What a mess they were in.

After Cal had gone around the entire perimeter of the car, he caught onto her and practically shoved them in

through the passenger's side. Jenna turned to put Sophie
in the rear-facing car seat, but a sound stopped her cold.

Footsteps.

Standing guard in front of her, Cal lifted his gun
and took aim.

"Don't shoot," someone whispered. It was a woman's voice, and Jenna expected to see Helena step from
the shadows.

Instead, it was Gwen Mitchell.

She lifted her hands in a show of surrender. She
didn't appear to be armed and unlike the meeting in the
grocery store, the woman didn't have a camera.

"I have to talk to you," Gwen said.

"This isn't a good time for conversation." Cal kept
his gun aimed at Gwen, and he shut the car door. However, he didn't leave her side to get in. He stood guard,
and Jenna made use of his body shield. She leaned over
and put Sophie in the infant seat. She strapped her in and
then climbed into the backseat with her in case she had
to do what Cal was doing—use her body as a final
defense.

"It's important," Gwen added.

Everything was important right now, especially
getting out of there. Jenna glanced around and prayed
that Salazar wasn't using Gwen as a diversion so he
could sneak up on them and try to kidnap Sophie.

"We should go," Jenna reminded Cal.

Gwen fastened her attention on Jenna. "A few
minutes ago I sent you a copy of the e-mail that I got
from Paul. Read it and you'll know why it's important
that we talk. Then get in touch with me."

Jenna hadn't brought her laptop, but she thought maybe her BlackBerry was in her purse. Once they were on the road and away from there, she'd check and see if the e-mail had arrived into her personal account. But for now, she continued to keep watch and wished that she had a weapon to defend Sophie and herself with.

"Keep your hands lifted," Cal instructed Gwen, and he began to inch his way to the driver's side of the car.

"Don't trust anyone," Gwen continued. "There's something going on. I don't know what. But I think Paul's left instructions for someone to play a sick game. I think he wants to pit each of us against the other."

Then Paul had succeeded. Five e-mails. Five people. And there wasn't any trust among them. It was too big of a risk to start trusting now.

"Did he say anything about me in the e-mail he sent to you?" Gwen asked.

"No," Jenna assured her.

"You're sure? Because I'm trying to figure out why he contacted me. Do you have any idea?"

Cal didn't answer. He'd had enough, and got into the car and started the engine. He drove away, fast, leaving Gwen to stand there with her question unanswered.

"The way she said Paul's name makes me think she knew him well," Jenna commented. She kept her eyes on the woman until she was no longer in sight.

"How well she knew him is what I need to find out. Right after I get you and Sophie to someplace safe."

With all the rush to leave her apartment, she hadn't considered where to go. First things first, they had to make sure no one was following them, or there wouldn't be any safe place to escape to.

Cal sped down Main Street. Thankfully, there was no traffic. It wasn't unusual for that time of night—Willow Ridge wasn't exactly a hotbed of activity. He took the first available side road to get them out of there.

Jenna continued to keep watch around them. She wanted to get her BlackBerry, but that could wait until she was sure they weren't in immediate danger. However, maybe she could get some answers to other questions. After all, her baby's life was in danger, and Jenna wanted to know why.

"What made your director think we couldn't trust Hollywood?" she asked.

Like her, Cal was looking all around. "He thinks Hollywood transferred some information he obtained through official message traffic that he was monitoring."

"Information about me?"

"Yeah," he answered as if he was thinking hard about that.

She certainly was. "I met Hollywood for the first time tonight. He doesn't even know me." But that didn't mean he couldn't be working for one of the other players in this. "You don't think Paul got to him, too?"

"I don't know. He was in Monte de Leon during your rescue, and he had access to any and all information flowing in and out of Paul's estate. There are plenty of people who would have paid for that information."

She considered that a moment while she stared back at the dark road behind them. The lights of Willow Ridge were just specks now. "Do you trust Hollywood?"

"Before tonight I thought I did." He shook his head. "But I can't risk being wrong. It's possible he got greedy and decided to sell your financial information to someone. If he's innocent, then what we're doing is just a waste of time."

But it didn't feel like a waste. It felt like a necessity.

"I changed all my passwords and account information after Paul was killed," Jenna explained. "So, unless someone's gotten their hands on the new info, those old codes won't do them any good." Of course, maybe Hollywood didn't know they were old.

"If someone were using this to set him up, it wouldn't matter if the codes were outdated. The unauthorized message traffic is enough to incriminate him."

So Hollywood could be innocent. Still, they were on the run, and that meant someone had succeeded in terrifying her.

"Any idea where we're going?" she asked.

Cal checked his watch and the rearview mirror. "I'm sure the director is making arrangements for a safe house. All previous arrangements will be ditched because Hollywood would have had access to the plans."

"So it could take a while." Jenna believed Cal would do whatever it took to keep Sophie safe, but she wasn't certain that would be enough.

"How far is your estate?" he asked.

She'd hoped there wouldn't be any more surprises tonight. "About two hours." But Jenna shook her head. "You're thinking about going there?"

"Temporarily."

Oh, mercy. She hated to point out the obvious, but

she would. "The reason I'm not there now is the threats from Holden."

"Holden might be the least of our worries," Cal mumbled. And she knew it was true. "How good is the estate's security system?"

"It's supposed to be very good." Her surprise was replaced by frustration. "In hindsight, I should have stayed put there, beefed up security and told Holden where he could shove his threats. Then we wouldn't be running for our lives."

Cal met her gaze in the mirror. "You were scared and pregnant. I don't think your decision to leave was based solely on logic."

"Pregnancy hormones," she said under her breath. She couldn't dismiss that they hadn't played a part in her going on the run. But hiding had made her pregnancy more bearable, and it'd saved her from having to explain to her friends that she'd gotten pregnant by an accused felon.

"I've spent a lot of my life running," she commented. Why she told him that she didn't know. But she suddenly felt as if she owed him an explanation as to why she'd left the safety of the estate and headed for a small town where she knew no one. "Before my parents were killed in a car accident, when we'd have an argument, I'd immediately leave and take a long trip somewhere."

He shrugged. "There's nothing wrong with traveling."

"This wasn't traveling. It was escaping." Heck, she was still escaping. And this time, she might not succeed. Sophie might have to pay the ultimate price for Jenna's bad choices. "I have to make this right for Sophie. I can't let her be in danger. She's too important to me."

"I understand," he said. "She's important to me, too."

And for some reason, that wasn't like lip service. He wasn't just trying to console her.

Cal had only known Sophie a few hours. There was no way he could have developed such strong feelings for her. Was there? Maybe the little girl had brought out Cal's paternal instincts. Or maybe he was just protecting them. Either way, it was best not to dwell on it. Once they got to her estate, Cal would leave. After all, he had a career to salvage.

Jenna checked on Sophie again. She was still asleep and would probably stay that way for several hours. With no immediate threat, it was a good time to check for that BlackBerry. Jenna climbed over the seat, buckled up and grabbed the purse that she'd tossed onto the floor.

It took several moments for the BlackBerry to load and for her to scroll through the messages. There was indeed one that Gwen had forwarded to her.

"Gwen, I expect you're surprised to hear from me," Jenna read aloud. *"When I was considering whom to give this particular task, I thought of several candidates, but you're the best woman for the job. Yes, this is a job offer. You see, I've been murdered, and if you're reading this, then my killer is still out there. I want you to use your skills as an investigative journalist and find proof of who that person is. Once you have the proof, contact Mark Lynch at the International Security Agency."*

"Mark?" Cal repeated. "Why would Paul want her to contact Hollywood?"

Jenna exchanged puzzled glances with him. "Obviously, Paul knew him. Or knew *of* him. But why would Paul trust Hollywood with that kind of information? Why not just turn it over to Holden or Salazar?"

Cal didn't say anything for several seconds. "Maybe he's giving each person one task. Or maybe Gwen is right and this is his way of dividing and conquering. If you're all at odds and suspicious of each other, then he'll get some kind of postmortem satisfaction. He sends Salazar after Sophie. Gwen, after the person who murdered him. And he somehow turns Helena against her own brother."

Yes. Jenna would have loved to know what Paul had written to Helena. Or to Holden. If they had all the e-mails, they might be able to figure out what Paul was really trying to do.

"Did you read the entire e-mail?" Cal asked.

"No. There's more." She scrolled down the tiny screen. *"If you find my killer, then my attorney will wire the sum of one million dollars to a bank account of your choice. I'm giving you one week. If you don't have the proof, the job will go to someone else."*

So this wasn't going to stop. If Gwen failed, then the investigation would continue.

"Maybe Hollywood will be offered the job," Cal speculated. "Or Salazar."

She heard him, but her attention was on the last lines of the e-mail. *"To make things easier for you, I want you to focus your efforts on my number-one suspect,"* she continued reading aloud. *"Actually, she's my only suspect. Her name is Jenna Laniere."*

That was it. The end of Paul's instructions.

Jenna had to take a moment to absorb it. "Paul obviously didn't trust me right from the start, or he wouldn't have written this e-mail."

"If he's the one who wrote it."

She turned in the seat to face Cal. "What are you thinking?"

"I'm thinking Gwen, Holden or Helena could be behind these messages from the grave." He hissed out a breath. "Even Hollywood could have done it. This could all be some kind of ploy to get Paul's estate."

Maybe. After all, Holden and Helena had shared Paul's money. Maybe one of them wanted it all. Or if Gwen was the culprit, maybe this was her way of ferreting out a story.

But how did Hollywood fit into this? Unless the man was just an out-and-out criminal, she couldn't figure out a logical scenario where he'd be collecting any of Paul's money.

"Maybe your friend's innocent," Jenna said, thinking out loud. "What if someone is setting him up so you can't trust him? That way, it would be one less person you could turn to for help."

Cal lifted his shoulder. "It's possible, I suppose. Once the director has gone through all the message traffic, we should know more."

Yes, but would that information stop her daughter from being in danger? Jenna couldn't shake the fear that Sophie was at the core of all of this.

Something caught her eye.

Headlights in the distance behind them.

Cal noticed it, too. His attention went straight to the rearview mirror. Neither of them said anything. They just sat there, breaths held, waiting to see what would happen.

He kept his speed right at fifty-five, and the headlights got closer very quickly. The other car was speeding. Still, that in itself was no cause for alarm. Combined with everything, however, her heart and mind were racing with worst-case scenarios.

"Get in the backseat and stay down," Cal insisted.

Jenna tried to keep herself steady. This could be just a precaution, she reminded herself, but she did as he asked. She climbed onto the seat with Sophie and positioned her torso over the baby so that she could protect her still-sleeping baby. But she also wanted to keep watch, so she craned her neck so she could see the side mirror.

The car was barreling down on them.

Jenna prayed it would just pass them and that would be the end to this particular scare. She could see Cal's right hand through the gap of the seats, and because of the other car's bright headlights, she could also see his finger tense on the trigger of his gun. He had the weapon aimed at the passenger's window.

The lights got even brighter as the car came upon them. Too close. It was a dark SUV, much larger than her own vehicle. Jenna braced herself because it seemed as if the SUV was going to ram right into them.

"Is it Salazar?" she asked in a raw whisper. Her heart was pounding now. Her breath was coming out in short, too-fast jolts.

"I can't tell. Just stay down."

Jenna didn't have a choice. She had to do whatever she could to protect Sophie. As meager as it was, her body would become a shield if the driver of that vehicle started shooting.

The headlights slashed right at the mirror when the car bolted out into the passing lane. She prayed it would continue to accelerate and go past them.

But it didn't.

With her heart in her throat, Jenna watched as the car slowed until it was literally side by side with them. Cal cursed under his breath and aimed his gun.

"Brace yourself," he warned her a split second before he slammed on the brakes.

She saw a flash of red from the other car. The driver had braked as well, and the lights lit up the darkness, coating their shadows with that eerie shade of bloodred.

Cal threw the car into Reverse and hit the accelerator. She didn't know how he managed, but he spun the car around so they were facing in the opposite direction, and gunned the engine.

There was another flash of brake lights from the SUV. The sound of the tires squealing against the asphalt. Jenna squeezed her eyes shut a moment and prayed. But when she looked into the mirror, her worst fear was confirmed.

The SUV was coming at them again.

If it rammed them or sideswiped them, it'd be difficult for Cal to stay on the road. It was too dark to see if there were ditches nearby or one of the dozens of creeks that dotted the area. But Jenna didn't need to see things like that to know the danger. If the SUV driver managed to get them off the road, he could fire shots at a stationary target. They wouldn't be hard to hit.

"Should I call the sheriff?" she asked. She had to do something. *Anything.*

"He wouldn't get here in time."

The last ominous word had hardly left Cal's mouth when there was a loud bang. The SUV rammed into the back of her car, and the jolt snapped her body. Jenna caught Sophie's car seat and held on, trying to steady it and brace herself for a second hit.

It came hard and fast.

The front bumper of the SUV slammed into them. The motion jostled Sophie, and she stirred, waking.

"Get all the way down," Cal instructed. "Put your hand over Sophie's ears and cover her as much as you can with the blanket."

She did, though Jenna had to wonder how that would help. A moment later, she got her answer. He didn't slow down. Didn't try to turn around again. He merely turned his gun in the direction of the back window and the SUV. Cal used the rearview mirror to aim.

And he fired.

The blast was deafening. Louder than even the impact of the SUV. That sound rifled through Jenna, spiking her fear and concern for her child. Even though she had clamped her hands around Sophie's ears, the sound got through and her baby shrieked.

Cal fired again and again.

The bullets tore through the back window, the safety glass webbing and cracking, but it stayed in place.

Thank God. Even though the glass wasn't much protection, she didn't want it tumbling down on Sophie.

Cal fired one more shot and then jammed his foot on the accelerator to get them out of there.

Chapter Eight

Cal sped through the wrought-iron gates that fronted Jenna's estate.

He'd spent most of the trip watching the road, to make sure that SUV hadn't followed them. As far as he could tell, it hadn't, even though they had encountered more traffic the closer they got to Houston. And then the traffic had trailed off to practically nothing once he was on the highway that led to Jenna's house.

Though the estate was only twenty miles from Houston city limits and there were other homes nearby, it felt isolated because it was centered on ten pristine acres.

The iron gates were massive, at least ten feet tall and double that in width. Fanning off both sides of the gate was a sinister-looking spiked-top fence that appeared to surround the place.

Even though there was no guard in the small red-brick gatehouse to the left, the builder had obviously planned for security, which made Cal wonder why Jenna had ever left in the first place. Yes, she'd told him she had a tendency to take off when things got rough, but the estate was as close to a stronghold as they could get. Somehow, he'd have to make Jenna understand that this was their best option. For now. He'd have to try to soothe her flight instinct so she wouldn't be tempted to run.

He stopped in the circular drive directly in front of the house and positioned the car so that Jenna would only be a few steps away from getting inside. He didn't want her exposed any longer than necessary. Salazar had expert shooting skills with a long-range assault rifle.

Like the rest of the property, the house was huge. There was a redbrick exterior and a porch with white columns that stretched across the entire front and sides. The carved oak front door opened, and he immediately reached for his gun.

"It's okay," Jenna assured him. "That's Meggie, the housekeeper. She's worked here since I was a baby."

The woman was in her mid-sixties with graying flame-red hair. Short, but not petite, she wore a simple blue-flowered dress. She didn't rush to greet them, but she did give them a warm smile when Jenna stepped from the car with a sleeping Sophie cradled in her arms.

"Welcome home. I have rooms made up for all of you," Meggie announced. Her words came out in a rushed stream of excitement. "When you called and said you were on the way, I got the crib ready in the nursery. The bedding is already turned down for the little angel. And I put your guest in the room next to yours."

"Thank you," Jenna muttered.

Once they were inside and the door was shut, Meggie patted Jenna's cheek and eased back the blanket a bit so she could see Sophie. She smiled again, and her aged blue eyes went to Cal. "She looks like you."

He wasn't sure what to say to that, so he didn't say anything. Meggie thought Sophie was his.

Cal forced himself to assess his surroundings. He'd expected luxury, and wasn't disappointed. Vaulted ceilings. Marble floors. Victorian antiques. But there were also a lot of windows and God knows how many points of entry. It would be a bear to keep all of them secure.

"We're exhausted," Jenna said to the woman, her voice showing her nerves. Maybe the nerves were from Meggie's comment about Sophie's looks but more likely from the inevitable adrenaline crash. "We'll get settled in for the night and we can talk tomorrow. There are things I should tell you."

Meggie nodded, and lightly kissed Sophie's cheek.

"Where's the main security panel?" he asked before Meggie could walk away.

She pointed to a richly colored oil landscape painting in the wide corridor just off the foyer. "The access code is seven, seven, four, one." Then she made her exit in the opposite direction.

Jenna let out a deep breath. A shaky one. Now that she was safe inside, the impact of what'd happened was hitting her. She was ready to crash, but Cal needed to take a few security measures before he helped her put Sophie to bed.

He aimed for some small talk so he could get some information about the place. And maybe get her mind off the nightmare they'd just come through.

"You were born here?" Cal asked, going to the

monitor. The painting had a hinged front, and he opened it so he could take a look at what he had to work with.

"Literally. My mother didn't trust hospitals. So my dad set up one here. In fact, he set up a lot of things here, mainly so that we'd never have to leave."

"They were overly protective?" Cal armed the system and watched as the lights flashed on to indicate the protected areas.

"Yes, with a capital Y. My mother was from a wealthy family, and she'd been kidnapped for ransom when she was a child. Obviously it was a life-altering experience for her. She was obsessed with keeping me safe, and over the years, Dad began to share that obsession. What they failed to remember was that my mother had been kidnapped from her own family's house."

Jenna followed his sweeping gaze around the room before her eyes met his. "There really is no place that's totally safe. Sometimes this estate felt more like a prison than a home."

That explained her wanderlust and maybe even the reason she'd gone to Monte de Leon. For months Cal had seen that trip as a near fatal mistake, but then he glanced at Sophie. That little girl wouldn't be here if Jenna hadn't made that trip. Maybe it was the camaraderie he'd developed with Jenna as they'd waited on that cantina floor. Whatever it was, that bonding had obviously extended to the child in her arms.

"Is the security system okay?" she asked.

"It looks pretty good." The back of the faux painting had the layout of the estate and each room was thankfully labeled not just for function but for the type of security that was installed. "The perimeter of the fence is wired to detect a breach. You have motion detectors at every entrance and exit. And all windows. This is a big place," he added in a mumble.

"Yes," she said with a slight tinge of irony. "Any weak spots you can see?"

"Front gate," he readily supplied. "Is it usually open the way it was when we came in?"

She nodded. "But it can be closed by pressing the button on the monitor or the switch located just inside the grounds." Jenna reached over and did just that. "There's an automatic lock and keypad entry on the left side of the gate."

Which wasn't very safe. Keypads could be tampered with or bypassed. Hollywood certainly knew how to do those things. Salazar likely did, too.

"What's this?" he asked, tapping the large area on the south side of the house that was labeled Gun Room.

"My father was an antique gun collector. He built an indoor firing range to test guns before he bought them."

Interesting. He hadn't expected that, but he would add it to his security plan. "You can shoot?"

"Not at all. The noise always put me off. But I'm willing to learn. In fact, I want to learn."

He just might teach her. Not so he could use her as backup. But it might make her feel more empowered. Plus, the room might come in handy, because it was almost certainly bulletproof. If worse came to worst, then he might have to move them in there. For now, though, he looked for a more comfortable solution.

"Where are the rooms we're supposed to stay in?" he

asked. When Jenna shifted a little, he realized that Sophie was probably getting heavy. He holstered his gun and gently took the baby from her. The little girl was a heavy sleeper. She didn't even lift an eyelid.

"Thanks." Jenna touched her index finger to a trio of rooms on the east side of the house. "That's the nursery, my room's next to it and that's the guest room."

He put his finger next to hers. Touching her. She didn't move away. In fact, she slipped her hand over his. It was such a simple gesture. But an intimate one. It was a good thing Sophie was between them, or he might have done something stupid like pull Jenna into his arms.

"There's a problem," he let her know.

The corner of her mouth lifted for just a second. "I think we're too tired to worry about another kissing session."

There was no such thing as being too tired to kiss. But Cal didn't voice that. Instead, he moved his hand away to avoid further temptation. "Your bedroom has exterior doors."

"Two of them. And another door leads to the pool area. The guest room has an exterior door as well."

From a security perspective, that wasn't good. "How about the nursery?"

"No exterior doors. Four windows, though."

He'd take the windows over the doors. "That's where we'll be spending the night."

She didn't question it. Jenna turned and started walking in that direction. Cal followed her, trying to keep his steps light so he wouldn't wake Sophie. Jenna led him down a corridor lined with doors and stopped in front of one.

"Don't turn on the lights," Cal told her when she opened the door. It was possible that Holden or someone else was doing some long-range surveillance, and Cal didn't want to advertise their exact location in the estate.

He took a moment to let his eyes adjust to the darkness, and he saw the white crib placed against an interior wall well away from the windows. That was good. Cal went that direction and eased Sophie onto the mattress. She moved a little and pursed her lips, sucking at a nonexistent bottle, and he braced himself for her to wake up and cry. But her eyes stayed closed.

"There isn't a bed in here," Jenna whispered. "Just that."

He spotted a chaise longue in the small adjacent sitting room just off the nursery. The chaise wasn't big enough for two people, but hopefully it would be comfortable enough for Jenna to get some sleep.

"I can have a bed brought in," she suggested.

"No. Best not to have any unnecessary movement." Nor did he want to alert anyone else in the household to their sleeping arrangements. Tomorrow, they'd work out something more comfortable.

Jenna walked mechanically to a closet and took out two quilts. The rooms were toasty warm, but she handed him one and draped the other around herself. Since she didn't seem steady on her feet, Cal helped her in the direction of the chaise.

"Get some sleep," he instructed.

She moved as if she were about to climb onto the chaise, but then she stopped. There was just enough moonlight coming through the windows that he could easily see her troubled expression.

"I've really made a mess of things," she said.

Oh, no. Here it was. The adrenaline crash. Reality was setting in, and she started to shake. He couldn't see any tears, but he had no doubt they were there.

She moved again. Closer to him. Until they were touching, her breasts against his chest. That set off Texas-size alarms in his head, and the rest of his body, but it didn't stop him from putting his arms around her.

She sobbed softly, but tried to muffle it by putting her mouth against his shoulder. Her warm breath fluttered against his neck.

"You'll get through this," he promised, though he knew it wouldn't be easy. She was in for a long, hard night. And so was he.

"You're not trembling," she pointed out.

"I'm trained not to tremble. Besides, I only shot an SUV tonight. Trust me, I've done worse." He tried to make it sound light. Cocky, even. But he failed miserably. The attack couldn't be dismissed with bravado.

She pulled back and blinked hard, trying to rid her eyes of the tears. "Have you ever killed anyone?"

Cal was a little taken aback with the question, and he kept his answer simple. "Yeah."

"Good."

"Good?" Again, he was taken aback.

Jenna nodded. "I want you to stop Salazar if he comes after Sophie."

Oh. Now he got it. Cal pushed her hair away from her face. "I won't let him hurt her. Or you."

Hell. He hadn't meant to say that last part aloud. It was too personal, and it was best if he tried to keep some barrier between them.

Her mouth came to his, and all that barrier stuff suddenly sounded like something he didn't want after all. He wanted her kiss.

Since it was going to be a major mistake, Cal decided to make the most of it. Something they'd both regret. And maybe that would stop them from doing it again. So he took far more than he should have.

He hooked his arm around her, just at the top of her butt. He drew her closer so that it wasn't only their chests and mouths that were touching. Their bodies came together, and the fit was even better than his fantasies.

The soft sound Jenna made was from a silky feminine moan of pleasure. A signal that she not only wanted this but wanted more. She wrapped her arms around him and gently ground her sex against his.

While the body contact was mind-blowing, Cal didn't neglect the kiss. This last kiss. Since he'd already decided there couldn't be any more of them, he wanted to savor her in these next few scorching moments. To brand her taste, her touch, the feel of her into his memory.

The kiss was already hot and deep. He deepened it even more. Because he was stupid. And because his stupidity knew no boundaries, he followed Jenna's lead.

Oh, man. Their clothes weren't thick enough. A wall wouldn't have been thick enough.

He could feel the heat of her sex. And his. The brainless part of him was already begging him to lower Jenna to that chaise and strip off her pants. Sex would follow immediately. Great hot sex. Which couldn't happen, of course. Sophie was just in the adjoining room and could wake up at any minute.

Cal repeated that, and he forced himself to stop. When he stepped back from her, both of them were gasping for breath.

"Good night," he managed to say.

"That was your idea of a good-night kiss?" Jenna challenged.

No. It was his idea of foreplay, but it was best not to say that out loud. "We can't do it again."

Why did it sound as if he was trying to convince himself?

Because he was.

Still, he was determined to make this work. He was a pro. A rough-around-the-edges operative. He could stop himself from kissing a woman.

He hoped.

She trailed her fingers down his arm and then withdrew her touch. "I wanted to kiss you on the floor of that cantina," she admitted. "Why, I don't know." Jenna shook her head. "Yes, I do. You're hot. You're dangerous. You're all the things that get my blood moving."

His pulse jumped. "So you like hot dangerous things?" he asked.

"I like you," she said, her voice quivery now. She sank down onto the chaise and looked up at him. "But liking you isn't wise. I've made a lot of bad choices in my life, and I can't do that anymore now that I have Sophie. If I fall for a guy, then it has to be the right guy, you know?"

"Sure." He wouldn't tell her that soon his job

wouldn't be that dangerous. If he got that deputy director promotion, he'd be doing his shooting from behind a desk. On some level Cal would miss the fieldwork, but the deputy director job was the next step in his dream to be chief. Maybe it was best that Jenna thought his dangerous work would continue. Maybe this was the barrier they needed between them.

"Sleep," he reminded her.

Jenna lay down on the chaise and covered up. Cal was about to do the same on the floor, but his cell phone rang. He yanked it from his pocket and answered it before it could ring a second time and wake up Sophie.

"It's Kowalski," his director greeted. "What's your situation?"

Cal got up, walked across the room and stepped just outside the door and into the hall. "Is this line secure?"

"Yes. I'm using the private line in my office."

Good. That meant if there was a leak or threat from Hollywood, then at least this call wouldn't be overheard. Cal had called Kowalski right after the SUV incident, but he hadn't wanted to say too much until he knew the info would stay private.

"I'm at Ms. Laniere's estate. Were you able to get anything on that SUV that tried to run us off the road?"

"Nothing. The Texas Rangers are investigating. There was a team of them nearby searching for that missing woman, and they got there faster than the FBI."

Well, Cal wasn't holding his breath that they'd find anything related to Salazar. If the assassin had been the driver, then the first thing he would have done was ditch the vehicle. He wouldn't have wanted to drive it around with bullet holes in it.

"And what about Salazar?" Cal asked, hoping by some miracle the man had been picked up.

"He's still at large."

Cal didn't bother to groan since that was the answer he'd expected. "What about the plates?" He had made a note of them and had asked the director to run them.

"The plates weren't stolen. They were bogus."

Strange. A pro like Salazar would normally have just stolen a vehicle and then discarded it when he was done. Bogus plates took time to create. "And Hollywood? Anything new to report?"

"Nothing definitive on him, either."

Cal was afraid of that. "How did he take the news that he's under investigation?"

The director took several moments to answer. "He doesn't know."

"Excuse me?" Cal was certain he'd misunderstood the director.

"Lynch doesn't know he's being monitored. I want to let him have access to some information and see what he does with it. If he does nothing, then maybe someone has set him up."

Or maybe Hollywood knew about the monitoring and was going to play it clean for a while.

"How's Ms. Laniere?" Kowalski asked, pulling Cal's thoughts away from all the other questions.

She's making me crazy. "She's shaken up, of course." Cal used his briefing tone. Flat, unemotional, detached. Unlike the firestorm going on inside him. "My plan was to stay here with her and her child until we can make other arrangements."

"Of course." The director paused, which bothered Cal. Was Kowalski concerned about this whole paternity issue? Was he worried that Cal was going to sleep with her? Cal was worried about that, too.

"Ms. Laniere is the main reason I'm calling," Kowalski explained. "We might have another problem."

This didn't sound like a personal issue. It sounded dangerous. Besides, they didn't need another problem, personal or otherwise. They already had a boatload of them. "What's wrong now?"

"The Ranger CSI unit is at Ms. Laniere's apartment in Willow Ridge now. About a half hour ago they found a listening device near the front door. It wasn't government issue. It was something you could buy at any store that sells security equipment. Still, Lynch could have put it there."

Holden or Helena could have done the same. All three had been there. Or maybe even Gwen had done it after Jenna and he had left.

"There's more," the director continued. "I had the CSI check your car as well, and they just called to say they'd found a vehicle tracking system taped to the undercarriage."

Cal cursed. "Someone wanted to follow me." He carried that through one more step. "And that means someone could have done the same to Jenna's car."

"Probably."

"But I checked the undercarriage when I looked for explosives." Cal started for the front of the house.

"You could easily have missed it. It's small, half the size of a deck of cards. But don't let the size fool you. It might be wireless and portable, but it's still effective even at long range."

"Stay put," he called out to Jenna. "I have to go outside and check on something."

Cal hurried toward the front of the house, disengaged the security system, unlocked the front door. He drew his weapon before he hurried out into the cold night. No one seemed to be lurking in the shadows waiting to assassinate him, but he rushed. He didn't want to leave Jenna and Sophie alone for too long.

Thankfully, the overhead porch lights were enough for him to clearly see the car. Staying on the side that was nearest to the house, he stooped and looked underneath. There was no immediate sign of a tracker. But then he looked again at a clump of mud. He touched it and realized it was a fake. Plastic. He pulled it back and looked at the device beneath.

His heart dropped.

"Found it," Cal reported. "Someone camouflaged it."

"So someone wired both cars," the director concluded. "The bad news is that anyone with a laptop could have monitored your whereabouts."

Cal's heart dropped even further. Because that meant someone had tracked them to Jenna's estate.

Salazar and maybe God knows who else knew exactly where they were.

Chapter Nine

Jenna checked her watch. It was nearly 6:00 a.m. Soon, Sophie would wake up and demand her breakfast bottle.

She took a moment to gather her thoughts and to reassure herself one last time that everyone was okay. The security alarm hadn't gone off. No one had fired shots into the place. That SUV hadn't returned.

But all of those things might still happen.

Cal hadn't come out and said that, but after he'd discovered the tracking device on her car, they both knew anything was possible. He'd considered moving them again, but had decided to stay put and hope their safety measures were enough to keep out anyone who might decide to come after them.

After Cal had disarmed and removed the tracking device, every possible function of the security system had been armed. Cal had even alerted all three members of the household staff, and the gardener, Pete Spears, had assured them that he'd keep watch from the gatehouse.

All those measures had been enough. They were still alive and unharmed. But the day had barely started.

With that uncomfortable thought, Jenna eased off the chaise and moved as quietly as she could so she wouldn't wake Cal. He hadn't slept much. She knew that because he'd been awake when she finally fell asleep around midnight. He was still awake when she'd gotten up at 2:00 a.m. to feed a fussing Sophie. He'd even gone with them to the kitchen when she fixed the bottle, and he'd taken his gun with him.

But he was thankfully asleep now.

He was sitting with his legs stretched out in front of him, so his upper back and neck were resting on the chaise. His face looked perfectly relaxed, but he had his hand resting over the butt of the gun in his shoulder holster.

She reached for her shoes, but Cal's hand shot out. Before Jenna could even blink, he grabbed her wrist, turned and used the strength of his body to flatten her against the chaise.

Their eyes met.

He was on top of her with his face only several inches away from hers. In the depths of those steel-blue eyes, she saw him process the situation. There was no emotion in those eyes. Well, not at first. Then he cursed under his breath.

"Sorry. Old habits," he mumbled.

It took her a moment to get past the shock of what'd just happened. "You mean combat training, not intimate situations?" She meant it as a joke, but it came out all wrong. Of course it did. His kisses could melt paint, and he was on top of her in what could be a good starting position for some great morning sex.

But there wouldn't be any.

Cal got off her with difficulty. He dug his knee into the chaise to lever himself up, but that created some interesting contact in their midsections.

"Dreams," he explained when he noticed that she was looking at the bulge behind the zipper of his jeans.

About me? she nearly asked but thankfully held her tongue. It was wishful thinking. Yes, he'd kissed her, but he hadn't wanted to. It'd been just a primal response. Now he wanted some distance between them. He wanted Sophie and her safe so he wouldn't feel obligated to help. And after all the trouble she'd caused for him, she couldn't blame him one bit.

Sophie's soft whimpers got her moving off the chaise but not before Cal and she exchanged uncomfortable glances. She really needed to make other security arrangements so he could leave. But that was the last thing on earth she wanted.

"Good morning, sweetheart," she greeted Sophie.

Jenna scooped her up into her arms and stole a few morning kisses. Sophie stopped fussing and gave her a wide smile. It wouldn't last, though. Soon her baby would want her bottle, so Jenna started toward the kitchen.

Cal was right behind her.

Meggie was ahead of them in the hall. The woman was walking straight toward them. "A fax just arrived for you." She handed Cal at least a dozen pages, but her attention went straight to Sophie. "I've got a bottle waiting for you, young lady."

Sophie looked at her with curious eyes and glanced up at Jenna. Jenna smiled to reassure her, and it seemed to work because Sophie smiled, too, when Meggie took her and headed for the kitchen.

Since Cal had stopped to look at the fax and since it seemed to have grabbed his complete interest, Jenna stopped as well. "Bad news?"

"It could be." He glanced through the rest of the pages and then handed her the first one. "These are reports I requested from my director. I asked for a background on Gwen Mitchell and I also wanted him to look for any suspicious activity that could be linked back to you."

She skimmed through the page and groaned. "There was a break-in at the pediatrician's office. Sophie's file was stolen." Jenna smacked the paper against the palm of her hand. "Holden is responsible for this. He's trying to prove that Paul's the father."

"What would have been in that file?" Cal asked.

"Well, certainly no DNA information, but her blood type was listed. It's O-positive."

Cal actually looked conflicted. "O-positive is the most common. It's my blood type."

Jenna immediately understood his mixed emotions. This might make Holden think she was telling the truth about Cal being Sophie's father. But this would also make his director have more doubts. She really did need to get a DNA test done right away.

Cal made his way toward the kitchen while he continued to read the fax. "Gwen Mitchell's been a freelance investigative reporter for ten years." He shuffled through the pages. "She's gotten some pretty tough stories, including one on a mob boss. And a Colombian drug dealer."

So they weren't dealing with an amateur. "She doesn't sound like the type of person to back off."

"She's not," Cal confirmed. He stopped again just outside the kitchen entrance. "According to this, when Gwen was working on that story in Colombia, a woman was killed."

Jenna nearly gasped. "Gwen murdered her?"

"Not exactly, but she was responsible for the woman's death. Gwen made the drug lord believe this woman had revealed sensitive information. The drug lord had her killed. Gwen managed to record the actual murder and that became the centerpiece of her story."

"Oh, God." So this was what they were up against. A ruthless woman who'd do whatever was necessary to get her story. And in this case her story was getting Jenna. Gwen would do anything to collect the one million dollars that Paul had offered her.

Cal walked ahead of her and checked the security system. It was identical to the check he'd made before and after Sophie's 2:00 a.m. feeding. When he was satisfied that everything was still secure, they went to the kitchen.

Meggie had Sophie in the crook of her arm and was trying to feed her a bottle while she checked something on the stove. Jenna went to take the child, but Cal caught her.

"I'll take her. You need to eat something."

Jenna's stomach chose that exact moment to growl. She couldn't argue with that. But she was more than a little surprised when Cal so easily took Sophie from Meggie. He sat down at the kitchen table and readjusted the bottle so there'd be an even flow of formula.

Jenna and Meggie exchanged glances.

"You're sure you haven't done baby duty before?" Jenna asked. She poured herself a cup of coffee, and Meggie dished her up some scrambled eggs.

"Nope," he assured her.

He was a natural. He seemed so at ease with Sophie. And willing to help. It made Jenna feel guilty—his willingness could be costly for him. If she hadn't told that lie to Holden, Cal would never have come to Willow Ridge, and he wouldn't be in this dangerous situation now. Of course, Jenna was thankful he was there. For Sophie's sake. But she hated what she'd done to him.

Jenna had only managed to eat one bite of the eggs when a shrill beep pulsed through the room. It brought Cal to his feet. He handed Sophie to her and drew his gun.

Just like that, her heart went into overdrive, and her stomach knotted. Jenna passed her daughter to Meggie so she could go with Cal and see what had happened to trigger the surveillance system.

Cal hurried to the security panel just as his cell phone rang. He answered it while he opened the panel box.

"You're here at the estate?" he asked a moment later. That sent him to the side windows by the front door, and he looked out. "Something's wrong."

It wasn't a question, but he must have gotten an answer because he hung up.

"Director Kowalski just arrived," Cal relayed to her. "He found Holden and Helena Carr outside. They were trying to get in the front gate."

CAL HAD HOPED that today wouldn't be as insane as the day before, but it wasn't off to a good start. Here it was, barely dawn, his director had arrived for an impromptu visit, and two of their suspects were only yards away. Cal didn't want those two in the same state with Jenna and Sophie, yet here they were.

Had they been the ones to put the tracking devices on Jenna's and his vehicles? Maybe. Or maybe they'd merely benefited from what someone else had done.

"Can your director arrest Holden and Helena?" Jenna asked.

"Probably not. I'm sure they'll have a cover story for their attempt to get through the front gate."

But maybe they could call the local authorities and have them picked up for trespassing. It wouldn't keep the duo in jail long since they'd have no trouble making bail, but it would send a message that they couldn't continue to intimidate Jenna without paying a consequence or two.

Cal grabbed his jacket and disarmed the security system so he could go outside and *greet* their visitors. Jenna picked up her jacket as well.

"I want to talk to them," she said before he could object to her going with him.

"That wouldn't be wise."

"On the contrary. I want them to know I won't cower in fear or hide. I want them out of my life."

Cal wasn't sure this was the way to make that happen, but he didn't want to take the time to argue with her. Director Kowalski might need backup.

"Wait on the porch," he instructed. "That way, they can see you, but you can get back inside if things turn ugly."

He hoped like the devil that she obeyed.

Cal walked down the steps and spotted the gardener, Pete, in the gatehouse. He was armed with a shotgun. Good. He'd take all the help he could get.

There were three cars just on the other side of the gate. Two were high-end luxury vehicles, no doubt belonging to Holden and Helena. Cal wondered why they hadn't driven together. The third vehicle was a standard-issue four-wheel-drive from ISA's motor pool.

The three drivers were at the gate, waiting. Cal didn't like the idea of his director being locked out with the Carrs, but he couldn't risk Sophie's and Jenna's safety. He needed to keep that gate closed until he was sure this visit wasn't going to lead to an attack.

Before he approached the gate, Cal glanced over his shoulder. Amazingly, Jenna was still on the porch. He doubted she'd stay there, but he welcomed these few minutes of safety.

"I didn't try to break in," Helena volunteered. "I merely wanted to speak to Jenna, and I was trying to find an intercom or something when that man with the shotgun sounded the alarm."

Kowalski was behind her. He had his weapon drawn in his right hand and held an equipment bag in his left. He rolled his eyes, an indication he didn't buy Helena's story.

Holden's eyes, however, were much more intense. He had his attention fastened to Jenna on the porch. "I need to talk to her, too," he insisted.

I, not *we.* Given the fact that the siblings had arrived

in separate vehicles, perhaps they were in the middle of a family squabble. Considering what Helena had said at Jenna's apartment in Willow Ridge, that didn't surprise Cal.

"Jenna's not receiving visitors," Cal said sarcastically. "But I'll pass along any message."

Holden continued to watch Jenna. "The message is that she's in grave danger." His voice was probably loud enough for her to hear.

Cal shrugged. "Old news."

"Not exactly," Holden challenged. He glanced at his sister.

Now it was Helena's turn to show some intensity. Anger tightened the muscles on her face. "My brother broke into my personal computer and read the e-mail Paul's attorney sent me. Holden seems to think that I'd be willing to do whatever Paul wants me to do."

Well, this had potential. "And what does Paul want you to do?"

Helena came closer and hooked her perfectly manicured fingers around the wrought-iron spindles that made up the gate front. "Paul seemed to believe that I would tie up loose ends if Salazar failed."

Holden stepped forward as well. "My sister's orders are to kill us all once Salazar has Sophie."

Oh, hell. Paul really had put together some plan. Kidnapping and murder.

"I'm not a killer," Helena said, her voice shaky now. "I have no idea why Paul thought I would do this."

"Don't you?" Holden again. He aimed his answer at Cal. "My sister was sleeping with Paul. She didn't think

I knew, but I did. And I also knew that they had plans to kill Jenna if she turned down his marriage proposal."

"That's not true," Helena protested.

Cal heard footsteps behind him and groaned. A glance over his shoulder confirmed that Jenna wanted to be part of this conversation. He didn't blame her. But he also wanted to keep her safe. He positioned himself in front of her, hoping that would be enough if bullets started flying.

"Paul didn't love me," Helena said to Jenna. She shook her head. "He didn't love you, either."

"I know," Jenna readily agreed. "He wanted my business. And you were in on his plan to get it?"

"Only the business." Helena's face flushed as if she was embarrassed by the admission of her guilt. "I never would have agreed to murder."

Cal wasn't sure he believed her. A flushed face could be faked. "How does Gwen Mitchell fit into the picture?" he asked.

Helena's eyes widened. "The reporter?"

"Yeah. Paul was sleeping with her, too." It was a good guess. After reading Gwen's background, Cal figured she'd do anything to get a story.

Helena shook her head again and a thin stream of breath left her mouth. "I didn't know."

"So Paul slept around," Holden snarled. If he had any concern for his sister's reaction, he didn't show it. "I don't think that's nearly as important as the fact that he's put bounties on our heads." Holden cursed. "He was my friend. Like a brother to me. And this is what he does?"

Kowalski came closer. "What exactly did Paul say in the e-mail he sent you?" he asked Holden.

Holden sent a nasty glare the director's way. "Well, he didn't ask me to kill anyone, that's for sure. He asked me to check on some accounts and old business connections. Nothing illegal. Nothing sinister. Obviously, Helena can't say the same. Paul made some kind of arrangement with my sister—"

"He didn't," Helena practically shouted. "And I didn't agree to do what he asked." She caught her brother's arm and whirled him around so he was facing her. "Have you ever considered that he could be doing this for some other reason? To get us at each other's throats? Paul had a sick sense of humor, and this might be his idea of a joke."

"My daughter is in danger," Jenna said, drawing everyone's attention back to her. "It's not a joke. Salazar is out there, and Paul is the one who sent him after Sophie."

Cal glanced at Holden and Helena to see their reactions. They were still hurling daggers at each other. It was a good time to interject some logic in this game of pointing fingers.

"If Paul wanted Sophie, but he also wanted all of you dead, then who would be left to raise her?" the director challenged. "Who would be left to manage his estate? Why would he want to eliminate the very people who could give him some postmortem help?"

Dead silence.

"Maybe he expected Gwen Mitchell to help him," Jenna mumbled. "Maybe they were more than just lovers."

That was exactly what Cal was considering. Gwen's ruthlessness would have endeared her to Paul. And for that matter, the e-mails could be a hoax. A way to drive them all apart. Gwen could have further instructions that Paul could have given her before he was murdered.

And that brought Cal back to something he wanted to ask. "How exactly did you two know that Jenna would be here?"

Holden shrugged and peeled off the leather glove on his left hand. "It wasn't a lucky guess, was it, Helena?"

The woman's shoulders snapped back, but she didn't answer her brother. She looked at Cal instead. "Salazar called me a few hours ago to tell me that he'd put a tracking device on Jenna's car. He said she was here."

Cal silently cursed and glanced around to make sure Salazar wasn't lurking somewhere. "Go back in the house," he instructed Jenna in a whisper. "Arm the security system."

"But if it isn't safe for me, it isn't safe for you," Jenna pointed out, also in a whisper.

"I won't be long," he promised, knowing that didn't really address her concerns. Still, he had some unfinished business. Concerns about his personal safety could wait.

"What else did Salazar say?" Kowalski demanded from Helena once Jenna started for the house.

"Nothing. I swear. He told me about the tracking device, said Jenna was at the estate, and that was it. He hung up." She slid an icy glance at her brother. "I didn't know Holden had tapped my calls. Not until I arrived here and realized that he'd followed me."

Cal stared at Holden, to see if he would add anything, or at least offer an explanation as to why he'd eavesdropped on his sister's conversations. But maybe this was the way it'd always been between them.

"You're not getting into the estate," Cal assured both of them. "You're trespassing."

Holden smacked the glove against the gate. "Arrest me, then. Go ahead. Waste your time when what you should be doing is stopping Salazar."

"Oh, I intend to do that." And he intended to stop Gwen if she was as neck deep in this as he thought she was.

"I don't think it'll be a waste of time if you report to the local FBI office for questioning," the director interjected.

"When there's a warrant for my arrest, I'll show up," Holden snarled. He headed for his car, got in and drove away. His tires squealed from the excessive speed.

"I'll go in for questioning," Helena told Kowalski. Her eyes watered with tears. "I'll do whatever's necessary to keep us all alive."

"Paul asked you to kill us," Cal reminded her. "What makes you think you're in danger?"

She glanced at her brother's car as it quickly disappeared down the road. "Holden won't show me the e-mail he got from Paul. My brother doesn't trust me. And why should he? Because of Paul, Holden thinks I'll try to kill him, and he's no doubt trying to figure out how to kill me first before I can carry through with Paul's wishes."

With that, she walked to her car. Her shoulders were slumped, and she swiped her hand over her cheek to wipe away her tears.

"Any idea what was in Holden's e-mail?" Cal asked once Helena had driven away.

Kowalski shook his head. "We're still working on that. But Helena didn't lie when she said what was in hers.

Paul did leave orders to kill Jenna, Holden and anyone else who got in the way of Salazar taking the baby."

Anyone else. That would be Cal. Somehow he would stop Salazar and unravel this mess that'd brought danger right to Jenna's doorstep.

He reached over and hit the control switch to open the gate. Kowalski walked closer and handed him an equipment bag. "I figured you might need this. There's an extra weapon, ammo and a clean laptop."

Cal appreciated the supplies, but knowing Salazar could be out there, he continued to keep watch. So did Pete. The lanky man with sandy blond hair shifted his shotgun and wary gaze all around the grounds. There weren't many places Salazar could take cover and use an assault rifle. Unless he actually made it onto the property. Then there were a lot of places he could use to launch an attack.

Cal glanced down into the unzipped bag and then looked at Kowalski. "Does this mean I'll be here for a while?"

"For now." He paused. "I know it's not protocol. Hell, it's not even legal. That's why you can't be here in a professional capacity. This is personal, understand? You're on an official leave of absence."

"I understand."

It was the truth. This had become personal for Cal.

"Last night after we talked, I worked to set up a safe house for Ms. Laniere and her child," Kowalski explained. "But then the communications monitor at headquarters informed me that my account might have been compromised. There was something suspicious about the way info was feeding in and out of what was supposed to be a secure computer. That means someone might have seen the message traffic on the safe house."

Cal cursed. "Hollywood?"

"Maybe. But it could also be a false alarm caused by a computer glitch. That's why I decided to come in person and tell you to stay put for now."

That's what Cal was afraid he was going to say. "But Salazar knows where Jenna is."

Kowalski nodded. "You might have to take him out if we can't stop him first. The FBI and the Rangers are looking for him. They know he's probably in the area."

Yeah. And for that reason, Cal didn't want to leave Jenna alone for too long. "I'll do what's necessary."

Another nod. The director glanced around uneasily. "What about the paternity issue? Did you get that DNA test done to prove you aren't the baby's father?"

Cal hadn't forgotten about that, but it was definitely on the back burner. "I figured it could wait until all of this is over. Besides, I want Holden and Salazar to believe the child is mine. That might get them to back off."

Though that was more than a long shot. Things had already been set into motion, and it would take a miracle to stop them.

Kowalski met him eye-to-eye. "You're sure that's the only reason you're putting off a DNA test?"

Cal stared at him and tried not to blast the man for accusing him of lying. "I've never given you a reason to distrust me."

"You have now." The director turned and started for

his vehicle. "Clear up this paternity issue, Cal, before it destroys everything you've worked so hard to get."

There was just one problem with clearing it up. Well, two.

Jenna and Sophie.

He closed the gate and stood there watching his boss drive away. Cal wondered if his chances at that promotion had just driven away, too. Without Kowalski's blessing, Cal wasn't going to get that deputy director job. Not a chance. He wouldn't even have a career left to salvage.

Cal grabbed the equipment bag and went back to the house. Jenna was there, waiting for him just inside the door. A few feet behind her was Meggie. She had Sophie cradled in her arms. The little girl smiled at him. She was too young and innocent to know the danger she was in.

Seeing Jenna and the baby was a reminder that his career was pretty damn small in the grand scheme of things.

"So, are we going on the run again?" Jenna began to nibble on her bottom lip.

"No." He hoped that was the right thing to do.

Still, he wasn't going to put full trust in his director's decision for them to stay put because Hollywood might still be getting access to any- and everything.

"I need backup," Cal mumbled to himself. More than just a gardener with a shotgun.

And it had to be someone he trusted.

His brother Max was his first choice. If Max was on assignment, then he'd call a friend who owned a personal protection agency. One way or another he wanted someone reliable on the grounds ASAP, and these were men he could trust with his life.

"So we stay put," Jenna concluded. She paused. "And then what?"

"We prepare ourselves for the worst."

Because the worst was on the way.

Chapter Ten

"Rule one," Cal said to Jenna. He slipped on her eye goggles and adjusted them so they fit firmly on her face. "Treat all firearms as if they're loaded."

He positioned the Smith & Wesson 9 mm gun in her hand and turned her toward the target. It was the silhouette of a person rather than a bull's-eye. Jenna didn't like the idea of aiming at a person, real or otherwise, but she also knew this was necessary. Cal was doing everything humanly possible to keep her and Sophie safe. She wanted to do her part as well.

"Rule two," he continued. "Never point a weapon at anything or anyone you don't intend to destroy."

There it was in a nutshell. Her biggest fear. She'd have to kill someone to stop all of this insanity.

Every precaution was being taken to prevent anyone, especially Salazar, from gaining access to the estate. Cal's friend Jordan Taylor had arrived an hour earlier. He was an expert in security. Jenna hadn't actually met or seen the man because he'd immediately gotten to work on installing monitoring equipment around the entire fence. Jordan had brought another man, Cody Guillory, with him, and the two were going to patrol the grounds. In the meantime, Director Kowalski and the FBI had assured Cal they were doing everything to catch Salazar and neutralize the threat.

However, Cal had insisted she learn how to shoot, just in case.

Jenna hadn't balked at his suggestion, but she had waited until Sophie was down for her morning nap. Meggie and the baby were in the nursery with the door locked, Meggie was armed and the rest of the house was on lockdown. No one was to get in or out.

"Rule three—don't hold your gun sideways. Only stupid people trying to look cool do that. It'll give you a bad aim and cause you to miss your target." Cal moved behind her.

Touching her.

Something he'd been doing since this lesson started. Of course, it was impossible to give a shooting lesson without touching, but the contact made it hard for her to concentrate. It reminded her of their kiss and the fact that she wanted him to touch her. She needed therapy. How could she be thinking about such things at a time like this?

Quite easily, she admitted.

It was Cal and his superhero outfit. Camo pants, black chest-hugging T-shirt. Steel-toed boots. The clothes had been in the equipment bag that the director had delivered, and in this case, the clothes made the man. Well, they made her notice every inch of his body, anyway.

"Okay, here we go," he said, pulling her attention

back to the lesson. "Feet apart." He put his hand on the inside of her thigh, just above her knee, to position her.

A shiver of heat went through her.

"Left foot slightly in front. Right elbow completely straight. Since you're new at this, look at the target with your right eye. Close your left one. It'll make it easier to aim." He stopped with his hand beneath her straight elbow and his arm grazing her breasts. "You're shaking a little. Are you cold?"

The room was a little chilly, but that wasn't it. Jenna knew she should just lie. It was right there on the tip of her tongue, but she made the mistake of glancing at him. Even through the goggles, he had no trouble seeing her expression.

"Oh," he mumbled. "Some women get turned on from shooting. All that power in their hands."

Jenna continued to stare at him. "I don't think it's the gun." She probably should have lied about that, too.

Cal chuckled. It was husky, deep and totally male. He dropped his hands to her waist to readjust her stance. At least that's how it started, but he kept his hands there and pressed against her. His front against her back.

That didn't help the shaking. Nor did it cool down the heat.

He grabbed two sets of earmuffs, put one on her and slipped the other on himself. "Take aim at the center of the target," he said, his voice loud so that she could hear him. "Squeeze the trigger with gentle but steady pressure."

Which was exactly what he was doing to her waist.

"Now?" she asked.

"Whenever you're ready." He brushed against her butt.

Sheez. Since this lesson was turning into foreplay, Jenna decided to go ahead. She thought through all of Cal's instructions and then pulled the trigger. Even with the earmuffs, the shot was loud, and her entire right arm recoiled.

She pulled off the earmuffs and goggles and had a look at where her shot had landed.

"That'll work," Cal assured her.

Jenna looked closer at the target and frowned. "I hit the guy in his family jewels."

Cal chuckled again. "Trust me, that'll work."

She replaced the earmuffs and goggles so she could try more shots. She adjusted her aim but the bullet went low again. It took her three more tries before she got a shot anywhere near the upper torso.

"I think you got the hang of it," Cal praised. He took off his own muffs and laid them back on the shelf. He did the same to hers and then took the gun from her. It wasn't easy—her fingers had frozen around it.

"You did good," he added, making eye contact with her.

His hand went around the back of her neck, pulling her to him, and his mouth went to hers.

Yes! she thought. *Finally!*

Maybe it was the fact she was a new mother and had learned to appreciate what little free time she had, but Jenna wanted to make the most of these stolen moments.

Cal obviously did, too. He kissed her, hungry and hot, as if he'd been waiting all morning to do just that.

He ran his hand into her hair so that he controlled the movement of her head. She didn't mind. He angled her so that he could deepen the kiss. And just like that, she was starved for more of him.

With his hands and mouth on her, Jenna's back landed against one of the smooth, square floor-to-ceiling columns that set off the firing lane. Cal landed against her. All those firm sinewy muscles in his chest played havoc with her breasts. It'd been so long since she'd been in a man's arms, and this man had been worth the wait.

His mouth teased and coaxed her. The not so gentle pressure of his chest muscles and pecs made her latch on to him and pull him even closer, until they were fitted together exactly the way a man and woman should fit. They still had their clothes on, but Jenna had no trouble imagining what it would be like to have Cal naked and inside her.

Her need for him was almost embarrassing. She'd never been a sexually charged person. She preferred a good kiss to sex, probably because she'd never actually had good sex. But something told her that she wouldn't have to settle for one or the other with Cal. He was more than capable of delivering both.

He slid his hand down her side, to the bottom of her stretchy top, and lifted it. His fingers, which were just as hot and clever as his mouth, were suddenly on her bare skin, making their way to her breasts and jerking down the cups of her bra.

Everything intensified. His touch. The heat. That primal tug deep within her.

Cal pulled back from the kiss, only so he could wet his fingertips with his tongue. For a moment, she didn't understand why. But then his mouth came back to hers, and those slick wet fingers went to her nipples. He caressed her, and gently pinched her nipples, bringing them to peaks.

Jenna nearly lost it right there.

Frantically searching for some relief to the pressure-cooker heat, she hooked her fingers through the belt loops of his camo pants and dragged him to her, so that his hard sex ground against the soft, wet part of her body.

It was good. Too good.

Because it only made her want the rest of him.

She reached for his zipper, but Cal clamped his hand over hers. Stopping her. "No condom," he reminded her.

Jenna cursed, both thankful and angry that he'd managed to keep a clear head. She didn't want a clear head. She wanted Cal. But she also knew he was right. They couldn't risk having unprotected sex.

She tried to calm down. She'd been ready to climax, and her body wasn't pleased that it wasn't going to get what it wanted.

Cal, however, didn't let her come down. He pinned her in place against the column and shoved down her zipper. He didn't wait to see how she would react to that. He kissed her again. And again, the heat began to soar.

While he did some clever things with his mouth, he tormented her nipples with his left hand. But it was his right hand that sent her soaring. It slid into her jeans. Underneath her panties. He wasn't gentle, wasn't slow. His middle and index fingers eased into the slippery heat of her body and moved.

It didn't take much. Just a few of those clever strokes.

Another deep French kiss. He nipped her nipple with his fingertips.

Their kiss muffled the sound she made, and his fingers continued to move, to give her every last bit of pleasure he could.

CAL CAUGHT HER to make sure she didn't fall. Jenna buried her face against the crook of his neck and let him catch her. Her breath came out in rough, hot jolts. Her body was trembling, her face, flushed with arousal.

She smelled like sex.

It was a powerful scent that urged his body to do a lot more than he'd just done. Of course, what he'd done was too much. He'd crossed lines that shouldn't have been crossed. In fact, he'd gone just short of what his director already suspected him of doing.

A husky laugh rumbled in Jenna's throat, and she blinked as if to clear her vision. Cal certainly needed to clear his. He made sure she was steady on her feet, and then he zipped up her jeans so he could step away from her.

She blinked again. This time, she looked confused, then embarrassed. "Oh, mercy. You could get into trouble for that."

He shrugged and left it at that.

"I keep forgetting that this has much stiffer consequences for you than it does for me." Still breathing hard, she pushed the wisps of blond hair from her face. A natural blonde. He'd discovered that when he unzipped her pants and pushed down her panties.

Now he needed to forget what he'd seen.

Hell. He just needed to forget, period.

"Of course, I'll get a broken heart out of this," she mumbled, and fixed her jeans.

A broken heart?

Did that mean she had feelings for him?

"Forget I said that," she mumbled a moment later. She looked even more embarrassed. "I'm not making sense right now."

So no broken heart. But still Cal had to wonder….

He didn't have long to wonder because his phone rang. The caller ID screen indicated it was Jordan.

"I was beefing up security by the front gate when a car pulled up," Jordan explained in the no-nonsense tone that Cal had always heard him use. "You have a visitor. She says her name is Gwen Mitchell and that she *must* talk to you."

"Gwen Mitchell's out front," Cal relayed to Jenna.

He wasn't exactly surprised. Everyone seemed to know where they were. But how should he handle this visit? He needed to question Gwen, but he didn't want to do that by placing Jenna and Sophie at risk.

"She says she has some new information you should hear," Jordan added. "She's refused to give it to me, but I can get it if you like. What do you want me to do with her?"

From Jordan, it was a formidable question. If Gwen had any inkling of the dangerous man that Jordan could be, she probably would have been running for the hills. Jordan was loyal to the end. He and Cal were close enough that he would trust Jordan to kill for him. Of course, he hoped killing Gwen wouldn't be necessary.

"Make sure she's not armed," Cal instructed. "And then escort her to the porch. I'll meet you at the front door."

"You're not going to let her in the house?" Jordan challenged.

"Not a chance."

Cal believed Gwen wanted one thing. A story. And even though he could relate to her devotion to duty, he was beginning to see that as a huge risk.

"You're meeting with her?" Jenna asked, following right behind him.

Cal locked the gun room door, using the key that Jenna had given him earlier. "I have a hunch that Gwen knows a lot more than she's saying. Plus, I want to hear what she considers to be important information."

"It could be a trap," Jenna pointed out.

"It could be, but if so, it's suicide. Jordan won't let an armed suspect make it to the door. Still, I want you to wait inside."

She huffed. For such a simple sound, it conveyed a lot. Jenna didn't like losing control of her life. But one way or another he was going to protect her.

"I'll stay in the foyer," she bargained. "Because you aren't actually going outside, are you?" She didn't wait for him to confirm that. "Besides, any information she has would pertain to me. Paul sent her after me because he thought I planned to murder him. I deserve to hear what she has to say."

He stopped at the front door, whirled around and stared at her. He had already geared up for an argument about why she shouldn't be present at this meeting, but Jenna pressed her fingers over his mouth.

"Don't let sexual attraction for me get in the way of doing what's smart," she said. Except it sounded like some kind of accusation.

"The sexual attraction isn't making me stupid."

"If you didn't want me in your bed," Jenna continued, "then you wouldn't be so protective of me. You'd let me confront Gwen." She frowned when he scowled at her. "Or you'd at least let me listen to what she has to say. I can do that as safely as you can. You already pointed out that Jordan will make sure Gwen isn't armed."

True. So why did he still feel the need to shelter Jenna from this conversation?

Hell. The attraction he felt for her could really complicate everything.

Cal scowled and threw open the front door.

Gwen was there, looking not at all certain of what she might have gotten herself into. Jordan probably had something to do with that. At six-two and a hundred and ninety pounds, he was no lightweight. He stood behind Gwen, looming over her. He was armed and had an extra weapon on his utility belt. In addition, he had a small communicator fitted into his left ear. He was no doubt getting updates from an associate somewhere on the grounds.

Jordan seemed to be doing a good job of neutralizing any threat from Gwen, but Cal took it one step further and made sure he was in front of Jenna.

"There's someone else waiting by the gate," Jordan informed them. "Archie Monroe. His ID looks legit. Says he's from Cryogen Labs."

Cal went on instant alert, and motioned for Jordan to

come inside. He shut the door, leaving Gwen standing outside, and lowered his voice to a whisper. "Could it be Salazar?"

"Not unless he's had major cosmetic surgery. This guy's about sixty, gray hair and he's got a couple of spare tires around his middle."

"It's not Salazar," Jenna provided. Jordan and Cal stared at her. "He's a lab technician. I called Cryogen this morning and asked them to send out someone to do a DNA test on Sophie."

Cal choked back a groan and geared himself up for an argument.

Jenna beat him to it. "The DNA issue is hurting your career. I can't let it continue."

Cal opened his mouth. Then he closed it and tried to get hold of his temper. "I will not let you put my job ahead of Sophie's safety. Got that?" Then he turned to Jordan. "Tell him there's been a misunderstanding, that his services are not needed."

Jordan nodded and opened the door to hurry toward the front gate. Jenna didn't say anything else, but she did send Cal a disapproving look. He knew she didn't want this test. Not really. She wouldn't want to do anything to increase the risk of danger for Sophie. That's what made it even more frustrating.

She was doing this for him.

That attraction had *really* screwed up things between them.

"Is there a problem?" Gwen asked, glancing over her shoulder at Jordan, who was making his way to the lab tech.

"You tell me," Cal challenged. "Why are you here?"

Gwen's attention went to Jenna. "I know you didn't murder Paul."

Not exactly a revelation.

"That's why you came?" Jenna stepped closer. "To tell me something I already know?"

"I have proof. I got Paul's attorney to e-mail me surveillance videos. There's not any actual footage of Paul being killed, but there is footage of you leaving the estate. Fifteen minutes later, there's footage of Paul coming out of his office to get something and then returning."

Cal knew all about that surveillance. The ISA had studied and restudied it. Well, Hollywood had. And Cal had reviewed it to make sure Jenna hadn't been the killer. The surveillance hadn't captured images of the person who'd entered Paul's office and shot him in the back of the head. Thermal images taken with ISA equipment had shown a person entering through a private entrance. No security camera had been set up there. Of course, the killer had to have known that.

"You could have called Jenna to tell her this," Cal pointed out.

Gwen shook her head. Her eyes showed stress. They were bloodshot and had smudgy dark circles beneath. "I think someone's listening in on my conversations. Someone's following me, too. I think it's because I'm getting close to unraveling all of this."

"Or maybe you're faking all this to cover your own guilt," Jenna countered.

Gwen didn't look offended. She merely nodded. "I could be, but I'm not." She gave a weary sigh. "I think there's a problem with the e-mails Paul wanted us all to receive."

"I'm listening," Cal said when she paused.

"I've been talking to Paul's attorney, and he told me that Paul wrote many e-mails and left instructions as to which to send out. For instance, if Jenna had had a baby, he was to send out set three. If any one of us, Jenna, Holden, Helena or Salazar, was dead by the time of the send-out date, then a different set was to be e-mailed."

"So?" Cal challenged. This wasn't news, either.

"So it wasn't the lawyer who determined which set was to go out. It was Holden."

"Holden?" he and Jenna said in unison. Whoa. Now, *that* was news.

"I asked him, and he confirmed it. But he said he had no idea what was in the other e-mails. He claims that they were encrypted when they went out and that in Paul's instructions to him, he asked Holden not to try to decode them, that he wanted each e-mail to be personal and private."

Well, that added a new twist, not that Cal needed this information to suspect Holden. Holden had a lot to gain from this situation, especially if he wanted to make sure he didn't have to share Paul's estate with his sister or any potential heirs.

But then, Gwen had motive, too. It could be that she just wanted a good story from all of this, but Paul had offered her a million dollars to find his killer. That was a lot of incentive to put a plan together. And there was another possibility: that Gwen hadn't just been involved in Paul's life but also his death.

Cal decided to go with an old-fashioned bluff.

"You didn't have any trouble getting Paul's lawyer to cooperate." He made a knowing sound. "Did you meet him when you were pretending to be Paul's maid? Are you the infamous Mary? And before you think about lying to me, you should probably know that I just read a very interesting intel report from an insider in Monte de Leon." That was a lie, of course, but Cal thought it would pay off.

Gwen's eyes widened, and she went a little pale. "Yes, I was Mary. I faked a résumé to get a job at Paul's estate, but he quickly figured out who I was."

The bluff had worked. Cal continued to push. "Is that when you killed him?"

"No." More color drained from her face, and she repeated that denial. "I didn't kill Paul."

"And why should I believe you?" Cal pressed.

"Because killing him wouldn't have helped me get a story. I wanted the insider's view to Paul's business. With him dead, my story was dead, too."

"Now you've resurrected it with a new angle. You don't care that you're putting Jenna and her daughter in danger?"

"I don't know what you mean." Gwen's voice wavered. "I haven't put them in danger."

"Haven't you?" Jenna asked, stepping closer so that she was practically in Gwen's face.

"Not intentionally." She seemed sincere. Of course, she was a reporter after a story, so Cal wasn't buying it.

Cal saw something over Gwen's shoulder, and he re-aimed his gun. But it was Jordan, who was quickly making his way back to the porch.

"Hell. It's like Grand Central Terminal around here," Jordan grumbled. "I sent the lab guy on his way, but someone else just drove up. He says his name is Mark Lynch. Hollywood. And he wants to see all three of you."

Gwen flattened her hand on her chest. "Me?"

"Especially you."

Chapter Eleven

Jenna didn't know which surprised her more—that Hollywood had shown up or that he wanted to see Gwen. It was definitely a development that she hadn't seen coming. It could be very dangerous.

Her first instinct was to tell Jordan to stop Hollywood from getting any closer to the house. Sophie would be waking from her nap at any minute, and even though Meggie had instructions not to leave the nursery until she checked with them, if they let Hollywood in the gate, he would be too close to her baby.

Gwen was already too close.

"We could take this meeting to the gatehouse," Jenna suggested. That way, they could ask Hollywood how he knew Gwen and why he wanted to see her. Or why he wanted to see Cal and her, for that matter. Even though he didn't know it, he was a suspect.

Cal glanced at her. She knew that look. He was trying

to figure out how to make this meeting happen so that she wasn't part of it.

"Hollywood asked to see me, too," Jenna reminded him.

"People don't always get what they want," Cal responded.

Before Jenna could challenge that, Gwen interrupted. "I don't want to see him." She managed to look indignant. Angry, even. "He's going to tell you that I'm behind the attempt to kill you. It's not true."

"Why would he tell us that?" Jenna demanded.

Silence. Gwen glanced over her shoulder as if to verify that Hollywood's car was indeed there.

"We'll go to the gatehouse," Cal insisted. "I'm interested in what Hollywood has to say about you. And himself." He turned to Jenna and took his backup weapon from an ankle holster. Cal handed it to her. "Stay close to me."

She nodded, taking the weapon as confidently as she could. Jenna didn't want Gwen to know that she didn't have much experience handling a gun.

Jenna also silently thanked Cal for not giving her a hassle about attending this impromptu meeting. That couldn't have been easy for him. His training made him want to keep her tucked away so she'd be safer. Part of Jenna wanted that, too. But more than her own safety, she wanted to get to the truth that would ultimately get her daughter out of danger.

Cal locked the front door before they stepped away from it. The chilly wind whipped at them as they went down the porch steps and across the front yard. Both

Cal and Jordan shot glances around the estate, both of them looking for any kind of threat. However, Jenna felt their biggest threat was the man waiting on the other side of the gate.

Hollywood was there with his hands clamped around the wrought-iron rods. He stepped back when Jordan entered the code to open the gate.

"Thanks for seeing me," Hollywood greeted Cal. He volleyed glances at all of them, except for Gwen. He tossed her a venomous glare.

Jordan stepped forward, motioning for Hollywood to lift his arms, and searched him. He extracted a gun from a shoulder holster hidden beneath Hollywood's leather jacket. Hollywood didn't protest being disarmed. He merely followed Cal's direction when Cal motioned for him to go inside the gatehouse.

The building was small. It obviously wasn't meant for meetings, but Cal, Gwen and Jenna followed Hollywood inside. Jordan waited just outside the door with his body angled so that he could see both them and the house. Good. Jenna didn't want anyone trying to sneak in.

Hollywood aimed his index finger at Gwen. "Anything she says about me is a lie."

"Funny, she said the same thing about you," Cal commented.

"Of course she did. She wants to cover her butt."

"And you don't?" Gwen challenged.

Jenna decided this was a good time to stand back and listen. These two intended to clear the air, and that could give them information about what the heck was going on.

"I slept with her last year in Monte de Leon," Hollywood confessed to Cal. "And when I told her it couldn't be anything more than a one-night stand, she didn't take it well. I figured she'd be out to get me. She's the one who's setting me up. She wants to make it look as if I've been feeding information to Salazar."

"Don't flatter yourself." Gwen took a step closer and got right in Hollywood's face. "I wasn't upset about the breakup. I was upset with myself that I let it happen in the first place."

Hollywood cursed. "You planned it all. You came on to me with the hopes I'd give you information about the ISA's investigation into Paul's illegal activities."

"I slept with you because I'd had too much to drink," Gwen tossed back.

Hollywood didn't have a comeback for that. He stood there, seething, his hands balled into fists and veins popping out on his forehead.

"So you slept with both Paul and Hollywood around the same time?" Jenna asked the woman.

Gwen nodded and had the decency to blush, especially since her affair with Paul had been a calculating way to get her story. That meant Hollywood might be telling the truth about Gwen's motives. But he still could have leaked information.

"How exactly could Gwen have set you up?" Cal asked, taking the words out of Jenna's mouth.

"I think she stole my access code and password while she was in my hotel room in Monte de Leon."

Jenna looked at Gwen, who didn't deny or confirm anything. But she did dodge Jenna's gaze.

"You reported that the code and password could have been compromised?" Cal asked.

"No. I didn't know they had been. Not until yesterday when I figured out that someone was tapping into classified information. I knew it wouldn't take long for Kowalski to think I was the one doing it."

"And you aren't?" Jenna asked point-blank.

"I'm not." There was no hesitation. No hint of guilt. Just frustration. But maybe Hollywood was true to his nickname—this could be just good acting.

"There's a lot going on," Hollywood continued. "Someone is pulling a lot of strings to manipulate this situation. Gwen wants a story, and she wants it to be big. That's why she's stirring the pot. That's why these crazy things are happening to all of us."

"Someone is out to get us," Cal clarified. "Someone tried to run me and Jenna off the road last night. And someone planted a tracking device on her car. You think Gwen is responsible for that?"

"Well, it wasn't me. I stayed back in Willow Ridge to look for that missing woman, Kinley Ford. Heck, I even called the FBI from town to let them know I'd learned the woman had been there. You can check cell tower records to confirm that."

Not really. Because with Hollywood's expertise, he could have figured out a way around that.

Hollywood swore under his breath and shook his head. "Gwen has the strongest motive for everything that's happening. She wants that story."

Gwen stepped forward, positioning herself directly in front of Hollywood. "Holden or Helena could be paying you big bucks for information. For that matter, the money could be coming directly from Paul's estate."

"I wouldn't take blood money," Hollywood insisted, ramming his finger against his chest. "But you would. So would Holden or Helena."

So this could all come down to money. That didn't shock Jenna, but it sickened her to know that her daughter could be in danger simply because someone wanted to get rich.

Cal glanced at Jordan to make sure the area was still safe. He waited until Jordan nodded before he continued the conversation with Hollywood. "Any reason you didn't tell me yesterday that you'd had sex with a person of interest in this investigation?"

The frustration in Hollywood's expression went up a significant notch. His chest pumped with his harsh breaths. "Before you judge me, I think you should remind yourself why you're here. You slept with Jenna while she was in your protective custody."

Jenna wanted to set the record straight for Cal's sake, but he caught her hand and gave it a gentle warning squeeze.

"I can't trust either of you," Cal said to Hollywood and Gwen. "I don't care what your motives are. I want you to back off and leave Jenna and Sophie alone."

"You should be telling the Carrs this," Gwen pointed out.

"Maybe you'll do that for me." Cal didn't continue until Gwen looked him in the eye. "You can also tell them that Jenna, Sophie and I are leaving the estate within the hour. We're already packed and ready to go."

Jenna went still. Had Cal really planned that, or was this a ruse to get everyone off their trail?

"You think that's a wise move?" Hollywood asked.

"I think it's a *safe* move. And this time, I'll check and make sure there aren't any tracking devices on the vehicle we use."

Gwen turned and faced Jenna. Her expression wasn't as tense as Hollywood's, but emotion tightened the muscles in her jaw. "No matter where you go, the Carrs will find you."

"And you, too?"

Gwen shrugged and folded her arms over her chest. "I plan to write a story about Paul's murder."

"Then this meeting is over," Cal insisted. He put his hand on Hollywood's shoulder to get him moving out the door.

"I'm innocent," Hollywood declared. "But I don't expect you to trust me. Just hear this, I'll do whatever's necessary to clear my name."

"If you do that, I'll be overjoyed. But for right now, I don't want you anywhere near Jenna or Sophie. Got that?" It was an order, not a request.

Hollywood nodded and walked out. So did Gwen. Both went to their respective vehicles, but Jordan didn't return Hollywood's gun until the man had started his engine and was ready to leave. Jenna and Cal stood inside the gatehouse and watched the duo drive away.

"Are we really leaving the estate?" Jenna asked.

"No," he whispered. "But I want to make it look as if we are. Then I can continue to beef up security here, and we can stay put until all of this is resolved."

Cal's plan seemed like their best option. She didn't like the idea of traveling anywhere while her daughter was a target.

They walked out of the gatehouse and started for the estate. After the battle they'd just had with their visitors, Jenna suddenly had a strong need to check on Sophie.

"You think Hollywood and Gwen will believe we're leaving?" She checked over her shoulder to make sure they were gone. Jordan was keeping watch to make sure they didn't double back.

"Jordan's employee will drive out of here in a couple of minutes," Cal explained. He caught her arm and picked up the pace to get them to the porch. "He'll be using a vehicle with heavily tinted windows. As an extra precaution we won't use any of the house phones. They might be tapped, and I don't want anyone to know we're here. We can use the secure cell phone that Director Kowalski gave to me."

Jenna hoped that would be enough. And that Kowalski hadn't given Cal compromised equipment. After all, someone had managed to put those tracking devices on their cars.

"Get down!" she heard Jordan yell.

Jenna started to look back at him to see what had caused him to shout that, but Cal didn't give her a chance. He hooked his arm around her waist and dragged her between the flagstone porch steps and some shrubs.

Jordan dove into the gatehouse. His eyes were darting all around, looking for something.

But what?

Jenna didn't have to wait long for an answer.

"Salazar's on the grounds," Jordan shouted.

Chapter Twelve

If Salazar was on the grounds, he had come there for one reason: to get Sophie. If the assassin had to take out Jenna and Cal, that wouldn't matter. A man like Salazar wouldn't let anything get in the way of trying to accomplish his mission.

Later, after Cal had gotten Jenna out of this mess, he'd want to know just how Salazar had managed to get through what was supposed to be the secured perimeter of the estate. But for now, he had to focus on keeping Jenna and Sophie safe.

He lifted his head a little and assessed their situation. Jordan was in the doorway of the gatehouse, but he hadn't pinpointed Salazar's position. But someone had. Probably Jordan's assistant, Cody Guillory. The man had spotted Salazar and relayed that info through the communicator Jordan was wearing. Since Cal didn't know the exact location of Jordan's assistant, that meant Salazar could be anywhere.

Cal glanced at the front door. It was a good twenty feet away. It wasn't that far, but they'd literally be out in the open if he tried to get Jenna inside. Besides, it was locked and it would take a second or two to open it. That'd be time they were in Salazar's kill zone. Not a good option. At least if they stayed put, the stone steps would give them some protection.

Unless Salazar planned to launch explosives at them.

"Call Meggie," Cal said, handing Jenna his cell phone. "Make sure she's okay. Then tell her to set the alarm and move Sophie to the gun room."

He didn't risk looking at Jenna, though he knew that particular instruction would be a brutal reminder of the danger they were in. Jenna already knew, of course, but by now she probably had nightmarish images of Salazar breaking into the house.

With her voice trembling and her hands shaking, Jenna made the call. Cal shut out what she was saying and focused on their surroundings. He tried to anticipate how and where Salazar would launch an attack. There were more than a dozen possibilities. Salazar might even try to take out Jordan first.

A shot cracked through the air and landed in one of the porch pillars.

Cal automatically shoved Jenna farther down just in time. The next shot landed even lower. It sliced through the flagstone step just above their heads. Salazar had gone right for them. Cal prayed that Meggie had managed to set that alarm and get Sophie into the gun room.

The third shot took a path identical to the second. So did the fourth. Each bullet chipped away at the flagstone and sent jagged chunks of the rock flying right at them.

Hell. Maybe staying put hadn't been such a good idea after all. Now they were trapped in a storm of shrapnel.

Cal pushed aside the feeling that he'd just made a fatal mistake and concentrated on the direction of the shots. Salazar was using a long-range assault rifle from somewhere out in the formal garden amid the manicured shrubs and white marble statues. There were at least a hundred places to hide, and nearly every one of them would be out of range for Cal's handgun.

Another shot sent a slice of the flagstone ripping across Cal's shirtsleeve. Since the rock could do almost as much damage as a bullet, he crawled over Jenna, sheltering her as much as he could. She was shaking, but she also had a firm grip on the gun he'd given her earlier. Yes, she was scared, but she was also ready to fight back if she got the chance. This wasn't the same woman he'd rescued in Monte de Leon. But then, the stakes were higher for her now.

She had Sophie to protect.

His only hope was that Salazar would move closer so that Cal would have a better shot or Jordan could get to him. One of them had to stop the man before he escalated the attack.

There was another spray of bullets, and even though Cal sheltered his eyes from the flying debris, he figured Salazar had succeeded in tearing away more layers of their meager protection. Cal couldn't wait to see if Salazar was going to move. He had to do something to slow the man down.

Cal levered himself up just slightly and zoomed in on a row of hedges that stretched between two marble statues. He fired a shot in that direction.

A shot came right back at Cal, causing him to dip even lower. From the gatehouse, Jordan fired a round. He was as far out of range as Cal. But between the two of them, they might manage to throw Salazar off his own deadly aimed shots. Not likely, though. Plus, they couldn't just randomly keep firing or they'd run out of ammunition.

But there was a trump card in all of this. Jordan's assistant. Maybe Cody Guillory was working his way toward Salazar so he could take him out.

The shots continued, the sound blasting through the chilly air and tainting it with the smells of gunpowder, sulfur and smoke. The constant stream of bullets caused his ears to ring. But the ringing wasn't so loud that he didn't hear a sound that sent his stomach to his knees.

The alarm. Someone had tripped the security system.

Which meant someone had broken in. Salazar or his henchman. Salazar normally worked alone, but this time he obviously hadn't come solo. There must be two of them. One firing at them while the other broke inside. Both trained to the hilt to make sure this mission was a success.

Jenna tried to get up. Cal shoved her right back down. And not a moment too soon. A barrage of bullets came their way. Each of the shots sprayed them with bits of rock and caused their adrenaline levels to spike. As long as those shots continued, it'd be suicide to try to get to the door and into the house.

But that was exactly what Cal had to do.

Meggie and Sophie were probably locked in the gun

room, but that didn't mean Salazar wouldn't try to get to them. Hell, he might even succeed. And then he could kidnap Sophie and sneak her out, all while they were trapped out front dodging bullets.

"I'm going in," Cal told her. "Stay put."

She was shaking her head before he even finished. "No. I need to get to Sophie."

"I'll get to her. You need to stay here."

It was a risk. A huge one. Salazar could have planned it this way. Divide and conquer. Still, what was left of the steps was better protection than dragging Jenna onto the porch. Cal took a deep breath and got ready to scramble up the steps.

But just like that, the shots stopped.

And that terrified him.

Had the shooter left his position so he, too, could get into the house?

"Cover me," Cal shouted to Jordan, knowing that the man couldn't do a lot in that department. Still, fired shots might cause a distraction in case the gunman was still out there and ready to strike.

Cal didn't bother with the house keys. That would take too long. He'd have to bash in the door and hope that it gave way with only one well-positioned kick.

Jordan started firing shots. Thick blasts that he aimed at the hedges and other parts of the formal garden.

"I'm going with you," Jenna insisted.

Cal wanted to throttle her. Or at least yell for her to stay put. But he couldn't take the time to do either. Jordan's firepower wouldn't last. Each shot meant he was using up precious resources.

"Now," Cal ordered since it seemed as if he would have a partner for this ordeal.

He climbed over the steps, making sure that Jenna stayed to his side so that she wouldn't be in the direct line of fire from anyone who might still be in those hedges. Cal reached the door and gave it a fierce kick. It flew open, thank God. That was a start. But it occurred to Cal that he could be taking Jenna out of the frying pan and directly into the fire.

Cal shoved her against the foyer wall and placed himself in front of her. He disarmed the security system to stop the alarm. Then he paused, listening. He tried to pick through the sounds of Jordan's shots and the house. And he heard something he didn't want to hear.

Footsteps.

Someone was running through the house. Hopefully Meggie was in the gun room. The obvious answer was Salazar.

"I have to get to Sophie," Jenna said on a rise of breath. She broke away from him and started to run right toward those footsteps.

JENNA BARELY MADE IT a step before Cal latched on to her and dragged her behind him.

Her first instinct was to fight him off. To run. So she could get to her baby to make sure she was safe. But Cal held on tight, refusing to let her go.

"Shhh," he warned, turning his head in the direction of those menacing footsteps.

Salazar had managed to break through security, and he was probably inside, going after Sophie.

Cal started moving quietly, but quickly. He kept her behind him as he made his way down the east corridor toward the gun room.

"Keep watch behind us," he whispered.

Jenna automatically gripped her gun tighter, and slid her index finger in front of the trigger. It was ironic that just an hour earlier she'd gotten her first shooting lesson, and now she might have to use the skills that Cal had taught her. She hoped she remembered everything because this wouldn't be a target with the outline of a man. It would be a professional assassin.

That was just the reminder she needed. It didn't matter if she had no experience with a firearm. She'd do whatever was necessary to protect Sophie.

Cal's footsteps hardly made a sound on the hardwood floors of the corridor. Jenna tried to keep her steps light as well, but she knew she was breathing too hard. And her heartbeat was pounding so loudly that she was worried someone might be able to hear it. Though with Cal bashing down the door, the element of surprise was gone. Still, she didn't want Salazar to be able to pinpoint their exact location.

Just in case, she lifted her gun so that she'd be ready to fire.

She and Cal moved together, but it seemed to take an eternity to reach the L-shaped turn in the corridor. Cal stopped then and peered around the corner.

"All clear," he mouthed.

No one was anywhere near the door to the gun room. Of course, that didn't mean that someone hadn't already gotten inside.

Her heart rate spiked, and she held her breath as they approached the room. The door was shut, and while keeping watch all around them, Cal reached down and tested the knob.

"It's locked," he whispered.

She released the breath she'd been holding, only to realize that Salazar could still have gotten inside and simply relocked the door.

Cal pressed the intercom positioned on the wall next to the door. "Meggie, is everything okay?" he whispered.

"Yes," the woman immediately answered.

Relief caused Jenna's knees to become weak. She had to press her left hand against the wall to steady herself. "Sophie's okay?"

"She's fine. What's going on?"

But there was no time to answer.

Movement at one end of the hall made Cal pivot in that direction. "Get down," he ordered her.

Jenna ducked and glanced in that direction. She saw the dark sleeve of what appeared to be a man's coat. Salazar.

Cal fired, the shot blistering through the corridor.

She didn't look to see what the outcome of that shot was because she saw something at the other end of the hall.

With her heart in her throat, she took aim. Waited. Prayed. She didn't have to wait long. A man peered around the corner. He had a gun and pointed it right at her.

Jenna didn't even allow herself time to think. This man wasn't getting anywhere near her daughter.

She squeezed the trigger and fired.

Chapter Thirteen

Cal forced Jenna to sit on the leather sofa of the family room.

He didn't have to exert much force. He just gently guided her off her feet. She wasn't trembling. Wasn't crying. But her blank stare and silence let him know that she was probably in shock.

Once the director was finished with the initial investigation and reports, Cal needed to talk her into getting some medical care. She'd already refused several times, but he'd keep trying.

Two men were dead.

Cal was responsible for one of those deaths. He'd taken out Salazar with two shots to the head. Jenna had neutralized Salazar's henchman. Her single shot had entered the man's chest. Death hadn't been immediate—he'd died while being transported to the hospital. Unfortunately, the man hadn't made any deathbed confessions.

Cal got up, went to a bar that was partly concealed behind a stained-glass cabinet door, and poured Jenna a shot of whiskey. "Drink this," he said, returning to the sofa to sit next to her.

As if operating on autopilot, she tasted it and grimaced, her eyes watering.

"Take another sip," he insisted.

She did and then finished off the shot. She set the glass on the coffee table and folded her hands in her lap. "Does killing someone ever get easier?" she asked.

"No."

He hated that this was a lesson she'd had to learn. What she'd done was necessary. But it would stay with her forever.

She glanced around the room as if seeing the activity for the first time. Director Kowalski was there near the doorway, talking to two FBI agents and a local sheriff. They were all lawmen with jurisdiction, but Kowalski was unofficially leading the show. This had international implications, and there were people who would want to keep that under wraps.

Jenna's eyes met his. The blankness was fading. She was slowly coming to terms with what had happened, but once the full impact hit her, she'd fall apart.

But Cal would be right there to catch her.

"Sophie," she said, sounding alarmed. She started to get up. "I need to check on her again."

Cal caught her. "I just checked on her a few minutes ago. Sophie's fine. Jordan's still with her and Meggie in the nursery. Even though there's no way she'd remember any of this, I didn't want her to be out here right now."

His attention drifted in the direction of the corridor where federal agents were cleaning up the crime scene.

Cal didn't want Sophie anywhere around that.

Jenna nodded. "Thank you."

He saw it then. Jenna's bottom lip trembled. He slid his arm around her and hoped this preliminary investigation would end soon so her meltdown wouldn't happen in front of the others.

"You did a good thing in that corridor," Cal reminded her. "You did what you needed to do."

The corner of her mouth lifted, but there was no humor in her smile. "You gave me a good shooting lesson."

Yeah. But he'd given her that lesson with the hopes that she'd never have to use a gun.

Kowalski stepped away from the others and walked toward them. He stopped, studied Jenna and looked at Cal. "Is she okay?"

"Yes," Jenna answered at the exact moment that Cal answered, "No."

The director just nodded. "I don't want any of this in a local report," he instructed Cal. "The sheriff has agreed to back off. No questions. He'll let us do our jobs, and the FBI will file the official paperwork after I've read through and approved it."

"I'll need to give a statement," Jenna concluded. Emotion was making her voice tremble.

"It can wait," Kowalski assured her. "But I don't want you talking to anyone about this, understand?"

"Yes." This would be sanitized and classified. No one outside this estate would learn that an international assassin had entered the country to go after a Texas heiress. The hush-up would protect Jenna and Sophie from the press, but it wouldn't help Jenna deal with the aftermath.

"Any idea how Salazar got onto the grounds?" Cal wanted to know.

"It appears he was here before your friend Jordan Taylor even put his security measures into place. There's evidence that Salazar was waiting in one of the storage buildings on the property."

Smart move. That meant Salazar had used the tracking device on Jenna's car to follow them to the estate, and he'd hidden out for a full day, waiting for the right time to strike. But why hadn't Salazar attacked earlier, when he and Jenna were outside meeting with the others? The only answer that Cal could come up with was that he had wanted as few witnesses as possible when he went after Sophie.

"Salazar and his accomplice broke in through French doors in one of the guest suites," Kowalski continued. "We believe the plan was to locate the child, kill anyone they encountered and then escape."

Jenna pressed her fingertips to her mouth, but Cal could still hear the soft sob. He tightened his grip on her, and it didn't go unnoticed. Kowalski flexed his eyebrows in a disapproving gesture.

Cal ignored him. "What about all the rest? Any idea who hired Salazar or if Hollywood had any part in this?"

The director shook his head. "There's no evidence to indicate Agent Lynch is guilty of anything. He might have been set up."

That's what Hollywood was claiming, and it might

be true. Still, Cal wasn't about to declare anyone's in-nocence just yet. "Who was paying Salazar?"

"The money was coming from Paul's estate, but his attorney will almost certainly say that he was unaware the payment was going to a hired killer."

"He might not have known," Cal mumbled.

Kowalski shrugged. "The ISA will deal with the attorney. But the good news is that Ms. Laniere and her child seem to be out of danger."

Jenna looked at the director. Then at Cal. He saw new concern in her eyes.

"I'm not leaving," Cal assured her.

That got him another flexed-eyebrow reaction from the director. "Tie things up around here," Kowalski ordered, "I want you back at headquarters tomorrow."

Cal got to his feet. "I'd like to take some personal time off."

"I can't approve that. Tomorrow, the promotion list should be arriving in my office. You'll know then if you've gotten the deputy director job." Kowalski's an-nouncement seemed a little like a threat.

Choose between Jenna and the job.

"I'm sorry," Jenna whispered. She stood, too, and this time moved Cal's hand away when he tried to catch her. "I'm going to check on Sophie."

No. She was going to fall apart.

"I'll be at headquarters tomorrow," Cal assured the director. "But I'm still requesting a personal leave of absence." Without waiting to see if Kowalski had any-thing else to mandate, Cal went after Jenna.

She was moving pretty fast down the corridor, but he

easily caught up with her. She didn't say anything. Didn't have to. He figured she was already trying to figure out how she was going to cope without him there.

Cal was trying to figure out the same thing.

Jordan stood in the doorway of the nursery. His gun wasn't drawn, but it was tucked away in a shoulder holster. "Everything okay?" he wanted to know.

Jenna maneuvered past him and went straight to her daughter. Sophie was awake and making cooing sounds as Meggie played peekaboo with her. Jenna scooped up the little girl in her arms and held on.

"The director and all the law enforcement guys will be leaving within an hour or two," Cal informed Jordan. He didn't go closer to Jenna. He stood back and watched as she held Sophie. "The threat might be over, but I'd like you to stay around for a while."

Jordan followed Cal's gaze to Jenna. "Is this job official?"

"No. Personal."

Jordan's attention snapped back to Cal. "You? Personal?"

"It happens."

Jordan didn't look as if he believed that. He shrugged. "I can give you two days. After that, it'll just be Cody. But he's good. I trained him myself."

Cal nodded his thanks. Hopefully, two days would be enough to tie up those loose ends the director had mentioned. Now if Cal could just figure out how to do that.

"Is she willing to take a sedative?" Jordan asked, tipping his head to Jenna.

Cal didn't have to guess why Jordan had asked that.

He could see Jenna's hand shaking. "Probably not." Even though it would make the next few hours easier.

"My advice?" Jordan said. "Liberal shots of good scotch, a hot bath and some sleep."

All good ideas. Cal wondered if Jenna would cooperate with any of them. But when she began to shake even harder, she must have understood that merely holding her baby wasn't going to make this all go away.

Cal went to her and took Sophie. The little girl looked at him as if she didn't know if she should cry or smile. She settled for a big, toothless grin, which Cal realized made him feel a whole lot better. Maybe he'd been wrong about the effects of holding her. He kissed her cheek, got another smile and then handed her to Meggie.

"See to Jenna," Meggie whispered, obviously concerned about her employer.

Cal was concerned, too. He looped his arm around Jenna's waist and led her out of the nursery. She didn't protest, and walked side by side with him to her suite.

"It's stupid to feel like this," Jenna mumbled. "That man would have killed us if I hadn't shot him."

Her words were true. But he doubted the truth would make it easier for her to accept.

"You're so calm," she pointed out, stepping inside the room. It was the first time he'd been in her suite. Like the rest of the house, it was big and decorated in soothing shades of cream and pale blue. He wasn't counting on those colors to soothe her, though. It'd take more than interior decorating to do that.

Cal shut the door. "I'm not calm," he assured her.

"You look calm." Her voice broke on the last word. Cal waited for tears, but she didn't cry. Instead, she moved closer to him. "My baby's safe," she muttered. "We're safe. Salazar is dead. And you'll be leaving soon to go back to headquarters."

He shook his head, not knowing what to say. Yes, he probably would leave for that morning meeting with Kowalski. He opened his mouth to answer, to try to reassure her that he'd be back. But Jenna pressed her hand over his lips.

"Don't make promises you can't keep," she said. She tilted her head to the side and stared at him. "I'm going to do something really stupid. Something we'll regret."

Jenna slid her hand away, and her mouth came to his, kissing him.

The shock of that kiss roared through Cal for just a split second. Then the shock was replaced with the jolt of something stronger—pleasure. His body automatically went from comfort and protect mode to something primal. Something that had him taking hold of her and dragging her to him.

He made that kiss his own, claiming her mouth. Taking her. Demanding all that she had to give.

His hands were on her. Her hands, on him. Their embrace was hungry, frenzied. Both of them wanted more and were taking it.

And then he got another jolt...of reality.

Sex wasn't a good idea right now. Not with Jenna on the verge of a meltdown.

He forced himself to stop.

With her breath gusting, Jenna looked at him. "No,"

she said. She came at him again. There was another fast and furious kiss. It was hard, brutal and in some ways punishing. It was also what she needed.

Cal felt the weariness drain from her. Or maybe she was merely channeling all her emotions into this dangerous energy. She shoved him against the door, fusing her mouth to his, her hands going after his shirt.

Part of him wanted to get naked and take her right there. But only one of them could get crazy at the same time. Since Jenna had latched on to that role, Cal knew he had to be the voice of reason.

But then her breasts ground against his chest. And her sex pressed against his.

Oh, yeah.

That put a dent in any rational thought.

Still, somehow, he managed to catch her arms and hold her at bay so he could voice a little of the reasoning he was desperately trying to hang on to.

"You're not ready for this," he insisted.

"I'm ready." There wasn't any doubt in her tone. Her eyes. Her body.

She shook off his grip, took his hand and slid it down into the waist of her loose jeans. Into her panties. She was wet and hot.

Oh, mercy.

Then she ran her own palm over the very noticeable bulge in his pants. "You're ready."

"No condom," he ground out.

Jenna's eyes widened, and she darted away from him. She ran to a dresser on the other side of the room, and frantically, began searching through the drawers. Several moments later, she produced a foil-wrapped condom.

Cal didn't give her even a second to celebrate. He locked the door and hurried to her. He grabbed the condom, and in the same motion, he grabbed her. He kissed her and backed her against the dresser.

The kiss continued as they fought with each other's clothes. He got off her top, and while he wanted to sample her breasts—man, she was beautiful—his body was urging him in a different direction.

With her butt balancing her against the edge of the dresser, he stripped off her jeans. And her white lace panties. By then, she was all over him. Her mouth, hungry on his neck. Her hands fighting with his zipper. She won that fight, and took him into her hands.

Cal didn't breathe for a couple of seconds. He didn't care if he ever breathed again. He just wanted one thing.

Jenna.

He opened the condom and put it on. "This is your last chance to say no."

She looked at him as if he were crazy. Maybe he was. Maybe they both were. Jenna hoisted herself up on the edge of the dresser.

"I'm saying yes," she assured him.

To prove it, she hooked her legs around him, thrust him forward and he slid hot and deep into her.

He stilled a moment. To give her time to adjust to the primal invasion of her tight body. He watched her face, looking for any sign that she might be in pain.

Angling her body back, she slid forward, giving him a delicious view of her breasts and their joined bodies.

She wasn't the pampered heiress now. She was his lover. Funny, he hadn't thought she would be this bold, but he appreciated it on many, many levels.

"Don't treat me like glass," she whispered.

"No intention of that," he promised.

He caught her hair and pulled her head back slightly to expose her neck. He kissed there and drove into her.

Hard.

Fast.

Deep.

Her reaction was priceless. Something he'd remember for the rest of his life. She grabbed him by his hair and jerked his head forward, forcing eye contact. And with her hand fisted in his hair, she moved, meeting him thrust for thrust.

Their mouths were so close he could almost taste her, but she was just out of reach. Instead, her breath caressed his mouth while her legs tightened around him.

Their frantic rhythm created the friction that fueled her need. It became unbearable. She closed around him, her body shuddering. The unbearable need went to a whole different level.

She sighed his name. "Cal." Jenna repeated it like some ancient plea for him to join her in that whirl of primitive pleasure.

Cal leaned in, pushing into her one last time. He kissed her and surrendered.

Even with his pulse crashing in his ears and head, he heard the one word that came from his mouth.

Jenna.

SHE WAS HALF-NAKED on a dresser. Out of breath, sweaty and exhausted. And coming down from one of the worst days of her life. Yet it'd been a long time since Jenna had felt this good. She bit back a laugh. Cal would think she was losing her mind.

And maybe she was.

This shouldn't have happened. Being with Cal like this only made her feel closer to him. It only made her want him more. But that wasn't in their future. She was well on her way to a broken heart.

"Hell," Cal mumbled. "We had sex on the dresser."

He blinked as if trying to focus and huffed out short jolts of breath. He was sweaty, too. And hot. Just looking at him made her want him all over again.

"You don't think I'm the sex-on-the-dresser type?" she asked, trying to keep things light for her own sanity. She couldn't lose it. Not now. Because soon, very soon, Cal would begin to regret this, and she didn't want her fragile mental state playing into his guilt.

With his breath still gusting, he leaned in and brushed a kiss on her mouth. It went straight through her, warm and liquid. "I thought you'd prefer sex on silk sheets," he mumbled.

Still reeling a little from that kiss, she ran her tongue over her bottom lip and tasted him there. "No silk sheets required."

Just you. Thankfully she kept that thought to herself.

He withdrew from her, gently. Unlike the firestorm that'd happened only moments earlier. Cal helped her to her feet, made sure she was steady and then he went into the adjacent bathroom.

Jenna took a moment to compose herself and remembered there were a lot of people still in her house. FBI, Kowalski, the sheriff. She started to have some doubts of her own. She should be focusing on the shootings.

But the shootings could wait. Right now she needed to put on a good front for Cal, spend some time with her daughter and try to figure out where to go from here.

Her old instincts urged her to run. To try to escape emotions she didn't want to face. But running would only be a temporary solution. She looked up and could almost hear her father saying that to her. Funny that it would sink in now when her life was at its messiest.

She needed to stay put, and concentrate on getting Helena, Holden and Gwen out of her life. While she was at it, she also needed to hold her daughter. Oh, and she had to figure out how to nurse her soon-to-be-broken heart.

With her list complete, she started to get dressed. She was still stepping into her jeans when Cal returned.

He looked at her with those scorching blue eyes and had her going all hot again. Jenna pushed aside her desire, reminding her body that it'd just gotten lucky. That wasn't going to happen again any time soon.

"You okay?" he asked.

Jenna nodded and was surprised to realize that it was true. She wasn't a basket case. She wasn't on the verge of sobbing. She felt strong because she had been able to help protect her baby.

He shoved his hands into his pockets. "When things settle down, you might want to see a therapist. There are a lot of emotions that might come up later."

She nodded again and put her own hands in her pockets. "Now that Salazar is dead, it's time to clear up Sophie's paternity with your director."

He looked down at the floor. "Best not to do that. We don't know who hired Salazar, and until we do, nothing is clear."

Confused, Jenna shook her head. "But certainly it doesn't matter if everyone knows that Sophie is Paul's biological child."

"It might matter." He paused and met her gaze. "Gwen was having an affair with Paul. Helena, too. Either could be jealous and want to get back at you. Either could have sent Salazar to take Sophie because they feel they should be the one who's raising her."

Oh, God. She hadn't even considered that, and she couldn't dismiss it. Both Helena and Gwen hadn't been on the up-and-up about much of anything.

"Holden could be a problem, too," Cal continued. "Paul might have told him to take any child that you and he might have produced. The child would be Paul's heir, and Holden would like nothing more than to control the heir to a vast estate."

Her chest tightened. It felt as if someone had clamped a fist around her heart. "So Sophie could still be in danger?"

"It's possible." He took his hands from his pocket and brought out his phone.

Alarmed, she crossed the room to him. "What are you going to do?"

"Something I should have done already." He scrolled through the numbers stored in his phone, located one and hit the call button. "Director Kowalski," he said a moment later. "Are you still at the estate? I need to speak to you."

Jenna shook her head. "No," she mouthed.

But Cal didn't listen to her. He stepped away, turning his back to her. "I'll meet you in the living room in a few minutes." He hung up and walked out the door.

She caught his arm. "What are you going to say to him?"

"I'll tell him that I lied. That Sophie is my daughter. I want to start the paperwork to have Sophie legally declared my child. I'll do that when I get to headquarters in the morning."

Oh, mercy. He was talking about legally becoming a father. Cal would make an amazing dad. She could tell that from the way he handled her daughter. But this arrangement would cost him that promotion.

"You don't have to do this," Jenna insisted. "We'll find another way to make sure she's safe."

"There is no other way." He caught her shoulders and looked her straight in the eye. "This is your chance at having a normal life. This way you won't always be looking over your shoulder."

"But what about you? What about your career?"

A muscle flickered in his jaw, and she saw anger flare in his eyes. "Do you really think I'm the kind of man who would endanger a child for the sake of a promotion?" He sounded disappointed. "I'm going to do this, Jenna, with or without your approval."

And with that, he walked out.

Chapter Fourteen

Cal hadn't expected Kowalski's ultimatum.

But he should have. He should have known the director wasn't going to let him have a happy ending.

He stood at the door and watched Kowalski, the FBI agents and the sheriff drive away. Now that the sun had set, a chilly fog had moved in, and the cars' brakes lights flashed in the darkness like eerie warnings. Jordan was there to shut the gate behind them. He gave Cal a thumbs-up before heading in the direction of the garden. He was probably going to give his assistant some further instructions about security.

The security measures wouldn't be suspended simply because everyone else had left the estate. Jordan, or one of his employees, would stay on as long as necessary. Of course, Cal still had to get out the word, or rather the lie, that Sophie was his child. Once that was done, he would deal with the ultimatum Kowalski had delivered just minutes before he left.

Cal closed the front door, locked it and reset the security system before he went in search of Jenna. He dreaded this meeting with her almost as much as he'd dreaded the one he'd just had with Kowalski. He felt both numb and drained.

He'd killed a man today. It was never easy even when necessary as this one had been. But his difficulty dealing with the death was minor compared to Jenna's. She'd killed a man, too. Her first. In fact, the first time she'd ever fired a gun at another human being.

This would stay with her forever.

Maybe that's why sex had followed. That was a surefire way to burn off some of her high-anxiety adrenaline. Cal shook his head.

It had felt real. And that was a big problem.

He'd compounded it by arguing with Kowalski. The conversation had been necessary, and Cal didn't regret it. But that wouldn't make his chat with Jenna any easier. She needed to know what the director had ordered him to do. And then he somehow had to convince her, and himself, that he could follow through and do what had to be done.

Cal found her in the kitchen. Meggie was at the stove adding some seasoning to a great-smelling pot roast. Jenna was seated at the table feeding Sophie a bottle. Jenna looked as tired and troubled as he felt.

Unlike Sophie.

When the little girl spotted him, she turned her head so that the bottle came out of her mouth. And she smiled at him.

He smiled right back.

Weariness drained right out of him. He wasn't sure how someone so small could create dozens of little daily miracles.

Sophie squirmed, pushing the bottle away, and made some cooing sounds.

"I interrupted her dinner," he commented. Cal sat in the chair next to them.

"She was just about finished, anyway." Jenna's tone was tentative, and she studied him, searching his eyes for any indication of how the conversation with Kowalski had gone.

Sophie reached for him, and Cal took her into his arms. He got yet another smile. It filled him with warmth and it broke his heart.

What the devil was he going to do?

How could he give up this child that'd already grabbed hold of him?

"Something's wrong," Jenna said. She touched his arm gently, drawing his attention back to her.

"Uh, I need to check on something," Meggie suddenly announced. She adjusted the temperature on the pot roast and scooted out of the kitchen. She was a perceptive woman.

"Well?" Jenna prompted.

Best to start from the beginning. "Kowalski didn't buy my story about being Sophie's father. The ISA has retrieved one of Sophie's pacifiers from your apartment in Willow Ridge and compared the DNA to mine. Kowalski knows I'm not a match. It's just a matter of time before he learns that Paul is."

"I see." She repeated it and drew back her hand, letting it settle into her lap. "Well, that's good for you. He doesn't still think you slept with me, does he?"

"No." Cal brushed a kiss on Sophie's cheek. "And Kowalski will keep the DNA test a secret."

He hoped. Kowalski had promised that, anyway.

"But?" Jenna questioned.

"I told him I still wanted to do the paperwork to have Sophie declared my child. I want the DNA test doctored. I want anyone associated with Paul to believe she's mine so they'll back off."

Jenna fastened her attention on him. "There's more, isn't there?"

Cal cleared his throat. "In the morning you'll go into temporary protective custody. Kowalski will leak the fake DNA results through official and unofficial channels, and you and Sophie will stay in protective custody until everyone is sure the danger has passed. He thinks it shouldn't be more than a month or two before the ISA finds out who's responsible for this mess and gets that person off the streets."

"The ISA?" she repeated after a long pause. "But you said your organization doesn't normally handle domestic situations."

"Sometimes they make exceptions."

"I see." Jenna paused again, studying him. Worry lines bunched up her forehead. "And what about you? How does all of this affect you?"

Cal took a deep breath. "Kowalski will tell the chief director the truth, that this is all part of a plan to guarantee your safety." Another deep breath. "In exchange for his guarantee of your safety, Kowalski wants me to extract myself from the situation."

Her eyes widened. "Extract?" she questioned. "What does that mean exactly?"

He'd rehearsed this part. "Kowalski thinks I've lost my objectivity with you and Sophie. He thinks I'll be a danger to both of you and myself if I stay." Cal choked back a groan. "It's standard procedure to extract an agent when there's even a hint of any conflict of interest."

Though nothing about this felt standard. Of course, Cal couldn't deny that he'd stepped way over a lot of lines when it came to Jenna.

Sophie batted him on the nose and put her mouth on his cheek as if giving him a kiss.

Cal took yet more deep breaths. "By doctoring the records and the DNA, Kowalski will be protecting you. But he wants me to swear that I won't see you or Sophie until there's no longer a threat to either of you."

Jenna went still. "But the threat might always be there."

Cal nodded and watched the pain of that creep into her eyes.

She quickly looked away. "Okay. This is good. It means you'll probably get your promotion. Sophie will be safe. And I'll get on with my life." Jenna stood, walked across the room and looked out the window. "So when do you leave?"

"Kowalski wanted me to leave immediately, but I told him I'd go in the morning when the ISA agents arrive."

She stood there, silent, with her back to him.

It was because of the sudden silence in the room that Cal had no trouble hearing a loud crash that came from outside the house.

He got to his feet, and while balancing Sophie, he

took out his phone to call Jordan. But his phone rang first. Jordan's name and number appeared on the caller ID screen.

"Cal, we've got·a problem," Jordan informed him. "Someone just broke though the front gate."

Before Cal could question him, there was another sound. One he definitely didn't want to hear.

Someone fired a shot.

JORDAN'S VOICE WAS LOUD enough that Jenna heard what he said. If she hadn't heard the crash, she might have wondered what the heck he was talking about. But there was no mistaking the noise of something tearing through the metal gates.

And then it sounded as if someone had fired a gun. It was too much to hope that the noise was from a car backfiring.

While Cal continued to talk with Jordan, Jenna reached for Sophie, and Cal reached for his gun.

"Try to contain the situation as planned," Cal instructed Jordan. "I'll take care of things here."

He shoved his phone back into his pocket and turned to her to give her instructions. But Meggie interrupted them when she came running back into the kitchen.

The woman was as pale as a ghost. "I saw out the window," she said, her voice filled with fear. "A Hummer rammed through the gate. Some guys wearing ski masks got out, and one of them shot the man that came here with Jordan Taylor."

Jenna's gaze went to Cal's, and with one look he confirmed that was true. "How many men got out of the Hummer?" Cal asked Meggie. He sounded calm, but he gripped Jenna's arm and got them moving out of the kitchen.

"Four, I think," Meggie answered. "Maybe more. All of them had guns."

Four armed men. Jenna knew what they were after: Sophie. Salazar had failed, but someone else had been sent to do the job.

There was another shot. Then another. Thick blasts that sounded like those that had come from Salazar. Someone was shooting a rifle at Jordan. He was out there and under attack. It wouldn't be long, maybe seconds, before the gunman got past Jordan and into the house.

Cal headed for the gun room. There was no escape route there, and Jenna knew what he planned to do. Cal wanted Meggie, Sophie and her to be shut away behind bulletproof walls while he tried to protect them. But it was four against two. Not good odds especially when her daughter's safety was at stake.

"I'm going to help you," Jenna insisted. She handed Sophie to Meggie and motioned for the woman to go deep into the gun room. Jenna grabbed two of the automatic weapons from the case.

"I need to make sure you're safe," Cal countered. Though he was busy grabbing weapons and ammunition, he managed to toss her a firm scowl. "You're staying here."

Outside, there was a flurry of gunfire.

Jenna shook her head. "You need backup." She wasn't going to hide while Cal risked his life. "If they get past Jordan and you, the gunmen will figure out a way to get into that room. They might even have explosives. Sophie could be hurt."

He shoved some magazines of ammo into his pockets, then stopped and stared at her. "I can't risk you getting hurt."

She looked him straight in the eye. "I can't risk Sophie's life. I'm going, Cal. And you can't stop me."

He cursed, glanced around the room at Sophie and Meggie. If her daughter was aware of the danger, it certainly didn't show. Sophie was cooing.

"Stay behind me," Cal snarled to Jenna.

She didn't exactly celebrate the concession, though she knew for him, it was a huge one. Jenna looked at Sophie one last time.

"Lock the door from the inside and stay in the center of the room, away from the walls," Cal instructed Meggie. Then he shut it.

Jenna didn't have time to dwell on her decision because Cal started toward the end of the corridor.

"What's the plan?" she asked.

"We go to the front of the house where the intruders are, but we stay inside until we hear from Jordan. He'll try to secure the perimeter."

"Alone? Against four gunmen?" Mercy, that didn't sound like much of a plan at all. It sounded like suicide.

"Jordan knows how to handle situations like these." But Cal didn't sound nearly as convinced as his words would pretend.

Jenna didn't doubt Jordan's capabilities, either. But he was outnumbered and outgunned.

"Jordan knows I have to stay inside," Cal added. He

headed straight for the front of the house, and Jenna was right behind him. "I'm the last line of defense against anyone trying to get to Sophie."

However, they only made it a few steps before there was another crash. It sounded as if someone had bashed the front door in.

Oh, God.

Jenna's heart began to pound as alarms pierced through the house. The security system had been tripped.

Which meant someone was inside.

Chapter Fifteen

This could not be happening.

He and Jenna had already survived one attack from Salazar, and now they were facing another.

He pulled Jenna inside one of the middle rooms off the corridor and listened for any sign that it was Jordan who'd burst through that door. But he knew Jordan would have identified himself. Jordan was a pro and wouldn't have risked being shot by friendly fire.

And that meant it was the gunmen who'd bashed their way in.

So Jenna and he had moved from being backups to primary defense. He sure as hell hadn't wanted her to be in this position, but there was no other choice. They might need both of them to stop the gunmen from getting to Sophie. The gun room was much safer than the rest of the house, but it wasn't foolproof. If the gunmen eliminated them, they'd eventually find their way to Sophie.

Cal was prepared to die to make sure that didn't happen.

He heard movement coming from the foyer. He also heard Jenna's breathing and then her soft mumbling. She was mouthing something, probably meant to keep her calm.

It wouldn't work.

Not with her child at risk. Cal was trained to deal with these types of intense scenarios, and even with all that training, he had to battle his emotions.

And that made this situation even more dangerous.

He forced himself to think like an operative. He was well equipped to deal with circumstances just like this. So what would happen next? What did he need to do to make this survivable?

At least four armed men had invaded the house. Even if they knew the layout, they wouldn't know where Sophie was. Which meant they'd have to go searching for their prize. They wouldn't do that as a group.

Too risky.

Too much noise.

They'd split up in pairs with one pair taking the west corridor. The other would take the east, which was closer to the gun room. The pairs would almost certainly search the entire place, going from room to room. That meant at least two would soon be coming their way. The other two wouldn't be that far behind.

Cal eased out of the doorway so he could see the west corridor entrance. Even though he didn't hear anything, he detected some movement and saw a man in a blue ski mask peer around the corner, so, "Blue" was already in place and ready to strike.

Cal didn't make any sudden moves. For now, he needed to stay put and stay quiet, all the while hoping the doorjamb would conceal him.

A moment later, "Blue" and his partner quietly stepped into the corridor. "Blue" ducked into a room to search it, and the other kept watch.

Cal was going to have to do this the hard way. He didn't want to start a gun battle in the very hallway of the gun room, but he didn't have a choice. He'd have to take out the guy standing guard, and the moment he did that, it would put his partner and the other pair of gunmen on alert. Of course, they already knew he was in the house. They already knew he was trained to kill.

The question was: how good were they?

And the answer to that depended on who had hired them.

If it was Hollywood, well, Cal didn't want to think about how bad this could get. Hollywood had as much training as he did. They'd be an equal match. And God knows how this would end.

Cal didn't want to risk giving away his position, so he hoped that Jenna would stay put and not make any sounds. He got his primary gun ready, and without hesitating, he leaned out just far enough to get a clean shot.

The one standing guard saw him right away as Cal had expected. And he turned his gun on Cal. But it was a split second too late. Cal fired first. He didn't want to take any chance that this guy would survive and continue to be a threat, so he went with three shots, two to the head, one to the chest.

The gunman fell dead to the floor.

Jenna's breathing kicked up a notch, and he was sure she was shaking. He couldn't take the time to assure her that they'd get out of this alive. Because they might not.

Those first shots were the only easy ones he would get. Everything else would be riskier.

Cal volleyed his attention between the room being searched and the other end of corridor. He needed help, and as much as he hated it, it would have to come from Jenna.

He angled himself in the doorway so that he was partly behind the cover of the door frame. "Watch," he instructed Jenna in a whisper. "Let me know when the gunmen come around the corner."

It was just a matter of time.

Cal's only hope was to take care of the "Blue" who was still in the room, and then start making his way toward the other pair. To do that, Jenna and he would have to use the rooms as cover. And then they'd have to pray that the second pair didn't backtrack and take the same path of their comrades. Cal didn't want them to be ambushed.

And there was one more massive problem.

While he watched for "Blue" to make an appearance from the room, Cal thought through the simple floor plan he'd seen on the security panel door. The east and west corridors flanked the center of the house, but there was at least one point of entry that the pair in the west hall could use to get to the side of the house where he and Jenna were.

The family room.

It could be accessed from either hall.

And if the pair used it, that meant they'd be making an appearance two rooms down on the right. He hoped that was the only point where that could happen. Of course, the floor plan on the security panel could have been incomplete.

But he couldn't make a plan based on what he didn't know. The most strategic place for Jenna and him to be was in that family room. That way they could guard the corridor and guard against an ambush. First, though, he had to neutralize "Blue."

There was still no movement near the dead gunman's body. No sound of communication, either. Cal couldn't wait too long or all three would converge on them at once. But neither could he storm the room. Too risky. He had to stay alive and uninjured so he could get Jenna, Meggie and Sophie out of this.

"Go back inside," he instructed Jenna in as soft a whisper as he could manage. "Move to your right and aim at the room where 'Blue' is. Fire a shot through the wall and then get down immediately."

She didn't question him. Jenna gave a shaky nod and hurried to get into position. Cal kept watch, dividing his attention among "Blue's" position, the family room and the other end of the corridor.

Cal didn't risk looking at Jenna, but there was no way he could miss hearing her shot. The blast ripped through the wall and tore through the edge of the door frame of the other room.

Perfect.

It was exactly where Cal wanted it to go. And Jenna did exactly as he'd asked. He heard her drop to the floor.

Cal didn't have to wait long for a response. "Blue" returned fire almost immediately, and Cal saw a pair of bullets slam into the wall behind them. He calculated the angle of the shots, aimed and fired two shots of his own.

There was a groan of pain. Followed by a thud.

Even though he knew his shots had been dead-on, Cal didn't count it as a success. "Blue" could be alive, waiting to attack them. Still, there was a better than fifty-fifty chance that Cal had managed to neutralize him.

"Let's go," Cal whispered to Jenna. He had to get moving toward the family room, and he couldn't leave her alone. As dangerous as it was for her to be with him and out in the open, it would be more dangerous for her to stay put and run into the gunmen.

Jenna hurried to the doorway and stood next to him. She had her weapon ready. He only hoped her aim continued to be as good as that last shot.

"We go out back to back," he said. "You cover that end." He tipped his head toward the dead guy and the room with the bullet holes in the wall. "When we get to the family room, I want you to get down."

Judging from her questioning glance, Jenna didn't approve. Tough. He didn't want to have to worry about her being in the line of fire, and he would have three possible kill zones to cover.

Cal took out a second automatic so he'd have a full magazine, and stepped into the hall. Out in the open. Jenna quickly joined him and put her back to his. He waited just a second to see if anyone was going to dart out and fire at them. But he didn't see or hear anything.

"Let's go," he whispered.

They got moving toward the family room. Cal didn't count the steps, but each one pounded in his head and ears as if marking time. He thought of Sophie. Of Jenna. Of the high stakes that could have fatal consequences.

But he pushed those thoughts aside and focused on what he had to do.

When they reached the family room, he stopped and peered around the doorway. The room was empty.

Or at least it seemed to be.

The double doors that led to the east corridor were shut. That was good. If they'd been open, the gunmen on that side of the house would have heard them. Cal was counting on those closed doors to act as a buffer. And a warning. Because when the pair opened them to search the room, Cal would hear it and would be able to shoot at least one of them.

"Check the furniture," Cal told her. "Make sure we have this room to ourselves."

She moved around him while he tried to keep watch in all directions. But Jenna had barely taken a step when there was a sound.

Cal braced himself for someone to bash through the doors. Or for one or more of the gunmen to appear in the corridor. But the sound hadn't come from those places.

It'd come from above.

He glanced up and then heard something else. Hurried footsteps. He spotted a lone gunman as he rounded the corner of the east corridor. Cal turned to take him out.

"Check the ceiling," Cal told Jenna as he fired at the man. But the man ducked into a room, evading the shot.

Cal made his own check of the ceiling then. Just a glance. The next sound was even louder. Maybe someone moving around in the attic.

He didn't have to wait long for an answer.

Two things happened simultaneously. The gunman

who'd just ducked into the room across the hall darted out again. And there was a crash from above. Cal hadn't noticed the concealed attic door on the ceiling. It'd blended in with the decorative white tin tiles. But he noticed it now.

THE ATTIC DOOR flew back, and shots rang out from above them.

Cal shouted for her to get down, but Jenna was already diving behind an oversize leather sofa. From the moment she saw that attic door open, she knew what was about to come.

An ambush.

At least one of the gunmen had accessed the attic, and now she and Cal were under attack.

She fired at the shooter in the attic and missed. He ducked back out of sight. She couldn't see even his shadow amid the pitch-darkness of the attic.

But shots continued to rain down through the ceiling. That alone would have sent her adrenaline out of control, but then she thought of Sophie.

Oh, God.

Was the ceiling in the gun room bulletproof?

She couldn't remember her father saying for certain, but she had to pray that it was. She hoped there was no attic access in there. But just in case, they needed to take care of this situation so they could make sure that Sophie and Meggie were all right.

Cal fired, causing her attention to snap his way. He wasn't aiming at the ceiling, but rather at someone in the east end of the hall. Mercy. They were under attack from two different sides.

Dividing her focus between Cal and the ceiling shooter, Jenna saw a bullet slice through Cal's shirt-sleeve. Bits of fabric fluttered through the air.

"Get down," she yelled, knowing it was too late and that he wouldn't listen.

Cal leaned out even farther past the cover of the doorway and sent a barrage of gunfire at the shooter in the hall. If Cal was hurt, he showed no signs of it, and there wasn't any blood on his shirt. He was in control and doing what was necessary.

Jenna knew she had to do the same.

She took a deep breath, aimed her gun at the ceiling and fired. She kept firing until the magazine was empty, and then she reloaded.

There was no sign of life. No sounds coming from above. She kept her gun ready, snatched the phone from the end table and pressed the intercom function.

"They might come through the attic," she shouted into the phone. She hoped the warning wouldn't give away Sophie's location.

Jenna tossed the phone aside and aimed two more shots into the ceiling. On the other side of the room, Cal continued to return fire.

The gunman continued to shoot at him.

Bullets were literally flying everywhere, eating their way through the walls and furniture. The glass-top coffee table shattered, sending the shards spewing through the room.

Cal cursed. And for one horrifying moment, Jenna thought he might have been hit.

Then the bullets stopped.

Jenna peered over at Cal—he wasn't hurt, thank God—and he motioned for her to get up. Since he no longer had his attention fastened to the corridor, that meant another gunman must be dead.

But there was still at least one in the attic.

Except with the silenced guns, she no longer heard any movement there. Had the person backtracked?

Or worse—had he managed to get into the gun room?

"Meggie, are you okay?" Cal shouted in the direction of the phone. He was trying to use the intercom to communicate.

While Cal kept watch of their surroundings, Jenna scurried closer to the phone that she'd tossed aside on the floor. She, too, kept her gun ready, but she put her ear closer to the receiver.

And she held her breath, waiting. Praying. Her daughter had to be all right.

"I hear something," Meggie said. "Someone's moving in the attic above us."

Oh, God. Even if that ceiling was bulletproof, it didn't mean a person couldn't figure out a way to get through it. If that happened, Meggie and Sophie would be trapped.

Jenna put her hand over the phone receiver so that her voice wouldn't carry throughout the house. "Someone's trying to get into the gun room through the attic," she relayed to Cal.

He cursed again and reloaded. The empty magazine clattered onto the hardwood floor amid the glass, drywall and splinters. He motioned for her to get up, and Jenna knew where they were going.

To the gun room.

It was a risk. They could be leading the other shooter directly to Sophie, but judging from Meggie's comments, he was already there.

"Take the phone off intercom," Cal mouthed. "Tell Meggie we're coming, but I don't want her to unlock the door until we get there."

That meant for those seconds, she and Cal would be out in the open hall. In the line of fire. But that was better than the alternative of putting her daughter at further risk.

Still keeping low, Jenna hurried back to the phone cradle and pushed the button to disconnect the intercom. She dialed in the number that would reach the line in the gun room. Thankfully, Meggie picked up on the first ring.

"Cal and I are on the way," she relayed. "Don't unlock the door until you're sure it's us."

"What's going on, Jenna?" Meggie demanded. "Where are Cal and Jordan?"

Jenna feared the worst about Jordan. They hadn't heard a peep from the man since the gun battle. Jordan must be hurt or worse.

Jenna heard a slight click on the line, and knew what it meant. Someone had picked up another extension and was listening in.

"I can't talk now," Jenna said to Meggie, hoping the woman wasn't as close to panic as she sounded. "Just stay put…in the pantry. We'll be there soon."

She hung up and snared Cal's gaze. "Someone picked up one of the other phones."

Cal nodded.

Jenna hoped the lie would buy them some time so they could get inside the gun room. She got up so she could join Cal at the doorway.

"We do this back to back again. And hurry," he whispered. "It won't take the gunman long to figure out that they're not in the pantry."

Jenna raced toward him and got into position. She would cover the left end of the corridor. He'd cover the right just in case the gunman was still in place. They had at least thirty feet of open space between them and the gun room.

However, before either of them could move, something crashed behind them. They turned, but somehow got in each other's way.

And that mistake was a costly one.

Because the ski-mask-wearing man who broke through the doors on the other side of the family room started shooting at them.

Chapter Sixteen

Cal shoved Jenna out of the doorway and into the corridor. She'd have bruises from the fall, maybe even a broken bone, but her injuries would be far worse if he didn't get her out of there.

He dove out as well, somehow dodging the spray of bullets that the gunman was sending right at them. He barely managed to hang on to his guns.

This wasn't good. Either the guy in the attic had gotten to them ridiculously quickly, or there were more men in the house than they knew.

Cal didn't dwell on that, though. With his gun ready in his right hand, he caught Jenna with his left and dragged her to her feet. He got them moving, not a second too soon. Another round of shots fired, all aimed at them. Because he had no choice, Cal pushed Jenna into the first room they reached.

It was a guest room. Empty, he determined from his cursory glance of the darkened area. Thankfully, there was a heavy armoire against the wall between the family room and this room. That meant there was a little cushion between them and the shooter.

Cal positioned Jenna behind him and got ready to fire. "Other than where we're standing, is there any another way to access this room?" he whispered.

She groaned softly, and the sound had a raw and ragged edge to it. "Yes."

Hell. He was afraid she would say that. "Where?"

"There's a small corridor off the family room," she explained, also in a whisper. "It leads to that door over there."

Cal risked glancing across the room. He figured it was too much to hope that it would be locked or, better yet, blocked in some way. But maybe that didn't matter— this gunman had a penchant for knocking down doors.

He peered around the door edge, saw the shooter and pulled back just as another shot went flying past him.

Well, at least they knew the shooter's location: inside the family room. "Make sure that door over there is locked," he instructed. "And drag something in front of it."

He'd keep the shooter occupied so that he didn't backtrack and go after them. Of course, that wouldn't do much to neutralize the one in the attic.

"Jenna?" someone called out.

It was Meggie. It took Cal a moment to realize her voice had come over the central intercom. Anyone in the house could hear her. Hopefully, they hadn't already pinpointed her location.

Cal glanced at Jenna, to warn her not to answer.

"Someone's trying to get in here," Meggie said.

Sophie was crying. She sounded scared. She probably was. It broke Cal's heart to know he couldn't get to her and soothe her.

God knew what this was doing to Jenna. The sound of her baby's tears had to be agony. This was a nightmare that would stay with her.

Cal wanted to check on her, but he needed to see if anyone was in front of that gun room door. It was a risk. But it was one he had to take.

He took a deep breath and tried to keep his wrist loose so he could shift his gun in either direction. He leaned out slightly, angling his eyes in the direction of the gun room. No one was there, which probably meant someone was still trying to get through the attic. He didn't have time to dwell on that, though.

A bullet sliced across Cal's forearm. His shooting arm. Fire and pain spiked through him, but he choked it back and took cover.

But for only a split second.

With the sound of Sophie's cries echoing in the corridor and his head, Cal came right back out with both guns ready, and started shooting. He didn't stop until he heard the sound he'd been listening for.

The sound of someone dying.

Still, he didn't take any chances. While keeping watch all around them, he eased out of the room and walked closer until he could see the fallen gunman on the floor. His aim had hit its mark.

The guy was dead all right. The bullet in his head had seen to that. His eyes were fixed in a lifeless, blank stare at the ceiling.

Cal glanced up and listened, wanting to hear the

position of the fifth and hopefully final gunman. He heard something. But the sound hadn't come from the attic. It'd come from the guest room where he'd left Jenna to block the door.

Hell.

He sprinted toward her, aimed his gun and prayed that the only thing he'd see was her trying to block that other door leading from the family room.

But that door was wide open.

Jenna was there, amid the shadows. Her face said it all. Something horrible had happened.

It took Cal a moment to pick through the shadows. Someone was standing behind Jenna.

And whoever it was had a gun pointed at her head.

JENNA REFUSED TO PANIC.

Her precious baby was crying for her. And Jenna wanted nothing more than to make sure that Sophie was okay. But she couldn't move, thanks to the ski-mask-wearing monster who'd come through the door off the family room.

It'd only taken the split-second distraction of Sophie's crying and the shots Cal had fired. Jenna had been listening to make sure he was okay. And because of that, she hadn't been watching the door. The gunman had literally walked through it and grabbed her. The gun had been put to her head before she'd even had time to react.

Now that mistake might get them both killed.

Cal stopped in the doorway, and Jenna watched him assess the situation. Either this person was going to kill them both, or he'd try to force them to give him access to the gun room.

That wasn't going to happen. Which meant they might die right here, right now.

"I'm sorry," Jenna said to Cal.

He didn't answer. He kept volleying his attention between her and the corridor, looking for the guy who'd been in the attic. Of course, that gunman could be the very person who now had a semiautomatic jammed to her head.

"I'm in here!" the guy behind Jenna suddenly yelled out. He ripped off his ski mask and shoved it into his jacket pocket. "Get down here now!"

Except it wasn't a man.

It was Helena Carr.

Jenna hadn't known whom to expect on the other end of that gun. Holden, Hollywood, Gwen and Helena had all been possibilities. All had motives, though they hadn't seemed clear. But obviously Helena's motive was powerful enough to make her want to kill.

"I'm stating the obvious here," she said, "but if either of you makes any sudden moves, I'll kill you where you stand."

"You're planning to do that anyway," Cal tossed back at her.

"Not yet. You're going to give me that screaming baby, and then you'll die very quick, painless deaths."

Oh, God. It was true. She wanted Sophie. Thankfully, her little girl's sobs were getting softer. Jenna could hear Meggie trying to soothe her, and it appeared to be working.

"Why are you doing this?" Jenna demanded.

"Lots of reasons." That was the only answer Helena gave before she started maneuvering Jenna toward the door where Cal was standing.

"Put down your guns," Helena ordered. "All of them."

Cal dropped the one from his right hand. He studied Helena's expression as she came closer. He must have seen something he didn't like because he dropped the other one, too.

Jenna's heart dropped to the floor with those weapons.

Cal wouldn't have any trouble defeating Helena if it came down to hand-to-hand combat, but Helena wasn't going to let it get to that point. She would use Jenna as a human shield to get into that gun room. Worse, she had a henchman nearby. After all, Helena had called out to someone.

With Jenna at gunpoint and Cal unarmed, this could turn ugly fast. It was a long shot, but she had to try to reason with Helena.

"Why do you want my baby?" Jenna asked. She hated the tremble in her voice. Hated that she didn't feel as in charge and powerful as Helena. She desperately wanted the power to save Sophie.

"I don't *want* your baby." Helena shoved her even closer to Cal. "But I need to tie up some loose ends."

So this was about Paul's estate. He'd left Helena some diabolical instructions as to what to do to her in the event of his death.

"I didn't do anything to hurt Paul," Jenna pleaded. "There's no reason for you to seek revenge for him."

"I'm not doing this for Paul."

Jenna heard footsteps behind her.

Helena's associate pulled off his ski mask and crammed it into his pocket. He was a bulky-shouldered man with edgy eyes. A hired gun, waiting to do whatever Helena told him to do.

"What?" Cal questioned Helena. "You don't have the stomach to kill us yourself?"

Jenna couldn't see the woman's expression, but from the soft sound that Helena made, she probably smiled. "I've killed as many men as you have—including Paul when I learned he was sleeping with both Gwen Mitchell and Jenna. The man had the morals of an alley cat."

"He slept with me to get his hands on my business," Jenna pointed out. "And Gwen slept with him to get a story. There was no affection on his part."

"That doesn't excuse it. I'm the one who set up your meeting with Paul. I'm the one who suggested he marry you so he could inherit your estate. Sleeping with you and getting you pregnant was never part of the bargain. He was supposed to marry you, drug you and then lock you away until the time was right to eliminate you completely."

"So why kill us? Why take Sophie?" Cal demanded.

Jenna could have sworn the woman's smile widened. "Oh, I don't want to take her. With my brother out of the way, I can inherit Paul's entire estate. Once any other heirs have been eliminated."

Helena's threat pounded in Jenna's head. She wasn't going to kidnap Sophie. She was going to kill her.

That wasn't going to happen. Rage roared through her. This selfish witch wasn't going to lay one hand on her child.

"Kill Agent Rico," Helena ordered the gunman.

Jenna heard herself yell. It sounded feral, and she felt more animal than human in that moment. She didn't care about the gun to her head. She didn't care about anything other than protecting Sophie and Cal.

She rammed her elbow into Helena's stomach and turned so she could grab the woman's wrist. Jenna dug her fingernails into Helena's flesh and held on.

A bullet tore past her.

Not aimed at her, she realized. The shot had come from the gunman, and it'd been aimed at Cal.

Jenna couldn't see if Cal was all right. Helena might have had a pampered upbringing, but she fought like a wildcat, clawing and scratching at Jenna. It didn't matter. Jenna didn't feel any pain. She only felt rage, and she used it to fuel her fight all while praying that Cal had managed to survive that shot.

The gunman re-aimed.

"It's me," someone shouted. Jordan. He was alive.

That only gave Jenna more strength. She latched on to Helena with both hands and shoved the woman right at her accomplice. But the gunman got off another shot.

It seemed as if everything froze.

The bullet echoed. It was so loud that it stabbed through her head and blurred her vision. But Jenna didn't need clear vision to see the startled look on Helena's face.

The woman dropped her gun and pressed her hand to her chest. When she drew it back, her palm was soaked with her own blood. Her hired gun had accidentally shot her.

Helena smiled again as if amused at the irony. But

the smile quickly faded, and she sank in a limp heap next to her gun.

Jenna forced her attention away from the woman. But she didn't have time to stop the gunman from taking aim at Cal again.

Another shot slammed past her, so close that she could have sworn she felt the heat from the bullet. A second later, she heard the deadly thud of someone falling to the floor.

The echo in her head was already unbearable and this blast only added to it. That, and the realization that Cal could be hurt.

Or dead.

She felt tears burn her eyes and was afraid to look, terrified of what she might see.

But Cal was there, his expression mirroring hers.

"I'm alive," Jenna assured him.

So was he.

He raced to her and pulled her into his arms.

Chapter Seventeen

Cal tried not to wince as the medic put in the first stitch on his right arm.

He'd refused a painkiller. Not because he was alpha or enjoyed the stinging pain. He just wanted to speed up the process. It seemed to be taking forever. He had other things to do that didn't involve stitching a minor gunshot wound.

"Hurry," he told the bald-headed medic again.

The medic snorted and mumbled something that Cal didn't care to make out. Instead, he listened for the sound of Jenna's voice. The last he saw of her, Kowalski was leading her out of the family room so he could question her.

Cal wasn't sure Jenna was ready for that. He certainly wasn't. Cal needed to see her, to make sure she wasn't on the verge of a meltdown. But Kowalski had ordered him to get stitches first. Cal had figured that would take five minutes, tops, but it'd taken longer than that just for the medic to get set up.

He heard footsteps and spotted Jordan in the doorway. The man looked like hell. There was a cut on his jaw that would need stitches, another on his head and he probably had a concussion.

Still, Jordan was alive, and an hour ago, Cal hadn't thought that was possible.

A fall had literally saved him. Jordan had explained that he'd climbed onto the gatehouse roof to stop the attack, but one of the gunmen had shot him. A minor scrape, like Cal's. But the impact of the shot had caused Jordan to fall off the roof, and he'd lain on the ground unconscious through most of the attack.

It was a different story for Jordan's assistant. Cody had been shot in the chest and was on his way in an ambulance to the hospital.

Of course, Cody was lucky just to be alive. Their attackers had obviously thought they'd killed him or else they would have put another bullet in him.

"All the gunmen are dead and accounted for," Jordan relayed.

"What about Jenna?" Cal wanted to know.

"Still talking to Kowalski in the kitchen." Jordan looked down the hall. "But you're about to get a visitor."

Cal winced. He was going crazy here. But he changed his mind when Jordan stepped aside so that Meggie could enter. She had Sophie in her arms.

"Hurry," Cal repeated to the medic.

"I'm done," the guy snapped. He motioned for Jordan to have a seat.

Cal gladly gave up his place so he could go to Sophie. The little girl automatically reached for him, and even though he had blood splattered on his shirt, he took her and pulled her close to him. Like always, Sophie had a magical effect on him. He didn't relax exactly, but he felt some of the stress melt away.

"You've seen Jenna?" he asked Meggie.

The woman shook her head. "She's still with your boss."

Enough of that. She shouldn't have to go through an interrogation alone. Cal shifted Sophie in his arms and started for the kitchen.

"Your boss has been getting all kinds of phone calls," Meggie said, trailing along behind him. "I heard him say that the guy who works for Jordan is going to be all right."

Good. That was a start. But God knows what Jenna was going through.

Cal got to the kitchen and saw Jenna seated at the table. Kowalski was across from her, talking on the phone. Jenna had her face buried in her hands.

"Jenna?" Cal called out.

Her head snapped up, and he saw her face. No tears. Just a lot of weariness.

"You're okay," Jenna said, hurrying to him.

She gathered both Sophie and him into her arms. Her breath broke, and tears came then. Cal just held on and tried to comfort her. However, the hug was cut short—Kowalski ended his call and stared at them. God knows what the man was thinking about this intimate family embrace.

And Cal didn't care.

"Holden Carr is dead," Kowalski announced.

Cal didn't let Jenna out of his arms, but he did turn slightly so he could face the director.

"Helena murdered him before she came here with her hired guns," Kowalski continued. "It appears from some notes we found in the Hummer that she eliminated her brother so he wouldn't be competition for Paul's estate."

"That's why she wanted Sophie out of the way," Cal mumbled, though he hated to even say it aloud. He had seen the terror in Jenna's eyes when she realized what Helena wanted to do. Cal had felt the same terror in his heart.

The director nodded. "Helena was going to set up Hollywood to take the blame."

"And what about Gwen Mitchell?" Jenna asked. "Did she have anything to do with this?"

"Doesn't look that way. She just wanted a story. Helena did everything else. She planted the tracking devices on your cars. Tried to run you off the road. Faked e-mails from Paul and sent Salazar after you. Helena wanted to get you and your daughter out of the way."

So it'd all been for money. No hand from the grave. No rogue agent. Just a woman who wanted to inherit two estates and not have to share it with anyone.

"With Helena dead, the threat to Sophie is over?" Jenna asked. Cal reached over and wiped a tear from her cheek.

"It's over. You and your daughter are safe." Kowalski tipped his head toward Cal's stitches. "How about you? Are you okay?"

"Yeah." Cal had already decided what to say, and he didn't even hesitate. "But I'm not going to stay away from Jenna and Sophie."

Kowalski made a noncommittal sound and reached into his jacket pocket. "That's the letter from the promotion committee. Read it and get back to me with your decision."

"I don't have to read it. I'm not going to stay away from them."

"Suit yourself." Kowalski strolled closer. "There's no reason for me to continue with that order. Ms. Laniere is no longer in your protective custody. What you two do now is none of my business."

It took Cal a moment to realize the director was backing down. There was no reason Cal couldn't see Jenna. Well, no legal reason, anyway. It was entirely possible that Jenna would want him gone just so she could have a normal life.

Cal couldn't give her normal.

But maybe he could give her something else.

Kowalski walked out, and Cal realized that Jenna, Sophie and he were alone. Meggie had left, too. Good. Cal had some things to say, and he needed a little privacy.

He was prepared to beg.

Cal looked at Sophie first. "I want to be your dad. What do you say to that?"

Sophie just grinned, cooed and batted at his face.

He nodded. "I'll take that as a yes." He kissed the little girl's cheek and turned to Jenna.

"Yes," she said before he could open his mouth.

"Yes?" he questioned.

"Yes, to whatever you're asking." But then her eyes widened. "Unless you're asking if you can leave. Then the answer to that is no."

This had potential.

"Wait," Jenna interrupted before he could get out

what he wanted to say. "I've just put you in an awkward position, haven't I?" She glanced at the letter. "You'll want to leave if you didn't get the promotion."

"Will I?"

She nodded. "Because it'll be my fault that you lost it. You resent me. Maybe not now. But later. And when you look at me, you'll think of what I cost you."

Cal frowned. "In less than a minute, you've covered a couple months, maybe even years, of our future. But for now, I'd like to go back to that yes."

"What about the letter?" she insisted. "Don't you want to know if you got the promotion?"

"Not especially."

But Jenna did. She snatched the letter from the table, opened it and unfolded it so that it was in his face. Cal scanned through it.

"I got the promotion," he let her know. Then he wadded up the letter and tossed it.

Jenna's mouth opened, and she looked at him as if he'd lost his mind. "Don't you want the promotion?"

"Sure. But it's on the back burner right now. I'm going to ask you something, and I want you to say yes again."

She glanced at the letter, at Sophie and then him. "All right," Jenna said hesitantly.

"Will you make love with me?"

Jenna blinked. "Now?"

Cal smiled, leaned down and kissed her gaping mouth. "Later. I'm just making sure the path is clear."

"Yes." Jenna sealed that deal with a kiss of her own.

"Will you move to San Antonio with me so I can take this promotion?"

"Yes." There was no hesitation. He got another kiss. A long, hot one.

Hmmm. Maybe he could talk Meggie into watching Sophie while they sneaked off to the bedroom. But Cal rethought that. He intended to make love to Jenna all right, but he wasn't looking for a quickie. He wanted to take the time to do it right. To savor her. To let her know just how important she was to him.

And that led him to his next question. "Will you marry me?"

Tears watered her eyes. "Yes."

Cal knew this was exactly what he wanted. Sophie and Jenna. A ready-made family that was his.

"Now it's your turn to answer some questions," Jenna said. "Are you sure about this?"

"Yes." He didn't even have to think about it.

"Why?"

Cal blinked. "Why?" he questioned.

"Yes. Why are you sure? Because I know why I am. I'm in love with you."

Oh. He got it now. Jenna wanted to hear the words, and Cal wasn't surprised at all that he very much wanted to say them.

He eased Jenna's hand away and kissed her. "I'm sure I love you both," Cal told them. "And I'm sure I want to be with you both forever."

Jenna smiled, nodded. "Good. Because I want forever with you, too."

It was perfect. All the yeses. The moment. The love that filled his heart. The looks on Jenna's and Sophie's faces. It wasn't exactly quiet and intimate with Sophie there, batting at them and cooing, but that only made it more memorable.

Because for the first time in his life, Cal had everything he wanted, right there in his arms.

* * * * *

TEXAS PATERNITY: BOOTS AND BOOTIES
continues next month with Secret Delivery,
only from Delores Fossen and
Mills & Boon® Intrigue!

PRINCE CHARMING FOR 1 NIGHT

BY
NINA BRUHNS

Nina Bruhns credits her Gypsy great-grandfather for her great love of adventure. She has lived and travelled all over the world, including a six-year stint in Sweden. She has been on scientific expeditions from California to Spain to Egypt and Sudan and has two graduate degrees in archaeology (with a speciality in Egyptology). She speaks four languages and writes a mean hieroglyphics!

But Nina's first love has always been writing. For her, writing is the ultimate adventure. Drawing on her many experiences gives her stories a colourful dimension and allows her to create settings and characters out of the ordinary.

A native of Canada, Nina grew up in California and currently resides in Charleston, South Carolina, with her husband and three children. She loves to hear from her readers and can be reached at PO Box 2216, Summerville, SC, 29484-2216, USA or by e-mail via her website at www.NinaBruhns.com.

To Dorothy McFalls, Judy Watts
and Vicki Sweatman: wonderful friends,
insightful critiquers, amazing writers
and rockin' concert buddies!

Chapter 1

"Hey, Vera, whatcha think?"

Vera Mancuso—or as the patrons of the Diamond Lounge gentlemen's club knew her, Vera LaRue—glanced over at her friend Tawnisha and nearly dropped her makeup brush.

"My God, Tawni! Kinky Cat Woman?"

When she looked closer, she *did* drop her jaw—all the way to the floor beneath her own four-inch crystal-clear heels. Why she continued to be surprised by her friend's outrageous outfits she'd never know. Vera had worked at the club for nearly four years now and Tawni's daring outfits still managed to shock her. Tawni always teased her for being too naive for an exotic dancer. Maybe she was right.

"Too much?" her friend asked.

Vera choked on a laugh. "Uh. Maybe too *little*?" Yikes. "Aren't there parts missing?" The black latex Cat Woman costúme—complete with whip—was minus several strategic bits. The outfit left pretty much nothing to the imagination.

But then again, Vera reminded herself, that was the whole idea here, wasn't it?

Tawni grinned. "Only the important parts."

"Too hot to handle, girl!"

"Just the reaction I'm going for." Tawni wiggled her hips in imitation of what she'd be doing onstage in a few minutes. "Rumor is there's a real hottie out there tonight."

Vera grinned. "Loaded, too, I hope? Because I could seriously use a few good tips tonight."

"You and me both." Tawni crooked her fingers playfully. "Come to mama, baby. Let's see you boys flash those twenty-dollar bills."

"Twenties? Damn. That outfit's gonna bring out the *fifties*."

"What I like to hear, girlfriend," Tawni said. "Those poor slobs don't stand a chance." She gave the mirror a final check, winked and strutted out of the dressing room.

Ho-kay, then. Great news for Tawni. Bad news for Vera. If the punters tossed all their cash at the Kinky Cat Woman during the first set, there'd be nothing left for Vera's Naughty Bride half an hour later. No, not good. Joe's retirement home payment was due in a few days, and after her vintage Camry finally broke down last week she was still three hundred bucks short, let alone her own expenses for the month.

Unbidden, her eyes suddenly swam at the thought of her once-burly stepfather lying in his antiseptic white room. He'd been so full of life, had so many friends, before. Now…she was his only visitor, and he hadn't even recognized her two nights ago.

She blew out a breath, fanning her misty eyes. *Don't go all weepy on me, Mancuso. Spoil your makeup and forget about those big tips. Buck up, girl!*

Besides, tears wouldn't help—they never did.

And if she got really desperate, she could always borrow the money from Darla, her sister. Well, half sister. Except Darla had taken off, and who knew when she'd be back. Maybe Tawni could help out if worse came to worst. *If* her friend hadn't already spent all her money on some outrageous new costume by that time. The woman went through expensive stage outfits like Vera went through romance novels.

Not that Vera should be complaining about the costumes. In fact, she was very grateful for them. Tawni was one of the big reasons the punters kept coming back night after night—and telling their friends back home in Des Moines about the great club they'd found in Vegas on their last business trip. *Diamond Lounge: Women in the rough, perfect and polished.* Yeah, that's what it actually said on the playbill out front. Seriously. With a sigh, Vera rolled her eyes. Lecherous Lou's idea, of course. Who else? Now *there* was a loser. Why couldn't *he* get Alzheimer's and forget all about Vera and his relentless campaign to get her to sleep with him?

Anyway, Tawni was one of the rough girls. Supposedly, according to Lecherous Lou. And Vera was polished. She snorted. Ha. Tawnisha Adams had graduated from UCLA magna cum laude and was one of the smoothest operators she knew. *Vera* was the only trailer trash around here, living the life her mother had lived before her. Mentally kicking and silently screaming.

Ah, well. It was what it was.

She leaned forward toward the big lighted mirror that covered an entire wall of the dressing room and critically examined her already generous eye makeup. Maybe a bit more mascara.

There was a fine line between virgin and whore. In her act, she was supposed to be a blushing, innocent bride who revealed her inner bad girl on her wedding night. Right. Like a *real* virgin would ever know those moves she did onstage. Hell, *she* barely did. But whatever. The punters loved it. Which kept Lecherous Lou from firing her even though she steadfastly refused to "do the dirty" with him, as he disgustingly referred to it. That's all that really mattered. Keeping her job.

At least until her Prince Charming came to sweep her away from all of this. Maybe tonight would be the night.

Uh-huh.

She sighed. More mascara it was.

"Vera!"

Her sister burst through the dressing-room door and skidded to a halt against the vanity counter, scattering bottles of nail polish and hair products willy-nilly.

Darla's expression was wild. "Thank God you're here!"

"Whoa!" Vera jumped up and steadied her. "Sis, what's wrong? Where have you *been* all week? You have to stop disappearing like that. Tell me what's going on!"

"Trust me, you don't want to know," Darla said, yanking open her purse.

Darla'd done one of her runners two weeks ago. Which in itself wasn't unusual. Her ditzy sister took off for parts unknown all the time, at the drop of a hat. But she always came back happier and even more relaxed than she normally was, never looking like hell warmed over. Or agitated.

Like this.

"Darla, you look something the cat dragged in," Vera said, genuine worry starting to hum through her. "Seriously, are you all right?" She'd never seen her chronically anesthetized and laid-back half sister so upset. Well, not since their poor excuse for a father had tried to throw Vera out of Darla's penthouse apartment for being a, quote, "money-grubbing gold-digging daughter of a streetwalker." But that was a whole different story.

"Yes. *No!* Oh, I don't know," Darla wailed. "Where the hell *is* it?" Stuff spilled all over the dressing table as she clawed desperately through her designer purse. A new Kate Spade, Vera noted. The real deal. Not like the knockoff Vera was carrying today, sitting on the counter next to Darla's purse. What a difference.

She caught a lipstick that went flying. "Sis, you're talking crazy. Where's *what?*"

"I gotta get out of town for a while, Vera. And I need you to do something for me—Yes! Here it is!"

Triumphantly, her sister held up a ring. A big sparkly one. Jeez Louise, was that a *diamond?* Nah, had to be fake. Even rich-as-Ivanka-Trump Darla St. Giles wouldn't have a rock that huge.

Darla thrust the ring at her. "Can you hide this for me back at our place somewhere?"

Despite their father's objections, Vera shared Darla's penthouse apartment, for which—at Darla's insistence—she paid a ridiculously small amount of rent. Amazingly generous, and a true godsend. Without it Vera'd be living in some low-rent dive in the burbs, an hour from work. Or on a sidewalk grate.

Half sisters, Vera was a product of their playboy father Maximillian St. Giles's legendary philandering. It pleased Darla—whom he basically ignored in favor of her older brother—Henry—to no end to throw their father's many faults and mistakes in his face. Sharing a penthouse with his by-blow ranked right up there. Why should Vera feel guilty about that? The man had treated them both like crap. And it was fun having a sister, even if Darla was a bit out of control at times. Okay, most of the time. They even looked alike. Superficially, at least. Darla meant a lot to her. She'd do anything for her sister.

She looked at the diamond ring in her hand. "Omigod, it's

gorgeous! Where'd you get it? Why do you want me to hide it?" Vera asked, instantly drawn in by the astoundingly beautiful sparkling jewel.

Darla scooped her stuff back into her Kate Spade. "Just as a favor. Lord, you're a lifesaver. I—" Her sister turned and for the first time noticed what Vera was wearing. Her eyes widened and a fleeting grin passed over her lips. "Dang, sis. *Great* corset. Man, that'll have 'em whackin' off in the aisles."

Darla always did have a way with words.

"Thanks, I think," Vera said wryly. Another thing about Darla: she might be an unholy mess, but she was an honest and genuine unholy mess—and never, ever judged Vera. About *anything*. "It is pretty spectacular, isn't it? I had it made to match my bride costume. What do you think? I designed it myself."

Seeing the fake wedding dress hanging from the mirror, a lightbulb went off behind eyes that looked so much like Vera's own. "Oh, it's fabulous," Darla exclaimed. "Hey! The ring'll blend right in! Go ahead, put it on," she urged.

She didn't have to ask twice. Vera slid the flashy ring onto her finger. "Wow. A perfect fit. It is so incredibly beautiful." And Darla was right. It went great with the bride outfit.

Again Vera's eyes were dazzled by the kaleidoscope of colors swirling in its center—green and blue and violet. Like one of those pinwheel whirly things used to hypnotize people in bad movies.

She shook her head to clear it of the weird feeling. "Seriously, what's the deal with the ring?"

A noise sounded out in the hall. Her sister darted a panicked glance at the door, then gave her a smile she knew darn well was forced. "No deal," Darla said. "Just hide it for me, okay?"

"Okay, but—"

"And whatever you do, do *not* talk to Thomas."

As in Thomas Smythe? Darla's ex-boyfriend? Before Vera could ask anything more, Darla pulled her into a quick, hard hug, then grabbed her Kate Spade and vanished out the door as quickly as she'd arrived.

Okay, *that* couldn't be good. Something was up.

Darla was *never* like that—all twitchy and in a rush. Darla never rushed anywhere. Or panicked over anything. Possibly because of the drugs she used far more than she should, but no doubt also because she had learned long ago that money could solve anything and everything. Even a messed-up life.

Tell her about it. Vera only wished *she'd* had the chance to learn that particular lesson.

Speaking of which, she'd better get her butt moving. If she missed her cue to go onstage, Lecherous Lou would pitch a fit. And have one more excuse to hit on her and expect capitulation. Gak. As if.

Luckily, because of her close association with the wealthy St. Giles family, Lecherous Lou—along with everyone else at the Diamond Lounge—was under the mistaken impression that Vera was loaded, too, and didn't need this job. That she just played at exotic dancing as a lark, to piss off conservative parents or whatever. Thank God for small favors. She knew other girls at the club didn't have that kind of leverage against Lecherous Lou to resist his overtures. Or other, shadier propositions. She'd heard about the "private gentlemen's parties" he ran off the books. It was really good money, and she'd been sorely tempted a time or two, but in the end, the thought of what else she'd be expected to do—according to those who did—made her just plain queasy. She shuddered with revulsion.

She might really, *really* need this job…and she might not have had sex in so long she'd probably forgotten how to do it…but she would never, ever, *ever*—

No. Way.

Hell, she wouldn't even do lap dances.

Brushing off the sordid feeling, she carefully shook out the satin skirt of her faux wedding dress and wrapped it around her waist, fastening it over the sexy white, beribboned corset she was wearing. Then she slid on the matching satin bolero-style jacket that made her look oh, so prim and proper, just like a blushing bride. Gathering the yards and yards of see-through veil—the punters particularly liked when she teased them with that—she attached the gossamer cloud to a glittering rhinestone tiara that held it in place on her head.

There.

She checked herself in the mirror. Not bad. The dress was actually gorgeous. In it, she felt like Cinderella stepping from the pumpkin coach. Every man's fantasy bride come to life.

For a split second, a wave of wistfulness sifted through her at the sight of her own reflection. Too bad it was all just an illusion.

She sighed. Oh, well. Maybe someday it would happen for real.

Sure. Like right after Las Vegas got three feet of snow in July.

Face it, Prince Charming was never going to sweep her off her feet and marry her. Who was she kidding? She knew when she got into this gig that no man she'd ever want to marry would look twice at her in that way again. Not after he found out where she came from, and on top of that, what she did for a living. It didn't matter that she'd graduated high school at the top of her class and could have gotten a full ride to any college—even Stanford. Wouldas and couldas didn't matter to men. Only perceptions. She knew that. Look what had happened to her own mother, a woman as smart and loving as any who'd ever lived, bless her.

She knew it would kill Mama, absolutely eviscerate her, if she were alive to see what Vera was doing.

But what choice did she have?

A mere high school graduate could not find an honest, decent job that paid enough to keep Joe in that pricey retirement home. And she'd be damned if she let the best man she'd ever met waste away his last years parked at some damn trailer park day care because she couldn't afford to pay for a proper assisted-living facility. No sirree. Never. Not as long as Vera had breath in her body. And boobs and an ass that could attract fifty-dollar bills. Heck, even the occasional hundred.

So. Off she went to the stage. And truth be told, she didn't even mind that much. Honestly. She *liked* her body. She'd been born with generous curves, and it did not bother her a bit to use them to her advantage. She'd never been shy. And if looking at her nude body could bring a few moments of pleasure to some lonely businessman jonesing for his far-off wife or girlfriend, well, hallelujah. Maybe she'd saved their marriage. Because men could look all they wanted, but they could not touch. That was a firm and fast rule. Both for the club and her personally.

"Two minutes!" Jerry, the bored UNLV senior and part-time stagehand, called from the hallway.

Pursing her bright red lips, she blew a good-luck kiss to the framed photo of Joe and Mama that sat at her spot on the dressing-room vanity, then hurried out and up the stairs toward the black-curtained wings of the stage. Tawni was just coming off.

"How's the house tonight?" Vera whispered.

Smiling broadly, Tawni shook a thick bundle of green bills in her fist. "Hot, baby, hot. Some real high rollers tonight. And, oh, those rumors were true. There's one singularly fine-lookin' man out there. You go get 'em, girl. Knock their little you-know-whats off."

Vera giggled. "You are *so* bad."

Tawni waggled her eyebrows and snapped her Cat Woman whip so it cracked the air. "And lovin' every minute." She raised a considering brow. "Though, Mr. Handsome didn't pay me no nevermind, so maybe he's ripe for a more frilly feminine type."

"One can only hope." *And* that he was rich as Croesus.

"Ten seconds, Miss LaRue." That came from Jerry.

Tawni gave her a wink, and Vera stepped up to the curtain.

"And now, gentlemen—" Lecherous Lou's smarmy, fake-Scottish accent crooned over the club PA system. Her music cued up with a long note from a church organ. "—you are in for a verra special treat, indeed. This next lass is guaranteed to make all you confirmed bachelors out there want to slip a gold ring on her finger and take her home for your verra own fantasy wedding night."

Stifling a yawn, Jerry stood with his nose buried in a textbook, curtain in hand, timing her entrance to exactly when the applause and male howling peaked. He didn't even look up. She didn't take it personally. Jerry'd just come out of the closet. Besides, he had exams this week.

"The Diamond Lounge is verra proud to present…"

She took a deep breath. The stage went black.

Showtime.

"Miss Vera LaRue!"

Chapter 2

Defense attorney Darius "Conner" Rothchild couldn't believe his luck.

What were the chances he'd go out on a little fishing expedition for the Parker case and end up running into Darla St. Giles, the very woman he'd been trying to track down for two weeks? At a strip joint, of all places…called, of all things, the Diamond Lounge.

The superb irony of the name did not escape him. Nor did the amazing coincidence of running into her there. Normally, Conner didn't believe in coincidences. But this just might be the genuine article.

Peeling a twenty from the roll of various bills he always carried in his pants pocket, he paid for another beer and scanned the dark club again.

Talk about two birds with one stone.

Being a Rothchild, a full partner in the family law firm of

Rothchild, Rothchild and Bennigan, and independently wealthy, all allowed him to take on a number of pro bono cases in between his paying clients. The Suzie Parker case was one of his current charity projects—a sordid affair concerning organized prostitution, unlawful coercion and sexual harassment. Several club managers on the Strip had gotten it into their minds to make their more desperate dancers attend infamous "gentlemen's house parties." Nothing more than sex parties. The girls were made to do disgusting things, often against their will, according to Suzie Parker. Unfortunately, the same reasons that led them into the coercion kept them from talking to Conner. And if he couldn't prove Suzie was telling the truth, she'd go to jail for prostitution, and her abusers would go scot-free.

But Darla St. Giles had nothing to do with the Parker case.

No. *She* was going to tell him what had happened to the missing Rothchild family heirloom, the Tears of the Quetzal, a unique chameleon diamond ring worth millions. She'd tell him, or he'd personally wring her spoiled-little-rich-girl neck. Or better yet, have her tossed into jail where *she* belonged.

He just had to find her first. Where had she disappeared to?

As Conner made a second circuit of the club looking for her, his mind raced over the facts of this case. Going into the Las Vegas Metropolitan Police Department headquarters last week, he'd literally run into Darla, one of two heirs to Maximillian St. Giles's billion-dollar fortune. Though they'd met many times socially because their families ran in the same lofty circles, Darla hadn't given Conner a second glance. She'd been too busy arguing with a cop on the sidewalk across the street from Metro headquarters. The pair of them had sounded like they were furious at each other, lost to the world in the throes of their disagreement. There'd also been something about the cop, Conner remembered thinking, something that didn't quite fit—other than his disgusting cheap cologne—although Conner hadn't been able to put his finger on it.

At the time he'd dismissed the incident as one of Darla's notorious public tantrums and continued on the errand his uncle Harold had sent him on: attempting to retrieve the Tears of the Quetzal diamond from police custody. The priceless ring was being held by LVMPD as material evidence in a high-profile murder trial—the victim being Conner's own cousin Candace Rothchild.

Her murder had hit the whole family hard, especially Conner's uncle. Hard enough to make Harold set aside a lifelong animosity and deliberate distancing of himself from all things connected with his rival brother—including his two nephews— in order to beg Conner for a favor. Get back the ring, or Harold was absolutely convinced terrible things would befall *everyone* in the family, due to some ancient curse connected with the ring. His daughter Candace had apparently been killed when she, against her father's strict orders, had "borrowed" the ring and worn it to a star-studded charity function at one of the big new casinos. She was just the first to die, Harold had warned. The man seemed genuinely terrified, convinced the so-called curse was real. He had become obsessed over retrieving the ring…especially after the near-fatal accident that befell his other daughter, Conner's cousin Silver, a few weeks back. An accident her new fiancé, AD, now suspected was a murder attempt.

Conner didn't believe in curses, but he did believe in family. He had a good relationship with his own parents and brother, but relations with Harold and his various offspring, Conner's cousins, had been more than strained for as long as he could remember.

Growing up, the deceased Candace and her coven of siblings and half siblings—Natalie, Candace's twin, who was now a Metro detective; Silver, the former pop star who'd recently made a stunning comeback; Jenna, the Vegas event planner; and the newest addition, Ricky, the devil child— every one of them used to bait him mercilessly about being born into the "wrong" side of the Rothchild family. Conner's highly respected attorney father, Michael Rothchild, was worth millions, but not billions like casino magnate Uncle Harold. Of course, that side of the family didn't even get along with each other, especially tabloid-diva Candace. Things had only gotten worse when she'd married and divorced a drunken loser drummer in a would-be rock band, leaving two beautiful but very neglected children in the constant care of nannies.

Wasn't family wonderful.

But to everyone's credit, things had changed dramatically after Candace's murder. Olive branches had been extended. Although, to be honest, he'd been reconciled with his cousins Natalie and Silver for a while now. They'd actually become good friends over the past few years…much to the chagrin of Uncle Harold. But he had changed now. And this was Conner's big chance to help bring the whole Rothchild family—imperfect as it was—back together. He did not intend to blow it.

Which was why he'd agreed to try to retrieve the ring from the police. Technically, the Tears of the Quetzal belonged to the entire family, having been unearthed in the Rothchild's Mexican diamond mine by his grandfather over five decades ago. But Uncle Harold had always been the ring's caretaker. And now with the ring's disappearance, he was obsessively worried it would bring danger to the family.

Although Conner still dismissed the ridiculous notion of curses, he did agree the diamond was not secure, even surrounded by hundreds of cops. As a lawyer, Conner knew firsthand that evidence disappeared from police custody all the time. Lost. Tampered with. Deliberately "misplaced."

And wouldn't you know it. Two weeks ago when he'd gotten to the evidence room, minutes after running into Darla St. Giles, he'd discovered, to his frustration, the unique and unmistakable chameleon diamond ring had vanished. Switched. Replaced with a paste copy that had gone missing from Harold's current wife's jewelry box. At Metro police headquarters, the theft had been pulled off by a cop who had apparently simply walked in and checked the real ring out of the evidence room on the pretense of having it examined for DNA, and left the clever fake in its place when he returned it an hour later.

Conner had gone ballistic. What was *wrong* with these people? Didn't they check ID? His cousin Natalie, the LVMPD detective, had led the search.

Then he'd remembered Darla arguing outside with that not-quite-right cop only ten minutes before he'd discovered the theft. And *that's* when he'd figured out what was wrong with the guy. His boots. They'd been brown and scuffed up. Regulation was black and spit-polished.

Conner was absolutely convinced that phony cop and Darla St. Giles were responsible for the theft of the ring from police headquarters. Damned unexpected, but not outside the realm of possibility. According to the tabloids, Darla had been scraping the proverbial bottom of the barrel of late, friend-wise and behavior-wise. Dating fake cops, stealing jewelry and hanging out at strip clubs would be right up her alley.

The question was, was the pair also involved in his cousin Candace's murder? He couldn't believe it of Darla. She was a wild party girl and definitely sliding down a slippery slope. A thief, yes. But a murderer? He could be wrong, but he didn't buy it. Still, he owed it to the family to find out for sure.

Naturally, after Conner raised the alarm, by the time Natalie had launched a search, Darla and the man had been long gone. Just in case, Conner had spent hours on the computer with Natalie by his side, looking at photos of every single police officer in Las Vegas. The man he'd seen was not among them. Therefore his instincts had been right—the culprit was not a real cop.

On that same day Darla had dropped out of sight completely, confirming his suspicions of her guilt. Despite Natalie assigning an officer to stake out her penthouse apartment 24/7, other than a single roommate, no one had seen hide nor hair of her there, or anywhere else, since.

Until now.

At least, ten minutes ago… But he'd lost her.

With mounting frustration, Conner had searched the Diamond Lounge from top to bottom for the illusive Darla. Twice. And come up empty.

Where the hell was she?

"Can I get you something, doll?" one of the waitresses asked him with a sultry smile. She was pretty. Blond. And topless.

Hello.

He glanced around, catapulted back to the present by the sight of so much skin. Whoa. Where had his famous powers of observation vanished to?

The Diamond Lounge was an Old Las Vegas landmark, a throwback to the times when total nudity was permitted along with serving alcohol. Naturally, he'd vaguely noticed the naked woman dancing on the stage. But how could he have been so angry and distracted that he hadn't noticed the all but naked women prancing around him carrying trays of drinks?

"You looking for someone special?" she asked, her smile growing even more suggestive.

Oy. He slashed a hand through his hair, composing himself. One always learned more playing nice than coming off like a demanding nutcase. And, hell, she was hot. No hardship there.

He smiled back. "Yeah. I thought I saw a friend of mine. Darla St. Giles. You know her by any chance?"

"Oh, sure," the waitress said, interest perking. He could practically see dollar signs flashing in her baby blues. As one of the rich and reckless, Darla's male friends were sure to be rich and reckless, too. Emphasis on the rich part. "She's in here all the time."

Popular landmark or not, that surprised him. "She is?"

"Uh-huh. To visit her sister. She works here."

He-llo. A St. Giles? Working at the Diamond Lounge as a topless waitress? Hell's bells. Ol' Maximillian St. Giles must be spitting disco balls over that one. Except now that Conner thought about it, he had never heard of a second St. Giles sister. There was a brother, Henry, but not... Unless... He tipped his head. "Are you *sure* they're sisters?"

"*Half* sisters, if you know what I mean. Although that's all hush-hush." The waitress waggled her eyebrows and leaned against the bar, folding her arms under her bare breasts so they pushed up toward him. Oh. Subtle. "Guess she likes walkin' on the wild side, or somethin'."

Or something. Whoa. All Conner's stress just oozed out of him. A deep, dark St. Giles secret, eh? A secret so hidden that Darla felt safe coming here tonight, even when she hadn't been to her apartment in two weeks and hadn't called her own family. Hell, all he had to do was put a watch on the secret sister and sooner or later Darla'd turn up here.

The Tears of the Quetzal was as good as found. And Natalie could bring her in for questioning about Candace's murder as well.

Damn, he was good.

"How 'bout you, doll?" the waitress asked, interrupting his thoughts again.

"Me, what?" he asked.

"You like walkin' on the wild side?"

He smiled at her. "Maybe." Then took a second look at what the blond waitress was offering up. He was used to women throwing themselves at him, one of the perks of his looks and his famous last name. Normally he was just too damn busy to take advantage. But what the hell, it had been a long time; maybe the Parker case could wait another night. But first... "Darla's sister, she around?" Just so he'd know who to look for. Tomorrow.

"Sure, she's coming on right now. That's her." The waitress pointed toward the stage.

The stage? He tore his eyes from her and turned. "You mean she's a—"

He froze, literally, instantly oblivious to everything else around him.

The sister... At first Conner thought it was Darla; they looked so much alike. But then she stepped into the spotlight, and all resemblance vanished. The woman was the most amazingly, lusciously gorgeous thing he'd ever seen in his life. She glided out on the horseshoe-shaped stage to the tune of Mendelssohn's *Wedding March*. Eyes cast demurely down, she was dressed in a frothy, whipped-cream wedding dress, complete with a long poofy veil covering her face and spilling over her shoulders and back clear to the floor like some kind of gossamer waterfall.

Wow.

Normally, the merest glimpse of a wedding dress made him break out in hives and sprint hell-bent-for-leather in the opposite direction. Not this one.

"Her?" he asked the waitress, totally forgetting that just seconds ago he'd been contemplating—

Never mind. What waitress?

Was he actually hyperventilating?

"Yeah. How about we—"

"What's her name?" he asked, his eyes completely glued to the perfect vision onstage.

The waitress was not pleased. He could tell by the way she huffed and turned her back on him. Working on autopilot, he dug out his ubiquitous roll, peeled off a bill and held it over his shoulder for her. "Her name?"

She gave a harrumph and snatched it. "It's Vera. Vera LaRue."

Vera... Wait. Wasn't that the name Natalie had said belonged to Darla's roommate? The *sister* was the roommate?

The churchy organ music morphed into a slow, grinding striptease number. Conner watched, beguiled, as Vera LaRue slowly started to move her body in a sinuous dance. And, damn, could the woman ever move her body. Her eyes were still cast innocently at the floor doing her vestal virgin bit, but there wasn't a man in the place watching her face.

Conner pushed off the bar and signaled a passing waitress, peeling off another few bills. Without saying a word, he was shown to a table, front and center. He sat down, and a glass of champagne appeared in his hand. Vera paused just above him on the stage. Oh. Man. She was close enough to touch. He was more than tempted to try.

She raised her lashes and looked down at him.

He looked up at her.

Their eyes met.

And sweet holy God. He was struck by lightning.

Or maybe just blinded by the flash of seven carats of chameleon diamond on her finger as she slowly unbuttoned the top of her gown. He almost fell off his chair. That was *his* seven carats of chameleon diamond! She was wearing the Tears of the Quetzal!

Well, hot damn. If this was Harold's so-called danger, bring it on.

The top of the white gown slid provocatively off Vera

LaRue's pale, pretty shoulders. Conner watched her slowly tug the sleeves down her arms, inch by tantalizing inch. For several moments his brain ceased to function.

Until he gave himself a firm mental kick. What was *wrong* with him?

She couldn't be nearly as innocent as she appeared, clutching the top of that dazzling white gown to her breasts like a blushing virgin. Hell, she *must* be involved with Darla in the theft of the ring. The evidence was right on her finger!

Logic told him she had to be innocent of involvement in Candace's murder. Only a complete, brainless idiot would kill someone, or even be remotely connected to a murder, and then flash the evidence in front of a room full of people. Obviously, she couldn't know of the link between Candace's murder and the ring she was wearing.

Come to think of it, maybe she didn't even know the ring was stolen. Now, *that* would make more sense. It could easily be she was just being used. Or set up.

In which case, he had to give Darla props. Hiding the unique ring in plain sight, as part of her sister's stage costume, was brilliant.

Too bad he was even more brilliant.

Brilliant and ruthless.

And did he mention intrigued as hell? Who *was* this Vera LaRue, Darla St. Giles's gorgeous, secret, illegitimate half sister?

And who'd have ever thought Conner Rothchild would be so captivated by a stripper? His snooty family would have a cow, every last one of them. Especially his dad, who'd always held Uncle Harold in contempt for his questionable taste in multiple women.

But thoughts of family vanished as Vera LaRue stopped in front of him and slanted him another shy glance. She held his gaze with a sexy look as she pulled at the waist of her wedding gown and the whole thing slid down around her trim ankles in a pool of liquid silk.

For a second he couldn't breathe. Sweet merciful heaven. All that was left was the most erotic, alluring bit of lace he had ever seen grace a woman's body. Parts of it, anyway. And a veil. Straight out of Salome.

Please don't let me be drooling.

Then, with a sultry lowering of her eyelashes, she scooped up the dress and let it fall provocatively right into his lap. Her eyebrow lifted almost imperceptibly.

Okay, seriously wow. A challenge? Clearly, she did not know him. Conner didn't lose. And if there was one thing he never lost, it was a dare.

Oh. Yeah.

He looked up at her and conjured his most seductive smile.

Still moving to the music, she knelt down on the stage. Right before him. With those melting eyes and amazing mile-long legs…encased in white thigh-high stockings and impossibly sexy crystal-clear high-heeled shoes. She dropped to her hands and knees. Just for him.

His brain pretty much disintegrated. The rest of his body was set to explode. He was hard and thick as one of those columns at the Forum. The *real* one in Rome.

The Rothchild heirloom flashed on her finger. His family's ring. A smile curved his lips.

She wanted his family jewel? Well, then. He just might have to be a gentleman and give it to her.

Oh, yes. This curse could prove to be very, very interesting, indeed.

Chapter 3

The applause for Vera LaRue was deafening. Conner watched mesmerized as she took her final bow and swished off the stage.

He let out a long, long breath. Lord, have *mercy*.

By the time she'd finished her incredible dance of temptation, she'd made her way all around the stage, weaving her erotic spell over the dozens of men who were pressed up to the edge like pathetic dogs panting for a treat. But Conner was the only one who'd rated personal attention from her. It was like she'd danced for him alone, even when she was all the way across the stage. Of course, probably every guy there thought exactly the same thing. That's what a good stripper did to a guy. Or maybe she singled him out because he was the only one who hadn't attempted to put his hands on her. Hadn't tipped her. Hadn't done anything but hold her sultry eyes with his and silently promise her anything she wanted. Anything at all.

On his terms.

She'd ended up gloriously, unabashedly naked. Or, as good as. Down to a G-string, stockings and those take-me heels…and the Quetzal diamond. Oh, yeah, and a thick layer of fluttering greenbacks stuck into her G-string, making it look like a Polynesian skirt gone triple X.

Her bridal veil was around Conner's neck. He was still sweating over the way she'd put it there.

Da-*amn.* The woman was Salome incarnate. But Conner fully intended to have her dancing to *his* tune before the night was over. Singing like a lark about how she'd ended up with his ring on her finger…without even benefit of dinner and a movie. Not to mention if she knew anything about Candace's death.

Conner was a damn good lawyer, skilled at making witnesses trust him enough to spill their guts. It was all about the approach. So…how to best approach this one…?

He looked around the room. And almost laughed out loud. The answer was beckoning from the back of the club. Aw, gee. He'd just have to sacrifice himself.

Throwing back the last of his champagne—not that he needed the Dutch courage—he signaled his waitress.

"I'd like Miss LaRue to join me," he told her as the fickle crowd roared for the new cutie who'd just come out onstage.

The waitress took the dress and veil from him. "Sure, hon. I'll have her come to your table."

He pulled off another bill. "No, somewhere private."

"Oh, sorry. I'm afraid Ms. LaRue doesn't do that."

"Do what?"

"Private parties. She's strictly a stage dancer."

"Really."

Now, *that* was interesting. Apparently being a St. Giles let her pick and choose her jobs. Normally the private VIP rooms upstairs were where the big money was made by these women.

And the big thrills. Personally, he'd never gotten into the whole lap dance thing. A nice sensual session in the privacy of your own home with a woman you knew and liked, sure. But an anonymous grind for cash? A bit sleazy if you asked him.

"Well," he told the waitress, "then it's good I only want to talk to her."

She rolled her eyes. "Sure you do, hon."

He could understand her skepticism. Hell, *he* was skeptical, and he knew he only wanted to talk to her. Honest.

He peeled off a few more bills and pressed them into her palm. "Tell Miss LaRue I have information about her sister. And that I'll match whatever she just made onstage."

Where she'd practically seduced him, by the way. But the woman didn't do lap dances. Something didn't add up about *that* picture.

The waitress shrugged. "You're wasting your time. Don't say I didn't warn you." She beckoned him with a crooked finger.

He strolled along behind her to the back of the club and followed her up the red-carpeted stairs to the second floor, where the inevitable small, "private entertainment" VIP rooms were located. Though gentlemen's clubs weren't Conner's favorite hangouts, one couldn't be a defense attorney in Vegas without doing a certain amount of business in them. Especially since his frequent pro bono work tended to involve hookers and runaways. So he was fairly familiar with the standard club setup.

Because of its enduring fame, Old Vegas reputation and pricey cover charge—and thanks to a complete renovation in the nineties—the Diamond Lounge wasn't too bad, compared to most. Clean. Sophisticated decor. Unobtrusive bouncers. Nice-looking, classy ladies. He supposed if you had to work in a place like this, the Diamond Lounge was definitely top drawer.

But once again he wondered why über-conservative Maximillian St. Giles let his daughter work at all, let alone take off her clothes for money. Even if she was illegitimate, and as far as he knew, unacknowledged, a negative reflection was still cast on the family.

Not that Conner was objecting to her taking off her clothes. Hell, no. The woman had an incredible body.

She also had his family's ring.

He wanted it back. That was his primary objective here. And nailing down Darla's involvement in his cousin's murder. Not nailing Vera LaRue. But if in the course of things, he ended up close and personal with her, well, who was he to protest? Especially considering the unmistakable signals she'd given him from up onstage. She had to be expecting this.

Handing the waitress his credit card, he did a quick survey of the tiny, soundproof room, then sprawled onto the heavy, red leather divan that took up most of one wall. Soft music played in the background. Scented candles littered the surfaces of two low tables at either end of the divan, as well as on the heavy wood mantel of the fireplace across from it. The tasteful cornice lighting was recessed and rose-colored, lending a pastel glow to Oriental rugs over cream-colored carpet and gauzy curtains that looked more like mosquito nets draped all around the walls of the room. It was like being cocooned in some exotic Caribbean bordello.

Oddly arousing.

The curtains over the door parted, and Vera LaRue suddenly stood there, holding a sweating champagne bottle and two crystal flutes. She'd put the wedding dress back on.

Hey, now.

"Hello," she said, her voice throaty and rich like a tenor sax. "I understand you wanted to speak with me about my sister."

Suddenly, talk wasn't at all what he wanted.

Wait. Yes, it was.

"Why don't you come in and open up that bottle," he suggested, indicating the champagne in her hand. The hand with the Tears of the Quetzal diamond on it. *Focus, Conner.*

"I, um…" She suddenly looked uncomfortable. "I'm sorry, sir. I really don't think so. Truth is, I don't do this."

He hiked a brow. "Drink champagne?"

She blinked. Flicked her gaze down to the bottle then back to him, even more flustered. "No. I mean yes, I drink champagne. Of course I drink champagne. Everyone does. But I *don't* do lap dances. I only came because you mentioned my sister. Now, what was it—"

"I understand," he cut in agreeably. Not having to endure her gyrating on his lap without being able to touch her was probably a good thing. If maybe a little disappointing. Fine, a lot disappointing. "Let's have some bubbly and then we can talk."

She gave him a look. What? She didn't believe him, either? "Sir, I'm serious. It's nothing to do with you. You seem like a nice guy. I just really don't—"

"Please. Call me Conner. If you don't want to dance for me, Ms. LaRue, that's fine. As appealing as that might be, it's not why I'm here." He held out his hand with a smile. "Here. I'll open it."

When she still balked, he stood up. That made her jump. But she recovered quickly. She gave him the bottle and pulled back her hand a little too fast. As though she were…afraid to touch him?

Impossible. The woman who'd practically had sex with him with her eyes from the stage could not possibly be nervous about physical contact, regardless of what he might or might not have had in mind for this tête à tête.

Which was *just* to talk.

Honest to God.

Or…did she perhaps realize who he was? *That* hadn't occurred to him. Had Darla warned Vera someone might come looking for the ring? Maybe asking questions about a murder? Was this modesty thing all a big ploy to throw him off?

Nah. If so, she would have run away, not flirted mercilessly and then locked herself and the ring in a tiny room with him.

The cork flew, startling her into raising the flutes to catch the golden liquid. Her satiny gown rustled against his legs as he stepped closer to fill the glasses. The scent of her perfume clung to the air around her—sweet and spicy. Very nice.

Suddenly, the most insanely irrational thought struck him. What if she really *were* his beautiful bride, that this really was their wedding night and he really *was* about to peel that bridal gown off her and—

Whoa, there, buddy. Hold on.

Where the hell had *that* come from?

Totally inappropriate temporary insanity, that was where. Obviously he'd gone without sex for *far* too long, and it was somehow damaging his brain's ability to function in the presence of a beautiful woman.

He eased a flute from her stiff fingers and clicked it with hers. Back to business.

But instead of a trust-inducing get-to-know-you question, what came out of his mouth was, "You do have some amazing moves, Ms. LaRue."

To make matters worse, his rebellious gaze inched boldly down her delectable body, all of its own volition.

Help.

"Um, thanks, Conner. I appreciate your…um, appreciation. But now you really need to tell me whatever information you have about my sister, or I'll be leaving."

Damn, she looked good. And so sweetly uncomfortable, he pulled out his roll, thumbed off two C-notes, held them up, and confessed, "Okay, you were right. I *would* like to see you dance up close."

Okay, way to go, you total moron. What was *wrong* with him? This was *not* the way he conducted business.

"I knew it." She shook her head, taking a step backward, away from him. "Look, I'm really sorry, but this is not happening. I'll just go find someone else—"

An incredible thought flew through his mind as she chattered on about getting him another girl. Could this befuddling change in his self-control be the mysterious power of the ancient Mayan legend-slash-curse Uncle Harold was always talking about? The part he was obsessed with portended terrible things would befall anyone who possessed the ring with evil intentions. But the *other* part said the spirit of the Quetzal would bring any truly worthy person within its range of influence true, abiding love.

For a second he just stood there, stunned.

He-*llo?*

Had he gone completely *insane?*

Mystical powers? True love? With an exotic dancer?

He gave himself a firm mental thwack.

And smiled at her. "No, it's you I want, and the room is already paid for." By the quarter-hour, no less. He held up his money roll. "Tell me, what did you make in tips onstage? I promised to match it." *To talk,* he tried to compel his mouth to say. But the words just wouldn't come out.

She didn't even blink. "That's very nice of you, but no. Thank you. As I said—" She launched into her spiel yet again.

But he wasn't listening. It was like he was standing next to himself watching as he was being taken over by pod people. He should be taking it slow. From arm's length. Gaining her trust. Not trying to jump her bones. Certainly not until after he'd gotten his answers. And his family's ring back. He *knew* that. But she was simply too delicious to resist.

Ah, what the hell.

He surrendered to it. Changed tactics. *Her* first. Answers later. Then the ring.

Yeah, that worked.

Determined, he thumbed out several more bills, bringing her chatter to a stuttering halt. He didn't doubt for a second she'd eventually capitulate. One thing his ruthless family had taught him—*everyone* capitulated. It was all just a matter of negotiation. "Four-hundred? Five?"

She swallowed. "Really. I don't think you under—"

He started peeling and didn't stop till he reached ten. "Let's say an even thousand, shall we?"

That really shut her up. She stared at the money, then shifted her gaze to stare at him for an endless moment. "Why?" she finally asked.

Good freaking question.

Vera LaRue was so different from the type of woman he was usually attracted to…this was completely unknown territory. Sure, he frequently worked with hookers, dancers and runaways in his legal practice. *Worked.* But he was definitely not attracted to them. Never slept with them. Ever.

So what was different about this woman? What made him want *her?* And no—hell, no!—it had *nothing* to do with mystical powers or curses.

A matter of pride maybe? Conner Rothchild wasn't used to being denied. The only time he took *that* without protest was in court.

Okay, bull.

Not pride. Not some stupid Mayan curse.

But chemistry. *Sexual* chemistry. Plain and simple. He wanted her in his bed, naked and moving on top of him. She was the sexiest woman he'd met in decades. Was this rocket science?

He wanted her. A lap dance seemed like a damned good way to convince her she wanted him, too. It was a start, anyway.

"Why?" he echoed. And gave her his best winning jury smile. "Let's just say you intrigue me."

She regarded him for another endless moment, her eyes narrowing and filling with suspicion. "Who are you, anyway?"

Uh-oh.

But as luck would have it, he never got the chance to answer. Because just then the door whooshed open and the mosquito net curtains blew aside as though from a strong wind. Two men in suits strode through and halted right inside, looking so much like federal agents that just on reflex Conner was about to warn Vera to not to say a word.

One of the men stepped forward. "Miss St. Giles?"

With a frown, Vera turned to the newcomers in confusion. "What?"

Conner frowned, too, when Forward Guy spotted the Tears of the Quetzal diamond on her finger, looked grimly smug, then officiously snapped up an ID wallet. "Special Agent Lex Duncan, FBI."

Oh, come on. Seriously?

But it was Special Agent Duncan's next words that really seemed to confuse the hell out of Vera. And him, too.

"Darla St. Giles, I am hereby placing you under arrest."

Chapter 4

"**Y**ou can't do that!" Vera exclaimed as an honest-to-goodness FBI agent spun her around, grabbed her wrists and snapped handcuffs onto them. "Hey! Watch the dress!" she cried. "What the heck—"

"Ms. St. Giles, you have the right to remain silent—"

"*What?* Are you kidding? I am *not*—"

"Vera," Conner, her would-be john, cut her off over the drone of the FBI agent—what was his name? Lexicon?—reciting her rights, "don't say anything. I'll take care of this."

Not only was the man annoying but he was a real buttin-sky, too. "You don't understand. I'm not—"

"I know you're not," Conner cut her off again. "But obviously *they* think you are."

"Move away from the suspect, sir," her second would-be arrestor admonished her would-be lawyer briskly, with just a touch of disdain in his voice, as Agent Lexicon continued his recitation. Great. Already with the attitude.

All at once his words registered. "Suspect?" she echoed, horrified. "*Me?* I'm *not* a suspect!" she insisted, growing more frustrated by the second. And more worried. She could see a crowd gathering outside the door. If Lecherous Lou got wind of this, her butt would be fired for sure.

One thing a club in this city did not need was bad publicity of any kind. Kept the tourists away. And her boss had just been waiting for a good excuse to fire her. Mainly because she refused his disgusting advances, but also because she wouldn't get involved in that shady business he was running on the side with a few other club managers, providing high-class dancers for private parties.

"That's right. You're no mere suspect," Agent Attitude agreed. "You've been caught red-handed, sweetheart, guilty as hell. Do not pass go, do not collect two-hundred dollars." He snickered at his own lame joke.

"What do you mean, guilty? I haven't done anything!"

"Vera," Conner headed off her impending tirade, "do *not* say another word." She snapped her mouth shut in irritation as he turned to Lex Luthor. "I'm Conner Rothchild, the lady's legal counsel. She is invoking her right to silence and to an attorney."

Wait. Oh, no. Conner *what?* Did he just say his name was—

"And by the way," Conner continued, "this woman is not Darla St. Giles. So if you would kindly take off the handcuffs and let her go?"

Rothchild! As in—

Agent Lucifer whipped around and peered closer at her. "Then who is she?" he demanded.

Rothchild! Oh, no. No way, Jose. She knew the reputation that went along with the name Conner Rothchild. She'd heard plenty of horror stories from his own cousins, tabloid-diva

Candace and pop star Silver, who used to be two of Darla's best friends. Not only was Conner a sleaze-bag shark of a defense attorney according to Candace, but according to Silver he was also possibly the biggest skirt-chaser in the state.

"She's—"

Hell, no. "I'm terribly sorry, but this man is *not* my attorney," she jumped in indignantly. "And I can answer for myself, thank you very much. My name is Vera Mancuso, and Darla St. Giles is my—"

"Stop!" Conner-freaking-playboy-of-the-year-Rothchild cut her off again with an exasperated glare. "I *said* not another word! I *am* her attorney, but since she is not the person you are looking for—"

"Oh, she's the right person, all right," the Devil's agent said resolutely. He pointed an accusing finger at her left hand. "Whoever she is, she's in possession of material evidence stolen from police custody. Therefore, Vera Mancuso, is it? I am placing *you* under arrest—"

"What?" The rest of his words faded out as Agent Attitude pried the ring from her finger and dropped it into a small Ziploc bag. "Oh. My. God. I cannot believe this." Her incredulity continued to pour out of her mouth all on its own as desperate thoughts bombarded her mind even faster.

Stolen? From the police? *Oh, Darla! What have you gotten yourself into this time?* Wait a second. Darla, nothing. Heck, what had her sister gotten *her* into this time? Now Darla's request to hide the ring made perfect sense. Stolen! She could go to jail!

Despair swept over her as the FBI agents pushed her out into the main part of the club, where every single person stood and gaped in avid interest as she was led through the room in handcuffs, tripping over the bridal gown because with the restraints she couldn't hold it up to walk. Even the new girl onstage stopped gyrating and stared wide-eyed. And, damn it, there was Lecherous Lou, looking murderous as he watched her being taken away.

Great. So much for *that* job.

What would she do for money now? How would she pay for Joe's retirement home from prison? Too bad she hadn't accepted gazillionaire Conner's proposition earlier…and gotten paid up front. That thousand bucks would at least have bought her a week or two respite. Then, oh, darn, got arrested, can't do the lap dance. Sorry, no refunds.

Yeah. Like her conscience would have let her do that, even if a thousand bucks to this man was merely a night's meaningless amusement. Honesty was such a bitch.

"You have a change of clothes in your dressing room?" Mr. Persistent Attorney asked as she was herded through the club's front door. She glanced back at him. And wondered what his real agenda was. He couldn't possibly care what happened to her.

Yeah, like she couldn't guess.

Conner Rothchild was a blue-blooded playboy who made the gossip columns nearly as often as Darla and Silver and their jet-setting, hard-clubbing cronies. Always with a different woman on his arm. He probably thought slumming it with Darla St. Giles's exotic-dancer sister would be a hoot. For about five minutes. Meanwhile, she'd be outed to the world at large, and good ol' Maximillian would be furious.

"I'll grab your purse and follow you," Conner said when she deliberately didn't answer. "Don't say anything until I get there. Nothing. I mean it."

"Look," she made one last stab at reasoning with him as she was being stuffed into the back of an unmarked SUV. The white frothy wedding dress filled the entire seat, and she had to punch it down. "Please don't bother following me. You can't be my attorney. I have no money to pay your fee, and even if I did, I—"

"Don't worry about the fee," he responded with a dismissive gesture.

Uh-huh. A girl didn't need a telescope to see exactly where this was going. "And I don't pay in kind!" she yelled just before the door slammed.

He grinned at her through the window. And had the audacity to wink.

She groaned, closed her eyes and sank down in the seat. Swell. Just freaking swell. Broke. Fired. Arrested by the FBI. And pimped out to the city's most charming keg of sexual dynamite.

What the hell else could go wrong today?

Special Agent Lex Duncan was being a real pismire.

Conner folded his hands in front of himself to keep from decking the jerk. They were standing in the observation room attached to interrogation out at the FBI's main Las Vegas field station. Vera was sitting at a table on the other side of the one-way mirror, looking tired, vulnerable and all but defeated. She hadn't started crying yet, but Conner felt instinctively she was close. Very close. Duncan had been interrogating her hard for over two hours, asking the same questions again and again. He hadn't even let her change out of that sexy breakaway bridal gown into the jeans and T-shirt Conner'd brought for her along with her purse from the dressing room. Pure intimidation. The bastard.

"Listen to me. She's not involved," he told Duncan for the dozenth time. He wasn't sure when he'd started being a true believer, but he was now firmly in the Vera-isn't-involved-in-the-ring-heist-*or*-Candace's-murder camp. In fact, he was pretty convinced she wasn't guilty of a damn thing, other than a crapload of bad luck.

"And you know this how?" Duncan asked, brow raised.

"It's *my* family's damn ring, and my own murdered cousin we're talking about. Not to mention possibly the same person nearly bringing down a theater scaffold on my other cousin Silver. Don't you think I want the guilty party or parties caught and fried?" he asked heatedly.

He and Candace might not have gotten along all that well, but she was still family. He'd see the killer hanged by his balls, no doubt about it. "But I want the *right* person caught and punished. Vera Mancuso is a victim of her half sister's bad judgment. Nothing more."

Duncan pushed out a breath. "Okay. Just for sake of argument, say I agree with you. My problem is, the stolen evidence was right on her finger."

"And she explained how it got there. About fifty times. I, for one, believe her story."

"So, what, I'm supposed to release her just because *you* have a damn hunch? Or more likely, have the hots for her and want to impress her with your prowess…as her attorney?"

Conner clamped his teeth. Okay, he might have the hots for Vera, but that would have ended abruptly if he'd still had the least doubt she was part of either the ring's theft or his cousin's murder. And, yeah, maybe he didn't have any real solid reason to believe that, but there you go. A man had to trust his gut instincts. Especially if he was a lawyer.

"Yeah," he said evenly. "Just release her."

Duncan started to shake his head. "No can do."

"I have an idea," Conner said, thinking fast. "We can use her. To get her sister. That's who you really want to question about the ring."

Duncan exhaled. "I'm listening."

"Darla trusts her. She gave Vera the Tears of the Quetzal for safekeeping. Believe me, she'll be back for it."

"And?"

"And when she shows up, I'll call you and you can come arrest her. You can get to the real truth. The *real* perps."

Duncan briefly considered. "Even if I went along with this, what makes you think Ms. Mancuso will let you stick around that long?"

Conner shrugged modestly. "I'm not without my charms."

The FBI agent's eyes rolled. "And yet, she keeps telling me you're *not* her lawyer. Besides, wouldn't your representing her be a conflict of interest?"

"Not if she's innocent."

And, damn, she really did look innocent sitting there in that bleak, gray interrogation room, holding back her tears by a thread. Innocent, and incredibly brave. While Duncan questioned her, Conner'd had his legal assistant do a quick workup on Vera Mancuso. Her background had been far from easy. He'd been all wrong about her relationship with her biological father, Maximillian St. Giles. The man didn't want to know her, was openly hostile to his illegitimate daughter and kept her existence deep in the closet. The scumbag.

Duncan raked a hand through his hair. "I don't know if you're aware of this, but the FBI is not in charge of your cousin's murder case. That's strictly Metro at this point."

Conner glanced at him in surprise. "Then why didn't *they* arrest Vera?"

"Because of that ring. My current investigation is a series of high-end interstate jewelry robberies for which Darla St. Giles is a prime suspect, along with a couple of her friends. Possibly even a family member," he added pointedly. "I got a tip from an informant that Darla was seen entering the Diamond Lounge, so we closed in. I thought she might be fencing some of her stolen goods. The manager there's had some illegal dealings in the past."

"So when you saw Vera wearing the Quetzal…"

"I recognized it right away. And she looks enough like Ms. St. Giles to have fooled me for a minute. I have good reason to believe Darla's gang had targeted the Rothchild diamond on the night your cousin was killed. You seeing her with that phony cop at the police station, and the ring showing up in her half sister's possession are both pretty strong evidence to connect her to the theft."

"But what about the phony cop I saw her with?" Conner said. "And didn't you say Luke Montgomery's new wife was there at the casino the night of Candace's murder, and was later stalked by someone wanting the ring?"

Duncan crossed his arms. "All true. But even if I agree with you in theory, my hands are tied. Until Darla is in custody and corroborates Ms. Mancuso's story, and Vera's alibi is checked out, I'd be insane to let the only suspect I have go free."

Conner stuck his hands in his pockets. "Okay, I see your point. Still, keeping Vera in custody is probably the best way to drive Darla so far into hiding you'll never find her. She certainly has the means to disappear for a good long time if she feels threatened."

"So what do you propose I do?"

"Let Vera out on bail. I'll pay it. Then we use her as bait, like I suggested."

Both of them turned to contemplate Vera through the mirrored window. She'd put her head down on the Formica table and buried her face in her arms. Had she finally broken down? Conner's heart squeezed in sympathy.

"If I agree to this crazy scheme," Duncan finally said, "I'd want something in return."

"Like what?" Conner asked.

"I'd want your help figuring out exactly who is part of the jewel theft ring I'm investigating. You move in the same social circles as Darla St. Giles. You go to the same parties and charity events, know the same people. I'd want you to nose around, ask questions. Narrow down my list of suspects." He turned to look Conner in the eye. "Help LVMPD figure out if your cousin's death was a jewel robbery gone bad, or something else entirely."

Conner raised his brows. "Kind of a tall order, isn't it?"

"That's the deal. Take it or leave it."

"Fine." Obviously, Vera wasn't going to get a better offer. Nor was he. "I'll take it."

Chapter 5

They were letting her go.

Vera couldn't quite believe it. But she wasn't about to question her good luck.

Right up until the devil's Agent Lex Luthor—whose name actually turned out to be Duncan—said to her as he handed over her bag of belongings, "Your attorney, Mr. Rothchild, has posted your bail and personally vouched for your whereabouts until the arraignment. As a condition of your release, you must agree to check in with him at least three times a day."

She stopped dead. "You can't be serious."

"Bear in mind you are a potential murder suspect, Ms. Mancuso," the agent said sternly. "Personally, I'm opposed to releasing you at all, but the Rothchild name wields a lot of influence—"

She handed him back her bag. "Forget it. If that's a requirement, I'll stay arrested, thanks."

The FBI guy's jaw dropped. "Excuse me?"

"No one ever listens to me. I've told you over and over, he's *not* my—"

"Actually, he is." Duncan held up a paper. "Court appointed. I have the order here if you need proof."

She blinked. Oh, for crying out loud. The man was totally relentless. "Let me see that."

It didn't matter that for some mysterious reason she found the loathsome Conner Rothchild so incredibly, toe-curlingly sexy that every time she looked at him she practically melted into a limp noodle at his feet. Or that the whole time he'd sat in the audience at the Diamond Lounge—*before* she knew who he was—she'd girlishly pretended he was the only man in the whole room, and danced for him alone. When had *that* ever happened before? With any man? Never, that's when.

But even so. She wasn't about to trade sex for lawyering. Or anything, for that matter. She knew what he must have in mind, and she wanted none of it. Well. Not like that, anyway. She probably wouldn't say no under other circumstances or if he were anyone else. But selling herself? No way. Regardless of how mouthwateringly and wrongly tempting he was. And how much she really wanted to find out what it would be like to lie under his ripped, athletic body and—

Oh, no. Banish *that* thought.

She looked over the paper that Duncan had handed her. Sure enough, it was a one-paragraph court order appointing Conner as her legal counsel.

What. Ever.

At least she didn't have to pay him. *Or* owe him in any other way. That was a huge relief.

But did she want to have to check in with Mr. Cutthroat Playboy Attorney three times a day like she was one of his low-life parolees? Heck, no.

"Have you ever been to prison, Ms. Mancuso?" the federal agent asked. Apparently mind reading was part of the FBI arsenal.

"Of course not."

"Trust me, you wouldn't enjoy it." He took back the paper and slid it into her file. "Mr. Rothchild seems like a decent attorney. Let him help you."

She regarded him. "Special Agent Duncan, if I were your little sister, would you be saying the same thing?"

He gazed back steadily. "If you were my little sister, you wouldn't be in this mess, and you sure as hell wouldn't be stripping for a living. You might think about what kind of future you want for yourself before choosing sides, Ms. Mancuso."

With that, he put her bag of belongings back in her hand, took her arm and hauled her down the hall and out into the reception area where Conner Rothchild was waiting.

Why, the arrogant bastard! She'd never been so—

"Everything okay?" Conner asked, eyeing the two of them. Vera was so mad she didn't trust herself to answer. Who knew what would come flying out of her mouth, landing her in even worse trouble?

"Just peachy," Duncan said, and unceremoniously handed her arm over to Conner, like a recalcitrant child turned over to her father for disciplining. "Make sure you know where she is at all times, Rothchild. If I were you, I wouldn't let her out of your sight."

"I'm sure we'll come to an understanding," Conner said, his face registering wary surprise.

"Just don't forget our agreement," Duncan admonished him, then without another word, he turned and stalked off.

"Okay, then," Conner said when he was gone. "What was *that* all about?"

She didn't know why she was so upset. This sort of thing

happened all the time, whenever anyone outside the business found out what she did for a living. She could call herself an exotic dancer all she liked. To everyone else she'd always be a stripper. She should be used to the disdain by now. But it still hurt every darn time.

"He doesn't approve of me," she muttered.

The lawyer frowned. "He said that?"

Some people could be so righteous and judgmental. They had no clue about the vicious cycle of poverty a woman could so easily fall into. She was one of the lucky ones who'd found a way out. Or at least a way to stay above water.

She sighed. *Get over it, girl.* "No. He said I should trust you."

"Well, you should," Conner said, brows furrowing. He glanced after the FBI agent. "Listen, if he said anything inappropriate, I'll go back in there and—"

"No, please—" She reached out to stop him…and got the shock of her life. The second she touched him, a spill of tingling pleasure coursed from her fingers—her *ring* finger to be exact—down her arm and through her torso, straight to her center.

She gasped.

He looked just as stunned.

She jerked her hand back. Too late. A flood of emotions washed through her. Not just physical desire, though God knew that came through strong and clear, but also a disconcerting mix of tenderness and trust. And…a kind of soul-deep recognition. That this man was *her* man. The man she'd been waiting for all her life. Her Prince Charming.

She swallowed heavily. Okay, so yikes. It was official. She'd totally lost her mind.

If only he'd stop staring at her like that. Like she had two heads or something.

"I'll take you home," he said abruptly.

"No," she said. "I can take a cab."

"Don't be ridiculous."

He put a hand to the small of her back and ushered her out the front entrance and into the night nearly as quickly as Duncan had dragged her through the field office's brightly lit inner corridors. Conner must have changed his mind about her, too. That was quick. Maybe that jolt knocked some sense into him. Too bad it hadn't for her. More like the opposite. He kept getting more and more attractive every minute that went by.

The shimmering heat of the Las Vegas nighttime enveloped her as she stepped into it, calming as always. It tamed the shivering in her chest and limbs. Filled her lungs with sage-scented comfort, like on long-ago evenings spent in her mama's lap in an old secondhand rocker in a tiny patch of garden behind their mobile home.

"Please," she said when they hit the parking lot. "Slow down. These shoes aren't really meant for walking in." Or maybe her knees still needed to recover from that Prince Charming nonsense.

He halted, glancing down at her four-inch-heeled glass slippers, which sparkled back at him in the reflected streetlamps.

Ah, jeez. The symbolism was just too damn perfect. She felt herself going beet red in embarrassment.

"Really, th-thanks for your assistance," she stammered, "but I'd prefer to take a cab home."

She turned toward the fenced perimeter and the street beyond and realized with a sinking feeling that taxis would be few and far between in this neighborhood, even during daylight hours. And it must be three in the morning by now. She'd have to go back inside and have them call—

Suddenly she found herself swept up in Conner's arms, her wrist looped around his neck.

"Hey! What are you doing?"

"Kick them off."

"Huh?"

"The shoes. Lose them. They're ludicrous."

"And expensive! No way!"

He made a face. "Lord, you're stubborn."

She mirrored it right back. "God, you're obnoxious."

They glared at each other for a moment.

"Fine," Conner said. "Keep the damn shoes."

"Thank you, I will. Now if you'll please put me down."

He actually snorted at her. "Can't you just accept my help gracefully?"

Before she had a chance to respond, he was carrying her toward a midnight-blue convertible sports car sitting in the first slot of the parking lot. It was the most dazzling car she'd ever seen in her life. And totally intimidating. Low, sleek, catlike in grace and Transformer-like in technology. It had to have cost more than she earned in a year. Or two. His hand moved and a couple of beeps sounded. The two car doors rose up like the wings of a giant bird.

"Holy moly. What is this, the Batmobile?"

"No, a Mercedes-Benz SLR McLaren Roadster." He lowered her into the passenger seat. She sank down into the buttery leather and it hugged her backside like a lover spooning her body. Softly firm and enveloping. "You don't like it?"

"It's, um…" Luxurious. Flashy and unreasonably sexy, like its owner. Totally out of her league. Like its owner. "Nice."

"Nice, huh?" He gave her a lopsided grin as he dropped down to sit on his heels next to her car door. He pulled the seat belt over her lap, leaned over and fought with the airy poofs of her faux wedding dress for a moment finding the socket to snap it into.

She heard the click. But his arms stayed lost in the voluminous folds of the gossamer fabric. Almost like he was looking for something else. His fingers suddenly touched her legs. A shiver of unwilling excitement shimmered through her body. Under the white silk skirt she was still only wearing her thigh-high stockings and a G-string. If he wanted, he could slip his hands up under and touch her. For one crazy second she almost opened her legs to let him.

Good grief, what was *wrong* with her?

Instead, his hands glided down her calves. Slowly. Deliberately. As though he were memorizing every inch of the descent. Her heart pounded. When he reached her ankles he paused, then wrapped his fingers around her crystalline shoes and tugged them off.

With a flick of his wrist they sailed into the narrow space behind the driver's seat. "There. That's better."

She couldn't decide if she felt more outraged, or breathlessly aroused. "Do you manhandle all your clients like this, Mr. Rothchild?"

"Only the ones who need handling," he said with a completely unrepentant smile. He came around and slid behind the wheel. "And it's Conner."

"Not if you're my lawyer, it isn't."

"What, because I'm your attorney we can't be friends?"

She searched his eyes. Which were the exact color of the morning desert, she noticed for the first time. A morning desert in the springtime, when the landscape was at its most beautiful. Falcon brown with flecks of rich green. Surrounded by long, dark lashes, and a sensual tilt to arched brows that matched his movie-star-perfect brown hair.

He was dazzling.

And so colossally out of her universe it made her stomach do crazy somersaults.

His smile widened. "I'll take that as a yes, we can."

Huh?

The engine revved and they took off, were waved through the FBI guard post and drove out onto the street. As they gained speed, the billowing skirt of the wedding dress fluttered up around her shoulders, filling the open convertible.

The night was dark and desert-warm, the winking lights of the Strip just ahead. Rusty mountains ringed the city, sometimes a cozy cocoon that circled the city in its own private haven, sometimes menacing omnipresent watchers of the multitude of sins that went down there in Vegas.

But for now, the bright lights reigned supreme, shiny and colorful, lending the city its famous carnival atmosphere.

As soon as they reached downtown, it started—the honking horns and the shouts and thumbs-up. Tourists waved and whistled. Obviously everyone thought she and Conner were newlyweds, coming straight from some outlandish Las Vegas wedding chapel with a preacher dressed as Elvis or some other zany impersonator.

She wanted to sink right through the soft leather seat and disappear forever. "Damn. I should have changed clothes," she said, chagrined. "Sorry."

Conner waved back to a blue-haired old lady walking with an equally old guy in a pair of screamingly loud plaid shorts. "Don't be. Haven't had this much fun since I drove the UNLV homecoming queen around the football field at halftime."

Figured he did that.

Probably dated her, too.

Probably last year.

Damn.

"How old are you, anyway?" she asked, suddenly irrationally, absurdly and completely inappropriately jealous.

The flashing neon lights of the Strip glinted back at her from his eyes as he smiled. "Thirty-three. You?"

"Twenty-four." Her mouth turned down. "Obviously a little too old for you."

He chuckled. "More like a little too young. I generally prefer my women older, more experienced. Fewer misunderstandings that way."

Red alert, girl. Well. At least he was honest about it. "I'm sure."

"That's a bad thing?"

She sank farther into the seat and scowled. "Not at all. Very considerate of you not to break all those young, impressionable hearts flinging themselves at you. I suspect you could do some genuine damage."

"Hmm. Sounds like you've had yours broken by some insensitive older guy."

The lawyer was too perceptive by half. She shrugged as casually as she could manage. Her heart was none of his damned business.

"I apologize on behalf of all older men," he said. "The jerk must have been a real idiot."

"Which one?" she muttered.

"Ouch." Somehow his hand found hers in the folds of her dress and squeezed it. "Every last one of them."

Their eyes met, and again that weird feeling sifted through her. Part longing, part relief, part visceral hope.

Totally insane.

She pulled her hand away. As seductions went, his technique was pretty low-key. But pretty darn effective. And very dangerous. Already she was wondering what it would feel like to be curled up in his arms, warm and replete after making love to him. To have those amazing feelings of tender belonging she'd gotten just a glimpse of, as they lay skin-to-skin and…

And heaven help her.

He stopped at the red light at Flamingo Road, just up the block from the faux Eiffel Tower. A clutch of tipsy tourists tumbled across the street in front of them. Naturally, the whole group noticed her white dress and started to cheer and clap.

"Kiss the bride!" one of them shouted. Soon they were all whistling and yelling, "Kiss her! Kiss her!"

He turned to grin at her.

Oh. No.

"Don't you dare even *think* ab—"

But his lips were already on hers. Warm. Firm. Tasting of sin and forever. She sucked in a breath of shock as his tongue touched hers, and he took the opening in bold invitation. His hand slid behind her neck and tugged her closer. His other arm banded around her, pulling her upper body tight against him. His tongue invaded her mouth, his fingers held her fast for a deep, lingering kiss the likes of which she'd never, ever experienced.

Oh. No.

The cheers of the onlookers faded as the world around them spun away. Wow. The man could *really* kiss. She was light-headed, dizzy with the taste of him and the feel of his body so close to hers. She couldn't help but want more. She wanted to crawl up into his lap and hold him tight and never let him go.

All too soon his lips lifted and the blaring of car horns and wolf whistles all around invaded her consciousness. She moaned. Unsure if it was the loss of his nearness or the reality of her immense stupidity that made the desperate sound escape her throat.

Oh, what had she done?

And, damn it, now he had that look on his face again. Like she was some kind of apparition or two-headed monster he couldn't quite believe he'd just kissed.

Nope, she sighed, as a slash of hurt ripped her heart once

again. Nothing quite so dramatic. Just an ordinary exotic dancer...make that *stripper*...from the wrong side of the tracks.

Way to go, Mancuso.

He revved the engine, and the car leaped forward. It took about three excruciating minutes to reach her gated apartment complex, where he zoomed into the underground garage and squealed into her parking spot. She was still too flustered and mortified to wonder how he'd known her address—or which slot was hers. He'd only opened his mouth again to confirm that she still lived with Darla. He shut off the engine and the headlights. The dim overhead garage fluorescents flickered and hummed.

She struggled to get the seat belt unfastened but naturally her fingers refused to work. Mentally she scrambled to prepare her Don't-Worry-I've-Already-Forgotten-It-Happened speech when he came around, reached in and unsnapped the belt. Then once again she was swept up in his arms.

"Conner!" she squeaked, clutching her bag of belongings to her chest uncertainly. "I can walk by myself!"

"Not with those ridiculous shoes, you can't. Pure instruments of torture." He looked down at her, an inscrutable look on his face. "Believe it or not, I *am* a gentleman."

His tempting, downturned mouth was dangerously close.

No.

No.

No.

The man had horrified himself by kissing her. Clearly, he didn't want her. She was *so* not going to embarrass herself even further.

He saved her the decision by looking away. And strode through the dark garage toward the lighted elevator without giving her a chance to protest. Her dress billowed. Her heart thundered. He didn't look like he wanted to seduce her. He looked like he wanted to devour her alive. And not in a good way.

The elevator whooshed open, and he carried her into it. He pressed the correct button for her floor—the penthouse, of course. Nothing but the best for Darla.

Darla, who wouldn't be home to run interference for her tonight. Was that why he'd asked?

Oh, great.

She was all on her own. To fend off this overpowering attraction for the most inappropriate man alive. Or…to let him in to break her heart.

She had to get a grip. Fast.

She was just under some weird, arrest-induced erotic spell. This wasn't like her. Not at all. She didn't do flings, or men she'd just met. She didn't even do men she knew well. How could she consider making such a fool of herself over this one who obviously didn't—

"Key," he broke into her chaotic thoughts before they reached the top floor. You couldn't get off at the penthouse without a special key. Naturally, he'd know that.

She juggled her purse out from the bag. Except—

"This isn't my purse. It's Darla's." Her sister must have grabbed the wrong one in her haste to get out of the club.

"Does she have a key?" he asked, his voice deep and dark. Something in his tone sent a shiver tripping down her spine.

She looked up at him. His eyes were smoldering. She faltered and dropped the belongings bag, but managed to hang on to the purse. What was going on here?

"Yes," she stammered, fumbling through its contents. "I—I th-think so."

"Let me have it."

Her pulse jumped a mile. "Conner," she managed, digging out the key and handing it to him. "You're not planning to come in, are you?"

"What do you think?"

He really didn't want to know what she was thinking…

"Please. This is really not a good idea."

"No damn kidding," he shot back. But then his mouth was on hers and she couldn't turn him away if her life depended on it. She moaned in surprise, opening herself to him, and wound her arms around his neck. This was *so* not a good idea. He swung her down so she was sitting on his forearm, and her legs instinctively wrapped around his waist.

The elevator doors opened, and they kissed madly, all the way across the square marble foyer to the penthouse entrance. Her back slammed up against it, and a moment later the door swung open and he followed the solid wood around with her, keeping her back pressed up to it as he devoured her mouth.

The sound of Velcro ripping apart was followed by a whoosh of cool air on her legs and bottom. A billow of white floated to the floor. Another rip and her breakaway top joined it. He groaned, pulling away to look at her spilling out of her lace corset, then his hands found her bare flesh.

They kissed and kissed, and he touched her everywhere. They ground their bodies together in a frenzy of desire. His fingers slid between her legs and parted her blossoming folds. She cried out as he found the center of her need and touched her there.

"That's right, give it to me," he whispered into her mouth. His fingers circled, driving a moan from her. "I want it all."

"Conner," she cried. "Please, I— Nhh…"

It was no use. He was too skilled, too perfect, and she was too aroused to stop the tidal wave of pleasure that crashed over her. She arched, her body shuddering over the edge, and surrendered to the sensation.

He drew it out as long as it would go, playing her flesh like a professional gambler caressed his cards.

By the time he let her slide to her feet, she was trembling

so hard she could hardly see straight. So at first she didn't even notice.

But when he demanded huskily, "Where's your bedroom?" and they turned into the living room, both of them halted dead in their tracks.

The place was in a complete shambles.

"Omigod," she whispered, barely catching her breath.

Someone had broken in. And ransacked the apartment.

On the wall, big sloppy letters had been scrawled in bright red paint.

GIVE IT BACK BITCH OR YOU'LL DIE NEXT.

Chapter 6

Conner took one look at the destruction in front of him and instantly visions of Candace's murder scene slammed through his brain. The wreckage. Her pale face lying in a stain of blood.

Oh, no, please not another victim.

He grabbed Vera and whisked her back out the door and pushed her against the foyer wall.

"Don't move," he admonished as he whipped out his cell phone and Lex Duncan's card from his pocket. "Someone may still be in there." Like Darla. Sprawled dead on the floor as Candace had been. Though he hadn't seen any blood or body in the quick visual scan he'd done. Thank God.

Vera looked like a deer caught in the headlights. "Someone like who?" she asked in a strangled croak, grasping his suit jacket sleeve with both hands.

"Whoever did this," he answered, punching buttons on the phone and trying not to think about what he'd just done with those same fingers. What he'd been *about* to do with them. *Damn.*

"Duncan."

"It's Conner Rothchild. Vera and Darla's place has been broken into," he told the FBI agent. "It looks bad."

Duncan swore. "Darla?"

"Not here that I could see."

"Exit the apartment and wait for me outside," he ordered, then hung up.

"I don't understand," Vera said, her voice cracking. Her eyes filled as he pulled her fully into his arms. "Why would anyone write something that horrible on my wall? Give *what* back?"

"I'm not sure," he said. Though he knew damn well. Silver had received a nearly identical message scrawled on her mirror about being the next one to die—just before someone maliciously brought a scaffolding down on her head. That someone must still be after the Tears of the Quetzal. And didn't know it was now in FBI custody. Until the culprit was found, Vera could be in danger.

Conner gathered her up in his arms again, heading for the elevator. "Let's get you away from here."

For a second she looked like she wanted to object. But then she just put her arms around him and clung to him. Not in a sexual way—despite the fact that she was nearly naked and just moments ago had all but given herself to him—but like a frightened woman would hold a man who made her feel safe.

His stomach roiled into a clot of opposing emotions. Anger at whoever had done this. And a strange, completely alien sense of wanting to protect her from all harm.

Okay, that and a gnawing sense of panic.

Something was going on deep inside him, in his heart, that he did not understand. Did not need. Definitely did not want.

The elevator opened and he swept in, pushed the button for the ground floor.

"Vera," he said. "I know you didn't want me as your lawyer, but I'm hoping you trust me as a friend, after—" He stopped, suddenly feeling awkward. Damn. If not for the break-in, they'd be in bed by now, naked, and he'd be deep inside her. Making love. He was still aroused, still aching for relief. Still wanting her like she was the last woman on earth and he hadn't had sex for at least a decade.

He cleared his throat. "In light of…what happened between us, I'll be turning over your case to my assistant in the morning. Meanwhile, I hope you believe I have your interests as my top priority in this incident."

For once she didn't argue. She bit her lip and nodded. It obviously hadn't occurred to her that her sister might be inside hurt—or worse. He didn't intend to enlighten her. But there were also other issues at hand.

"Here's the thing. The FBI is on its way. Vera, think hard. If there's anything, any reason at all, they shouldn't go into your apartment, you need to tell me now. Before they arrive."

She gazed up at him, her green eyes wide and uncomprehending. Man, she was guileless. Did that mean his instincts were right about her?

"You mean…like drugs or something?" she asked.

Again he cleared his throat, not understanding why it was so damn important to him that she be innocent. "For example, yeah."

She continued to worry her lip. "Um. Darla might not want them in her room. There could be…some illegal substances."

He nodded. No shock there. "They'll probably look the other way on that, this time. Anything else?"

"Like…?"

"Did Duncan tell you any of his suspicions about your sister?" he asked carefully.

"Suspicions of what?"

Okay, apparently not. "I'm not really sure how much I should be revealing to you, but since you're still my client, I feel I should be up-front and warn you. That ring you were wearing isn't the only thing Darla is suspected of stealing. There may be more."

"Stolen jewelry?" she asked, her jaw dropping. "That's not possible. Darla is rich! An heiress. Why would she ever…" Vera's words trickled to a stop.

He gazed down at her. "Could it be true? Because if the FBI finds stolen goods in your apartment, it could get really ugly."

"I don't know," she said worriedly. "Really. I wouldn't have thought so, but…Darla is… Well, sometimes she gets these crazy ideas. For thrills, she says. Or to get back at our father. For his neglect. I suppose…" She looked miserable. "I suppose it could be true. I just don't know. But I don't think anything would be kept here. I would know."

"Fair enough." The elevator doors opened and suddenly he remembered what she was wearing…or rather, *not* wearing. He was about to slip off his jacket to give her when he realized the bag of belongings she'd dropped on the ride up was still lying in the corner of the elevator.

He grabbed it and pressed it into her hands. "Here. Better get dressed before someone sees you."

"Oh, jeez," she said, glancing down at herself. "Not exactly street attire."

More's the pity. He admired how she was so totally comfortable in her own bare skin. The women he knew would be dying of embarrassment to be seen like this in public, every last one, convinced their bodies were too fat or too skinny or had some other terrible imagined flaw, making them unduly

self-conscious. Women could have such hang-ups about their
self-image. It was refreshing to be around one who so obviously liked how she looked.

She quickly pulled on the jeans and T-shirt. He forced
himself to concentrate. "You stay down here in the lobby and
wait for Duncan. I'll go back to the apartment and take a quick
look around. If there's anything that shouldn't be found, I'll
deny him permission to search there. Okay?"

Fear leaped into her eyes. "You're leaving me alone? Why
can't I go with you?"

"Just in case," he said, and she looked even more
panicked. "Don't worry, you'll be fine. Duncan will get here
in a few minutes." Unable to help himself, he bent down and
kissed her. The taste of her lips swirled on his tongue, and a
painful ache of arousal swept through him again. *Too good.*
He pulled away.

"Conner, wait," she began. She glanced down at his mouth,
and then his body, and something shifted in her expression.
Uh-oh, trouble ahead. "I, um, don't—"

He put a finger to her lips. "Shh. We'll talk later, all right?
I've got to go up."

She nodded reluctantly. "What if someone's up there with
a gun?" she asked nervously.

"Anyone's probably long gone," he assured her, then led
her out of the elevator, gave her a last kiss and got back on.

Watching him unhappily, she wrapped her arms around her
middle. "Please, be careful."

He smiled, touched by the sincere worry in her eyes.
"Count on it."

Once up in the apartment, he was able to give the whole
penthouse a cursory search before the FBI showed up. No
Darla, thank heaven. Nothing else out of the ordinary was
visible in the piles of debris left by the break-in or in any of

the bedrooms, either, so granting Duncan and his CSI techs access would not compromise his client.

He took one last look around. If the place hadn't been such a mess, it would have been really nice. If nothing else, Darla had good taste. At least in interior decorating. In friends and lifestyle, maybe not so much.

Of course, an exotic dancer would normally be included in his general condemnation. In the Las Vegas legal community, aside from his take-no-prisoners ruthlessness in the courtroom, Conner was known for a generous pro bono policy toward the homeless, drug addicts and sex workers. But he'd never considered them his equals in any sense of the word. His family would disown him if they even suspected he was considering a serious liaison with a stripper...even if she was the illegitimate daughter of billionaire Maximillian St. Giles.

Hell, *especially* if she was the illegitimate daughter of Maximillian St. Giles. Or any other woman not in his social class or better. The key word there was *illegitimate*. His father had given Uncle Harold a lifetime of grief for marrying beneath him. More than once. Conner had no intention of repeating that mistake and lowering his father's respect for him. Or giving his blue-blood family any reason to question Conner's loyalty to their highbrow ideals, even if he thought they were at times silly and sometimes destructive.

He'd seen firsthand what those kind of elitist notions could do to families. Look at Candace. He was convinced she'd still be alive today if she hadn't been summarily dismissed from the family fold after marrying Jack Cortland, the druggie rock-star boy. Those two poor kids of hers. God only knew what would become of them without the support of family, with only a questionable father to raise them, stuck out on some ranch in the middle of nowhere.

Anyway. Under all the broken glassware and china, disheveled books and shelf items and knife-slit, unstuffed cushions and furniture, Conner recognized a beautiful living space, subtly sophisticated and timelessly chic. He didn't know why that surprised him, but it did. Pleasantly so. *Some* of Darla's wealthy upbringing must have rubbed off on her, after all.

He gave a wry sigh. That probably explained why she'd gone after the Tears of the Quetzal. The ring was the classiest piece of jewelry he'd ever laid eyes on. And now it had passed from Vera's finger straight into FBI custody. Forget about retrieving it any time soon. *That* place was like Fort Knox. Uncle Harold was not going to be pleased.

The sound of the elevator approaching pulled Conner back to the situation at hand. He went out to the foyer and met Special Agent Duncan as he exited the lift, followed by two other men in white jumpsuits carrying CSI cases. Vera popped out like a nervous jack-in-the-box.

"Are you okay?" she asked him before Duncan could open his mouth. "Did you see anyone? Any more messages written on the walls? Talk to me!"

"Whoa, slow down," he admonished gently and put an arm around her shoulder. "No more graffiti. No sign of the intruders," he told Duncan, and gave a surreptitious shake of his head at the agent's silent query about Darla.

Duncan looked relieved, then gave Conner's protective arm a brief, disapproving frown.

"Not that it's any of your business," Conner said to stave off any comments, "but I'm turning over Vera's case to an associate so there's no conflict of interest."

Duncan's frown deepened as he signaled the CSI techs to proceed into the penthouse to get started. "That wasn't part of our deal," he said.

"What deal?" Vera asked.

"Nothing's changed," Conner assured him. "Can we just—"

"What deal?" Vera asked again, more insistently. She turned under his arm to look up at him.

"Never mind—"

Duncan addressed her. "For your release."

"What about it?" she asked, eyes narrowing.

Damn. *So* not good.

"Rothchild agreed to help us bring Darla St. Giles into custody. He promised to call us when she contacts you."

Ah, hell.

Shock went through her expression. She stepped away from him angrily. "Oh, really. What makes you think she'll contact me? And even if she does, what makes you think I'll tell you? How dare you! What would make you agree to such a thing?" Her voice was getting louder and louder.

"Vera, please believe me, it was for your own good."

"My own *good?*" she spat out. "Are you *kidding* me? Betraying my sister?"

"He's right," Duncan interjected stonily. "You were apprehended with the Rothchild's diamond on your finger. Until it can be established exactly how it got there, *you* are our—"

"Wait just a cotton-picking minute!" Her expression went even more furious. She glared at Conner. "The *Rothchild's* diamond? That was *your* ring?"

He was in *such* deep trouble. "My family's, yes. But—"

She looked like he had slapped her across the face. Hard. "And you were going to tell me this little detail *when?*"

"Vera, who the ring belongs to is not what's important here."

"My God, Conner! If *that's* not a conflict of interest, I don't know what is! And you expect me to trust you? What else are you lying to me about?"

It was his turn to be indignant. "That's not fair. I never lied to you."

"I may not be some rich, fancy-schmancy lawyer, but even I know what lying by omission means," she ground out. "And to think I—" Her mouth snapped shut, and she squeezed her eyes closed.

He fisted his hands on his hips, ignoring the all-too-personal dig. "Do you recall in the club when I said I had information about your sister? I was going to tell you then, but was interrupted when…let's see…oh, yeah, you got *arrested!*"

"Speaking of which." Duncan stepped between them. "Why exactly were you at the Diamond Lounge in the first place, Rothchild? Quite a coincidence, wouldn't you say?" The FBI agent's tone was neutral, but his meaning was unmistakable.

Conner tamped down on his quickly rising hackles. Forced himself into composed, professional lawyer mode. "Are you by any chance asking me for an alibi?" he asked coolly. "For this?" He swept a hand toward the mess in the apartment.

Duncan lifted a shoulder. "It occurs to me that a Rothchild would have the strongest motive to search Miss St. Giles's home. Missing family heirloom, and all. And you being convinced she stole it." He looked smug. "It would also explain your presence at the Diamond Lounge. You didn't find the ring when you searched the apartment and Darla had disappeared, so you took a chance her sister might know where she went."

Damn. It all sounded *far* too plausible.

Except it was all bull, and Duncan knew it. They both knew whoever did this was the same person who'd stalked and almost killed Silver. And possibly Candace. But, okay, he played along.

"Just one thing wrong with your theory," Conner said evenly. "I had no idea Darla had a sister. Oh, and the fact that I *do* have an alibi. I was working another case. The Parker case, if you want to call my firm. I spent the whole afternoon asking questions of the dancers up and down the Strip. At least a couple hundred witnesses, plus video surveillance, I'm sure. The Diamond Lounge was my next stop." He held up a hand. "And, yes, I do have a checked-off list to prove it. Thank you. Thank you very much."

At least Duncan cracked a smile. Vera was still glaring at Conner.

"Okay," Duncan said. "I'll get that checked out, but I believe you're telling the truth. Meanwhile, I still have the problem of Ms. Mancuso. Because if *you* didn't do the break-in…"

Conner nodded. "It was most likely the same guy who's been after the ring since it disappeared from Candace's hand the night she died."

Duncan nodded, too. "A thief whom Darla seems to have double-crossed. And since the FBI now has the ring in its custody—"

"He didn't find it in his search. And since Darla has disappeared—"

"He'll be looking for Ms. Mancuso next, thinking she knows where to find her sister, and therefore the ring."

Vera had been watching the back-and-forth like a spectator at a tennis match, but now she finally caught on with a gasp. "Are you saying…I could be in danger?"

"Did you *read* the message he left on the wall?" Conner queried.

"This man has already gone on the attack for the ring," Duncan said. "Don't take any chances with your safety."

"So what am I supposed to do?"

"Ms. Mancuso was released into your recognizance, Rothchild." Duncan turned to remind him. "And the terms of her bail still stand. But if you prefer, I'll take her back into custody. I can't risk losing my only suspect. In any manner."

"What? Hold on!" Vera exclaimed. "His recognizance or police custody? There has to be a door number three here."

"I respect your dilemma, Ms. Mancuso," the agent said. "But the only reason you are not in a cell right now is because of Mr. Rothchild's spotless reputation as an attorney and his formidable social standing in the community. I've already stretched the law as far as I'm willing to go in that regard. He stays with you or you come with me."

There was a pregnant pause, the silence in the marble foyer only broken by the sounds of the CSI techs' cameras clicking inside the apartment.

"Fine," she said at length, but obviously mad as a hornet. "I'll move a futon for him out into the vestibule." She rounded on Conner. "You can set it up in front of the elevator so there's no way I—or anyone else—can slip past—"

His brows shot up. *Excuse me?* He shoved aside the insult. "You *want* to stay in a ransacked apartment?"

"Like I have a choice?" she fired back.

"Sorry," Duncan interrupted. "Not possible. No one's allowed into the apartment until the techs are finished processing for trace and fingerprints. That'll take at least a few hours."

"She'll stay at my place," Conner said through clamped teeth, ready to strangle the woman. A freakin' futon? He didn't *think* so.

She opened her mouth to protest but he nipped it. "I have plenty of room. And can provide an armed guard," he added pointedly.

"Good," Duncan said, passing Conner his notebook. "Write down the address and phone number."

Almost sputtering, she crossed her arms over her ample chest. Sending an untimely reminder through his body that he was still more than half-aroused. But her vehement, "I am *not* going anywhere with you," jerked him right out of his momentary hormonal stupor.

Which probably made him point out more sharply than

strictly necessary, "I happen to know you have no money and nowhere else to go." He ignored her gasp and went on, "And if you think I'm paying for a hotel when I have ten bedrooms sitting empty at my house, you're dead wrong."

She blinked and her eyes shuttered. He realized too late he'd reacted like a defense attorney, trampling her objections like a charging rhino. And he'd hurt her.

Well, too damn bad. She'd hurt him first.

He pushed out a calming breath, chagrined at his childish outburst.

God.

Was he actually whining like a two-year-old?

"I'm sorry," he said gruffly. "That was a thoughtless and unnecessary remark. But the reality is, it's my house or jail."

She looked like a Nile cat chased into a tree by that charging rhino. Angry. Cornered. But undefeated. "In that case," she said with chin held high, "I'll take jail."

Chapter 7

Vera stared up at the stunning mansion in front of her.

Holy mackerel.

The rising sun was just peeking over the desert horizon, spreading a magical spill of golden light over the soft coral-colored adobe walls and arches of the Southwest-inspired manor house and surrounding lush green lawns and gardens.

"You live here?" she asked her jailer. *"Alone?"*

They were the first words she'd spoken to Conner Biggest-Bully-in-the-Universe Rothchild since she'd grudgingly hunched into the passenger seat of his ridiculously ostentatious car to be driven here. To his house. Where he lived.

How she'd let herself get talked into going *anywhere* with the lying jerk, let alone his own home, she'd never know.

Okay, not true. It was the work of the usual catch-22: absence of money, family or personal influence.

Story of her life.

"Alone, yes. But I have a lot of friends who visit," he answered her rhetorical question.

She just bet he did.

Never mind that ninety-eight percent of the women in the state of Nevada would kill to take her place. Or that *Las Vegas Magazine*'s official Most Eligible Bachelor was undoubtedly the sexiest, most attractive man breathing on this earth. Vera knew very well when she was outclassed, outplayed and miles out of her comfort zone. About ten-and-a-half miles to be exact—the distance between the mobile home park where she'd grown up and Conner Rothchild's sprawling, multimillion-dollar neighborhood.

No, Vera Mancuso had no freaking business being in this place, with this man.

"Must be nice," she responded as he drove through the ten-foot-tall iron security gate, which closed automatically behind the car. "And you have a lot of family, too, from what I hear. Quite the Las Vegas dynasty, the Rothchilds."

"Don't believe everything you read in the tabloids," he said, pulling to a stop under the entry's porte cochere.

"I don't," she assured him. "My information comes straight from the horse's mouth."

"Oh?" He gave her a mildly curious hike of an eyebrow as he opened the car door for her and helped her out.

"Darla was good friends with your cousins Candace and Silver. I still have lunch with Silver occasionally."

"Ah."

She stopped suddenly and turned back to his car. Before leaving the apartment, the CSI techs had packed her a small overnight bag, including a pair of flip-flops, but she needed her stage shoes for work tonight. They were still behind the seat where he'd tossed them back at FBI headquarters. "I'd like my shoes back, please. From last night."

"Of course." He leaned over the side of the car to fish them out.

Oh, boy.

His suit pants stretched over his tight backside, revealing every luscious dip and muscle of that tasty bit of anatomy. She had to stuff her hands under her armpits to keep from touching.

He handed her the glasslike shoes with a wry smile. "Don't lose one, Cinderella," he teased.

She made a face and snatched them from his hand. "You know, she talked about you all the time. Your cousin Candace."

"Did she, now." He took her overnight bag and led her up the mansion's sweeping front steps.

"She didn't like you very much."

"Now there's a shock." He did something with his key chain, and the ornately carved entry door swung open.

"She said you're mean, stubborn and ruthless and will do anything to get your clients off."

"Never a good thing in a lawyer," he said dryly. "After you."

She met his amused gaze, so strong and confident. Not to mention devoid of shadiness or deceit. With a sinking feeling she suddenly knew Candace was completely wrong about him.

She shouldn't be surprised. The rivalry between the Rothchild family cousins was legendary in Vegas, where each sought to outdo the other in glamour, media notoriety and wild living. Conner was no exception. He regularly figured in the gossip columns.

But Vera, of all people, was acutely aware that a public image did not always reflect the real person. Although she got along with Candace okay, and Darla adored her, Candace always did have a family ax to grind.

"Touché," Vera acknowledged, thinking just maybe *she'd* been wrong about Conner, too.

Not good. She did *not* want to like this man. Bad enough

she was so hopelessly attracted to him physically. How depressing would it be to have him turn out to be honorable and principled, too?

He ushered her in. "Welcome to my home."

Said the spider to the fly.

"Wow," she murmured, stepping into a stunning showplace of glossy, contemporary elegance. Clutching her shoes in her hand, she walked from the soaring foyer into a grand salon and did a slow three-sixty, totally awestruck. She'd decorated Darla's penthouse because when she'd moved in it had white walls and hotel furniture, and she'd been darn proud of the results. But this…this was utterly gorgeous. "Nice place," she managed.

He chuckled. "Apparently I live for nice."

Just then, an older woman in a fuzzy robe hurried into the room. "Oh, Mr. Conner, sir! I didn't expect you back tonight."

"Sorry to wake you so early, Hildy," he said in warm apology. "This is Vera. She'll be spending a few days with me."

Days?

"Certainly, sir."

The housekeeper didn't even bat an eyelash. Obviously not unusual for her employer to bring home women at the crack of dawn and announce they'd be spending more than one night chez Conner. Vera ground her teeth. Well, what did she expect?

"Will you be needing anything, sir? Coffee, or…?" Hildy asked.

"No, nothing, thanks. Just sleep." He handed her Vera's overnight bag, and the woman turned to go.

"Uh," Vera interjected before it was too late, "by 'with me' what Mr. Rothchild really meant was 'here.' As in 'here,' but in a separate bedroom. And 'here,' but as far away as possible from where he sleeps." She pasted on a smile.

This time Hildy did blink. And glanced at Conner for confirmation.

His mouth quirked. "As the lady says. You can put her in the guest cabana. That should be far enough away."

Hildy's eyes met hers for a split second, and Vera could have sworn the older lady was holding back a smirk. Vera wondered idly if she'd just joined the ranks of Too-Stupid-To-Live, or Girl Folk Hero....

"Oh, well. I need the sleep anyway," he said philosophically when the housekeeper had gone. "You'll like the cabana. It's very private out there. But don't get any bright ideas about escaping. I was serious about the armed guard. I've already called the security company."

She didn't know whether to be insulted or flattered. "Don't worry. I took Agent Duncan's warning to heart."

Before leaving the penthouse, the FBI man had cautioned her against going anywhere alone, or without Conner's permission, for her own safety. After finding out about the connection between the stolen ring and the murder of Candace Rothchild and attack on Silver Rothchild, the whole 'Give it back or you'll die next bitch' thing was plenty to convince Vera not to take any chances.

"I don't know why you didn't just let Duncan put me in jail," she said without thinking.

Then she remembered.

Whoops. Yeah, she did know. Because Conner'd expected to have sex with her, that's why. Which would surely have happened had it not been for the timely interruption of the break-in and the subsequent revelations into his motives for seeking her out in the first place.

She'd so totally lost her mind in that elevator. Thank God she'd found it since.

More or less.

Though being reminded of the delicious things he'd done to her during her temporary insanity wasn't helping.

She looked up and realized he was gazing at her sardoni-cally, his thoughts as transparent as hers apparently were.

"Forget it." She wagged a finger. "No bodyguard necessary. Literally or otherwise. I saw the size of the fence around this place, and the only person I'm in danger from here is you." And possibly herself.

"Only thinking of your safety," he said amenably.

"Sure you are."

Seeking a distraction, she glanced around the glamorous room, filled with the trappings of wealth, and was suddenly struck with a pang of regret. What would it be like to be part of this world, even for a few days…or nights? Would it be such a sacrifice to sleep with him, to find out?

God, no. Not in the least. The man was to die for. And she'd be using him just as much as he was using her. But…

"I'm sorry, casual sex isn't something I do." She felt the need to explain, but it came with a belated inward wince. "Embarrassing evidence to the contrary."

He smiled. "Nothing embarrassing about it. In fact, it was pretty damn hot if you ask me. For, you know, not being casual sex."

She actually felt a flush work its way up her throat to her cheeks. Good grief. When was the last time she'd blushed?

Help.

"You said something about a guest house? I really should get some sleep or I'll be a mess at work tonight." She sighed. "Assuming I still have a job."

He looked surprised. "You're going back there?"

"Hell, yeah. If the boss will let me. I have no choice, Conner. I have bills to pay. Money doesn't grow on trees." She glanced around again. "Well, for some of us anyway."

He ignored the barb and rubbed a hand over his mouth. "Okay. I guess I can do that."

"You? What do you mean?"

"So quickly they forget."

"Oh. Right." They were stuck like glue until Special Agent Duncan decided to arrest her. Which meant Conner'd have to come to the club with her.

A memory washed over her, of him sitting in the front row sipping champagne like a dissolute sultan, watching her take off every stitch of clothing. And—oh, God—how turned on she'd been. By him. By his negligent air of wealth and power. And the hungry look in his eyes as his gaze had caressed her nude body. No wonder she'd gone off like a rocket when he touched her later on.

She swallowed. "I suppose you'll insist on going with me."

"Oh, absolutely. Wouldn't miss it." He winked.

That's what she was afraid of.

That, and the nutcase who might now be after her because of that damn ring. Maybe it wasn't such a bad idea he went with her, after all.

Bad enough she'd invaded his dreams all night like some kind of teasing succubus, but even now, the next morning, sun shining, birds singing, the little witch was still torturing him. Deliberately. With malice aforethought.

Conner frowned, taking in the sight that had nearly made the tray of coffee and croissants he was carrying spill all over the Mexican patio tiles. The French doors to the cabana had been flung open. Sheer curtains billowed out from them in the hot desert breeze. Inside the dim room, the scene was straight out of one of the erotic dreams he'd been haunted by all night.

Vera. Nude. Sprawled on her stomach across her bed... Except in his dreams of course it had been *his* bed. Sheets in a tangle. Her skin moist with a sheen of sweat. Her hair in a

mess as though from his fingers… Except his fingers had unfortunately been nowhere near her last night.

Seeing her like that, he'd been shocked enough that his first
thought was that she was dead. Lying there brutally murdered,
like his cousin Candace. The memory of that crime scene had
streaked through his mind, nearly tipping the tray in his hands.
Thankfully she'd stirred immediately at the sound of the
rattling dishes so he knew she was okay, or he would really
have lost it.

As it was, he was now close to losing it for an entirely different reason.

The woman was a sensual vision. Her hot body even sexier
than in his dreams.

Easy, boy.

She'd made it clear last night she was no longer interested
in sex with him. He'd honored her wishes and hadn't pushed
it, although he was pretty sure he could have changed her
mind with very little effort. They obviously had chemistry.
Potent chemistry. And lots of it.

But this…this was unfair.

Or maybe it was an invitation? Had she gone to bed naked,
hoping he would come to her?

What an idiot. He should at least have tried…

"Conner?"

He started at the sound of her throaty, sleep-muzzy voice.
The dishes rattled, and he had to catch the tray for the second
time to keep from dumping it.

"Yeah. It's me."

She turned over in the bed, and he gripped the tray even
harder. *Pure torture.* "What have you got?"

Besides a hard-on? "Breakfast," he croaked. "Interested?"

"Mmm." Her arms rose in a languorous stretch. "Coffee,
I hope?"

Lord, help him.

"Yep." He reached a nearby patio table just in time, depositing the tray on the round glass top with a clatter. After righting the cups and returning the croissants to the plate, he turned, ready to abandon all pretense and just go in and devour her, when she strolled by with another stretch, heading for the pool.

"I feel divine! Haven't slept so well in ages," she declared, pushing her mane of chestnut hair back from her face. "I love sleeping with the doors open, with the warm air and the smell of the desert. Haven't been able to do that since I sold the mobile home."

He paused, nonplussed. Okay. Obviously *not* an invitation. He grappled for a thread of conversation that didn't involve the words *condom* or *go down*. "Mobile home?" he asked.

She shot him a look, stopping at the edge of the pool and dipping a toe into it. A toe that was bare, just like the rest of her. "I grew up in the Sunnyvale Mobile Home Park, just outside of town."

He knew that. He was just momentarily brain-dead. "No air-conditioning?" he ventured.

She smiled. "No."

She executed a perfect dive into the water. He let out a long, long breath, and for a few minutes he watched her expertly cut through the water, the joy in her movements contagious. He wanted to join her in the worst way, but in a sense it would have been like some fool painting daisies into a Monet. Perfection spoiled. He forced himself onto a patio chair, peeled off his shirt because he was suddenly far too warm and poured coffee instead.

She bobbed up at the side of the pool, folding her arms along the coping. "Hope you don't mind. I couldn't resist a quick dip. We have a pool in our apartment building, but it's indoors." She wrinkled her nose as though that were a cardinal sin.

"Take all the time you like. I'm enjoying the view."

She tilted her head. "Not misinterpreting, I hope."

"I'll have to admit," he said, taking a sip of strong black coffee to jolt his mind back up where it belonged, "your…lack of inhibition did take me in a certain direction. I now stand corrected."

She smiled and lithely hoisted herself from the water and onto the deck in one fluid movement. Like Venus rising from the sea. She padded to the table with water flowing from her lightly tanned skin like drops of molten gold, and reached for his cup. She put it to her lips with eyes closed and long lashes sparkling with water droplets. He had to grip the arms of his chair to keep from surging to his feet to lick them off. Along with the rivulets trickling down her perfect breasts.

He stifled a groan.

She set the cup down on the table. "Give me a minute," she said. "I'll get dressed." Then she disappeared into the cabana.

He cleared his throat, found his voice and called after her, "Don't bother on my account!"

And he knew then if he hadn't before—which deep down he had, but up until this very moment had chosen total, blind denial. One thing was for damned certain.

He had to have her.

Really *have* her. All to himself. For a few days. A week. Maybe even a month. Long enough to explore that chatterbox mouth with its guileless smile, that amazingly sensual body and the wonderfully sassy woman inside it.

Oh, yeah. He'd have her, all right.

He'd find a way to make her want him.

And the sooner the better.

Or he might just go completely out of his mind.

Chapter 8

"I have a proposition for you."

Vera halted her coffee cup halfway to her mouth and glanced at Conner. "What kind of proposition?" she asked. Like she couldn't guess.

Frankly, she'd been expecting this. She was actually surprised he'd managed to hold out as long as he had. Nearly a whole hour. While they'd talked of her childhood, his crazy relationship with his famous cousins and what it was like to stare up at the night sky out in the vast desert and see a billion gazillion stars up there and wonder if there was any other life in the universe.

Nevertheless, disappointment sifted through her. For some unfathomable reason, she'd thought he might be different from all the other men who tried to get in her pants. She'd *hoped* he was different. He'd been lost in thought for the past few minutes, and she'd really believed he was adjusting his perception of her. Starting to see her as a whole person and not just a nude body onstage or an easy seduction in an elevator.

Oh, well.

"More like an exchange of services," he explained.

"Uh-huh."

Her expression must have betrayed her skepticism, because he rushed to say, "I'd pay you, of course."

She set down her cup very, very carefully. "For what, Conner?"

He exhaled. "You know that deal I made with Duncan for your release? Well, there was more to it than just reporting in on Darla's movements."

Okay, he'd managed to surprise her. Not that this sounded much better than some kind of sexual favor. "Like what?" she asked cautiously.

"I promised I'd help him find out about the jewel theft ring Darla's allegedly part of. Try to narrow down suspects for him."

"I told you I don't know anything about that."

"But I'd like your help investigating."

"Me?"

"I've been thinking about how much you look like Darla. It's obvious you're her sister. You could get people to talk to you. A lot easier than I could."

"But I don't know anyone involved," she said. "Who would I talk to?"

"That's what I need your help figuring out. I'll bet someone from her circle of friends is either in on the jewelry thefts or knows something about the ring of thieves doing them. You've met most of her friends, right?"

"Well. Not really. Only the ones who've been to parties at our apartment or who we've occasionally gone out with together, like to casinos or clubs. But that doesn't happen very often. And very few know I'm her sister. We've mostly passed off our resemblance just as a fun coincidence."

He tilted his head. "Really? And she didn't invite you to other people's parties? Social events? That sort of thing?"

She glanced away. To her credit, Darla *had* invited her to lots of things. Vera had even gone. Once. And stood in a corner the whole time paralyzed with feelings of inadequacy. "I don't really fit into her social stratosphere."

He regarded her for a moment. "Her evaluation or yours?"

"Mine," she admitted with a shrug. "And my father's. He threatened to disown Darla if she spread it around that he'd spawned an illegitimate child. He'd make my life hell if it got out."

"I assume you're talking about Maximillian St. Giles."

"Daddy dearest." She sighed. After twenty-four years, you'd think she'd be used to the hurt. But it still cut like a shard of glass to the heart when she thought about his categorical rejection.

"What could he possibly have against you?" Conner asked, echoing the question she'd asked herself a thousand times. Always with the same answer.

She looked back at Conner. "I take my clothes off for a living. And I suppose I remind him of his vulnerability. Or failings. Or both."

"And whose fault is all that? Not yours." He shook his head. "The man's a dolt. If I had a daughter as smart, gorgeous and determined as you, I'd be showing her off to everyone, not hiding her away like she was something to be ashamed of. I wouldn't care how she came into the world."

Vera blinked, blindsided by the sincere indignation in Conner's voice…on her behalf. No one had ever defended her honor so vehemently. No one.

She swallowed the lump that welled up in her throat. "Thanks. Too bad he's not quite as broad-minded as you are."

"That settles it," Conner said, folding his arms over his chest and surveying her with a resolute smile. "No argument. You're coming with me."

Alarm zinged up her spine. "Where?"

"The Lights of Las Vegas Charity Ball on Friday night."

He had to be kidding. The Lights of Las Vegas Charity Ball was the biggest annual charity fund-raiser in the city; everyone who was anyone went—provided you were a gazillionaire or a famous star of some sort.

"What, *me?* No! *Hell,* no. Are you nuts?"

"All of Darla's friends will be there. It's the perfect opportunity for you to ask questions. Hey!" he exclaimed with growing excitement. "Maybe the thieves are planning to work the event and we can catch them in the act."

"One small problem."

"What's that?"

"Aside from the fact that I'd never in a million years be able to pull it off, I work Friday. It's our biggest night."

He waved a hand in the air dismissively. "I'll pay you better. Name your fee."

"*And* I have nothing to wear that doesn't fasten with Velcro," she added wryly.

"With a clothes allowance."

God, so tempting. He waggled his eyebrows, and for a nanosecond she actually considered it. Then she shook her head. "I can't. Honestly. I'd be lost at one of those fancy society bashes. I wouldn't have the faintest idea what to do or how to conduct myself. People would laugh—"

He took her hand in his over the table and gazed intently at her. "Trust me, no one will laugh. Not after I'm done with you."

Her eyes widened. "What do you mean?"

"Ever see *My Fair Lady?*"

She gave him a withering smile and yanked back her hand.

"Yeah, and look what happened to Eliza Doolittle at the horse race. I rest my case."

He chuckled. "The difference being, you wouldn't need to change a single thing. Just be yourself as you ask around after Darla. Say she's disappeared and as her roommate, you're worried about her."

"I wouldn't be lying. I *am* worried."

"Good. Then you'll do it."

She pushed out a breath, still unconvinced. "What if my father shows up?"

"You leave Maximillian St. Giles to me. C'mon, Vera. Take a chance. Be Cinderella for a night. Hell, you've even got the perfect shoes."

She laughed at his handsome, open face and charmingly amused smile. And felt herself weaken.

She shouldn't.

God knew, she had no business even pretending to belong at a highbrow event like that. Let alone with a man like Conner Rothchild.

"You're wrong about Darla," she said. "If I go to that ball, it's only for one reason. To prove my sister isn't a criminal."

"Fair enough," he said. "It's a deal." He looked at her triumphantly. "So, when can we go shopping?"

Silk. Satin. Lace. Bamboo, for crying out loud. When had they started making clothes out of bamboo, anyway?

Vera had never felt so uncomfortable in her life. Not even the first time she'd gone onstage at that seedy titty bar five years ago and taken off every stitch in front of a pack of drooling men had she felt this vulnerable. At least onstage *she* was in control.

"Utterly stunning," the duchesslike boutique owner said with a satisfied smile at her creation. Meaning the slinky, floor-length evening gown clinging to Vera's every curve. "What do you think, Mr. Rothchild?"

He considered. "I think the neckline could be lower."

"No way," Vera muttered. "Any lower and you'd have to call it a waistline."

"So charming," the duchess cooed. "Your lady friend's modesty becomes her, my dear."

Get me out of here.

"Yes," he deadpanned. "It's one of my favorite things about her."

"I'm standing right here, you know," she said evenly, shooting him a warning glare.

"Well, which gown do you like best? The blue, the red, the gold or the white?" he asked with an unrepentant smile, motioning with a twirled finger for her to spin around one more time in the blue one she was wearing. She grudgingly obliged.

She'd tried on about a thousand different dresses over the past three hours at a dozen or more trendy boutiques before finding a designer Conner approved of, and he had narrowed it down to four choices. Vera hadn't dared voice an opinion other than about the ones she didn't care for, because she had no clue what was expected at the Lights of Las Vegas Charity Ball. Each event on the Vegas social calendar had its own dress code, known only to the city's Chosen Ones. If you violated the Code, people knew and smirked at you behind your back. Or so she'd surmised from the stories of fashion faux pas Darla had come home telling with a superior air of glee.

"They're all exquisite," Vera said. And meant it. "And all far too expensive." And meant that, too. The dresses in this store were so expensive they didn't even have price tags. "You should donate the money to the charity instead."

He signaled the boutique owner to give them a minute alone, then smiled at Vera indulgently. "I've already made out the check, and trust me, this wouldn't even put a dent in it. Besides, I want my assistant to be the most stunning woman there."

Assistant? Oka-ay.

"You wouldn't deny me that satisfaction, would you?" he asked.

She ignored the deliberate hint his slight emphasis on the word *that* carried. "So I take it this isn't a date," she casually said.

"Definitely not. I'm paying you," he said oh-so-reasonably. "I wouldn't want there to be any…misinterpretations."

Ha-ha. The man was hilarious. And transparent as glass.

"Good," she said with a quick smile, not falling for the ploy. "Keeping it business is for the best." Though that did make her stomach sink a little with disappointment. "And since this is on your dime, boss, *you* choose which gown you like best."

"Very well. If you insist."

He studied her again from head to toe, taking so long she was in danger of melting under his scrutiny. The man had a way of undressing her with those dreamy bedroom eyes that made her toes curl and her mouth go dry. Which was a pretty good trick, considering her profession.

"You are so incredibly beautiful," he said at last and looked up with a funny little smile.

Surprise washed through her at the heartfelt compliment. "Thank you," she said, flustered by the admiration lingering in his eyes as he continued to gaze at her. "For everything." She went up on her tiptoes and gave him a soft kiss on the mouth. "You're being so generous, I don't know what to say."

He smiled and kissed her back—a gentle, easy kiss. Then pushed a lock of hair behind her ear. "You've said it. Thank you is plenty."

"I really do feel like Cinderella getting ready for the ball."

His smile went roguish. He brushed his knuckles down her

bare arms, producing a shower of goose bumps. "So, if you're Cinderella, who does that make me?"

He was so fishing. "My fairy godmother?" she suggested impishly.

He made a face. "Not exactly what I was going for."

She grinned, her heart spinning in her chest. "I don't recall reading anywhere that Cinderella was Prince Charming's *assistant*."

"And I don't remember her being such a smart-aleck." He tapped her on the end of the nose. "Get changed and I'll settle up."

"Aren't you going to tell me which dress you chose?"

"Nope. It'll be a surprise."

"No fair."

He winked. "Who said anything about fair?" Then he was gone from the dressing room.

She eased out a long breath to slow her fluttering heart. Who, indeed? Nothing was fair about this whole situation. Not Darla involving her in felony theft. Not having to go to this stupid ball and make a fool of herself. Certainly not the fact that she was falling hard and fast for Conner Rothchild, a man so breathtakingly wrong for her it defied all odds. Talk about a fairy tale! Too bad Cinderella was just a story. The kind that *didn't* happen in real life.

She really had to make herself remember that. Because after Conner was finished with her, no longer needed her help to fulfill his obligations to the FBI, she knew darn well the magical bubble she'd been floating in would morph back into a pumpkin. It would leave her standing alone, right back where she'd always been. And the only glass slippers she'd be trying on would be on a stage along with a fake wedding dress.

But in the meantime, she had no choice. She must go

through with this. Darla would be the one to suffer if she wimped out and didn't help prove her sister's innocence.

No, she was well and truly stuck in this crazy situation. So she may as well try to enjoy the ride as best she could. Prince Charming and all.

She just hoped she could hang on to her heart—and not let Conner Rothchild steal it along the way.

Chapter 9

Traffic was a bitch. Parking was even worse.

"Just drop me off," Vera told Conner after glancing at the dashboard clock for the tenth time in as many minutes.

He knew she was worried about being late for her shift, convinced her boss was looking for an excuse to fire her after she'd been hauled off by the FBI yesterday. To tell the truth, Conner wished she *would* get fired. She was better than that job. Did not belong at the Diamond Lounge—or anywhere else she had to bare her breasts to make a decent living.

Oh, she'd told him all about her lack of education and her stepfather's Alzheimer's and thus the need to keep him in an assisted-living facility. Conner understood her reasons. He did. He was just unconvinced she had no other recourse. She'd simply had no one tell her about other options.

He planned to. As soon as they'd put this FBI mess behind them, he'd show her how she didn't have to continue in the same vicious cycle as her mother'd been stuck in. There were ways out. To that end, this afternoon he'd paid the bill for the retirement home for the next month. Call it a bonus for her help. That would give her a few weeks' breathing room to help him. It was the least he could do.

Actually…it was far more than he *should* be doing. More than he'd ever done for a client before. He'd always prided himself on staying aloof from the all-too-unfair predicaments life had heaped upon many of his clients…hell, most of his clients. He was a defense attorney. People who did crimes had myriad reasons for committing them, but none of those reasons were fair or happy. Like a doctor with his patients, a good attorney needed to distance himself from the world of hurt he dealt with every day. Treat everyone as a case number, even as he helped them.

But Vera was different. She affected him like no one ever had. As a representative of the law—and as a man. She was incredibly smart, grounded and determined. Not to mention the hottest woman he'd ever met.

He was in deep trouble here.

"Seriously," she said, "I can walk to the club. It's just a couple of blocks. It'll be faster than this mess."

No doubt correct. Sundown on the Strip was a giant traffic jam. "All right," he said, though he didn't like the notion of her being on her own for even a minute. Whoever was stalking the Tears of the Quetzal was still out there. Conner had checked in with Lex Duncan, but no new leads had turned up. "Promise me you'll go in through the front of the club, not from the alley."

"You know I have to use the stage door," she said as she ducked under the car's gull-wing door as it rose to let her out. "Lecherous Lou will have a fit if I—"

"Tell him you have a new sugar daddy who's coming to

spend lots of money in his club—but only if you walk in through the front entrance."

She rolled her eyes and pulled her garment bag from the backseat. "Sugar daddy?"

He shrugged with a grin. "Sounds better than fairy god-mother."

She laughed. "You're crazy, you know that?"

Yeah, about her. "More so every minute."

He watched her walk away on the tourist-crowded side-walk in a simple pencil skirt and blouse, and a pair of sexy, do-me shoes that should be illegal, her hips swaying entic-ingly. Leaving a trail of turning male heads in her wake.

He wanted to jump out of the car and strangle every one of them for looking at her that way.

Damn, he was in *such* deep trouble.

Traffic barely inched along, so he fell farther and farther behind her. For a moment he lost sight of her in the moving throng. His pulse jacked up. He didn't like this. He shouldn't have let her get out of the car. To his relief, she got stuck at a Do Not Walk sign at the next corner and actually obeyed it. Meanwhile his lane jerked forward half a block so he almost caught up with her. She didn't know it, though, and he smiled at her impatient foot tapping as she waited.

Suddenly, he noticed someone else watching her. Closely. From the sidewalk just behind her. A man. Tall, muscular, with an olive complexion, thick black hair and a furtive look about him. A *familiar* furtive look. The guy stepped closer to Vera's back. *Too* close. As the man surreptitiously checked the crowd to both sides, Conner saw high cheekbones that gave him an exotic Hispanic or maybe Native American look.

And then it struck him. It was the man who'd been arguing with Darla! In front of police headquarters!

Alarm zinged through Conner's insides. Just as Vera's

stance went straight and rigid. Slowly, she put her hands out to her sides.

Holy hell! The bastard had a gun to her back!

Conner leaped from the car and barreled down the street to her aid, knocking people aside, apologizing as he ran. It took him about seven seconds flat to reach her. They were the longest seconds of his life.

"Hey!" he yelled just before flinging himself onto the douchebag's back. "Get away from her!" A mistake. The man was quick. He spun, saw Conner and took off, just missing being tackled. Conner managed to avoid mowing down Vera, but when he veered, he slammed into the streetlight post. Stars burst in his head.

"Conner!" Her voice echoed like he was in a tunnel. "Oh, my God! Conner! Are you okay?"

He gave his head a shake to clear it as well as his hearing. "Did someone catch that guy?" he demanded, scanning the area around them. Concerned tourists looked back at him blankly.

Damn.

"That was him, wasn't it?" Vera said, obviously totally freaked out. "The guy who broke into my apartment. He had a gun, Conner! He was going to shoot me!"

The circle of tourists glanced nervously in the direction the man had run, and started to back away. Out on the street, car horns started honking.

"Damn. I left the car running down the block." He grasped her elbow firmly. "Come on. We're going back home."

She dug in her heels. "No, Conner," she protested. "I have to go to work!"

He towed her along unwillingly. "You were nearly mugged, woman! Or worse. How can you even consider—"

"I told you. I don't have a choice. I *need* my job. Please,

Conner. Let me go. He just wants the ring, and I don't have it. I'll be fine."

Silver had thought she was safe, too. Right before a thousand tons of pipe and wood had crashed down on her. She was still emotionally traumatized by the attack.

Damn it, he didn't want Vera in danger, too. But that determined look was back in her eyes. He knew he'd lose this argument. "All right. But I don't care how long it takes. You're not walking. Get in the car."

Thankfully she didn't argue but slid back into the car, if reluctantly.

"Did you get a close look at his face?" Conner asked her once he'd calmed down enough to think rationally. "Would you recognize him again?"

She shook her head. "No. I didn't dare turn around when he had his gun in my back. I didn't see his face at all. Did you?"

"Just from a distance, and I only caught a glimpse of it. But I think I've seen him before. I'll have Duncan pull video from the traffic cam." He pointed to the unobtrusive camera pointed at the intersection. "With luck, it got a good shot of him, and we can identify the bastard once and for all. At least see if he's the same guy I suspect of taking the Quetzal from police headquarters."

And hurting Silver.

And possibly murdering Candace.

"Damn it! I don't want you going to work tonight," Conner said, slamming his fist on the steering wheel. "I'll pay your salary—whatever you would have made."

She stared at him for a moment, then smiled weakly. "I know you just want to help, but…I can't do that."

"I'm not trying to buy you, Vera."

"I know that. But, no, thanks."

It took them ten minutes to drive the block and a half to

the Diamond Lounge parking lot. By the time they got out of the car and he escorted her to the stage door, she'd composed herself completely. He didn't know how she could be so calm. Or so stubborn about accepting his help. A man had just tried to kill her!

Since Conner wasn't an employee of the club, the guard wouldn't let him in the side entrance.

"Be careful," he admonished Vera, giving her a worried kiss. "I'll be in the audience all night. If you need me just yell."

She smiled and touched his cheek. "My hero."

He knew it was just teasing, but her endearment made him feel warm all over. Or maybe it was just the hot Las Vegas night wind. People had given him a lot bigger compliments, accompanied by far more substantial rewards than a smile. So why did every little thing this woman do affect him so deeply?

He made his way around to the front, directly to the head of the line of schlubs waiting to get into the exclusive club. As an Old Las Vegas landmark, the Diamond Lounge was extremely popular with tourists and locals alike. But it didn't surprise him that the bouncer immediately recognized him, either from the society pages, or because he'd been part of the stir last night.

"Evening, Mr. Rothchild. Welcome back," the brawny man said, ushering him past the velvet rope.

After paying his exorbitant cover, he was immediately shown to the same table as last night, right in front of the stage. He suppressed a chuckle of amusement. Had Vera really told them he was her sugar daddy? He wouldn't put it past her. She had a wicked sense of humor, that woman.

This time a whole bottle of champagne appeared on his table, served by a pretty petite brunette who displayed her nearly nude body invitingly for him as she poured.

He was so not interested.

A beautiful redhead came out onstage in a sexy French maid's outfit and for the next fifteen minutes did a very energetic number with the center pole. The men perched on the bar stools arranged against the edge of the stage cheered and groaned in approval.

Conner drained a glass of champagne and was actually bored. He was only interested in seeing one certain, particular woman take off her clothes. And the thought of her doing it in front of all these clowns was making him want to swallow the whole damned bottle.

He checked his watch. Eight-thirteen.

Vera didn't come on until eleven.

Hell. It was going to be a really, really long night.

He was out there.

Conner.

Why did the thought of that one man being in the audience put butterflies in Vera's stomach and impossible feelings in her heart? Feelings of warmth and affection, and sadness and regret, all balled up in one giant knot?

She was falling in love with the man. That's why.

Despair filled Vera as she prepared to go out onstage. For the first time ever, she didn't want to do this. Wished she'd chosen a more conventional means of making a living. Hadn't let a thousand men see her wearing nothing more than a G-string.

Stop it! she told herself.

There was nothing wrong with what she did. And it wasn't as though she'd had a lot of choice.

As Jerry the stagehand pulled back the curtain for her, she thought about all the times she'd strutted out onstage and enjoyed the heck out of it. She'd loved the power of her female body over the punters. Loved the effect she'd had on them, reducing strong, intelligent men to blithering bundles of testosterone willing to give her everything they had for just one more peek. Loved that she was giving a thrill to those who had no one, and to those with someone waiting for them a reason to go home and give that woman a thrill of her own.

And then she thought of Conner, out there, waiting for her to come out and perform. How terrifying was that? Because suddenly she realized there was nothing she wanted more than to have him take her home and give *her* a thrill.

She was nothing if not realistic. She knew a man like him would never love her back. But that didn't mean she couldn't enjoy him while he still wanted her. And he did want her. Anyone with eyes could see that.

So why was she wasting time? The man was out there, waiting, needing to be seduced. Quickly. Before Agent Duncan found Darla and the Quetzal-crazed maniac, and Vera had to go back to her old life.

This life.

Without Conner.

The long chords of her organ music started. Her cue.

She fluffed the skirt of her faux wedding gown and gave her breasts an extra push up.

Okay. This was it.

The man didn't stand a chance. When she was done with this performance, he'd be putty in her hands.

At least for a little while. Longer if she was lucky. Until life intervened and he came to his senses.

But in the meantime he'd be hers. All hers.

Her very own Prince Charming.

For one magical night.

Chapter 10

Conner sat back in his seat, exhaled a long, long, *long* breath and willed the goose bumps running up and down his arms to go away.

His body was painfully aroused, throbbing hard and craving satisfaction.

The woman was a witch, pure and simple. She'd bewitched him. Again. Totally. Thoroughly. Unabashedly. She'd danced her dance of the seven veils with that gossamer white wedding costume, and he'd been as lost as King Herod, ready to throw whatever she wished at her feet. Money. Fame. His heart on a platter.

Damn. How pathetically cliché was this? Rich man falling for a much younger stripper, willing to alienate his family, his friends, his entire social circle, to be with her.

How could he even consider it?

He'd be on the front page of every tabloid, laughed at

behind his back. His career would suffer. His family would be embarrassed. Probably end up being disowned by his overly socially conscious father.

All because he suddenly couldn't imagine his life without Vera Mancuso in it.

And yet, there it was.

He wanted her anyway.

He wanted her.

But he just couldn't. Couldn't do that to his family. Couldn't toss aside everything he'd worked so hard to achieve.

There had to be another way.

A way to have her, all to himself, but not expose either of them to the severe downsides of a relationship like theirs.

Relationship.

He shuddered, and even more goose bumps broke out on his flesh. What was he *thinking?* There must be a—

"Mr. Rothchild?"

With a start, he came back to the present. Vera had left the stage ages ago, and another girl had replaced her. Ever since, he'd just been staring into space, his mind whirling in a chaos of growing panic.

He turned to see a middle-aged man with an obviously expensive but still oddly ill-fitting suit standing by his table. "Yes?"

The man extended his hand. "I'm Lou Majors, the manager, Mr. Rothchild. Welcome to the Diamond Lounge."

Ah. If it wasn't Lecherous Lou himself. Conner projected his voice over the bass-heavy stripper music blaring from the loudspeakers, "Thank you. Won't you join me?" It never hurt to schmooze the enemy.

"Don't mind if I do." The manager snapped his fingers at a hostess, who hurried over with another bottle of champagne. This time it was Cristal. Nice.

Also pretty nervy, because Conner was the one who'd end

up paying for it. Not that he cared. Beat the hell out of the cheap stuff he'd been drinking.

"Enjoying the floor show?" Lou asked politely, leaning in so he could be heard.

"Absolutely. Some parts more than others." Conner sent him a knowing, male-bonding-type smile.

Lou smiled back amiably. "Couldn't help but notice. You're acquainted with Miss LaRue, I take it?"

LaRue? Oh, right. Vera's stage name. "Yes. Met her here, actually. Yesterday."

At the reminder of the disruption, a shadow of annoyance passed through the manager's eyes but was quickly gone. "Her lawyer, I take it."

Conner winked lasciviously and leaned in closer. "Who could resist?" May as well go for broke. If the scumbucket thought she had a wealthy protector, he'd never dare fire her. "But I'm no longer her lawyer. I passed her case to a colleague." He lowered his voice, confidential-like. "Conflict of interest, if you get my drift."

He did. Lou couldn't have looked more pleased if Conner'd just handed him a stack of hundred-dollar bills. Which no doubt was exactly what the old roué had in mind. "I see." Several seconds went by as the manager regarded Conner. Finally he said, "Mr. Rothchild, I have a very special offer to make you."

"Yeah? What's that?"

Lou beckoned, rose and led him through the club to the sweeping red-carpeted staircase that led upstairs. On the way up, he refilled his champagne flute and handed it back. "I think you'll be very interested in this unique opportunity."

They ducked into the same VIP room as yesterday. Conner raised a brow questioningly. "What's this all about?"

Lou cleared his throat. "Are you the kind of man who likes…private parties, Mr. Rothchild?"

His brows rose higher. "That depends on who's invited."

"Men such as yourself. Wealthy. Discriminating. Discreet."

Suddenly, it hit him. *Good Lord.* If this was going where he thought it was going, the Parker case just got a huge break. "Go on."

"The ladies are of the highest caliber, of course. Only the best, most beautiful women are in attendance. Women who will cater to your every whim."

Lou looked at him expectantly, the man's crude excitement coming through loud and clear. Whether it was excitement over the prospect of the power he wielded over helpless beautiful women, or the prospect of all the money Conner would have to spend to attend that shindig, he couldn't guess. Suzie Parker had told him the attendees paid five thousand dollars each for an invitation to these exclusive gentlemen's house parties.

But Conner was a very, very rich man. He could get any woman he wanted for no more than the cost of a drink. His reputation was well-known.

He shrugged, playing it cool. "There's only one woman I'm interested in catering to me," he said, feigning indifference to the whole thing. "And I've been told in no uncertain terms she doesn't do private parties. Of any kind."

Lou's eyes narrowed, his lip curling. After a brief pause, he said, "What if I could change her mind?"

Whoops. Not the direction Conner'd meant to go. He scrambled for a reason to refuse, but Lou beat him to the draw.

"I'll make you a deal. If she'll do a party here in the VIP room with you, you'll give my other invitation a try." Because he was so sure after one visit, Conner'd be sucked into the decadence.

Hell, that's what a man got for cultivating his reputation as a player and a heartbreaker all over town. Which, ironically enough, he'd done in order to *avoid* breaking hearts. He'd never been interested in hanging with one woman for more than a few days.

Before now.

Temptation loomed large. On both counts.

This was an unprecedented opportunity to help Suzie Parker by witnessing firsthand what she'd been forced to do. To gather hard evidence against the culprits running these parties and shut them down for good. So other innocent girls weren't caught in the trap, lured by the money into selling themselves short.

Not to mention being able to have Vera all to himself in the VIP room, driving him crazy with her delectable body, dancing up close and personal.

Except she'd be madder than a coyote if Lou made her do it. She'd probably never speak to Conner again.

Which could, of course, solve that other problem. The one where he was about to throw away his whole life to have her. No sense doing that if she wasn't even speaking to him.

He hesitated. Just long enough for Lou to pull out his cell phone and make a three-word call. "Send her up."

Oh, crap.

Vera was sitting at the dressing-room mirror touching up her makeup and listening to Tawni prattle on about some man she'd just met. Some computer IT guy from New Orleans.

"Always wanted to visit the Big Easy," Tawni said. "Do you think I should go?"

"Is he married?" Vera asked.

Tawni flung out a hand. "Who cares? We're not talking about having the guy's kid, here, just a little fling!"

"Which can lead to all sorts of heartache for everyone involved, especially if he's married," Vera pointed out. "I'd ask before I even considered it."

Tawni sighed. "I suppose you're right. Wouldn't want to have my eyes scratched out by some dumb punter's irate wife."

"Very sensible."

"What about your guy?"

"I have no guy."

Tawni snorted. "Yeah? Then who was Mr. Tall, Rich and Handsome in the front row drooling into his champagne? For the second night in a row, I might add. The one whose ten-million-dollar mansion you happen to be staying at?"

Vera swiveled on her stool to face her friend. "We haven't slept together." Well. Not technically. It didn't count when only one of the parties got off and there was no bed involved. Right?

Tawni's eyes bugged out. "Are you *insane?* What are you waiting for?"

Vera sighed dreamily. "Nothing, anymore. I decided to seduce him tonight."

"Good plan," Tawni said in exasperation. "Jeez, girl, the man is worth megabucks. You've got to hurry up and soak him for all he's worth!"

She shook her head, feeling a loopy smile spread on her face. "No. I couldn't. It's not like that. He likes me. Respects me."

Tawni slapped her hands to the sides of her face. "Are you out of your mind? *Respects* you? Look at yourself in the mirror, Vera May Mancuso. Does that look like the sort of woman a man has any kind of honorable thoughts about? Mark my words, he's after something you've got, but it ain't R-E-S-P-E-C-T."

"Maybe. Maybe not. It doesn't matter. I've decided to give it to him anyway."

Something in her voice must have given her away. Tawni gasped. "Oh, sweet heaven. You're *in love* with the man! My God, girl, you just met him yesterday!"

"I know. Totally insane, isn't it? I took one look at him, and it was like…like I'd been zapped by a magic wand or something. Bells rang. Stars exploded." Or maybe that part was just the stage lights reflecting off the incredible ring she'd been wearing. The Tears of the Quetzal. She'd been blinded by its hypnotic brilliance. No wonder some lunatic had become obsessed by it.

Tawni was still staring at her incredulously.

Vera held up a hand. "I know. I'm certifiable. Believe me, I wasn't going to touch him—" much "—but oh, God, Tawni, I want him. I want to feel what it's like to be with him. Just once. Don't worry, I'm not fool enough to think it'll last."

Sympathy filled Tawni's gaze. "Oh, sweetie, you do have it bad. Come here, girl." She stretched out her arms, and Vera went into them, grateful for a hug, grateful for a friend who knew exactly what she was going through. No matter how jaded they pretended to be, their hearts still broke like everyone else's.

"You're right, sweetie," Tawni murmured. "Don't you worry about the future. You go for it. Get all the loving you can out of him. Just hang on to that precious heart of yours. Don't you give that to any man, you hear?"

Vera nodded. "I won't."

But it was too late, and they both knew it.

Still, she told herself, at least she'd have some amazing memories.

She pulled back from Tawni's hug, filling with a jittery kind of excitement. She really *was* going to go for it.

Jerry poked his head in the door just then. "Miss LaRue?"

She looked up, surprised. She wasn't on again for another two hours. "Yeah, Jerry?"

"Lecherous Lou wants to see you. Upstairs. Room seven."

Now what? Lou knew she was absolutely adamant— Okay, wait. Maybe… "Do you know if there's anyone with him?" she asked Jerry.

"That rich dude's been panting after your bod."

Excellent. "Tell him I'll be there in a minute." Jerry left. She met Tawni's I-told-you-so gaze in the mirror. "Don't say a word. Not a blessed word."

"Did I say anything? Here, look, this is me not saying a single damn thing." Tawni made a zipping motion over her lips as Vera gathered her skirts and headed out the door. "You go get 'im, girl," she called after her. "Make the boy wish he'd never been born with that thing between his legs."

That was the whole idea. For now. But later, after they went home, she'd make him glad again. Oh, so very, very glad.

And her, too.

"There you are, my dear," Lecherous Lou said when she swept into the VIP room.

Conner was standing next to him, looking too handsome for his own good. Damn, the man was fine, as Tawni would say. Broad shoulders; square jaw; long, hard, muscular legs; strong hands. And those eyes. She'd never known eyes so bone-quiveringly sexy as those hot-as-the-desert hazel ones gazing at her from under his perfectly shaped masculine brows. "Vera," he said in greeting.

"Hello, Mr. Rothchild," she said with demure formality. "Lou. What can I do for you gentlemen?"

"I think you know what Mr. Rothchild would like, Vera," Lou said. Subtlety had never been his strong suit.

She allowed herself a coy smile at her would-be lover. "I'm pretty sure that would be illegal. Wouldn't want to get any of us into trouble with the law, would we?"

Those perfect brows flicked. She'd caught him by surprise. He'd been expecting her to flatly refuse, as she had yesterday.

"Of course not!" Lou blustered. "Nothing illegal. Just a standard lap dance, that's all. The VS1 Special."

Which was code for total nudity.

She swallowed.

She'd avoided this for so long that the words almost stuck in her throat. "All right," she said.

Omigod, what was she doing?

What they both wanted. That's what.

Lou almost fell over. He'd been expecting a total refusal, too, and to have to threaten her with her job. "Get lost," she told him. "Before I change my mind."

He was out the soundproof door, and the gauzy curtains were drawn closed faster than she could blink.

"Surprised?" she asked Conner when they were alone.

The lingering shock and the slight parting of his lips belied his causal stance. "I could have sworn you don't do lap dances."

"This isn't a lap dance."

"Strange. I'm pretty sure that's what you just agreed to."

She smiled. And took a step toward him. "Then, it'll be our little secret—" and another step "—what we really do."

That's when he started to get nervous. And in spite of himself, excited. She could see his body reacting to the fantasies in his mind. The ones she'd planted there. "Vera? What's going on?"

"I hope you're prepared, Mr. Rothchild," she said, lowering her voice to a throaty purr, and with one finger pushed him backward onto the divan. "To be seduced."

Chapter 11

Vera seduced him slowly, minute by minute, inch by inch, the way she'd done onstage earlier. If Conner had any notion of resisting her, the man could just forget it.

She was an expert at very few things, but this was one of them. She knew how to make a man want her.

Not that he needed any help in that department. He'd made no secret of his desire to sleep with her. He hadn't pressed her on it, but only because she'd told him no. The man was a true gentleman, just as he'd said.

And now he would get his reward.

Well. Sort of. She knew he'd do his damnedest to follow club rules and not touch her. It would be pure torture on him. Heck, for both of them. But it would make the coming night all the sweeter, once they got back to his place.

She adjusted the music to a low, bluesy song she loved, and took her place in the middle of the small room. He sat sprawled on the divan, looking like a tiger who couldn't quite believe a kitten had wandered into his cage.

"You don't have to do this," he said.

Making her fall for him all the more.

"I want to," she assured him. "Just relax and enjoy the show."

"I already did. You were incredible onstage. It felt like I was the only man in the room and you were dancing just for me."

"You were." She smiled and started to sway her hips to the music. "And I was."

His eyes darkened, his smile going sexy. "What brought on the change of heart?"

"You," she said simply. And let her body take over.

She knew all the moves, but suddenly they had a whole new meaning for her. She wanted to seduce this man, body and soul. Wanted to entice him. Enthrall him. Make him pant. Make him sweat. Make him never, ever forget this dance of temptation…

Or her.

Slowly, she peeled off her wedding gown. Taking her time. Moving her body to the music. Teasing him. Provoking him. Making the anticipation last and last. Until she was left wearing only the lace corset, stockings and shoes. The G-string of tiny seed pearls she'd selected for tonight hardly counted as attire.

His gaze devoured her, lingering on the special wax job her line of work demanded.

"Like what you see?"

"I'd like it a whole lot better closer up."

She smiled. "Yeah?"

He looked relaxed, arms lying along the back cushions of the sofa, his legs spread wide. But she knew it was a hard-won facade. There was a film of sweat on his forehead that had nothing to do with the outside night heat, and the pulse on the side of his throat throbbed wildly. Not to mention that solid ridge in the front of his pants. "Oh, yeah."

She moved closer. He swallowed.

He couldn't touch, but there were no such restrictions on her. She put a knee to each side of his, kneeling on the red leather divan with her hands on his shoulders, and straddled his lower thighs. Keeping distance between them.

"This better?" she asked.

"Not nearly close enough," he murmured darkly.

The fabric of his suit was smooth and luxurious, cool to the touch. But the man in it was sizzling. She ran her fingers down his shirtfront. "Mmm. You're hot," she observed.

"Burning up," he agreed.

She peeled off his jacket and tossed it aside. Loosened his tie.

"Take it off," he ordered huskily.

"Why, Mr. Rothchild…"

"The tie."

She obliged, using the length of silk like a sex toy. Drawing it off slowly, teasing him with the end, glancing at his wrist debating whether to tie him up to the iron ring attached to the wall above his head.

"Don't even think about it," he warned.

She smiled, setting it aside. "Later, then."

"We'll see about that."

One by one, she teased his shirt buttons open. Touched his broad chest. Reveled in the feel of his skin under her fingers. In the soft scratch of the curls of masculine hair. He shifted under her, and she could feel the slight trembling of his thighs.

She wet her lips and brushed them over his. He groaned softly. "You're killing me here, you know that."

She put her hands to his chest, rubbed her thumbs over his tight nipples. "Hope you have nine lives."

He sucked in a breath, lifted his knees and tipped her into his chest. "Not fair," he gasped.

She tilted her head up, taking her time pulling her body away from his. "Who said anything about fair?"

He gave a strangled laugh. "Witch."

"Candy-ass."

"You are so getting a spanking when we get home."

She winked. "Promises, promises."

His eyes cut down to hers, darkened to the color of a forest in a storm. "You are a naughty girl."

"Want to see how naughty?" she whispered in his ear.

"I'm your lawyer. I need to know these things."

Her corset was held together in front by a row of bows. She reached down, found the end of one of the ribbons, and tugged it almost open. Then she put the ribbon to his lips. With a jerk of his head, he finished the job. Her breasts spilled out of the garment…just enough to be a tease.

She lifted up on her knees a little. Like lightning he grasped the end of the next ribbon with his teeth and tugged that one open, too. Her breasts tumbled out, brushing his face. He groaned, trying to catch a nipple with his tongue and teeth.

"Uh-uh," she scolded, wagging a finger. Feeling the intimate contact like a wave of shivers.

"Let me," he pleaded.

"Finish undoing the bows. Then we'll see."

His hot breath puffed over her skin, his wet tongue grazed her flesh as he bent to his task. Her nipples spiraled harder. Achy coils of desire tightened around her center.

He made quick work of the bows. Clever man. The corset slid to the floor. On impulse, she unclasped her G-string and let it slither off, too. She wanted to be completely naked for him.

His expression was pure sin as his gaze caressed her.

"You are so damn beautiful," he whispered.

Still up on her knees, she bent forward, offering him her breasts. She wanted to feel his mouth on her. He latched on like a hungry babe, suckling one then the other, until she was panting with need.

With a groan, she pulled herself away. "Any more and I'll come," she murmured.

"Do it," he urged. "I want to see you come apart for me again."

"Not here." She eased out a shuddering breath.

He blinked and glanced around, as though he'd completely forgotten where they were. He'd dug his fingers deep into the divan back, holding on to the cushions with a death grip, but now he eased them off and flexed them. "God. You're right. What was I thinking?" He nuzzled his lips against her throat. "Let's get out of here."

"I still have another show."

"Forget it. You're coming home with me." He stood up, sweeping her into his arms. *"Now."*

She didn't protest, other than to insist on picking up her discarded costume and his jacket and tie. He and Lecherous Lou seemed to have some kind of understanding. Hopefully she wouldn't lose her job over this.

Not that it would change her mind if she did. She was ready to be his. In every way. More than ready.

Conner drove like a madman, making the trip to his house in less than twelve minutes. He didn't want to waste a single second. He wanted to be inside her, now, finding release for this volcano of desire roiling inside his body.

Before leaving the club, he'd allowed her to slip back into her pencil skirt, peasant blouse and do-me shoes, but nothing else. He could see her tawny nipples through the almost-sheer fabric of the blouse. He was dying. He needed her under him.

As soon as they got inside the door of his mansion, he had her up against the wall, his mouth to her breast. She moaned, clasping his head in her hands, pulling him closer.

"Conner," she pleaded, her voice strangled, writhing against the wall as he ground the silk blouse onto her nipple with his wet tongue.

"I'm here, baby." He threw aside his jacket and practically ripped the buttons from his shirt, ridding himself of it. She lifted her shirt up over her ample breasts, baring them for him. They were breasts a man could lose himself in. Soft, round, full. Perfect.

He could smell the feminine scent of her desire, lightly musky and spicy, an alluring aphrodisiac that made him twitch in an agony of want.

With a growl, he banded his arms around her and carried her into the living room, swept the things off a low coffee table, and lowered her onto her back on it. Wrenching her legs apart, he tasted her, covering her with his mouth and tongue.

She gasped, arched and splintered apart. So fast he didn't have time to enjoy it. So he did it again.

When he finally climbed up on the table and lowered himself on top of her, she was totally wrung out and he was ready to detonate. He grasped under her knees and spread them.

"Protection?" she managed to murmur.

"Taken care of," he told her. Thank God he'd tucked a few condoms in his trouser pocket. Just in case.

"Mmm."

He thrust into her. The feel of her hot flesh surrounding him burst through his consciousness like a kaleidoscope of erotic sensation. He froze. If he moved a muscle he'd be lost. She held him tight, her chest expanding and contracting against him. It wasn't helping. He groaned.

"Conner?"

"Yeah, babe?"

"Is anything wrong?"

"Other than me being about to shame myself and totally ruin my macho reputation?"

She let out a surprised laugh. Her muscles contracted around him.

Jeez-uz.

"Baby, have mercy," he begged.

Her eyes softened, joy suffusing her whole face. She was so lovely his breath caught in his lungs. Was it really possible *he* had done that to her? Made her so happy she glowed with it?

"Kiss me," she whispered.

So he did. Long and wet and thorough as a spring downpour in the Mojave. She wrapped her legs around his waist and held him tight and used her heels on his backside to push him deep, deep, deep into her. So deep he found he couldn't hold back.

"It's okay. Let yourself go," she whispered into his mouth, her voice low and thready with emotion.

He shuddered, fighting it. Not wanting it to be over so quickly. "Too soon," he gritted out.

"We have all night," she refuted breathily.

Which was a good thing, because he had no more strength to resist.

An overwhelming surge of pleasure crashed over him. And he surrendered. Surrendered to the carnal bliss. Surrendered to the emotional rightness. Surrendered to the deep inner knowledge that after this night, he would never be the same man again.

This was just the beginning.

Chapter 12

"No, Dad. Because I don't—" Speaking on the phone, Conner did not look like a happy camper. In fact, he looked downright angry. "What about Mike? Why can't he—"

Vera wrapped the silk robe Conner'd lent her a bit tighter around her body and sank a bit deeper into the leather recliner she was curled into, trying to make herself invisible. They were in his study while he'd put out a fire or two at work. This didn't sound like work, though.

"Yes, Dad. Of course I am. But—"

They'd made love all night. And all morning. And half the afternoon. They'd shared passions and done things together she'd never done with another human being. He'd claimed her body; she'd given him her heart and her soul.

But she still felt like a trespasser in his world.

"Fine, Dad. Yes, I understand." He slammed the phone down with a curse, a scowl etched on his face.

She didn't dare ask him what was wrong. Not her place.

"Too early for a drink?" she ventured. It was just past four. Hell, it was five o'clock just down the road in Denver. At least she thought it was. Of course, one never knew with Mountain Time.

He looked up, apparently surprised to see her sitting there. *Oops.* Should have kept her mouth shut.

"Come here," he ordered.

She untangled her legs and did as he bid. Normally she wasn't such a "yes" girl, but last night she'd quickly realized the considerable benefits of doing as he asked.

He patted the desk blotter in front of him, and she duly climbed up and sat.

"Open your robe."

She smiled. The man was truly insatiable. Okay, this she could do. Her body already quickening, she unbelted the robe and held it open in anticipation of whatever he had in mind to make himself forget the conversation he'd just had with his father.

He didn't touch her. Just looked. And looked.

"You have the body of a goddess," he finally said. "You could have any man you want at the charity ball tonight."

"Why would I want anyone else when I have you?" she asked, reaching out for his hand and raising it to her cheek. She kissed his palm. He frowned.

She knew it was the wrong thing to do. Men didn't like it when a woman got all clingy after sex. But she just couldn't help herself.

Heart on her sleeve? Look it up. Her picture would be right there under the definition.

Did she care?

Ask her tomorrow.

She brought his hand to her breast. He cupped her,

running his thumb gently over the nipple. Shivers of pleasure went up her spine.

"And you make love like a god," she murmured.

Abruptly, he rolled his chair forward and leaned her backward onto his arm, bracing her as he took her other nipple in his mouth. Using his tongue, he imitated what his thumb was doing to the first one.

She sucked in a sharp breath, already rushing toward climax. Her body had gotten so tuned to him, physically, all it took was a touch or a kiss and she was practically there.

He withdrew, kissing her on the mouth instead. A sweet, tender kiss.

Her stomach sank.

A goodbye kiss.

Momentarily stunned, her heart squeezed painfully. Wow. That had happened more quickly than she'd thought.

But okay. She was a big girl. She could handle it.

She steadied herself, physically and mentally, for the inevitable.

"Are you ready for the ball?" he asked. "You still okay with what you have to do?"

The question caught her off guard.

In between their lovemaking and occasional foraging trips from the bedroom to the kitchen, they'd talked about what she would do tonight, how she'd go about getting the information about Darla that they needed. How to lure Darla's accomplices in the jewelry theft ring out into the open. *Alleged* accomplices.

Vera was still convinced Darla was innocent. But she'd sworn to do her best for Conner and she would. She'd rather know the truth about her sister, either way.

"Of course," she answered. She was nervous as hell about it but ready as ever. She thought about that phone call. "Why? Has something happened?"

His gaze dropped to her breasts again, and he stroked his hands over them possessively. "No," he said. "Nothing that affects anything important."

Now, there was a nonanswer if ever she'd heard one.

"What was that argument with your father all about, Conner?" she asked, a sick foreboding knotting in her stomach. "What did he want?"

Her lover leaned over and pressed his lips to her abdomen, trailing down to her belly button. He flicked his tongue into it. "Nothing important," he repeated.

Which probably meant it was. So important he didn't want to tell her. Which probably meant she wouldn't like it, whatever it was.

His tongue trailed lower still. "Spread your legs."

"Conner—"

"Open them."

He was definitely trying to distract her.

It was working.

She moaned as his tongue slipped between her folds, still swollen from hours of lovemaking. It felt warm and silky on her tender flesh. *So good.*

Ah, well. She'd find out soon enough what the problem was. No sense borrowing trouble.

Meanwhile, she planned to enjoy every minute she had left with him. And this was a very, very good start.

He had to tell her.

Consumed with guilt—and fury at his meddling father—Conner helped Vera into the white stretch limo he'd ordered to take them to the Lights of Las Vegas Charity Ball.

She looked like a princess in the strapless sapphire-blue satin gown he'd selected for her tonight. Worldly, sophisticated, stunning. He wanted her to be on his arm. All evening.

So there'd be no possibility of other men charming her, dancing with her, tempting her away.

Unfortunately, that was not to be. Dear old Dad had unknowingly made certain of it.

The old bugger'd be even more delighted if he actually knew what he'd done. Conner's father was a stand-up guy, but completely unreasonable when it concerned the family's reputation. Dad had tolerated Conner's rakish behavior—barely—up until now only because he was young, single and male. But he couldn't imagine Michael Rothchild ever in a million years condoning his son taking a stripper to a high-profile social event like this one. Much less dating one. No matter how amazing a person she was. Or how incredibly gorgeous.

Conner took his place beside her in the limo and tucked her under his arm. She nestled against him, resting her hand on his thigh.

"Nervous?" he asked.

She nodded. "Terrified."

"Don't be. You'll do fine. And you look exquisite."

She smiled up at him as she had so often today. Happy. Trusting. "Thank you." Her long lashes swept shyly downward, making his heart squeeze.

"You take my breath away, Vera Mancuso," he said and gave her a lingering kiss.

"The feeling's mutual, Conner Rothchild," she whispered.

He reached into his pocket for the velvet pouch he'd had his secretary deliver to the house that afternoon. From it he pulled a solid gold Byzantine rope necklace that had been his grandmother's. "I thought this would go nicely with your dress."

"Oh, Conner, it's beautiful!" she exclaimed, fingering it reverently after he'd fastened it around her neck. "But—"

"There's more."

When he pulled out the ring, her eyes went wide as saucers. "My God! Where did you get that? I thought the Tears of the Quetzal was stolen!"

He slipped it on her finger.

"It's a copy. Paste. The thief left it in place of the original when he stole that from police evidence. Not sure how he got hold of this one. It was supposedly in my aunt's jewelry box in her bedroom. My grandfather had it made decades ago for family members to wear out in public. Before he decided the ring was cursed and locked it away for good in a vault some-where. Anyway, LVMPD turned over the paste ring to the FBI, too, and Duncan said we could borrow it tonight, thinking its appearance might help lure the thieves."

Conner had debated long and hard with himself about this. Having Vera wear the fake Quetzal could potentially put her in danger from the psycho thief. But as long as she only wore it at the ball, where security would be ultratight, and went home with him afterward, she should be safe. It also reassured him knowing that Duncan would have his men watching his property all night, too.

As an extra precaution, Conner had hired a bodyguard to discreetly follow her around at the ball, because Conner wouldn't be able to watch over her personally.

She held her fingers up to the limo's overhead light. Even in the dim wattage, the faux chameleon diamond shot off a shower of purple and green sparks, almost like the genuine article. "Wow. If I hadn't had the real thing on my own finger, I'd sure be fooled. It's nearly identical."

"Not many could tell the difference," he agreed.

Just then, the limo made a turn into a circular driveway. Damn. His time was up.

Vera peered out the tinted windows at the private mansion they'd pulled up in front of. "Where are we?" she asked.

"My brother's house," Conner said, steeling himself to meet her eyes. "We're picking him up, along with his date. And mine."

She did her best to hide her visceral reaction, but he clearly saw the flash of shock and devastation in her eyes before she managed to mask them. Her lips parted, then closed. "Your…date?"

Damn his father. "The daughter of an important client. She flew in from Paris yesterday and—"

Vera held up her hand. "No, it's okay," she said, though she couldn't quite squelch the strain in her voice. "You don't have to explain. We agreed I'd be coming as your assistant, not date. It's more believable this way."

So much for happy and trusting.

"Vera—" He reached for her, but she scooted away, all the way to the other side of the limo. He moved to go after her.

"Don't," she said, just as the door opened.

He halted, torn. She was his lover. He should never have let his father bully him into this farce. And yet…there was a microscopic part of him that was secretly relieved not to have to reveal their relationship just yet—and bear the brunt of social and familial disapproval.

He was such a damn coward.

"Howdy, bro," his brother, Mike, stuck his head in the door that had been opened by the chauffeur and greeted him. "Hey, now, what have we here?" Mike's confusion was obvious when he spotted Vera sitting in the corner. Then he really looked at her, and his face lit up. "A threesome? You dirty old man, you."

Mike, or Michael Rothchild Jr., was the older brother, but acted like a kid sometimes. He had no emotional radar.

"Just get in the damn car," Conner said evenly.

Mike stepped aside and his striking blond fiancée, Audra, slid into the seat opposite Conner. She leaned over and air-kissed him on the cheek. "Hi, Conner. Good to see y—" She also spotted Vera and halted in mid-word. "Hello," she said, glancing between her and Conner. "This is, um, interesting."

"My assistant, Vera Mancuso." Conner cut off her blatant rampant speculation. She was as bad as his brother. The perfect pair. "Vera's helping me with a case tonight."

Audra's brows rose delicately. But she refrained from comment, because Conner's date had just glided onto the seat next to him. She was model-thin with shiny black hair and long legs exposed by a slit running up the side of her gown. *Way* up. Aristocratic features, olive skin, a long neck and slim arms dripping with jewelry. The woman oozed class and sophistication.

His father knew him well. She was just his type.

Up until two days ago.

She raised her hand, European style. "Annabella Pruitt," she said in a cultured voice. *"Enchanté."*

He knew he was expected to kiss her hand, but he couldn't make himself do it. He shook it awkwardly instead, introducing himself, trying to subtly ease his body closer to Vera, who sat primly on the other side of him, maintaining a perfectly blank face.

"Did I hear you say assistant?" Mike queried after he'd climbed in and gotten settled next to Audra. He smiled at Vera when Conner introduced her to him and Annabella. "Just like my little brother to be working a case on a night like this," he said with good-humored disapproval.

"That's why he brought me," Vera said smoothly, the first peep she'd uttered. "So he wouldn't have to work. Now he can devote all his time to his lovely date." She smiled genially at the other woman, but Conner knew better than to think he'd been forgiven.

"Now *that's* a waste of a beautiful woman," Mike

remarked disgustedly, and Audra smacked him in the arm—but there was no heat in it. "So what kind of case does one work at a fancy ball?" he asked, patently intrigued by the whole situation.

"The confidential kind," Conner interrupted before Vera could answer. He sat back and folded his arms over his chest irritatedly. This was *so* not the night he'd envisioned.

Audra hadn't taken her curious eyes off Vera. "I didn't know Conner had hired an assistant," she ventured. "You're very young. Are you a junior associate in the firm? Paralegal maybe?"

"Confidential informant." Conner cut off whatever Vera'd opened her mouth to say. "She knows people."

"You do look familiar," Mike said with a curious tilt of his head. "Have we met somewhere? At another charity event perhaps?"

Vera's glued-on smile didn't waver. "You probably know my sister, Darla St. Giles."

Mike's brows shot into his scalp. "Good God. Darla has a sister? How did I not know that?"

"Vera isn't into Darla's social whirl," Conner supplied.

"I prefer to stay out of the tabloids." She folded her hands in her lap.

And that's when Mike noticed the fake ring on her finger. His eyes bugged out, and his shocked gaze snapped to Conner.

Annabella apparently noticed it, too. "What an unusual ring you have," she said. "May I see it?"

"Of course," Vera said, and held out her hand. Annabella let it rest on her fingers as she examined it. Over his lap. His brother peered at him over their fingers. Conner peered back, grinding his jaw.

"Extraordinary. Where on earth did you get it?" Annabella asked.

"Why," Vera said innocently. So innocently he knew he was

in trouble the second the word left her mouth. "From your date." Her lips smiled up at him, but her eyes were shooting daggers. "Conner gave it to me earlier tonight."

Chapter 13

She pretended she was onstage.

That was the only way she could get through this. Being onstage gave her permission to be someone else: a brave, confident woman whose power came from deep within her. Not the terrified, heartbroken, barely hanging on woman she really was.

She could do this.

She *had* to do this.

The thought of everyone's shock in the limo when she'd announced Conner had given her the Tears of the Quetzal gave her the boost she needed to pull this off. They'd naturally all jumped to the same wrong conclusion. Oddly enough, Conner hadn't corrected it. He'd actually glanced at her just as surprised as the others, but she could have sworn she'd seen him hide an amused smirk. Anyway, she'd set them straight herself, five seconds later, by adding, "For the investigation, of course!" in an innocent exclamation. But those five seconds had been glorious.

What. Ever. Now she was on her own, Conner having wandered off with his glamorous date, leaving Vera standing alone in the middle of a huge ballroom full of high-society mucky-mucks. And the uneasy feeling that someone was watching her. Conner had warned her to be on the lookout for the man who'd attacked her on the street. Thank you *so* much for that.

Damn, she needed a drink.

"Darla?" A surprised male voice assaulted her. "Is that you, babe?"

This one, at least, didn't sound dangerous.

She turned. Nor did he look like the Hispanic guy from the fuzzy traffic cam photo—but that was fairly useless. He was a raffish man about her own age, all decked out in the latest trendy Eurotrash style, blond hair going every which way.

"No," she said, taking a breath of relief and putting on her brightest smile. "I'm Vera, her roommate. Have you seen her by any chance?"

"Wow. You sure look like her. I'm Gabe. No, I haven't…"

And so it started. If she thought she'd be left alone, she'd totally misjudged Darla's friends. They might be wild and crazy, but they circled wagons for one of their own. She'd met some of them at the apartment already, so she wasn't totally out to sea. They took her under their wing, pulling her along with the flow as they made the social rounds, laughing, dancing and speculating madly with her over where Darla could have disappeared to this time. No one was worried about Darla. While everyone remarked on her ring, and a few had even read the newspaper reports that linked the ring to Candace Rothchild's murder, no one seemed overly interested in it other than as a ghoulish souvenir of that tragedy.

Unique, expensive jewels with a history were a way of life for these people. And everyone had on their most unique and expensive pieces for tonight's ball. Hers was just one more fabulous diamond to admire, gossip about, then forget.

And speaking of forgetting…she didn't think about Conner more than once, all night.

Okay, once a minute, all night.

But she was proud of the fact that she didn't track him all over the ballroom, keeping tabs on his movements, how many drinks he had, how many times he danced with that bitc—er, date, or if he ever looked across the room, searching for Vera.

She *so* didn't care.

At least, that's what she kept telling herself.

Once a minute, all night.

"Ms. Mancuso?"

She almost choked on her drink. Despite the uneventful evening so far, she'd still had the creepy feeling someone had been watching her the whole time. But probably not this guy.

A tall, elegantly dressed man with salt-and-pepper hair, who looked so much like Conner he could only be his father, or uncle, gazed down at her pleasantly.

"Y-yes," she stammered, all her hard-won poise and confidence vanishing in a fell swoop.

He extended his hand. "I'm Michael Rothchild. I understand you came with my son tonight."

Oh, God. More than once, she thought with half-hysterical irreverence. And last night, too.

She blinked, frozen by the howlingly inappropriate thought, with her hand in his. The one with the ring on it. *His* ring. "Um. Yes. But, uh, not as— I mean, I'm just working—"

He glanced at the fake Quetzal, then up again. "I just wanted to thank you." At her deer-in-the-headlights look, he added, "for helping with—" he glanced around "—well, you know." She did. She was just surprised *he* did. "Your discretion is appreciated."

"My, um—" She was about to say "pleasure," but it wasn't really, was it? So she just let the inane half comment hang there.

"*Greatly* appreciated." Michael Rothchild was still holding her hand. So firmly she couldn't politely extract it. He kept looking at her, taking in her whole person, expensive outfit and all, and it was like he saw straight through her charade. "I don't approve of your sister," he said. "but I respect family loyalty. I hope you find what you're looking for."

He released her hand, gave a little bow and walked away to join a petite ashen-haired woman who must be Conner's mother. The woman smiled at her uncertainly, then they both turned and vanished into the crowd.

Okay. That was very weird. Talk about cryptic.

"Who was that old geezer?" Gabe asked.

"Michael Rothchild."

"Dude! You know them, too? Man, Vera, for someone who doesn't get out much, you sure get around."

He had no idea.

She turned to Gabe. It was getting late, and she was ready to call it a night. She'd been dancing around the topic of Darla and her craziness with everyone all night and gotten nowhere. So she decided to just come out and ask. "Gabe, have you ever heard of Darla being involved in anything illegal?"

He regarded her skeptically. "Like what?"

"Like stealing jewelry."

"Whoa, dude." He shook his head. "No, nothing like that."

Vera nodded. "Good. I'd heard a rumor. But I just couldn't believe it myself." She met his eyes. "If you ever hear of her being involved in—"

"What the *hell* are *you* doing here?" The furious words were growled from behind. A firm male hand clamped around her arm and yanked her away from the group, then pushed her off toward a large potted palm that was part of the decor. She could hardly keep up and nearly tripped several times. Alarm zoomed through her. He wouldn't let her turn to look at him. But he didn't have the right color hair. It was thick and silver. Like—

She gasped. *Please, anything but this.*

They were attracting stares, so he slowed down until they reached the palm, then spun her to face him.

God help her. It *was* him.

Maximillian St. Giles.

Her father.

Vera's heart thundered so hard she was afraid it would pound out of her chest. She opened her mouth, but didn't know what to say. "Hello, Daddy," somehow didn't seem appropriate. So she firmly shut it again.

"You little gold-digging whore," he snarled, his piercing green eyes identical to her own glaring at her in hatred. "What do you think you're doing here?"

The *bastard*.

She resisted the urge to slap him across his sanctimonious face. For the insult. For all the insults she'd endured over the past twenty-four years. For snubbing her her entire life. For abandoning her mother, leaving the poor woman pregnant and alone with only a token cash settlement as compensation for a ruined life. But mostly for being a selfish, womanizing, egotistical prick.

She resisted, but her control was hard-won. She started to shake with bitter fury. And a stinging hurt that refused to be ignored.

"Why I'm here is none of your business," she snapped, glaring at his hand on her arm. She'd dealt with plenty of men like him. Bullies covering up their insecurities with threats of violence. "Let me go, or I'll call security."

He finally let her go. And leaned his anger-reddened face right into hers. "It *is* my business if you've come here to make trouble for me and my family."

"Trust me, you are not worth the bother," she spit out, keeping her chin up, shoulders straight. She *wouldn't* let him intimidate her.

"You've been asking questions about my daughter," he accused. "My *real* daughter."

More pain sliced through her chest. How could he *say* that? She fought to keep tears from filling her eyes. She wouldn't give him the satisfaction. "Darla's disappeared. I'm worried about her."

He snorted. "More like upset she's not there for you to leech off."

She curled her hand into a fist to keep from smacking him. But maybe she should give in to her first impulse. A fist in that hypocritical, self-righteous face sounded really good about now.

"Get out of here," her father sneered. "Go back to that strip club where you belong. And if I catch you asking questions about my daughter again, I'll hit you with legal action so hard you'll be living on a grate for the rest of your life."

With that, he turned on a heel and stormed off.

She stood watching his wake disappear into the crowd, fighting to control the trembling in her limbs.

Okay, then.

Another sentimental family reunion. Always a fun time.

"Are you all right?"

She looked up to see Conner. Her tongue tied in knots and she couldn't speak. Because suddenly, she had a blinding insight.

Conner Rothchild was just like her father.

Oh, not abusive, or overtly insulting. Nothing like that. But he was the same kind of man. With the same kind of lifestyle. And the same kind of prejudices. Against people like her.

Conner was *ashamed* of her.

That was why he'd insisted she come to the event as his assistant. Why he'd accepted a date with Ms. *Paris Vogue*. Why he hadn't told his brother, or anyone, the true nature of his relationship with Vera. If you could call two days of monkey sex a relationship.

"N-no," she stammered. Shook her head. "I mean yes. I'm fine. Really. Go back to your date."

"I don't want to—"

"Conner, please. I'm tired. There's nothing more to learn here. I'm going home now."

He frowned, managing to look concerned. Maybe he really did care. Yeah, that she'd blow their cover and reveal herself to his blue-blood family. She'd seen him with his famous hotel magnate uncle, Harold Rothchild, and his young trophy wife. Wouldn't they get a kick out of—

No, stop it. Conner wasn't like that.

Except he was. And now finally both of them knew it.

"I'll call the limo for you," he said.

"No. I'll take a cab."

"Don't be ridiculous." He pulled his cell phone from his tuxedo pocket.

"All right, fine." She didn't want to argue. She just wanted to be gone from this nightmare of a night.

"The driver has the pass code for the gate."

For a second she didn't know what he meant. Then it hit her. He expected her to go back to *his* home.

Can you say no way in hell? But she decided not to tell *him* that. "Yes, I remember."

"Good. I'll tell Hildy to be expecting you."

It occurred to her that this must be a huge relief for him. Now he wouldn't have to come up with lame excuses as to why he needed to drop his assistant off *after* he dropped off his date. She'd just be waiting for him at home. Preferably in bed. Preferably nude.

No wonder he hadn't protested.

She went to take off the ring. "You should take this."

"No, keep it for now," he said.

She couldn't argue or he'd know she had no intention of going to his place. She'd just have to send it back to him tomorrow.

"All right. Go." She made a shooing motion. "Your friends will be wondering where you are."

He hesitated, his brow furrowed. "Are you sure you're okay? You look…"

"I'm fine," she lied. "Go find your lady."

"She's not—"

But Vera was already walking away, not listening. *Back straight, head up,* she told herself as she threaded through the throng. How many of these strangers had witnessed Maximillian's tirade against her? It didn't matter. She just had to make it to the door without being stopped. *Pretend you're on the catwalk. You're not naked,* they *are.*

"Vera?"

Oh, God, now what?

She resolutely ignored the unfamiliar male voice and went right on walking.

Long fingers grasped her shoulder. "Vera, wait."

She suddenly remembered the thief. She opened her mouth to scream. But then she recognized who it was. From pictures. In her living room.

"I'm Henry St. Giles," he said, removing his hand. "Darla's brother."

Fortyish with thinning hair, he was still good-looking in a boring businessman sort of way. Darla was always telling stories about his out-of-control, crazy youth, but somehow he'd ended up selling out to their father and going to work for him after he was cut off for a year. Which explained why they'd never met.

"I know who you are," she said curtly, bracing herself for round two. "What do you want?"

He looked abashed. "I'm sorry, Vera. I just wanted to apologize for what happened back there. With my father."

"Why?" she asked suspiciously.

"We don't all think the way he does."

She arched a brow but didn't comment.

"I know you have no reason to believe me," he continued, "but I honestly regret not getting to know you like Darla did. You're my little sister. I should have made the effort, not cowed under to my father's…stupidity."

Wow. She hadn't known what to expect from Henry St. Giles when he stopped her, but this definitely wasn't even on the list.

"That's, um, very nice of you to say." Not that she particularly believed him.

"You look like her," he said, with a little smile.

"Yeah. So we've been told."

The man actually looked bashful. Either he was a hell of an actor or he was sincere. You could have knocked her over with a feather.

He held out a business card to her. "This is me. I've written my private line on the back. Call me. I'd love to get together for lunch or dinner. Get to know you. If you like."

She decided to be flattered. "Thanks. Maybe I will." Could she actually be getting a brother? She reached for the card. The second he spotted the ring on her finger, Henry's eyes popped. "What the—" They shot to hers in shock, even wider. "Vera, is that what I think it is? The ring from Candace Rothchild's murder?"

She smiled at his bewilderment and shook her head. "No. It's paste. Pretty good copy, though, don't you think?"

"Where on earth did you get it?" he asked, still awestruck by the jewel.

"Long story," she said with a laugh.

"I thought it was stolen?"

"No, the original was stolen. Well, actually both. But now they're back—"

"Miss Mancuso?" the doorman interrupted. "Your limo is here, miss."

"Thanks, I'll be right there." She tucked Henry's card in her beaded bag and held out her hand to him. "It was nice to finally meet you, Henry. And I will call. I look forward to lunch."

He nodded and waited just inside the entrance, watching as she walked to the white stretch limo and got in. He waved as the chauffeur closed the door.

Vera let out a long sigh of relief, bending down to pull off her shoes and wiggle her toes on the plush limo carpet. Thank God the night was over. Just one more thing to do. She picked up the phone to the driver.

"Yes, Miss Mancuso?"

She gave him her home address.

"But Mr. Rothchild said—"

"Change of plans," she said. "Just take me to the address I gave you."

"Very well, Miss Mancuso."

She didn't want to think about Conner right now. Didn't want to let herself be depressed about their doomed affair. Or her bastard of a father. Or even about not making any headway on the investigation of Darla and the theft ring.

She did smile when she thought of Henry. Well, at least the night hadn't been a total disaster.

Her brother. Who'd have thought he'd want to get to know her after all this time?

It was so amazing, it almost made up for losing Conner. Almost.

Chapter 14

"Babe? Where are you?" Conner jetted out an impatient breath. "Vera, pick up the damn phone!"

Her answering machine clicked on. Conner slammed down his receiver and paced back and forth in frustration. "Damn it!" Where *was* she? She must be there. Ignoring him.

He *knew* he'd be in trouble over that freaking date.

He ripped off his bow tie and threw it onto his bed. The bed Vera should be tucked into, waiting for him.

Not that he blamed her, if he were honest. He wouldn't have been nearly as civilized about it as she was if *she'd* turned up with a date for the evening. He would have ripped the guy's throat out.

Or at least kicked him out of the limo onto his damn ass.

He picked up the phone again and dialed the number of the bodyguard he'd hired to follow her tonight.

"Barton."

"Where is she?" he demanded, not bothering with the niceties.

Barton rattled off the address of her apartment. "Limo dropped her off just over an hour ago. She's still up there."

"You sure? She's not answering her phone."

Barton was wise enough not to comment. "I'm camped out in the lobby, and I paid the security guy to keep an eye on her, too. I'll know if she budges."

"Good. Anything else I should know about tonight?"

"Some guy spoke to her as she was leaving the event." Conner heard the sound of notebook pages being flipped. "Name of Henry St. Giles. Gave her a business card."

Darla's brother? Hell, *Vera's* brother. What did *he* want? "Was it amicable?"

"Seemed to be."

As opposed to her confrontation with Maximillian. Her own father. "You'll be there all night?"

"That's the plan."

"Good. I'll expect your full report in the morning."

"Will do, sir."

Thoughtfully, Conner put the phone back in its stand. Should he go check on her? Or just let her cool off… He wasn't too worried about her safety, not with Barton there standing guard all night. And Conner'd hired a cleaning crew to tidy up the apartment after the FBI was done with their evidence collecting, so she didn't have to deal with that.

But, damn it, he *missed* her.

He'd been bored stiff all night, stuck at that stuffy ball with his stuffy family and the stultifyingly sophisticated Annabella Pruitt, slowly drinking himself numb. Or trying to. Unfortunately, he'd remained distressingly sober the entire time, despite the copious amounts of alcohol that had passed through his system.

Guilt?

Possibly.

Probably.

He wasn't proud of the way he'd treated Vera. In fact, he was downright ashamed. What was wrong with him? Was he such a damn wuss that he couldn't just tell his socially paralyzed father to take a flying leap if he didn't like Conner's choice of women?

Not to mention the whole Maximillian St. Giles thing. Conner should have pounded him into the dance floor like a wooden peg. Or at least shamed him into apologizing to his daughter, admitting he was being an ass.

So, why hadn't he?

Because Conner was an even bigger ass, that's why.

Setting his lips in a thin line, he strode into the hall. "Hildy!" he yelled. "Get the limo back here! I'm going out again."

Naturally, Vera refused to answer the intercom. So Conner had to talk the security guard into letting him into the penthouse.

Luckily, he'd been introduced as Vera's lawyer the other day after the break-in, so he didn't have too much trouble convincing the man he was worried about his client and wanted to check on her well-being. The C-note deposited discreetly in his uniform pocket didn't hurt either.

Conner found her in the bathtub. Up to her neck in bubbles, the mirrors steamed up and a dozen scented candles lit. The room smelled like a hothouse filled with damask roses. A bottle of red wine was propped on the edge of the tub. Half-empty. No glass.

The fake Quetzal was sitting on the tub's front rim, winking in the candlelight like a multicolored disco ball.

"Go away," she mumbled, not opening her eyes.

"How do you know who it is?" he asked, chagrined that she wasn't worried and didn't even check. He could be the thief returning, for all she knew!

"I can smell you," she said thickly. "The demonic scent of wealth and temptation."

Had he just been insulted? He made a mental note to change his cologne.

He stepped into the room and closed the door. "Sweetheart—"

"Don't!" Her hand shot up from the water, fanning out a cascade of droplets. "Don't you 'sweetheart' me, you…"

His eyes widened as she called him a *very* bad name.

Ho-*kay*, then. Looked like he wasn't the only one drinking himself into oblivion. "Been watching reruns of Deadwood?" he muttered. Walking over, he plucked the wine bottle from the tub and deposited it on the marble vanity counter.

"Hey!"

"Any more of that stuff and you'll drown yourself," he said.

"Drown *you*, you mean," she muttered. Then called him that word again.

Okay, so maybe he deserved the moniker. But he couldn't help smiling. She was even more beautiful when she was calling him bad names.

"Vera, I'm sorry."

"Tell it to someone who cares."

"Look, honey, I know you're mad, but—"

"Mad? Me?" She cracked an eyelid, gave him a gimlet eye and made a really rude noise.

"I can see you're not going to make this easy on me."

"Sure, I am. What part of 'go away' don't you get? I'll be happy to e'splain it to you." She hiccupped.

He desperately wanted to chuckle. But he figured it would be the last thing he ever did. So he did the second best thing. Toed off his shoes and socks and climbed into the tub with her. They'd have to cut his tuxedo pants off him, but what the hell, he didn't like this suit anyway.

"What the—" she sputtered, wheeling her arms to get away from him. But he just grabbed onto her and held tight as he slid down behind her into the water, leaning his back against the end of the oversize spa tub. "You are such a freaking Neanderthal," she gritted out.

"So sue me. But I warn you, I'll win."

Damn, it felt weird taking a bath in his clothes. But she really would have screamed bloody murder if he'd gotten undressed.

Besides, he didn't want to give her the wrong idea, either. He wasn't here for sex. He was here for forgiveness. For her.

At least she wasn't fighting him anymore. With a huff, she let herself fall back against his chest, closed her eyes again and refused to look at him.

Progress.

She sighed. "Conner, what are you doing here?" she asked him, sounding suspiciously uninebriated.

"Apologizing."

"That's not what it feels like," she said dryly.

He realized his hand had unconsciously found its way to her breast and was gently fondling it. Since she hadn't clawed his eyes out, he didn't stop.

He kissed the top of her head. "I'm sorry, Vera. I acted like a jackass. You have every reason to be angry with me, and I wouldn't blame you if you never spoke to me again."

"Good, because I don't plan to."

"Which would be a damn shame, because I'd really miss you ordering me around when we're in bed."

Instead of snorting and telling him *he* was the one who did all of the ordering around, as he'd hoped she would, she just sighed again.

"Conner, you and I, we're not going to work," she said quietly. "I don't fit into your world. I'd never be accepted by your family. What's the point?"

He hugged her closer, leaning his cheek on her head. "Because I don't want to give you up."

"You did a pretty damn good imitation of it tonight."

Guilt assailed him anew. "I know. And I couldn't be sorrier. I was wrong. It'll never happen again. I swear."

"You're positive?" she asked bleakly. "Because if it came down to a choice between me or Rothchild, Rothchild and Bennigan, I have a feeling I know which way it would go."

"I'm not so sure." He fell silent, and for the first time he seriously thought about what would happen to him if he left the family law firm. Or was asked to leave.

Would he be sad? Sure, he would. Would it take a while to regroup and start over? Undoubtedly. But he had more than enough money in the bank never to have to work another day in his life. So would his world fall apart? Definitely not.

The only question was, if it came down to a choice between Vera and his *family,* which way would *that* go?

"You're jousting at windmills," she murmured.

She sounded tired. And he was totally beat himself.

"Let's get out of this water," he said. "And go to bed. We can talk about all this in the morning."

"Conner…"

He kissed her on the temple. "We don't have to make love if you don't want to. Just let me hold you while you sleep."

She hesitated, then let out a resigned breath. "You're a real bastard, you know that?"

He'd been upgraded. A good sign. "I'll take it," he said, kissing her ear. "As long as I can be with you tonight."

The next morning Vera got breakfast in bed. It was Saturday, and Conner didn't have to work.

The sun was streaming through the floor-to-ceiling bedroom windows looking out over the city below and the mountains beyond. The sky was so blue it hurt. A lone hawk rode the thermals that rose off the desert floor, scouting for its morning meal…or maybe just windsurfing for the sheer joy of it.

She had no right to be so happy. She knew the bliss wouldn't last. Conner was fooling himself if he thought they had a prayer.

But it was enough that he wanted to try.

Or said he did.

That was a miracle in itself.

He'd made no declarations of love, given her no vows of forever. She could live with that. For now. Just having him here with her was more than she'd ever expected.

"Coffee?"

"Mmm." It smelled delicious. "Who made the French toast?"

"I did," he said proudly.

She was impressed. "A man of many talents."

He leaned over and gave her a slow, thorough kiss. "And a woman of rare appetite," he said in a low rumble.

They'd made love. Of course they had. Like she could take him to her bed and not touch him. Not have him touch her. Impossible.

He'd been so tender it nearly broke her heart. It almost felt like… No, she wasn't going there.

They'd just nestled together into the propped-up pillows to eat the savory breakfast, when his cell phone rang. He checked the screen.

"It's the office. Guess I'd better get it." They rarely called him on weekends, so when they did it was usually important.

"Conner here."

"It's your father."

Hell. "Hi, Dad. What's up?"

"You got an e-mail about a surveillance from someone named Barton."

Conner glanced at Vera and smiled. "Yeah?" How the hell had his father gotten hold of that?

"It came in on the general e-mail account," his dad said, answering the unspoken question. "You're surveilling Vera Mancuso? What's that all about?"

Double hell. "Hang on, Dad." He climbed out of bed, giving Vera a kiss. "Reception's bad in here. I'm gonna take this outside." He grabbed a towel to wrap around his waist and trotted out the double sliders to the huge tiled patio that circled the penthouse, closing them firmly behind him.

"I told you about the case she's helping me on. The whole Quetzal thing. She could be in danger, so I'm making sure she's safe."

"From between her sheets? Mike says—"

Anger shot through Conner. He tamped it down. "That's none of Mike's business, Dad. Or yours."

"It is if I think you're getting personally involved with his woman."

"Why would that matter?"

"You have the family name to think of."

"Oh. You mean like Uncle Harold? Or Candace, or Silver?" All stars of the local gossip columns due to their endless "inappropriate" love affairs. Although Silver seemed to have settled down now that she was a newlywed and expecting a baby.

"That's not our side of the family. *Our* side—"

"I know, I know. We're the respectable ones. We only defend murderers and rapists. But we marry decent women."

His father made a choking noise. "If you have a problem being a defense attorney—"

"I don't. But if I want to date a stripper, I'll date a stripper. Besides, it's not serious." Yet. "I just met the woman. No doubt I'll get tired of her soon, just like I get tired of all the women I date."

It was disturbing how easily the half-lie slipped out. Half, because he *did* go through women like popcorn at the movies. But he didn't want to deal with his father now. He *had* just met Vera, and although his feelings about her were totally different than for any other woman he'd ever dated, how could he be so sure she was The One? That this affair was forever? Why alienate his dad until he was a hundred percent certain?

That wasn't being a coward. That was being prudent.

"Did you at least get the paste Quetzal back from her? That's an extremely valuable piece of jewelry."

"Yes, Dad. I got it back," he said exasperatedly. And made a mental note to retrieve it from the tub.

"All right. Good. Anyway, just be careful, son. Women like her—"

"I will, Dad. Don't worry. Just forward the e-mail to my private account, okay?"

"Your mother is asking if you'll come to dinner tonight. Ms. Pruitt and her father will be here."

Saints preserve him. "Sorry, can't make it. I've got a good lead on the Parker case and will be working it tonight until all hours."

"The Parker case?"

"One of my pro bonos."

"I see. Conner, I really wish—"

"I know, Dad. Give Mom a kiss for me."

He punched the end button on the cell phone with an annoyed curse. He knew his dad meant well. But he was all grown up now—thirty-three years old. He could run his own life.

And if he wanted Vera in it, that was *his* decision to make, no one else's.

Chapter 15

It's not serious... No doubt I'll get tired of her soon...

Vera hadn't meant to eavesdrop. She really hadn't. She'd just gone into the bathroom and noticed it was still humid from last night's bath and opened a window. Could she help it if Conner was talking on the phone practically right under it?

And now his casual pronouncement was seared into her brain.

Nothing she hadn't already known. Nothing she hadn't been telling herself over and over for the past three days.

But hearing it spoken out loud like that, from her lover's own mouth in such a matter-of-fact manner, well, that really brought it home with a sick thud in her heart.

Everything he'd said last night was a lie. She really was just a temporary plaything for him.

As her mother had been for her father.

For the first time ever, she finally understood why her mother had done what she had. Thrown away her life for a man who didn't care about her for more than a few nights of pleasure. She'd been in love with wealthy, powerful Maximillian St. Giles, just as Vera was in love with wealthy, powerful Conner Rothchild. And love made women do foolish, foolish things.

Taking a deep cleansing breath, Vera quickly finished up and slid back into bed before he knew she'd overheard his conversation.

For now it didn't change anything. Outwardly. But she was so glad she'd found out his true feelings. Or she might have believed his pretty lies and allowed herself to dream of the impossible. Heartbreaking as it was, better to know the truth.

Putting on her best smile, she greeted Conner with a kiss when he came back to bed.

"Mmm," he hummed approvingly. "You taste sweet."

"You'll never guess what I found on the breakfast tray."

He grinned against her mouth. "Yeah? What's that?"

She held up a can of whipped cream. "Funny, I don't remember this being in the kitchen yesterday."

"I found it in the limo fridge. Those chauffeurs do think of everything, don't they?"

She squirted a dollop on her finger and slid it into her mouth suggestively. "Gee, and I thought you didn't come here for sex last night."

His grin widened. "A man can always hope, can't he? I did apologize. Abjectly and sincerely. *And* I ruined my tuxedo getting back into your good graces."

"Or pants, as the case may be."

"As I recall, there were no pants involved."

"Hmm." She flipped back the covers, revealing his magnificent naked body. His magnificent and *aroused* naked body. "It appears you're right."

His eyes went half-lidded. "I was talking about you."

"And I," she said, giving the can a shake, and then a well-aimed squirt, "was talking about you."

He moaned as she bent to lick the sweet cream from his shaft, melting back onto the pillows in willing surrender to her tongue.

He may well give her up in the end, but when he did, he'd be giving up the best damn lover he'd ever had. She'd make sure he remembered her for the rest of his life, seeing her face in the face of every future lover, feeling her touch in every brush of their fingertips.

He might give her up. But he'd always regret letting her go.

Almost as much as she did.

Conner was totally wrung out.

Ho. Lee. Batman.

The woman was amazing. Agile. Clever. Mind-blowing. Among other things.

Last night they'd done tender and loving. The night before had been hot and ravenous. This morning had been...well, every one of his fantasies come true.

Yeow.

She'd left him sprawled limply in bed, waving at him from the door with her fingers and a wicked smile, and gone to visit her stepfather, Joe. It was Saturday, her usual day to have lunch with him at the assisted-care facility.

Conner had a feeling she wouldn't be all that hungry. She'd eaten a ton of whipped cream at breakfast.

Oy.

The woman would be the death of him yet.

But what a way to go.

He *really* did not want to do this.

But he had no choice. It was the only way to get the

evidence he needed to exonerate Suzie Parker and put the scumbags who'd abused her away for good.

Conner reluctantly hit the "Pay Now" button on the PayPal invoice he'd received from Lecherous Lou for tonight's private gentlemen's party. He'd much rather be watching Vera dance at the club. And he was still worried about her safety. So much so he'd put Barton back on her tail after letting him get a few hours of sleep. He'd just called in after catching up with her at the assisted care. The guy was good. And thorough. The report he'd e-mailed this morning was detailed as hell, including background sketches on all the people she'd spent more than five minutes with last night at the charity ball. Apparently, Barton liked to while away his hours on stakeout doing research on the Internet from his BlackBerry.

From his notes, Darla's friends seemed to be mostly aging spoiled rich kids who seemed harmless enough, with no huge red flags among the bunch of them. Her brother, Henry, on the other hand... The guy was a real piece of work. His record up until his early thirties read like a Primer for Troubled Young Men. Everything from joyriding without permission, to a dismissed assault charge for beating up a love rival, to a variety of drunk-driving charges. All dismissed as well. His daddy had very deep pockets.

Conner shot off a note to his secretary to give Barton a raise, then reached for the phone to call Vera's cell.

"Where are you?" he asked when she picked up.

"Are you stalking me, by any chance?" She sounded more amused than irritated.

He sat back in his chair and grinned. "Hell, no. Well Maybe. But in a good way."

"Good," she said. "Then I know I've got you hooked."

"Hook, line and sinker, baby."

She chuckled softly, but he detected a sadness lurking in the tone.

"Something wrong?" he asked. "Your stepdad okay?"

The question elicited a sigh. "No, not really. He's getting worse. It's so depressing to watch."

"I'm so sorry, sweetheart. I know he means a lot to you."

"Yeah." There was a pause. "So what's up? Where are *you?*"

"At the office catching up. And I'd like to point out, you never actually answered where you are."

She laughed gently. "On the way home. I have *got* to get some sleep before work tonight."

"I've got a few hours free," he said suggestively. "I could come over and—"

"Forget it, Batman. I can barely walk as it is. God knows how I'm going to perform tonight."

He gave a bark of laughter. "That bad?"

She made a throaty moan. "That good."

He sat there beaming. You could pull down the blinds and the room would still be fully lit. "Yeah," he said. "For me, too." He made a frustrated noise. "I sure wish you were here so I could kiss you."

"Me, too. Maybe later?"

"Absolutely." Suddenly, he remembered why he'd called. "Listen, about later. I'm going to have to work until pretty late. There's a lead I need to follow on another case, but it'll only happen tonight."

"Oh. I understand," she said, trying to hide her disappointment but failing. God, she made him feel good.

"I've assigned you a bodyguard," he continued. "His name is Barton, and he'll stay with you at the club until I can get here."

"Really? You think that's necessary?"

"I hope it's not, but I won't take any chances."

She hesitated, then, "Okay."

He breathed a sigh of relief. "Thank you for not arguing."

"I can still feel that gun sticking into my back. Something I'd just as soon not experience again."

"Beautiful *and* smart," he said. "Just do what Barton says, okay?"

"Everything?" she teased.

"Ha-ha. Only if you want me in prison for homicide."

"Sweet-talker."

"You have no idea."

He heard a soft puff of breath. "I'll be waiting for you."

"Your place or mine?"

Her voice went low and throaty. "Where would you like me?"

A loaded question, if ever he'd heard one. He matched her tone. "Where haven't I had you yet?"

"You are so bad."

"That's why you love me."

Suddenly there was an awkward pause.

Ah, hell. Why had he said *that?* He covered quickly. "If I don't get to the club before your shift ends, go to my place, okay? I'll be there as soon as I can. Barton will keep me informed with what's up."

"Right," she said. "I'm home now. Gotta run. Bye."

"Be careful, honey."

But she'd already hung up.

He took a deep breath.

Way to go, idiot. Talk about almost stepping in it. He knew she was deliberately keeping her distance from him emotionally. Which was a *good* thing. Because he was, too. This affair between them was too new, too potentially disastrous, for either of them to take it lightly. Dropping the L-bomb like that…already…not good timing on anyone's clock.

Maybe she hadn't noticed.

Uh-huh.

Which was why she'd been in such an all-fired hurry to hang up.

Damn.

Vera lay in bed staring at the ceiling for two solid hours, trying to take a nap.

It was no use.

Thoughts whirled in her head, around and around at the speed of light, keeping her wide awake. Because when Conner had made that joke about her loving him, she'd almost blurted out and told him the truth. That she really did.

Love him.

Thank God she'd had the presence of mind to stop herself. What a joke. Yeah, on her.

She finally gave up and got ready for work instead. May as well go in and pick up an extra set. At least she'd be using her insomnia productively. She needed all the money she could make.

Joe was worse. A lot worse. He'd picked up an infection in his lungs, and if it didn't get better, it could easily turn into pneumonia. His nurse said a lot of Alzheimer's patients died of pneumonia. So he needed a lot of extra medications. Which cost a lot of extra money.

When she got down to the lobby, a man rose to his feet.

"Are you Burton?" she asked. When he nodded and showed her his ID, she suggested they carpool. "Seems silly to take two vehicles when we're going to the same place."

"Good idea. I'll drive," he said, and made a notation on a small spiral pad.

When they arrived at the Diamond Lounge, Lecherous Lou called her into his office right away. Barton insisted on following her and standing guard outside the door.

Seemed a bit obsessive. But it did make her feel safe.

"So," Lecherous Lou said as soon as the door was closed, "you on for tonight?"

She frowned in confusion. "Well, yeah. That's why I came in early."

He smiled, all teeth. "Great! I knew you'd come around eventually." He leered at her. "Nothing like a big spender to open a woman's eyes—and her legs—I always say."

Wait. "What are you talking about?" Obviously not the same thing she was.

"The private party tonight. You are coming, right?"

Disgust straightened her spine. "No. I've told you a million times—"

"That was before your sugar daddy signed up," he said smugly. He lifted a shoulder. "Naturally, I assumed you'd want to reap the full benefit of his generosity, and not let some other girl in on the action. After all, it's only because of your performance in the VIP room he decided to take me up on my offer."

Conner?

Shock hit her square in the gut. "You're talking about Conner Rothchild? He's going to one of your parties?"

Lou dangled a PayPal receipt in her face. "Want to change your mind? I'm telling you, the man's got a thing for you, babe. Play your cards right and your take-home pay for the night will be in the thousands. Guaranteed."

But her mind was still reeling over the fact that Conner was attending a private stripper party. *Her* Conner!

Okay, so apparently not as hers as she'd thought.

He'd lied to her! He'd said he was working tonight!

What else had he lied about?

No doubt I'll get tired of her soon...

Obviously, not about that part.

She'd been right. He *was* just like her father.

"So, you in?"

Fuming, she gave herself a severe reality check. The jerk wanted a private party? Fine. She'd give him a damn private party.

And then she'd give him a big fat piece of her mind. Right before she left him and his lying self high and dry.

For good.

"Sure," she declared, already planning her exit strategy. "Count me in."

Chapter 16

Conner was wearing a wire. Well, technically, not a wire but a tiny video camera and wireless transmitter, a handy gizmo he'd had a techie friend build into an old Rolex watch a few years back. The device beamed sound and video images to a small laptop, which he'd set up back in his room to record everything. The laptop was being monitored by a Metro vice officer recommended to him by his cousin Natalie.

Lou's party was being held in a luxurious multibedroom suite in one of the most exclusive hotels in Vegas. Unbeknownst to upper management, Conner assumed. He'd registered for a room of his own on the floor directly below, where he'd gotten ready, made sure the vice officer was comfortable and well-stocked for the night, then ridden the elevator up to the party suite.

Imagine his surprise when he found Barton standing guard outside the door.

What the—

He scowled. Heading him off, Barton jammed a thumb in the direction of the door. "Sorry, sir. She took my BlackBerry. I didn't want to leave my post to find a phone."

Conner ground his teeth. What the freaking hell? "It's okay. You did the right thing."

He rang the buzzer and waited for a long minute until the door was answered. When it finally opened, his worst fears were realized.

Vera. Wearing red silk lingerie and red satin high heels.

She looked ready to work. Hell, she looked ready to sin.

"Hello, Mr. Rothchild," she said smoothly. "Welcome."

The unforeseen development threw him for a total loop. Hadn't she said she refused to dance at these parties? "What the *hell* are you doing here?" he demanded under his breath.

"I could ask the same," she said pleasantly, crooking her arm around his elbow and drawing him inside. Except her arm was stiff and her smile glued on.

Which was his first clue that she was furious. *Really* furious.

Oh.

Hell.

Lou must have bragged to her that he was coming tonight. And invited her to join the fun. Damn. He should have anticipated that and told her himself.

"I can explain," he said.

"I'm sure you can," she said, piercing him with a look that would wither flowers. "Although I could have sworn you told me you'd be working on a lead tonight. You know, lawyer stuff."

He glanced around the large, opulent room populated with a dozen well-dressed wealthy men and maybe twenty mostly undressed girls—a couple of whom were not looking happy to be here—making sure they weren't being overheard. Behind them, the buzzer sounded and another man was ushered in by a different lady.

"I *am* working on a lead," he whispered, starting to get ticked, himself. After what they'd shared together, she should have a *little* faith.

She stared at him in abject disbelief.

Conner raised his wrist, pretending to check his Rolex. "Smile for the camera," he gritted out under his breath, and pointed the face at her. "Click."

At least she had the grace to look taken aback. "But…I thought—"

"You thought what?" he quietly demanded, leading her to the side of the room. "That I'd go off looking for a good time somewhere else? That I'd betray you like that? That I can't be *trusted?*"

Her suddenly remorseful face said it all. No. She *hadn't* trusted him.

"Great." He raked his fingers through his hair, not knowing whether to be more hurt or angry. "Thanks for the overwhelming vote of confidence."

"I'm sorry," she whispered contritely. "I didn't know. Lou said—"

"And naturally you believed him, not me. Because *he's* so trustworthy."

Definitely hurt.

Her lips turned down unhappily. "I'm sorry, Conner. The men in my life haven't had the best history for being icons of trust."

His heart zinged. Right. How could he forget? Especially after the scene last night with her own father.

With a monumental effort, he pushed back his anger. Given her background, she had every right to be wary, and he had no right to chastise her for it. With a sigh, he put his arms around her and pulled her into an embrace. "No, *I'm* sorry, honey. This is my fault. I should have told you the whole truth. I just thought—"

"You couldn't trust me?"

He gave her a sardonic smile. "No, I thought maybe you'd get jealous and want to be here for me, regardless of personal consequences. You know, so I wouldn't go with another woman."

She stared at him, chagrin clouding over her pretty green eyes. "Touché." Then her gaze darted to the door, where another pair of men had arrived, and back to him. "What lead *are* you following?"

He sent her a warning look. "Whatever it is, I can't do it with you here," he said in a low voice. "You need to leave."

"But I could help."

He set his jaw. "I don't want you involved."

"But—"

"You should go. Now. Unless you want to wind up arrested, or faced with testifying in open court."

She shook her head, eyes wide. "No."

"I didn't think so." He brushed his fingertips down her cheek. "Go home. Wait for me there." He tilted her chin up and gave her a kiss.

"Okay, I—"

"Well, well, well." They looked up at the nasty tone of an all-too-familiar figure standing next to them. "If it isn't the little gold-digging stripper again."

Conner's back went right up.

Maximillian St. Giles. He should have known a reprobate like St. Giles would show up at one of these things.

Vera's father continued his harangue of her, barely taking a breath. "What's the matter? Didn't find a big enough sucker to leech onto at the ball last night?" He puffed up and tried to look down his nose at Conner but was several inches shorter. He only succeeded in showing off his nose hairs. "Rothchild, isn't it? Michael's oldest. I see you've met my bastard daughter. Careful, she'll—"

Conner couldn't take another word. "The only bastard around here is *you,* St. Giles," he growled, easing Vera protectively behind his body. His hands were literally itching to flatten the jackass. "Tell me, if you're so high and mighty, why are *you* here?"

Maximillian glared. "I have every—"

Conner knew he shouldn't draw attention to himself, but he just couldn't stop from saying, "Not getting it at home? Is that it? The wife finally had enough and cut you off?"

"Why you—"

For every syllable Conner uttered, he was getting angrier and angrier. "Maybe you should try being a little less hypocritical, eh? And clean up that mouth of yours around a lady."

"How dare you! She's no lady."

"Vera is your *daughter,*" Conner spat out. "Your own flesh and blood! You should be loving her, taking care of her. Not heaping her with your scorn and two-faced disdain. Forcing her into this lifestyle because you refuse to take responsibility for your own actions. You are one damned poor excuse for a man, St. Giles. You're not fit to clean this woman's shoes."

He turned to find Vera covering her mouth with both hands, tears brimming over her eyelashes. She looked up at him with such an expression of misery, Conner's heart broke right in two. "Ah, sweetheart. Forget him. He's not worth your anguish." He pulled her close, turned her away from the jerk.

Another man hurried up to them anxiously. "Mr. St. Giles, are you having a problem with this girl?" The pimp du jour, no doubt. Without waiting for an answer, the pimp discreetly took her arm and urged her toward one of the bedrooms, presumably to get her things. "We can't have any disruptions. I'm afraid I'm going to have to ask you to leave immediately, Ms. LaRue."

"I understand." She glanced back at Conner, tears glistening on her cheeks. "Thank you," she said, her voice cracking, her heart in her eyes.

"Go on and get your things. I'll take you home," Conner said.

"Oh, but—" She shook her head, wiping her tears, and straightened her shoulders. "No. I'll be fine. You stay, Mr. Rothchild. I know you were looking forward to a night of pleasure." She pretended to toss it off and smile carelessly. "Please don't let this spoil your evening."

"Vera, I really—"

"Here." To his shock, she reached out and unclasped his Rolex, then took Pimp Man's wrist and put the watch on him. She gave Conner a meaningful look. "Mr. Black here is in charge of all the night's entertainment. He'll see to it you have everything you could ever wish for, Mr. Rothchild. Isn't that right, Mr. Black?"

The pimp's eyes were glued greedily to the expensive Rolex. Thank God it actually still functioned. "Everything and more," he assured Conner, glancing at a group of girls who were nervously looking on.

Conner knew what Vera was doing. The vice officer downstairs was probably having an orgasm about now. With the audio-video transmitter on the very man who set the price for every criminal act being committed here tonight, they'd have ample ammunition to make the man testify against the club managers who ran the show, and all the evidence needed to shut down these parties for good.

But Conner had never been so torn in his life. He *had* to stay. Make sure nothing went wrong. Set Black up to get the best evidence possible and protect the girls who didn't want to do the things they were being coerced into doing. But if he stayed, Vera would go home alone and crushed. Again. He'd seen how hard she'd taken her father's rejection yesterday. He didn't want to think about the tears she would surely shed tonight if he wasn't there to help her through the emotional turmoil.

"Vera—"

"It's okay, Mr. Rothchild. We'll hook up next time." She went up on her toes and gave him a long, sensual kiss filled with warmth and promise. "And I'll be sure to thank you properly."

He kissed her back, barely able to keep the love and concern spinning around inside him from bursting out of his chest. He whispered, "Promise you'll go to my place."

She nodded and gave him one last hug, then was whisked away by Mr. Black.

A few moments later, head held high, dressed and carrying her purse, she was escorted out of the suite.

He turned to see Maximillian St. Giles watching her with a look of guarded unease on his face.

The bastard.

Conner couldn't help himself. He clamped his jaw, pulled back his fist and punched the man as hard as he could.

Miraculously, Conner's not-so-little outburst did not cost him the Parker case. For some reason, St. Giles didn't press charges. In fact, he was strangely docile about the whole thing. He got up, brushed himself off, excused himself with as few words and as much dignity as he could muster and left the hotel.

After things settled down, for the next several hours Conner walked a tightrope between pretending to be a conscienceless lecher who was interested in the dozen or so women thrust at him by Mr. Black and pretending to drink copious amounts of the champagne they kept filling his glass with. He sure hoped the potted geraniums survived. All the while convincing everyone he really didn't give a damn about Vera other than her body. That Sensitive New-Age Guy performance earlier? Just him trying to get laid.

It would have stretched the thespian skills of a seasoned actor, let alone a lawyer whose skills in that direction came solely from the drama of the courtroom.

Somehow he managed to pull it off, though, and by around three in the morning the officer downstairs had gotten enough evidence to send the Metro vice squad bursting into the suite to take down the whole operation. Everyone got arrested except Conner. But he nevertheless spent the rest of the night arranging bail and deals for the handful of dancers who'd been coerced into working the private party. They'd be good witnesses, and their testimony would corroborate the story of his original client, Suzie Parker, and her prostitution charges would be dismissed.

All in all, a very good night's work, but by the time he got out of there, it was almost noon.

He should be proud, and heading home to a well-deserved night's…well, midday's…sleep. Instead, he was breaking all speed limits to get back home to Vera. He was worried about her and couldn't wait to pull her into his arms and sink down into his bed and just let out a long sigh of relief that she was okay. Maybe get a little sleep before showing her how hard he was falling for her.

Maybe even telling her.

Wow. How terrifying was *that?*

He was just passing the Luxor when his cell phone rang. It was Barton.

"Hey, what's up? Is Vera okay?"

"She's fine, Mr. Rothchild. As I texted you, I drove her to your place last night, and your Miss Hildy took good care of her. Put her to bed, and I sat outside her door the whole night. No suspicious activity at all."

"Excellent."

Barton continued, "But this morning she got a call from

Mr. Henry St. Giles and apparently made plans to go out to lunch with him in a few minutes. I'm sorry, sir, I didn't find out until just now. Do you want me to follow them?"

Hell's bells, Barton must be dead on his feet. Conner definitely was, and he'd actually been able to catch a long catnap in an empty LVMPD conference room while everyone was being processed into the system.

He pushed out a breath. "Where are they going, do you know?" Barton named a small restaurant just off the Strip. "Okay, can you make sure she gets there safely? Then you're done for the day. I'll meet you and take over from there."

"Sure thing, Mr. Rothchild."

He thanked the man for his diligence and made a quick right, heading for the restaurant.

He got to the parking lot before Vera and didn't see Henry waiting. Which gave Conner time to figure out how to handle this. It would be stupid for him just to sit in his car and stake out the place. Aside from which, he might easily fall asleep. Or something could happen to her inside the restaurant.

Because to be honest, Conner was a bit concerned about Henry's motives in courting Vera's favor. His sudden appearance in her life out of nowhere was more than a little suspicious.

Conner was not forgetting his assignment for Special Agent Lex Duncan, to narrow down possible suspects in the interstate jewelry theft ring the FBI was trying to crack—the same ring Duncan highly suspected Henry's sister, Darla, of being part of.

Vera was hoping Darla was innocent, but Conner wasn't so sure she was. What would be more natural than a brother-sister team of high-end thieves?

And if either of them was involved in his cousin Candace's murder, Vera could be in genuine danger meeting with Henry. Conner'd already seen Darla arguing with the man he was convinced stole the Quetzal from the police—likely the same man who later attacked Silver and then Vera, searching for the illusive diamond after he'd failed to hang on to it while he had it. Duncan was waiting for more concrete evidence, but Conner was convinced that man was the link between the ring and Candace's murder.

Would it be such a stretch if Henry somehow had his fingers deep in this mess, too? Even if he didn't, he was Maximillian St. Giles's son and heir. What did he want with Vera after all these years? Nothing good, Conner figured.

Conner decided to let Vera and Henry go into the restaurant after they arrived and got seated; then he'd casually walk in and spot them like his being there was a pure coincidence. Vera would probably twig, but after her quick uptake and play-along last night, he wasn't worried she'd give him away.

That way he could simply join them for lunch. Vera would be safe. And he could subtly pump Henry for information while they ate.

Problem solved.

Except, unfortunately, that's not how things worked out.

Henry arrived first, not unexpectedly. He should have realized something was up when the other man didn't let the valet park his car. But Conner was distracted by Barton cruising past the McLaren and giving Conner a thumbs-up, indicating Vera was right behind him.

Henry, leaning against the door of his Lexus, waved to Vera when she drove into the lot and let the valet whisk her Camry away. Conner raised a brow at the touching hug they exchanged, Henry smiling broadly as he then teasingly touched her earlobe. *Oh, please. Don't fall for it, sweetheart.* The guy had serious bloodsucking scum written all over him. How could Vera possibly miss that transparently fake smarm?

Because she was looking for something else in the man. Like acceptance. Affection. Warmth.

Family.

But still, Conner was not prepared when Henry went around and opened the passenger door for her and she climbed into the Lexus. With a spin of the wheels, Henry peeled out of the parking lot.

Whoa! What had just happened? Had they decided to go to a different restaurant? Or was something else going on?

Conner jackknifed up, gunned the engine and took off after them.

When Henry made a sharp turn onto an all-too-conve-niently-situated freeway ramp onto the I-15 south, the major route heading out of the city, Conner really started to worry. So much so that he pulled out his phone and speed-dialed Duncan and then his cousin Natalie.

He wanted backup. Just in case.

Because suddenly, he had a really, really bad feeling about this whole thing.

Chapter 17

"Where are we going, again?" Vera glanced around at the downtown area fast disappearing behind them and bit her lip. "I thought you were taking me to lunch."

"I am!" Henry grinned over at her. "There is this amazing little bistro up in the mountains above Henderson I want you to try. Very chichi. The food there is so incredible, and the view is spectacular. You can see all the way to Lake Mead."

"Okay…" Vera knew Henderson was a growing tourist destination all on its own, but she'd never heard about a fantastic restaurant in the mountains *above* the Vegas suburb. But Henry—she couldn't believe she was finally getting to know her brother!—was presumably a lot more dialed into the hideaways of the rich and famous.

"You're not in a hurry, are you?" he asked politely, even though he was driving like a speed demon.

"No, of course not," she rushed to say. She didn't want to

annoy him the first time they did anything together. Either about his choice of restaurants or his driving habits. She smiled over at him. "I can't wait."

But still... When he bypassed the main exit to Henderson but took a long back road in, she started getting concerned. Not nervous, exactly. More like...uneasy. But he was happily chatting about the Lights of Vegas Charity Ball and how he wished he'd known earlier she was there, and how terribly embarrassed he'd been about his father's—*their* father's, he quickly corrected himself—behavior that night, and how he'd heard so many good things about her from Darla. He seemed so kind and attentive that Vera just couldn't interrogate him about their destination.

Nevertheless, she wished she'd called Conner to tell him where she was going.

Lord, she'd been so upset last night when he never came home. She'd stared at the ceiling until the sun was streaming through the windows and still he hadn't gotten home. In her mind she knew why. She understood what he was doing. That he was not cheating on her. That he hadn't gotten tired of her already and was out having fun with another woman. He was working. He'd probably gotten caught up in...well, God knew what. But whatever it was, she was sure he had a good reason why he couldn't be there for her.

But she'd needed him so badly. She'd been devastated by her father's renewed attack on her and had desperately wanted Conner's warm, comforting presence to soothe the razor-sharp pain in her heart. And in that same hurting heart, she'd felt the slightest bit betrayed.

Even though she knew it was wrong to blame him, that he had an important job to do, she'd been mad enough to arrange this lunch with her brother and take off without paying any heed to Barton's warnings that she shouldn't leave Conner's house. She saw now she'd been acting like a selfish baby.

Surreptitiously, she glanced in the side mirror to see if she could catch a glimpse of Barton following her. But she hadn't seen him since before leaving the restaurant where she'd met Henry. At least she didn't think so. She thought there might have been someone following far behind them, but it wasn't the same color car as Barton had been driving and had since disappeared. Probably wishful thinking on her part. Last night she'd tried to get him to lie down on the sofa, but he'd insisted on sitting up the whole night on a chair outside her door punching buttons on his ubiquitous BlackBerry. No doubt Barton had figured she was safe having lunch with her own brother and had gone home to get some sleep.

So she was on her own here.

Her heartbeat kicked up as Henry turned the car onto an old macadam road heading up into the craggy desert bluffs. "Doesn't this go up to where all those old quarries are located?" she asked.

He glanced at her in surprise. "You know about those?"

"Doesn't everyone?" She gripped the car seat with her fingers. "Are you *sure* this is the way to the bistro?"

"Actually, we're making a quick stop first."

Okay, now she was officially nervous. "Where?" She hadn't been able to stop her voice from squeaking.

He glanced over at her, an enigmatic look on his face. "To see Darla."

"What!?" Confusion coursed through her. Along with a tingling of fear. Why wouldn't he have said that in the first place? *Oh, God.* Had she made a horrible mistake trusting him?

Her pulse doubled. She should bail. Even though the car was climbing up a steep incline and on her side a sheer cliff dropped a hundred feet practically straight down, she should jump out right now. Take her chances on foot—if she survived the fall—while they still weren't too far from civilization and she had a shot at making it back alive.

A shot...

Cold fear surged through her veins. What if he had a gun?

"I had to hide her where no one could find her," he said all-too calmly. "You'll understand when you see her."

Yeah, because she was probably *dead*. The man was a sociopath!

Blind panic had her grabbing the door handle and yanking hard. It didn't budge. *Ohgodohgodohgod*. He had the child safety locks on.

"What are you doing?" he barked, slashing her a glare. "Are you nuts?"

"No, but *you* are if you think I'm just going to sit here and—"

Suddenly, he swung the car behind a huge boulder and pulled to a halt amid a cloud of dust that nearly obscured the silhouette of an ancient mining hut.

"Don't be stupid, Vera," he said, unlocking the doors.

She jerked it open and lunged out, taking off at a run. And immediately tripped in the gravelly sand. Hell! She'd wanted to impress Henry so she'd dressed to the nines, including the pair of exorbitantly expensive high heels she'd borrowed from Darla's closet for the ball. The spike heels pierced the sand like tiny jackhammers, and one of them broke off, hurling her forward into a warm body.

She screamed.

"Vera! Oh, thank God you've come!" wailed Darla, grabbing onto her and giving her a death-grip hug, then pulling away to peer frantically into her eyes. "You've got to help me!" Her voice was filled with desperation.

And her face was covered by knuckle-size cuts and livid purple bruises, her wrist wrapped in a discolored bandage.

"Oh, God, Darla! What has that monster done to you?"

"He beat me up," she wailed, "and I didn't know what to do. I'm so sor—"

Behind her, the car door slammed. Vera didn't wait to hear more of Darla's explanation. She kicked off the ruined shoes, and at the same time as she spun to face Henry, she swooped down and grabbed a fist-size rock from the ground, shoving Darla behind her.

"Vera? No! Wait!" Henry rushed toward them, reaching into his pocket. Going for his gun!

She raised her arm, prepared to fling the rock at his head.

"Vera!" Darla grabbed her wrist. "What are you *doing?!*"

Vera hesitated in confusion. Just as a loud gunshot rang out, cracking the air like thunder.

To her shock, Henry cried out and jerked backward, a cloud of red blossoming around his right shoulder as he fell to the ground.

"Henry!" Darla shrieked. "My God, *Henry!*"

He'd been *shot!*

It hadn't happened often, but there had been one or two shootings at the clubs where she'd worked, so Vera knew enough to hit the dirt. She pulled Darla down with her and immediately started tugging her toward Henry and the car.

"What the hell is going on?" she asked, keeping the panic at bay by a thread as they scurried. "Who's shooting at us?" And from where? The hut?

"It's Thomas! Oh, Vera, I'm so sorry I got you into this! He threatened to kill me if we didn't get you up here! You have to believe me, we didn't want to, but he swore he wouldn't hurt any of us if you only came."

Thomas? Darla's ex-boyfriend, Thomas? "*Me?* Why me?"

Another shot erupted and whined off the boulder just above her.

"The ring!" Darla cried in despair. "He wants the diamond ring! You know, the one I told you to hide for me?"

They sprinted the last few feet. "But I don't have it! The police do!"

"What?" Darla looked at her in horror. *"Noooo!* Now we're dead for sure."

But there was no time to explain. They'd reached Henry. "Grab his feet!" she ordered her sister as she put her arms around her brother's chest to drag him to safety behind the vehicle. As she did, a newspaper clipping fluttered from his fingertips. Not a gun.

"Oh, Henry," she murmured distraughtly. He hadn't wanted to kill her. Some maniac was trying to kill *him!*

Three shots in succession punched through the windshield of the Lexus as she and Darla frantically hauled Henry around to the other side between the car and the boulder.

Correction: someone was trying to kill *all three of them.*

Lord. How had she gotten things so wrong?

Darla was sobbing, and if Vera weren't so terrified, she'd be dissolving into tears herself. But her instinct for self-preservation was too strong. It kicked in big time. One advantage of growing up hard and fast, she thought sardonically.

She pulled off her summer jacket and pressed it to Henry's bleeding shoulder. "Here, hold this here," she told Darla, taking her hand and pushing it firmly onto the cloth. "Harder, or he'll bleed to death."

Darla shuddered out a sob but obeyed. "What are you going to do?"

"Get my cell phone."

Vera reached up from the ground and eased open the Lexus door. Immediately a shot took out the driver's window. Lord, how many shots did that gun have? She tried desperately to remember how many Clint Eastwood counted before he asked the bad guy if he felt lucky...

Okay, that *so* didn't matter. *Focus!*

Sucking down a deep breath, she opened the door wide and snaked onto the car's floor on her belly, snagged her purse from the other side and wiggled out again. Success!

She whipped out the phone and frantically hit speed-dial number one. *Conner.*

"Please answer. Please, please, please," she prayed. "I swear, I'll never doubt you again. Or get mad at you. Or do anything to make you—"

"Ver...? Where the...ll are...?" His anxious voice surged across time and space to yell at her. Well, space anyway. Sort of. Static broke up the words, but she got the drift.

She sobbed with relief. "Thank God. Oh, thank God."

"...alk to me, damn it! I...rd *shots*....where the h...id he take...ou?"

"We're on a little road up in the mountains behind Henderson!" she said, exchanging a desperate look with Darla when Henry moaned in agony. "Nearly up to those old gravel quarries!"

"...reaking know that! *Where?*"

Two more shots blasted through the noon heat, plinking through the car hood and zinging off the engine block right above them.

She and Darla both let out bloodcurdling screams.

"Vera! V...! Are y...ight?" Conner's voice shouted through the phone.

"Yes! Sorry! We're just so scared!"

"Wh...'s wit...ou?"

"Darla and Henry are with me. Henry's been shot! Oh, Conner, he might die if he doesn't get—"

"Vera, list...me! H...the...rn!"

"What?"

"...orn! Hon...e horn!"

"Horn?" What did he— "Oh!" Suddenly hope blasted through her chest. Was he that close by? "Hang on!" She thrust the phone into Darla's lap and crawled partially into the car again. She reached up and gave the horn a hard blast.

This time the bullet came through the passenger door and thwacked into the driver's seat, not twelve inches from her head. She smacked a hand to her mouth to muffle her terrified scream and hit the horn again two more times, then slammed herself down onto the ground. She met Darla's wild, tear-filled eyes again. A bullet must have severed some wires because the horn continued to blare like a siren. Or was it the car alarm?

"Vera! *Vera!*"

She whipped her gaze to the phone in Darla's lap. But Conner's voice wasn't coming from there. It was coming from—

His car fishtailed around the boulder, blasting its horn and spraying gravel all around it like a machine-gun turret. Conner hung out of the driver's-side window shouting her name.

"Conner!" She jumped up and ran straight for him as he dove from the car, rolled and came up sprinting. Belatedly she realized running to him wasn't the smartest move. He grabbed her and lunged back behind the Lexus.

"Get the hell down!"

But no more bullets came at them. No more shots. As they held their breath, the only sounds to be heard were the distant cry of a hawk, the warm breeze rustling through the creosote bushes and the ticking of Conner's car engine.

"Is he gone?" Darla half sobbed in a pathetic whisper.

"Yeah," Conner finally said after a few more tense moments. "I think he is."

And that's when Vera lost it. Sinking down in his arms, she collapsed in a flood of tears.

Chapter 18

Agent Duncan wheeled up ten minutes after Conner in an unmarked SUV, followed closely by Conner's cousin Natalie, who wailed up in a LVMPD cruiser with lights spinning and sirens blaring. Thank God he'd called them when he did.

By now, Conner'd gotten Vera reassured and Darla's hysterics under control, and the three of them had managed to stop Henry's bleeding and make him comfortable until the ambulance could arrive. He was going in and out of consciousness, but Conner was pretty sure he'd live.

Before the cavalry arrived, Conner had refrained from asking more than two questions, since he knew they'd all just have to go through the story again with Duncan. But his mind burned with theories.

Especially after he found a newspaper clipping on the ground. It was an article about the charity fund-raiser held at Luke Montgomery's Janus Casino several months ago. Next to the column was a photo taken at the event, of Candace showing off the Tears of the Quetzal for the camera. On the night of her murder.

Coincidence?

He didn't think so.

That's what had prompted his two questions. That, along with Darla's badly bruised face.

"Did you beat up your sister?" he asked Henry during one of his lucid moments.

Pain flared in the other man's eyes, though Conner couldn't say if it was physical or mental. "No," Henry rasped. "I'd never hurt Darla."

Darla had gasped softly at the question and nodded at her brother's answer. "He wouldn't," she assured Conner brokenly. "Ever."

Satisfied, Conner accepted that and returned his gaze to Henry. "Did you kill Candace Rothchild?" he asked evenly.

Henry's eyes squeezed closed, and he hacked out a dry laugh. "No. She almost got *me* killed." He opened his eyes. "And my sister." He glanced at Vera apologetically. "And now almost my other sister, too."

Baffled, Conner furrowed his brow. "Candace is dead. How could she possibly be behind the shootings today?"

Okay, so three questions.

But Henry slipped into unconsciousness, his mouth going slack, and didn't answer.

"This wasn't Henry's fault, Conner," Vera said. "He was trying to save Darla's life."

But she didn't have a chance to explain further because just then Duncan and Natalie had gotten there and leaped from their vehicles, weapons drawn and shouting orders to their subordinates to fan out and start searching for the gunman Conner had alerted them to as soon as he'd heard the first shots fired.

"Conner! Are you okay?" His cousin Natalie came running up at full tilt, double-fisted grip on her service revolver, looking like a lean, mean cop on a mission.

Conner rose and swept one arm around her waist and gave her a big hug. "I'm good, Nat. Thanks for coming. I know it's not Metro jurisdiction."

She holstered her weapon and squeezed him back. "Are you kidding? Family's family."

It hadn't always been that way. Natalie was Candace's twin sister and had participated fully in the disparagement of young wrong-side-of-the-family Conner. However, Natalie had matured emotionally faster than her twin; she'd realized their taunting was wrong and hurtful and stopped her part of the torment around the time they graduated high school. Candace never had. But then, by that time, Conner had realized she was an equal-opportunity bitch. Family, foe, friend, stranger: she didn't care who she ripped apart. Anyway, over the past ten years or so, he and Natalie had actually become good friends.

Which was probably why her brows hit her hairline when he noticed that his *other* arm was firmly around Vera and that Vera was clinging to him like a limpet to a ship's hull.

Ah, hell.

He knew damned well that whatever Natalie knew, the whole damn Rothchild clan would soon know…which meant word would get back to his parents in about, oh, ten seconds flat.

He really wasn't prepared for this now.

"Natalie, this is Vera Mancuso. Vera, my cousin Natalie," he said to stave off any immediate pointed inquiries, and left it at that, despite Natalie's crazy eye gyrations, and the fact that he refused to let go of Vera even if it meant he was so freaking busted.

"Nice to meet you, Vera," Natalie said. "Wish these were more pleasant circumstances."

"Thanks, me, too," Vera murmured softly.

"Were you and Ms. St. Giles injured?" Natalie asked.

Vera swallowed and darted a glance at Darla, who was holding Henry's hand as the EMTs loaded him onto a stretcher. "I wasn't. Darla was beaten, but I don't have it exactly straight who did it. Not Henry, though," she said and looked up to Conner for support.

"That's what they both claim," he affirmed. "I believe them on that point. But they're obviously involved in some seriously bad stuff. And…" He dug in his pocket and wordlessly handed Natalie the newspaper clipping.

She froze, absorbed the implications in a nanosecond and motioned to Darla to hold out her wrists. "Sorry," she said bringing out her handcuffs. "I've gotta do this."

"Whatever," Darla said bleakly.

"Come on. You can say goodbye to your brother before he's taken to the hospital."

"Wait!" Vera said and stepped away from Conner to give her sister a mutually tearful hug.

"Thanks, sis," Darla said, choking up. "He really was going to kill us. You saved our lives."

"No," she denied, wiping her tears. "It was Conner who saved the day. I just beeped the horn."

Nevertheless, Darla said, "You've always been my biggest hero," and kissed Vera's cheek as Natalie, for some reason, smiled at *him,* then led Darla away.

"Beeped the horn, my patoot," Conner said, turning back to Vera, who was suddenly preoccupied with wiping the dust off her ruined skirt. "You're far too humble." That's when he noticed she was barefoot. "And what *is* it with you and shoes?" he asked with a tender smile, and swept her up in his arms just to be able to hold her tight. He was so damn proud of her. "I always seem to be carrying you around. Not that I'm complaining," he added in a low murmur in her ear. "Gives me a chance to cop a feel."

She gifted him with a sweet, watery smile. "You really don't have to carry me. If it embarrasses you, I can—"

"Don't be silly. Why would it embarrass me?" Where had *that* come from? He started walking toward the car, then paused. "Um, listen, I'd like a quick word with Duncan. You want to come with? Or…?"

"Would you mind if I just sat in your car and waited?" she asked, nibbling on her lip. "My knees are still shaking so hard I don't know if they'll hold me up. And to be honest…it makes me cry to see my sister in handcuffs."

"My poor darling." He sneaked a kiss onto her hair, brought her to his car and deposited her gently in the passenger seat. "You just relax. There's a bottle of water behind the seat, if you want it."

She nodded, and he could feel her eyes on him as he made his way over to the ambulance where Natalie was still holding the newspaper clipping with her arms folded over her chest. Duncan was talking to Darla while Henry was loaded into the back of the bus.

Duncan turned to Conner as he came up. "I probably shouldn't tell you this…." His lips quirked in resignation. "But I figure you'll hear it all from Detective Rothchild, here, anyway. Besides, I owe you one…seems you've broken my case wide open for me."

"Always happy to be of service to our friends at the Bureau." He winked at Natalie.

Duncan snorted. "Anyway, Ms. St. Giles has corroborated Ms. Mancuso's statement as to how she came into possession of the stolen Tears of the Quetzal ring and has also absolved her sister of all involvement in any jewelry thefts."

Conner smiled. "Vera will be relieved to hear that. Listen,

would you mind if I asked Darla a question?" The ambulance carrying Henry pulled away, and Duncan turned back to Conner, looking uncertain. "I've already read Ms. St. Giles her rights. She doesn't have to say a word."

"I understand."

"Well. Then it's up to her."

"Ask me," Darla said. "I owe you that much for showing up when you did."

Since she'd been read her rights, he also assumed she'd waived her right to an attorney.

"Okay, your brother said *Candace* nearly killed you both. What did he mean by that?"

A dark shadow passed over her face. "As I've already told Special Agent Duncan…if it weren't for her, we wouldn't be in this mess. My brother and I may have stolen a few pieces of jewelry, but we've never hurt anyone. Jeez. We did it for the thrills, not to get ourselves shot at."

"So how'd that happen?"

She unconsciously worried the bandage on her arm. "This guy, Thomas Smythe, approached us maybe six months ago, wanted to join in our—" she shrugged "—you know, the jewelry thing. He and I hit it off at first and we hooked up for a while. But it turns out he was only using me to get close to Candace."

"Why?" Conner asked. Not that anyone ever needed a reason. Candace had been a force of nature, attracting all sorts of people—weirdos and saints alike. They all wanted to bask in the light of her stardust and notoriety. "What did this Thomas guy want with her?"

"Not her," Darla explained. "Thomas was obsessed with the Tears of the Quetzal. I'm telling you, the guy was bonkers. He talked Henry into trying to steal it." She shrugged again. "Hell, why not? Even cut up into smaller stones, it would bring millions. I'd finally be free to do anything I wanted. With or without the approval of my father."

Aha. So Conner's theory about her had been right.

"Anyway, since I was friends with Candace, my job was to persuade her to sneak it out of her daddy's safe." Darla rolled her eyes. "Talk about obsessive. Her old man is nearly as crazy as Thomas about that ring." Suddenly, she remembered who she was talking to and winced at Natalie. "Sorry. I forgot he's your dad, too."

"No, you're right. He does have a major bug up his nose about that ring. He's convinced it's cursed."

Darla nodded vigorously. "Yeah! So did Thomas. But he's got it in his head the ring will give him some sort of special powers. Something about revenge or some nonsense like that. He was never real coherent when he talked about that stuff." Her mouth turned downward. "I should have listened to my instincts. After a while I broke up with the nutcase and stopped baiting Candace to borrow the ring, but Henry still had this deal with him to fence the diamond if he stole it from her."

"So what went wrong?" Conner asked.

She covered her mouth with a trembling hand, then slid it down to unconsciously touch the bruises on her throat. "The night of that big charity deal at Luke Montgomery's casino, it was all over the local news. You know—" she made quote marks with her fingers "—'Film at six! Live from the red carpet!' God, and there she was, wearing the damn thing on national TV! I mean, we knew Thomas would go for it that night."

"Did he?" Duncan asked grimly.

Tears welled in Darla's eyes. "I honestly don't know. When we heard Candace had been murdered and the ring was missing…" She swallowed.

Natalie burst out accusingly, "My God, Darla! He killed her and you didn't come forward? She was your friend!"

"I would have, honest, but Thomas swore he didn't do it!" Darla wailed. "He was furious, and he didn't have the ring, so I believed him!"

That fit, unfortunately. The ring had disappeared after the murder, but then was found in the possession of Luke Montgomery's fiancée, Amanda, hidden in her purse unbeknownst to anyone. There was rampant speculation as to how it had gotten there, but as soon as it was found, Amanda Patterson had turned it over to the police. She hadn't even been in Las Vegas at the time of Candace's murder, so she was never a suspect.

"After the ring turned up in that woman's purse," Darla continued, "the papers all said the police were holding it as evidence. So Thomas hatched this crazy plan to disguise himself as a cop and walk right in there and check it out of the evidence room! And damned if it didn't work!" She sounded amazed.

Conner could see Natalie gritting her teeth. He knew heads had rolled over *that* one. He'd personally seen to it.

"So," Conner asked Darla, "why were you arguing with him outside the cop shop after he pulled it off?"

Her jaw dropped. "How did you know about that?"

"I saw you. I was on my way in."

"So *you're* the one who figured out so quickly he'd left the paste ring in its place!"

Conner nodded. "I recognized the copy. How did he get hold of it, anyway?"

"He claims he posed as a reporter to gain admittance into Harold Rothchild's mansion. Candace had once told him he stepmother kept an old paste copy of the Tears of the Quetza in her jewelry case in the bedroom upstairs."

Naturally.

Harold's fourth wife was of the trophy variety and not th brightest bulb on the Christmas tree. It was hard to imagin a rational person keeping a million-dollar jewel in a box on the vanity. Oy. She probably thought just because it wasn't the original it wasn't valuable.

"Pretty clever of him," Conner conceded. "Might have worked, too, if Harold hadn't insisted I go and try to get the ring out of police custody."

"Dad never did trust cops," Natalie muttered. An understatement. Harold had not been happy when she became one.

"Apparently not just cops," Darla said. "Candace told us your father refuses to let anyone near the Tears of the Quetzal, ever."

"Yes, but it isn't about trust, it's about that stupid curse," Natalie said with a hint of annoyance.

"Anyway…" Darla cast her eyes downward again, looking honestly distressed. "If I thought for a minute he'd killed Candace, I would have called you, even though it meant getting heat on the jewelry thing. But he swore he didn't touch her." Her eyes welled. "But now, after he did this to me—" she looked up, gestured to her battered face, and her voice grew thready "—and trying to shoot us today…" Her tears spilled over her lashes.

"You think it was him doing the shooting?" Duncan asked.

"I *know* it was. Who else would it be? The man is a damn lunatic. He's *dangerous*. I'll sign a sworn statement, whatever you need to arrest this guy, but I want protection for Henry and me in exchange, until he's behind bars."

"I'll see what I can do to get you a deal," Duncan said. "Rothchild, you coming down to Metro? LVMPD is taking the suspects into custody for now. But I'll need your statement, along with Ms. Mancuso's."

"Sure thing." Hell, Conner'd gone *this* long without sleep, what was another few hours? He was on about his third…or maybe fourth wind, by now. "We'll meet you there."

Natalie waved to him as she led off her prisoner, then

darted a glance over to his car. "By the way, will we see you at dinner tomorrow, Conner?" she called.

"Not sure. I'll let you know," he called back, heading to the driver's-side door.

Lately he'd gotten into the habit of having dinner at the "other" Rothchilds' on Monday nights. But frankly, he'd rather spend the time with Vera. He slid into the car and smiled across at her, but…she was fast asleep. He leaned over and quietly snapped her belt over her lap, planting a kiss on her temple as he did so.

"Conner?" she murmured sleepily, her eyes still closed.

"Yeah, babe."

"You're not my Prince Charming anymore."

He raised his brows in amusement. Was she talking in her sleep? "No?"

"Nmn-mmnh. That was just for one night." She sighed dreamily. "Now you're my knight in shining armor."

He'd take it. "Okay."

"Know who that makes me?"

"No. Who?"

She giggled softly, still not opening her eyes. "Sleeping Beauty." She sighed and snuggled down into the soft leather of the bucket seat. Totally oblivious.

He laughed, marveling at the ability of this amazing woman to take a horrible situation and pluck the one positive note from its depths. Even in her sleep she was relentlessly optimistic and charmingly romantic.

God, he loved her.

Now if he could just get his family to love her the same way…to see all the good in her…to accept her as worthy of the Rothchild name.

Was that too much to ask?

Unfortunately, he feared it just might be.

Chapter 19

Vera was too wiped out to protest when Conner carried her up from his car to her penthouse.

"We've got to stop meeting like this," she murmured.

"Why?" he asked with a grin.

She couldn't think of a damn reason. So she reached up and kissed him. He winked back at her and carried her into the apartment. They were just here for a quick stop on the way to the police station. For shoes. And a change of clothes. The ones she had on were covered in dirt and blood.

"Maybe a quick shower, too?" she asked.

"Only if I can watch."

She smiled demurely. "Or you could join me."

"How quick are we talking here?"

"That all depends."

"On?"

"How good you are at lathering up."

He made a very male sound deep in his throat. "Oh, honey, I'm *real* good."

"I somehow knew that," she said, wrapping her arms around his neck and kissing him all the way to the bathroom.

He set her down and closed the door behind them with a firm click. Then advanced on her, murmuring, "Baby, prepare to be thoroughly lathered."

Conner's cousin Natalie, the homicide detective, only blinked once when he and Vera walked into Metro headquarters still damp from their not-quite-so-quick shower. She did, however, raise an eyebrow in salute to Vera.

Good thing *Conner* wasn't a detective, because he was totally clueless to the whole female-to-female exchange.

Vera was feeling so good, she couldn't help but smile back at the woman. She hoped there wouldn't be fallout because of Natalie's astute observation. She knew Conner's rich family would not be pleased he was dating someone like her. Her own father's ubiquitous "gold-digger" insults rang a constant reminder in her head of how people like the Rothchilds thought of people in her social class. As in poor. Dirt poor.

Whatever. She still had him for today, and that's all that mattered. What tomorrow brought, she'd deal with tomorrow.

Special Agent Duncan was there, too, and took Conner into a conference room to get his statement. Natalie led Vera over to her desk to take hers.

"Sorry about the luxurious accommodations," she quipped snagging them each a cup of coffee along the way. "Interrogation rooms are all full. Sugar?"

"Just cream," Vera said. "Thanks. No problem."

Natalie very professionally went through the statement procedure, making sure she wrote everything down just right

Then she handed the papers off to a junior officer to get them typed up for signature.

"So," she began, leaning back in her creaky office chair while they waited, "you and Conner, eh?"

"Um." Ho-boy. She should have known this was coming. Now what? "It's not serious," Vera echoed his words from yesterday morning to his dad, as much as she wished she dared say otherwise. "We just met, really."

Natalie nodded. "I figured as much. Since you weren't at the Lights of Las Vegas Charity Ball with him."

"Oh, I was there," she said without thinking. *Oops.* "Um. Just not *with* him."

Natalie stared at him. "So, you, like, met him there? Or earlier today?" She blinked again. "Please tell me not at the crime scene." She could tell the woman wanted to be scandalized but was only succeeding in being greatly amused. And trying valiantly to hide it.

"Not at the crime scene," Vera confirmed with a half smile. "Actually it was…four days ago." Had it been such a short time? It seemed like she'd known him a lifetime already. And yet…for only hours.

"Yeah? Where'd you meet?"

Vera felt like she was being interrogated.

Oh, wait. She *was* being interrogated. By a homicide detective concerning her favorite cousin. Territory didn't get much more dangerous than that.

Better play this straight, not only because Natalie would see right through lies, but…she may as well know the truth so she wouldn't get all excited about cuz's new girlfriend and blab to the family. Maybe this way she'd keep it to herself, and Conner wouldn't be embarrassed.

"He saw me dance," Vera said. She went to take a sip of

coffee. Except her hand was inexplicably shaking, so hot liquid sloshed over the rim. She hurriedly put it down again.

Natalie opened her top desk drawer and tossed her a napkin. "Can't take me anywhere, either," she said with a commiserating grin. Still trying to be friends. Vera wanted to cry. "So you're a showgirl. Cool. What show do you work?"

Oh. Crap.

She gave up, and looked Conner's cousin in the eyes. "The Diamond Lounge."

"Oh." Then it really registered. "Oh!" Natalie's eyes got wide. "You mean… A *dancer.* That's, um. Nice."

Yeah.

Thank God, the junior officer returned with her statement. She took as little time as possible to read and sign the thing, then rose and held out her hand. "Good to meet you, Detective. I should be going now. Got to get ready for work."

"Oh. Of course. Sure." She shook her hand, mumbled a thanks for the statement and escorted her back to the waiting area out front. "But you do know we shut down the Diamond Lounge last night, right?" she said as Vera was about to leave.

Vera halted. Frowned. "Closed down?"

Natalie said, "Yeah, Conner orchestrated this big sting of club managers over some call-girl deal, and the clubs all shut down until owners can get other management in place. It'll probably be a few days before the club reopens."

"Oh. I had no idea."

"Not surprising. Been a bit busy today," Natalie said wryly.

"Yeah. Well. Thanks for the heads-up. Guess I'll have the night off."

"Oh, and Vera?"

She paused. "Yes?"

"Conner's coming over to our house for dinner on Monday

Kind of a new tradition, since…" She cleared her throat. "Anyway, we'd love for you to join us, too, if you can make it."

Disbelief sifted through her. Surely, she was kidding.

Just then, the desk sergeant called over to her, "Ms. Mancuso?"

She tore her gaze from Natalie. "Yes?"

"Can you wait for just a moment? There's someone who wants to speak with you before you go."

Rats. Conner must be finished, too. She wasn't sure she could handle being scrutinized next to him, not now that his cousin knew who she really was. Especially not after that unexpected invitation. *He'd* have to field that one. Vera dare not touch it with a ten-foot pole.

But it wasn't Conner who wanted to talk.

The door opened and out walked the last person on earth she wanted to see.

Her father.

No. No, no, *no*. Not here. Not right now.

She spun on a toe and practically sprinted for the door.

"Vera! Wait!" His voice boomed across the reception area.

She fought to hold back sudden tears. Of all days. Why did he *always* have to—

She fumbled with the door handle, unable to get it open. He reached her and put a hand on her shoulder. She stiffened, waiting for the verbal abuse to start.

"Vera. Please. I know I don't deserve it. But for the love of God, please let me say something to you."

He didn't deserve it? More like *she* didn't. Mutely, she took a cleansing breath and turned to face the barrage.

She was shocked at what she saw. His face was gray, haggard, his eyes bloodshot and rimmed with red. One of them was bruised by a half moon of purple.

He swallowed, his Adam's apple bobbing several times. "I just want to say…thank you," he said, shocking her even more.

Was this some kind of cruel trick? She felt her lips part but for the life of her couldn't think of what to say. It was like she'd landed in some kind of weird parallel universe. Dinner invitations from detectives. Thank-you's from her father. What next?

"Darla told me what you did," he choked out. "That you saved her life. And my son's. That they would both be dead now if it weren't for your calm thinking and unselfish bravery."

"She e-exaggerates," Vera stammered. Still waiting for the other shoe to drop.

"Somehow, I don't think so," he said, voice cracking. "I've been wrong about you, Vera. Your whole life, I've treated you like trash because of my own cowardly refusal to confront my feelings about—" He halted. Cleared his throat. "In any case…words can't express how truly sorry I am."

Wow.

Her throat tightened, almost squeezing the air from her windpipe and sending a flood of emotions cascading from her heart. Almost. But she would *not* let herself break down.

Nor would she fling herself into his arms and cry, "Daddy!"

Or even succumb to the shameful temptation of being a mean to him as he'd earned through his own despicable behavior over the years.

"Okay," she managed, thoroughly shell-shocked.

He looked at her desperately. "Please," he begged softly. "Forgive me?"

Tears stung the back of her eyelids, screaming to come out. This was so damn unfair. How could she forgive him after he'd caused her a lifetime of misery? *And* her mother?

How could she not?

"Sure," she rasped out. "I'll forgive you." Someday. "I've got to go now."

She turned, grabbed the entry door handle to escape, then turned back to Natalie, who'd been watching the entire exchange silently, with a studiously neutral look on her face. "Detective Rothchild," Vera said, her voice barely working. "About that dinner tomorrow? I think I'll have to send my regrets. But thanks."

Then she stumbled out the door, gasping down deep, stinging lungfuls of hot desert air as it surrounded her body.

My God. Her whole life she'd been waiting for this very moment. And now that it had come and gone, all she wanted to do was throw up.

She thought briefly of Conner. Oh, how she wanted his arms around her! But this was one thing she had to process on her own, without his nurturing cocoon of emotional protection.

She just needed to think.

"Ms. Mancuso?" A black-haired LVMPD officer waved and approached her.

Oh, God. *No more.* Please!

He smiled genially. "Ms. Mancuso, Detective Rothchild sent me out to give you a ride home. She said you don't have your car with you. Right?"

"Oh. That was thoughtful." Vera almost sagged with relief. Now she wouldn't have to stand here and flag down a taxi.

The officer led the way to a gray sedan parked on the street. "Sorry about the unmarked car. All the cruisers are out."

"It's okay. I'd just as soon not get dropped off at my building by a police car with lights flashing anyway," she said, making a stab at a normal conversation while her insides were still shaking and churning.

He chuckled and opened the passenger door for her, his strong cologne making her nose twitch. "I hear you."

She got in. But instead of going around to the other side,

he said, "I'm afraid I'm going to have to ask you to slide over and drive, Ms. Mancuso."

Her mind went blank. "What? Why?"

He drew his service revolver from its holster and pointed it at her head. "Because if you don't, I'll kill you."

Chapter 20

"Where's Vera?" Conner asked Natalie. He'd
[...] see his lover chatting amiably with his cousin,
[...]or Duncan and him to wind up their business. Of eve[...]
[...]n his family, he trusted Natalie not to prejudge a per[...]
[...]ased on her job, so he'd felt comfortable leaving Vera i[...]
[...]er charge.

"She left a good while ago," Natalie said, sitting back in
[...]er squeaky chair to regard him.

"Oh. Okay." Disappointed, he poured himself another cup
[...]f coffee. It was his... Hell, he had no idea, he'd downed so
[...]any cups. He was wired, but at least he was awake. Duncan
[...]ad kept him longer than anticipated...but he thought she'd
[...]ait for him anyway.

"There was an incident," Natalie reported.

Conner stopped mid-sip and held his cup still. *Ah, hell.*
[...]et me guess. Her father." He'd seen Maximillian gliding

past the conference-room window, and ped the bastard
wouldn't run into Vera. Apparently ho in vain.

"How'd you know?" arred and feathered."

"The man is an ass. He shoul coffee cup. "The incident
Natalie peered at him over hat I gathered."
was not in the usual vein, f gain why I can't just shoot the

Worse? Jeez. "Remin
jerk?" Conner asked prison," she said without missing

"Unspeakable er head. "Though, as a notorious
a beat. Then c close connections to the underworld.
defense atto ed the worst humiliations. Except by the
e."

you migh . "Okay, I get the drift. I'll be good. So. Wha
guards ual about the incident?"

ologized to her. Said she'd saved important lives
ed 'calm thinking and unselfish bravery,' I think were
xact words."

"*Seriously?* Max St. Giles?"

"Said he'd misjudged her."

"Wow. That's huge."

"So," Natalie said, eyeing him.

"Spit it out," he said.

"A *stripper?*"

"Please. Exotic dancer."

"Conner. Have you *lost* your mind?" she asked, lifting he
cup to her lips.

"Possibly," he answered just as evenly. "Nat, I love her."

She sprayed coffee all over her desk.

He opened her top drawer and tossed her a couple o
napkins. "What do I do?"

Her gaze said it all. Total, paralyzing astonishment. "Well…
Just then her phone rang. Saved by the bell.

She grabbed it, bobbled it, recovered. "Rothchild." After a second, her eyes seemed to focus sharply. She stopped breathing—never a good sign. Her gaze sliced to him. "One moment." She handed him the receiver. "It's for you."

As soon as he took it, she jumped up and started making frantic hand movements at the officers across the room. What the—

Suddenly, his heart stalled.

"This is Conner," he barked into the receiver.

"I have something you want, *Conner,*" the male voice sneered. "And you have something I want. Trade?"

Conner's blood chilled. "What do—"

There was a muffled sound, and Vera's desperate voice came on. "Conner? Oh, my God, Conner, it's him, it's—"

"Do we have a deal?"

"What is it you want?" Conner forced himself to calmly ask while his pulse pounded through his body like a kettledrum. Natalie was still moving like a blur, listening in while organizing a trace, he assumed.

"The Tears of the Quetzal," he spat out. "You're at the police station, and I know they have it," he said. He, being Thomas Smythe. It had to be him.

The man's next words confirmed it. "One hour. Bring it to the same place you were this morning. Alone. No games. Or your little stripper dies." Then he hung up.

Conner let loose a string of violent curses.

Natalie, being the ever-practical one, swiped up the phone and punched in buttons like it was on fire. "Duncan!" she said. "Get out here. We have a situation."

"This isn't going to work."

Conner loosened his death grip on the steering wheel of the McLaren and flexed his fingers, taking another hairpin turn up the gravel road to the quarry where the shoot-out had taken place earlier.

"It'll work," came the muffled reply from the trunk, where Duncan was curled into a Kevlar ball, probably roasting in there like a pig at a luau. "It has to."

Tell him about it. He'd kill himself if anything happened to Vera because of this stupid, obnoxious ring.

Maybe Uncle Harold was right. Maybe it *was* cursed.

"Sure you can open the trunk from inside?" Conner asked for the dozenth time.

"Got the safety latch in my hand and my gun in the other, just in case."

"Okay." Conner took a deep breath. "Okay."

"Sitrep?" Duncan prodded.

"Almost there," Conner reported. "Just around the bend." He scanned the road and cliffs around him. "Don't see him yet."

"Vera?"

"No sign." All sorts of awful images flowed through Conner's head as he searched the mountain for any sign of anything.

He slowed to maneuver around the giant boulder, pulled up in front of the old mining hut and cut the engine. After the bustle, whistles and constant ka-ching of every venue in Vegas, the lonely mountaintop was disturbingly silent. Had it been this preternaturally quiet this morning?

He got out of the car. A dust devil twirled past. Nothing else moved.

"Smythe!" he shouted. "Thomas Smythe! I have the ring. Let Vera go!"

"Oh, I'll let her go, all right," came the maniacal reply.

Conner whirled toward the voice. Looked up. And his legs almost gave out from under him. "Vera!" he cried.

He could just make her out, dangling over the side of the cliff a hundred feet above them by a rope tied around he wrists. The rope had been threaded through the arm of an old, rickety piece of quarry equipment, a pulley-type affair on the top of the cliff, from which the rope pulled taut down the cliff to the front of the old hut, ending up winding around an old-fashioned hand crank and shaft. A black-haired Hispanic-looking man was holding on to the handle of the crank. For a split second Conner was confused. The man was dressed as a cop.

Then it hit him. Hell. How stupid could he get? Smythe had done it once and gotten away with it. Why not twice?

Sure enough, it was the same man he'd seen arguing with Darla in front of LVMPD. And who had attacked Vera on the street.

The bastard Thomas Smythe. Or whatever the hell his real name was. Duncan had run a check and found no one matching his description with that name. Figured.

In a flash, Conner saw that if Smythe let go of the rusty crank handle the rope would spin off like greased lightning and Vera would plunge down the cliff. To certain death.

Conner was rigid with fear. "Don't do anything rash, Smythe," he said as calmly as he could manage. "I told you I have the ring."

"Show it to me!"

Moving slowly away from his car, Conner reached carefully into his pocket and brought out the jewel. He held it up for the other man to see. Even in the dimming light of the setting sun, the stone glittered and shone, flashing green and blue and purple like a sparkler on the Fourth of July. Almost like the real thing.

For several seconds, Smythe seemed hypnotized by the light, his eyes blinded with lust and greed, a look of ecstasy coming over his whole face. Conner took the opportunity to move closer. He had to get to that crankshaft before the deranged man let it go. Which Conner was absolutely certain he would do. Darla was right. He was already over the edge.

Conner cringed. Bad analogy. Really bad.

"Hand it over!" the man yelled, letting the crank unwind a whole revolution.

Vera screamed as she plunged several feet down the cliff.

Smythe's muscles strained to stop the movement. "Now! Or I let her go all the way!"

"All right, all right!" Conner said, taking a few steps closer. Close enough to see the gun tucked in the waistband of the man's jeans, the whites of his crazy-wild eyes, the beads of sweat drenching his face…and the deadly intent in his glazed expression as he started to let the handle go for good.

"Nooo!" Conner shouted, and threw the ring in a high arc over Smythe's head at the same time he made a flying leap for the crank's handle, just as it left the other man's hands.

He grabbed it. It whacked him in the chin going around, knocking him silly.

Vera screamed in terror.

He lunged for it again. This time it dug into his stomach, but he managed to hang on. Vera was still screaming and thrashing, making the rope pull all the harder on the handle. Conner could feel it slipping in his sweaty hands.

"Duncan!" he yelled in desperation. The plan had been for the FBI agent to chase Smythe down, shoot him or at least be able to tell the herd of Metro officers waiting below which direction he'd fled in. That wasn't going to happen. "I need your help!" he shouted.

In a flash, the agent was there, helping to hang on to the crank. Between the two of them they got it under control, then let the rope play out slowly to let Vera down without scraping her up too badly.

"Sorry," Conner grunted as they let out the rope. "I'm sorry I couldn't handle this myself. Now you've lost him again."

"Forget it. Vera's life is all that matters," Duncan said grimly. "Don't you worry. We'll get the bastard. And won't he be surprised when he realizes the ring he has is the fake."

They lowered Vera nearly to the ground, and at the last minute, Conner grabbed her. He hugged her fiercely to him, tears blurring his vision as she clung to him and let out a hic-coughed sob. She was shaking like a leaf.

Hell, so was he.

"You're okay now, you're okay now," he told her over and over, as much to convince himself as her.

She was so damn brave.

And at that moment he realized. It didn't matter what his family thought. Or the risk to his career. Or his social position.

Nothing else mattered.

She was his. And he would never, ever let her go.

Chapter 21

Conner didn't think he'd ever be alone again with Vera.

But after waiting an endless amount of time for the trackers to find Thomas Smythe—and failing—Lex Duncan decided they may as well go home for now.

Thank God.

Vera was on the verge of emotional collapse, and Conner hadn't had a wink of sleep in close to forty-eight hours, putting him near the limit of his endurance both physically and mentally. Lex seemed to recognize that.

"I'll take you two home," Natalie told him, looking more than exhausted herself after tramping up and down the steep mountains for hours. "Wouldn't want any more fake-cop incidents."

Vera glanced at her wide-eyed, and Conner managed a weary laugh, appreciating his cousin's stab at black humor.

"Thanks, Nat," he said, and turned over the McLaren's keys to an awestruck young officer. "Scratch it and you'll be washing my cars for the rest of your life," he warned the kid with mock seriousness. Okay, not so mock. Conner loved his car.

Almost as much as he loved the way Vera looked at him when he climbed into the back of Natalie's cruiser with her instead of getting in the front seat.

He just prayed they'd make it back to his place before he passed out. They did. Just barely.

"We'll be expecting you for dinner tomorrow night," Natalie said as a parting shot when they stumbled out onto his driveway. "*Both* of you."

"Nat—"

"Don't argue with me, boy," she said gruffly. "I have a gun, and I know how to use it."

He gave her a halfhearted grin and a tired wave, and she drove away. Ah, well. He could always cancel tomorrow.

He put his arm around Vera. "I'm about to fall over. How 'bout you?"

"I want to spend a week in bed."

And he had a feeling she meant actually to sleep. He'd probably be of a different opinion tomorrow, but right now that sounded like paradise. They went straight to his bedroom, shedding clothes along the way. Five minutes later they were in bed, snuggled up together like puppies in a basket.

Small tremors still sifted through her. He wrapped his body around her in a sheltering, protective shield. So she'd know without a doubt that, if anyone wanted to get to her, they'd have to go through him first.

She sighed, and finally her tense muscles began to relax. Skin to skin, warm and smooth, primal and visceral, he soaked in the feel of her, the smell of her, the sound of her soft, even breathing. And recognized on a soul-deep level that this was something special. Something once-in-a-lifetime. He kissed her brow, and she nestled closer. She put her lips to the curve of his neck, and whispered, "I love you, Conner Rothchild."

He looked down at the woman in his arms, his heart filling with an unexpected burst of joy and longing, and he wondered if she was talking in her sleep again. But then she opened her eyes and smiled up at him.

"Yeah?" he said.

"Yeah," she said.

"I'm glad," he said, and held her close. "So very glad, Vera Mancuso. Because I love you, too."

"We are well and truly screwed," Conner said, flopping back in the McLaren's bucket seat.

"Well," Vera mused, "not the most romantic way of putting it, but I suppose you could say that."

She thought back over the relaxing day. Without a doubt the happiest day of her life to date. They'd slept over twelve hours the night before, then slowly awoken to take advantage of their renewed energy, the glorious weather streaming in through the windows and the fact that Hildy did not put a single phone call through to his suite.

Well, until that last one. The *summons,* coming around midafternoon. Apparently *nobody* told Harold Rothchild he couldn't speak with his nephew. Whereupon he had told Conner in no uncertain terms he was to gather his "young lady" and bring her to dinner that night. Seven o'clock promptly.

They'd gotten ready and left at five o'clock. Conner had said he wanted to make a stop on the way. Something to give him the courage he needed to face his family with her on his arm. She hoped it had worked for him. *She* felt wonderful.

Vera followed Conner's gaze now as he surveyed the Rothchild driveway, brimming with Jaguars, Mercedes, Porsches and even a Lamborghini. "Looks like they've invited a few people over," he said nervously.

Poor Conner. He wasn't used to being the object of gossip or disapproval. "We can still leave," she told him. "Do this another time."

He glanced at her, pretending not to be scared. He was so sweet it made her heart ache with love. "Hell, no," he said. "If Uncle Harold wants to meet my young lady he's going to damn well meet my young lady." His mouth tilted up. Half of it, anyway.

She was still getting used to the thought of being Conner's anything, let alone romantically linked to him. *His young lady.* She glanced down at her hands. It had a certain ring to it.

He'd said he loved her. More than once. And as unreal as it felt, she believed him. Oh, how she believed him.

But inside, her heart was doing the quickstep. She had to say it. "What if they don't approve of me? What if they tell you you can't—"

"They won't." He cut her off. "And even if they did, I wouldn't care. I don't need their approval."

"But you want it."

He gazed at her. And nodded. "I want them to love you as much as I do. I have to believe they will."

Her heart swelled. "Okay, then let's go find out."

"Right."

He drove up to the house and left the car in the care of a young man who, a hundred years ago, would have been called a stable hand. She wondered vaguely what they called them nowadays...since they took care of cars, not horses.

God. She was mentally babbling again. It happened whenever she was nervous. She really had to quit wandering off into left field or she'd end up like Joe.

At the thought of her stepfather, a rush of warmth filled her. And wonder. The care facility had called her today, informing her that an anonymous donor had set up a fund to pay Joe's bills there for the rest of his life. She'd been shocked. And immediately assumed it was Conner, all set to hang up and tell him thanks but no thanks. But the director had told her in confidence the secret benefactor had been Maximillian St. Giles. After debating with herself all day, she was inclined to accept his generosity. After all, he owed Joe for taking over his role in her life for the past twenty-four years. This was small payment in recompense, but perhaps it would assuage his guilt just a tad. She could give him that much. Forgiveness would take longer, but this was a place to start at least.

"Ready?" Conner asked her.

She squared her shoulders and nodded. "If you are."

"Oh, I'm ready," he murmured, pulling her close to his side, leaning over and putting his lips to hers. He smiled down at her, and her heart did a perfect swan dive into the warm oases of his eyes.

And somehow she knew it would all be okay.

They walked into the Rothchild mansion arm in arm and were immediately surrounded by all of Conner's various cousins. Even his brother, Mike, with fiancée, Audra, were there—a first, apparently—invited by Natalie, whose skill as a detective Vera was growing to admire greatly. Natalie, it turned out, was getting married to her college sweetheart Matt Shaffer, on June fourteenth, just two short weeks away. Matt was there standing next to her, looking all tall and lean and muscular like the security chief he was.

Hanging a bit back, observing the crowd, was another man, Austin Dearing, whom Vera immediately recognized from the tabloids. Brawny, tan, chiseled as a sculpture and built like a Delta Force god, he and Vera's friend Silver had created quite the scandal last month by announcing first their baby, and *then* their whirlwind marriage.

Silver was the first to come over and give Vera a big welcome hug. "You and Conner!" Silver exclaimed with a grin. "What a surprise!"

She had no idea.

They were immediately joined by the only cousin Vera hadn't already met. Jenna, the youngest of the half sisters, who was Vera's age. Jenna was an event planner, party princess, an absolute knockout and clearly the apple of her daddy's eye. Harold's gaze followed her proudly from the foot of the foyer staircase as she said hello to Vera then was drawn into the midst of the other arriving guests.

For a family dinner, there was quite a crowd gathering. Through which Conner expertly steered her, until they got to the staircase and Harold Rothchild, who'd been joined with perfect timing by his current wife, Rebecca.

Harold gave Conner a slap on the back. "Glad you could make it, boy. Come see who's here."

Vera saw Conner pale when he turned and found himself eye-to-eye with Michael and Emily Rothchild, his parents. Uh-oh. He *hadn't* been expecting that.

"Thought it was time to bury the hatchet," Harold said, then sobered. "When Candace died, I realized what was important in life. And that's family." He turned to Conner and brightened up. "Isn't that right, boy?" He slapped him on the back again.

Conner glanced over at her. She smiled, so filled with love for the man she was bursting at the seams. Even as he fought for his own happiness, he never forgot his love and duty to his parents and family. Never forgot that his decisions affected more than himself, or even her. It made her love him all the more to know he was willing to sacrifice for his family. She'd never known that kind of loyalty and was awed that it was now all directed toward her.

As was his attention. He held out his hand to her, she took it and he pulled her up the staircase a few steps, so he towered over the noisy throng crowding the massive foyer.

He let out a piercing whistle. The talking and laughing stopped abruptly. Everyone turned to stare at him in surprised expectation. Suddenly, her knees felt weak. *Oh, God.* This was worse than dangling a hundred feet over a cliff.

Okay, not really. But almost.

But his gaze met hers, and she could feel all the love and support she'd need for a whole lifetime pouring through them into her. He squeezed her hand. Then turned to the crowd.

"Before we go in to dinner, I'd like to introduce someone very special to me." He glanced at his parents and uncle. "Mom, Dad, this is Vera. Uncle Harold, you invited us here tonight because you wanted to meet my young lady. Well, I'm afraid that's not possible." Harold's bushy brows rose. "You see," Conner continued, "Vera is no longer my young lady. As of an hour ago, she's much more to me than that."

Gasps went through the room. He smiled down at her.

"Everyone, I'd like you to meet Vera Mancuso Rothchild. My new wife."

Epilogue

Two weeks later

Tears trickled down Vera's cheeks as she watched Natalie Rothchild and Matt Shaffer say their wedding vows. The church was packed, and there wasn't a dry eye in the house. Natalie and Matt had written the words themselves, and there was no doubt in Vera's mind that they meant every single word. It was movingly beautiful, the whole ceremony.

Afterward, as the organ music swelled and everyone stood wiping tears and cheering the bride and groom out of the church, Vera realized Conner, who'd held her left hand in both of his the whole time, was watching her instead.

She gave him a watery smile, dabbing with a tissue. "I'm such a sucker for weddings," she said with a happy sigh.

He raised her hand to his lips, kissing her ring finger, where two weeks ago he'd placed a simple gold band. "Are you sorry?" he asked softly, his eyes filled with emotion. "That I didn't give you a day like this? With flowers and a white dress and a big party? A day to remember for the rest of your life…"

She met his gaze, and her eyes brimmed over anew. Didn't he know stopping at that Vegas wedding chapel on the way to dinner at the Rothchilds had been the happiest moment of her entire life? The shock, the utter joy, the amazing realization that he truly loved her, wanted to spend his life with her, was worth more than anything in the universe.

"Oh, Conner. You *did* give me a day to remember for the rest of my life. I wouldn't have changed a thing. Not one. Not for the world."

He bent down and kissed her tenderly. "Sure?"

She gently touched his cheek. "Positive." She smiled. "And believe me, the white dress thing? Been there, done that. Not a big deal."

His lips curved up at that, as she'd hoped they would. She kissed him lovingly. "Conner, don't think for a single moment that—"

"Hey, you two," an amused male voice interrupted from behind Conner. "No smooching in church. You're holding up traffic."

She rolled her eyes at Lex Duncan, who'd sat next to them in the pew. It was their turn to exit. "You're just jealous because you didn't bring a date to smooch with."

He made a face. "Date? Remind me again what that is?" He followed them out of the church into the bright sunshine. "Aside from which, technically, I'm working."

Conner shook his head. "Buddy, you need to forget that job of yours for an afternoon and take advantage." He swept an appreciative glance around. "Check out all the gorgeous women, all dressed up and all choked up on love, just waiting for a handsome man such as yourself to make their dreams come true. Have you never seen *The Wedding Crashers?*"

Duncan gave a short laugh. "Funny. Anyway, I don't dare get distracted. Aside from keeping watch for our escaped stalker, I'm deathly afraid war is going to break out at any moment."

Conner winced. "You mean among the guests?"

Duncan nodded, surveying the large area in front of the church where the reception line was forming.

Vera looked, too. "What do you mean?"

Conner put his arm around her and squeezed. "Your new brother-in-law comes from the biggest mob family in Las Vegas. See all the hard-eyed men in dark suits? And you can't miss the sea of khaki uniforms."

True. Half the Metro force had turned out for the wedding of one of their own. And Matt had mentioned his notorious family on a couple of occasions.

"Yikes," she said. "I hadn't thought of that."

"I better get to work."

As Duncan left, Natalie's sister Jenna came up and gave Conner a kiss on the cheek. "Don't worry, cuz. Matt assures me his family will be on their best behavior."

Jenna had done an amazing job putting together the whole wedding. Her eyes scanned the proceedings critically, never resting, ready to head off any problem before it arose.

"The church flowers were lovely, Jenna," Vera said. "Everything was so gorgeous."

"Thanks. Wait'll you see the reception hall. Dad gave me an unlimited budget." She grinned. "I took blatant advantage. But speaking of receptions, you two are wanted in the reception line now. Get your butts over there."

"Us?" Vera asked in alarm.

"Favorite cousin, and all." Jenna's eyes landed on Duncan's

receding back. "Say, who was that guy? I thought I knew everyone on the guest list."

"Lex Duncan. The FBI agent who's been helping us with the Tears of the Quetzal. He just took over Candace's case, too."

Vera secretly winked at Conner. "Handsome, isn't he? And single, too."

Jenna's gaze lingered appreciatively on him for a second, then moved on distractedly. "Whatever. Come on, you two. Reception line."

Terrified at the prospect, Vera looked to Conner for support. "I really don't think—"

"Nonsense. It's time I introduced my wife to society. No time like the present."

Jenna smiled encouragingly. "It'll be fine."

And as it turned out, it was. More than fine.

When they joined the line right next to Conner's parents, his father shook Vera's hand and kissed her cheek, and his mother actually hugged her. The first couple of days after Conner's surprise announcement at dinner had been rocky. But they'd been more shell-shocked than disapproving. Once they accepted the idea of a married son, they'd made an honest effort to get to know his new wife. That was all Vera could ask, and it seemed like they had accepted her, too.

His parents weren't the only ones stunned by the news that Conner Rothchild had gotten married. He did, after all, have a reputation as a confirmed bachelor who played the field with gusto. She'd learned that was mostly media hype, a facade cultivated to help his tireless work for those less fortunate than himself. Nothing like society connections to change society. But even his close friends were surprised. When had a workaholic like him had time to fall in love?

Sixty seconds was all it took, he'd assured them all. One look, and he was a goner.

There were a few sideways glances at Vera from those guests who'd heard about her questionable background. But there were many more who'd read about the press conference Maximillian St. Giles had held about Darla and Henry, and his unexpected announcement that he'd discovered he had another daughter, one who had risked her life to save his other children. And that he'd acknowledged being her father and written her into his will as an equal heir to the other two.

Congratulations flowed from both sides, Conner couldn't stop beaming and her heart was filled with joy.

Talk about a Cinderella moment.

Things like this *did* happen to people like her!

"I am so incredibly happy," she said to Conner when they were in the Batmobile, driving to the reception, which was being held at the Rothchild Grand Hotel. "How did I get so lucky to find you?"

He grinned over at her. "Uncle Harold said it must be the curse of the Tears of the Quetzal. Or in this case, the blessing. Rothchilds are falling like dominoes. In love, that is."

She grinned back. "Well, it's true, I *was* wearing the ring the first time I saw you," she teased as they pulled in at the Grand.

"That's about *all* you were wearing," he teased back. "Who could help falling in love with you at first sight? Every last man in the room was in love with you." He pulled into the parking lot, leaned over to grasp her behind the neck and kissed her. "I was just the lucky guy who got you all for myself."

"Yes," she said, loving the taste of her new husband, loving the feel of his muscular body, loving the honor in his heart most of all. "You did."

The wedding party limo pulled up with a blare of horns and a rippling of crepe paper bunting. Natalie and Matt emerged, glowing and smiling and kissing like two people so in love the earth spun around the axis of it. Just like Vera and Conner.

She returned his kiss with all the love within her heart and soul. Then told him sincerely, "Flowers and white dresses and parties are wonderful, darling. But none of those things matter. We already have what's important. We have each other, and we have love. I love you so much, Conner. That's all I'll ever need."

His eyes looked down at her so tenderly her heart simply overflowed. "I love you, too, Vera. So very much."

Again, he raised her fingers to his lips and kissed them, and then he slipped another ring on next to her wedding band.

She looked down at it in surprise. A perfect diamond winked back at her, blazing with green, purple and blue sparkles. Just like a miniature Quetzal.

"So we can make our own magic," he whispered. And kissed her again.

Oh, yes. The magic of love.

* * * * *

*Mills & Boon® Intrigue brings you
a sneak preview of…*

Carla Cassidy's The Rancher Bodyguard

*Grace Covington's stepfather has been murdered, her
teenage sister the only suspect. Convinced of her
sister's innocence, Grace turns to her ex-boyfriend,
lawyer Charlie Black, to help her find the truth.
Although she is determined not to forgive his betrayal,
the sexual tension instantly returns as their
investigation leads them into danger…and back
into each other's arms.*

Don't miss the thrilling final story in the
WILD WEST BODYGUARDS
*mini-series, available next month from
Mills & Boon® Intrigue.*

The Rancher Bodyguard
by
Carla Cassidy

As he approached the barn, Charlie Black saw the sleek, scarlet convertible pulling into his driveway, and wondered when exactly, while he'd slept the night before, hell had frozen over. Because the last time he'd seen Grace Covington, that's what she'd told him would have to happen before she'd ever talk to or even look at him again.

He patted the neck of his stallion and reined in at the corral. As he dismounted and pulled off his dusty black hat, he tried to ignore the faint thrum of electricity that zinged through him as she got out of her car.

Her long blond hair sparkled in the late afternoon sun, but he was still too far away to see the expression on her lovely features.

It had been a year and a half since he'd seen her, even though for the past six months they'd resided in the same small town of Cotter Creek, Oklahoma.

The last time he'd encountered her had been in his upscale apartment in Oklahoma City. He'd been wearing a pair of sports socks and an electric blue condom. Not one of his finer moments, but it had been the culminating incident in a year of not-so-fine moments.

Too much money, too many successes and far too much booze had transformed his life into a nightmare of bad moments, the last resulting in him losing the only thing worth having.

Surely she hadn't waited all this time to come out to the family ranch—his ranch now—to finally put a bullet in what she'd described as his cold, black heart. Grace had never been the type of woman to put off till today what she could have done yesterday.

Besides, she hadn't needed a gun on that terrible Friday night when she'd arrived unannounced at his apartment. As he'd stared at her in a drunken haze, she'd given it to him with both barrels, calling him every vile name under the sun before she slammed out of his door and out of his life.

So, what was she doing here now? He slapped his horse on the rump, then motioned to a nearby ranch hand to take care of the animal. He closed the gate and approached where she hadn't moved away from the driver's side of her car.

Her hair had grown much longer since he'd last seen her. Although most of it was clasped at the back of her neck, several long wisps had escaped the confines. The beige suit she wore complemented her blond coloring and the icy blue of her eyes.

She might look cool and untouchable, like the perfect lady, but he knew what those eyes looked like flared with desire. He knew how she moaned with wild abandon when making love, and he hated the fact that just the unexpected sight of her brought back all the memories he'd worked so long and hard to forget.

"Hello, Grace," he said, as he got close enough to speak without competing with the warm April breeze. "I have to admit I'm surprised to see you. As I remember, the last time we saw each other, you indicated that hell would freeze over before you'd ever speak to me again."

Her blue eyes flashed with more than a touch of annoyance—a flash followed swiftly by a look of desperation.

"Charlie, I need you." Her low voice trembled slightly, and only then did he notice that her eyes were red-rimmed, as if she'd been weeping. In all the time they'd dated—even during the ugly scene that had ended *them*—he'd never seen her shed a single tear. "Have you heard the news?" she asked.

"What news?"

"Early this afternoon my stepfather was found stabbed to death in bed." She paused for a moment and bit her full lower lip as her eyes grew shiny with suppressed tears. "I think Hope is in trouble, Charlie. I think she's really in bad trouble."

"What?" Shock stabbed through him. Hope was

Grace's fifteen-year-old sister. He'd met her a couple of times. She'd seemed like a nice kid, not as pretty as her older sister, but a cutie nevertheless.

"Maybe you should come on inside," he said, and gestured toward the house. She stared at the attractive ranch house as if he'd just invited her into the chambers of hell. "There's nobody inside, Grace. The only woman who ever comes in is Rosa Caltano. She does the cooking and cleaning for me, and she's already left for the day."

Grace gave a curt nod and moved away from the car. She followed him to the house and up the wooden stairs to the wraparound porch.

The entry hall was just as it had been when Charlie's mother and father had been alive, with a gleaming wood floor and a dried flower wreath on the wall.

He led her to the living room. Charlie had removed much of the old furniture that he'd grown up with and replaced it with contemporary pieces in earth tones. He motioned Grace to the sofa, where she sat on the very edge as if ready to bolt at any moment. He took the chair across from her and gazed at her expectantly.

"Why do you think Hope is in trouble?"

She drew in a deep breath, obviously fighting for control. "From what I've been told, Lana, the housekeeper, found William dead in his bed. Today is her day off, but she left a sweater there last night and went back to get it. It was late enough in the day that William should have been up, so she checked on him. She immediately called Zack West, and he and some of his deputies responded. They found Hope passed out on her bed. Apparently she was the only one home at the time of the murder."

Charlie frowned, his mind reeling. Before he'd moved back here to try his hand at ranching, Charlie had been a successful, high-profile defense attorney in Oklahoma City.

It was that terrible moment in time with Grace followed by the unexpected death of his father that had made him take a good, hard look at his life and realize how unhappy he'd been for a very long time.

Still, it was as a defense attorney that he frowned at her thoughtfully. "What do you mean she was passed out? Was she asleep? Drunk?"

Those icy blue eyes of hers darkened. "Apparently she was drugged. She was taken to the hospital and is still there. They pumped her stomach and are keeping her for observation." Grace leaned forward. "Please, Charlie. Please help her. Something isn't right. First of all, Hope would never, ever take drugs, and she certainly isn't capable of something like this. She would *never* have hurt William."

Spoken like a true sister, Charlie thought. How many times had he heard family members and friends proclaim that a defendant couldn't be guilty of the crime they had been charged with, only to discover that they were wrong?

"Grace, I don't know if you've heard, but I'm a rancher now." He wasn't at all sure he wanted to get involved with any of this. It had disaster written all over it. "I've retired as a criminal defense attorney."

"I heard through the grapevine that besides being a rancher, you're working part-time with West Protective Services," she said.

"That's right," he agreed. "They approached me about a month ago and asked if I could use a little side work. It sounded intriguing, so I took them up on it, but so far I haven't done any work for them."

"Then let me hire you as Hope's bodyguard, and if you do a little criminal defense work in the process I'll pay you extra." She leaned forward, her eyes begging for his help.

Bad idea, a little voice whispered in the back of his brain. She already hated his guts, and this portended a very bad ending. He knew how much she loved her sister; he assumed that for the last couple of years she'd been more mother than sibling to the young girl. He'd be a fool to involve himself in the whole mess.

"Has Hope been questioned by anyone?" he heard himself ask. He knew he was going to get involved whether he wanted to or not, because it was Grace, because she needed him.

"I don't think so. When I left the hospital a little while ago, she was still unconscious. Dr. Dell promised me he wouldn't let anyone in to see her until I returned."

"Good." There was nothing worse than a suspect running off at the mouth with a seemingly friendly officer. Often the damage was so great there was nothing a defense attorney could do to mitigate it.

"Does that mean you'll take Hope's case?" she asked.

"Whoa," he said, and held up both his hands. "Before I agree to anything, I need to make a couple of phone calls, find out exactly what's going on and where the official investigation is headed. It's possible you don't need me, that Hope isn't in any real danger of being arrested."

"Then what happens now?"

"Why don't I plan on meeting you at the hospital in about an hour and a half? By then I'll know more of what's going on, and I'd like to be present while anybody questions Hope. If anyone asks before I get there, you tell them you're waiting for legal counsel."

She nodded and rose. She'd been lovely a year and a half ago when he'd last seen her, but she was even lovelier now.

She was five years younger than his thirty-five but had always carried herself with the confidence of an older woman. That was part of what had initially drawn him to her, that cool shell of assurance encased in a slamming hot body with the face of an angel.

"How's business at the dress shop?" he asked, trying to distract her from her troubles as he walked her back to her car. She owned a shop called Sophisticated Lady that sold designer items at discount prices. She often traveled the two-hour drive into Oklahoma City on buying trips. That was where she and Charlie had started their relationship.

They'd met in the coffee shop in the hotel where she'd been staying. Charlie had popped in to drop off some paperwork to a client and had decided to grab a cup of coffee before heading back to his office.

She'd been sitting alone next to a window. The sun had sparked on her hair. Charlie had taken one look and was smitten.

"Business is fine," she said, but it was obvious his distraction wasn't successful.

"I'm sorry about William, but Zack West is a good man, a good sheriff. He'll get to the bottom of things."

Once again she nodded and opened her car door. "Then I'll see you in the hospital in an hour and a half," she said.

"Grace?" He stopped her before she got into the seat. "Given our history, why would you come to me with this?" he asked.

Her gaze met his with a touch of frost. "Because I think Hope is in trouble and she needs a sneaky devil to make sure she isn't charged with a murder I know she didn't commit. And you, Charlie Black, are as close to the devil as I could get."

She didn't wait for his reply. She got into her car, started the engine with a roar and left him standing to eat her dust as she peeled out and back down the driveway.

© Carla Bracale 2009

2 FREE BOOKS
AND A SURPRISE GIFT

We would like to take this opportunity to thank you for reading this Mills & Boon® book by offering you the chance to take TWO more specially selected books from the Intrigue series absolutely FREE! We're also making this offer to introduce you to the benefits of the Mills & Boon® Book Club™—

- **FREE home delivery**
- **FREE gifts and competitions**
- **FREE monthly Newsletter**
- **Exclusive Mills & Boon Book Club offers**
- **Books available before they're in the shops**

Accepting these FREE books and gift places you under no obligation to buy, you may cancel at any time, even after receiving your free books. Simply complete your details below and return the entire page to the address below. You don't even need a stamp!

YES Please send me 2 free Intrigue books and a surprise gift. I understand that unless you hear from me, I will receive 5 superb new stories every month, including two 2-in-1 books priced at £4.99 each and a single book priced at £3.19, postage and packing free. I am under no obligation to purchase any books and may cancel my subscription at any time. The free books and gift will be mine to keep in any case.

Ms/Mrs/Miss/Mr _____ Initials _____

Surname _____

Address _____

_____

_____ Postcode _____

Send this whole page to: Mills & Boon Book Club, Free Book Offer, FREEPOST NAT 10298, Richmond, TW9 1BR